THE SNAKE IN THE SIGNAL BOX

Book 1

Published by Fish Eagle Books
Eshowe, Rosslare Strand,
County Wexford, Republic of Ireland.

ISBN 978-1-54957-837-3

Also available as a Kindle ebook
ISBN 978-1-84396-424-7

A catalogue record for
this book is available from the British Library
and the American Library of Congress

Cover photograph
Richard's Bay picnic, 1919.

Pre-press production
eBook Versions
27 Old Gloucester Street
London WC1N 3AX
www.ebookversions.com

Acknowledgements

I am indebted to those who provided invaluable background material and guidance, without which this story could not have been told: Yvonne Altman, Irish Jewish Museum, Dublin, for clarifying the transliteration of the Kaddish; Ross Anderson for his kind permission to quote an excerpt from *The Forgotten War 1914-1918: The East African Campaign* in the Prologue to Book Two, *What Happened at Yonder*; David Arguile, College Head of St Anne's Diocesan College for permitting a reference to the college; Max Arthur, for permission to adapt a short extract from his book *Lost Voices of the Royal Navy*, originally published as *The True Glory: The Royal Navy 1914—1939* being first-hand accounts of action in the RN; Anne Archer, Senior Archivist, Lloyds Bank Group, for information on the Capital & Counties Bank; Anna Baggalay and my wife Patricia – Anna for a complete and independent edit of the first edition and Patricia for her painstaking transfer of the revisions to the manuscript; Jan Bezuidenhout, Webredakteur of *Landbouweekblad* and his colleague Koot Louw of *Cotton South Africa* for vital information about cotton cultivation; Dr Bill Bizley, author of the article *Unsung heroes: the trek ox and the opening of*

Natal, which appeared in the Natal Society's journal *Natalia* *#34*, upon which my description of oxen and wagons is based; likewise for permitting me to draw from his article *U-boats off Natal*, which was published in *Natalia #23* and #24, and which will surface in Book Three; Alec Bozas, Chairman of T M Loftheim (Pty) Limited for his permission to use the store name of Loftheim's in these pages. Loftheim's is arguably the oldest company in Zululand and still going strong, nowadays as a property-owning company; Vusi Buthelezi, erstwhile Senior Museologist of the Killie Campbell Collections, University of Kwa-Zulu Natal (Durban) who so kindly checked my descriptions of the Killie Campbell Collection and did not find them wanting; Steve Cook of the International 12-foot Dinghy Class Association, Switzerland for correcting material on sailing the BRA (Boat Racing Association) – particularly about the strategic use of the centreboard when running this dinghy before the wind; Peter Croeser, Trustee & Administrator of the Natal Society Foundation in Pietermaritzburg for his ready help in locating elusive information on matters Natal; Nestlé, for permission to mention KLIM in several places. KLIM is a registered trademark of Société des Produits Nestlé S.A., Vevey, Switzerland; Peter Ducasse, Headmaster of Hilton College for permitting a reference to the college; Tara Forster, niece of Killie Campbell, who challenged and corrected my characterisation of Killie; Howard Freeman, Assistant at the Irish Jewish Museum, Dublin for the phonetic transcription of the Mourners' Kaddish and pointing out the number of Jewish adults that must be present before it can be said; Mark Henderson, owner of *The Zululand Times* printing company, who had no objection to my mentioning the newspaper of that name (no longer published), often called 'The Sausage Wrap' and for the assistance of Noel Ashburner; Professor Shannon Hoctor, School of Law, University of Kwa Zulu Natal (Pietermaritzburg) and his colleague Dr Rose Kuhn, Librarian (Law) for investigating regulations governing mandatory inquests in Natal during 1919; Allan Jackson and Gerald Buttigieg of *Facts About Durban*, an interactive website, who provided a lot of information and continue to mine the rich seam of Durban history; Kevin Joseph, Deputy General Manager Food & Beverage of the Oyster Box Hotel, Umhlanga for use in full of his famous curry recipe which appears just after the bibliography in Book One, with the kind approval of his General Manager, Wayne Coetzer; Brendan Lillis, retired banker, for cutting through the mystery of local banking; Senzosenkosi Mkhize, Senior Librarian of the Campbell Collections for locating details of payments to Indentured Indians; The Reverend Sally Muggeridge, International President of The Malcolm Muggeridge Society for insights into Malcolm Muggeridge's activities in Lourenco Marques during the Second World War and allowing me to use Muggeridge's name in Book Three, although the narrative in the novellas strays from the actual facts; Richard Nicholson, Manager, Economic Research at the South African Cane Growers; Members of the Council, Clan Gregor, for reviewing passages about the Clan; David Savides, Editor and Kyle Cowan, journalist, Zululand for helping to track down Ashley Peter, co-author of *Centenary of the North Coast Railway*, who had the facts at his fingertips about the Mtubatuba railhead in 1919; Artur Stehli, writer in Schwiizerdütsch; Dr J C van der Walt, for allowing me to draw on an anecdote from his book, *Zululand True Stories 1780 to 1978*; Dalene Worrall for sending me a magnificent fistful of anecdotes gathered from her Zululand relations, many of whose memories have found their way into these pages in disguised form. I must make the point that this had nothing to do with the passages on the Broederbond, which came from a completely different source. A few words in the passage about the mixed-goods milk train were borrowed from *Night Mail* by W H Auden. References to the Sunlight Soap and Bovril advertisements are by kind permission of Unilever PLC and group companies; United Agents LLP is thanked on behalf of Jean, Lady Tweedsmuir, The Lord Tweedsmuir and Sally, Lady Tweedsmuir for permission to include eight words from John Buchan's novel, *The Thirty-Nine Steps*; Lines from *The Dodo*, a poem in Hilaire Belloc's Bad *Child's Book of Beasts*, are reproduced by permission of Peters Fraser & Dunlop (www.petersfraserdunlop.com) on behalf of the Estate of Hilaire Belloc. Graphics for the Natal railway map, adapted from an HTOL original and the cover of Book One were by Tom Kelleher, ThINK, Wexford, Ireland.

For Patricia

THE SNAKE IN THE SIGNAL BOX

Book 1

WILLIAM PATERSON

FISH EAGLE BOOKS

Contents

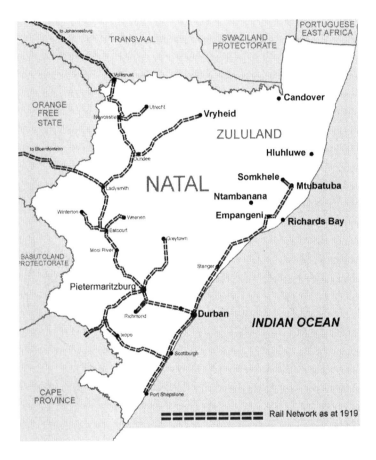

Natal Rail Network 1919

List of Characters

Donald Kirkwood	Brother died in France 1916 Sisters Winnie and Jean Tam settler
Judy Eriksen	Donald's original girl / Barbican
Dorothy Eriksen	Judy's older sister / Barbican
Toby Strafford	Good friend / co-farmer/ Sisters Phoebe and Hannah Jenny, the maid
James (Jim) Bell	Empangeni farmer
Edna Bell	His wife
Emily Bell	Their daughter
Andrew Bell	Son
Nigel Bell	Son
Noel Reed	Empangeni farm manager
Lucy Reed	His wife
Eric Schnurr	Ntambanana cotton man / American
Marie Schnurr	His French (Madagascar) wife

Sonya Broccardo	Emily's good friend
Zeno Broccardo	Sonya's twin brother
Joy Broccardo	Sonya's younger sister
Paolo Broccardo	Their father (Accountant)
Bianca Broccardo	Their mother
George Moberly	Editor, *Zululand Times*
Ivana 'Poppy' Popov	Typesetter / Married Eshowe butcher
Jan Mocke	Wagoner / Wagon Builder
Johan Myburgh	Tam settler
Herina Myburgh	His wife
Susannah Myburgh	Young daughter
Angelien & Katrien Myburgh	Very young children
Piet & Hannah van Jaarsveld	Tam store owners
Eben Brink	Vet
Hendrik Louw	Dutch Reformed Church
Jean-Pierre Meyer	Dinghy sailing friend
Caroline Meyer	His wife
Prudence Jardine	Librarian Daughter of Harbour Master
Kim Logan	Logan's Import & Export
Howard Creighton	Agent
Fritz du Quesne	Alias Capt. Stoughton Opsaal Brandy salesman

Hubie von Weldenburg	Swiss Farmer
Frieda von Weldenburg	His wife (Braille teacher)
Vishnu	Indentured Indian
Deepika	Vishnu's wife
Ivan Cohen	Musical instrument shop owner
Joelle Cohen	His wife
Masheila Reddy	Daughter of Indentured Indian at Bells
Luna de Villiers	Prostitute
Danielle Joubert	Braille teacher, Durban
Layani	Shangaan farm worker

Preface

There is a beautiful land in Africa, cradled by the Drakensberg, the Lebombo Mountains and the Indian Ocean, where this story begins and ends. There never was a Masonic Hotel in Empangeni and the characters that people these pages are creatures of fiction.

Except for a few public figures, long gone, any resemblance to actual persons, living or dead, or events related to them is purely coincidental.

Nowadays, the words 'native' and 'Kaffir' are regarded as insults and pejoratives, but, in 1919, that was not so.

A few of the people shown in the List of Characters only put in appearances in *What Happened at Yonder* (Book Two) and *Children of the Mist* (Book Three).

Chapter One

The small Indian was mumbling away behind his moustache at the corner of the General Post Office with eyes raised to the clock tower, a carnation flower in the palms of his cupped hands. Donald was surprised that he was still there at dusk. He had often wondered what he was mumbling about and assumed he was just plain dilly.

Mynah birds had returned to their roosts in the palm trees and were as raucous as ever. Some were still perched on the statues in Farewell Square while others were chattering away in the giant fig trees beside the town hall.

He avoided the Indian flower-sellers opposite the station entrance who were packing up for the night, the pavement wet and the heady smell of carnations almost overpowering, and crossed Railway Street to where his cabin trunk was being guarded by Punyane standing beside the café-de-moveon.

His trunk, on which he had painted the initials DWK in white before leaving England on the last day of February 1914, still bore faded Garth Castle mail ship Tourist Class stickers. It had to be presented at the luggage counter further down towards the engine workshops, so Punyane commandeered a helper to lug the case there, where oblong stickers marked 'Empangeni' received a splash of gum from

3

a large pot before being plastered on the tops and sides of the case. He would next see the trunk at his destination.

Armed with a chit for his cabin trunk and having tipped Punyane and his helper for their services, he was left to clutch a lighter case, now worse for years of battering, to study the list of names against compartments on the rack beneath the clock. A high barrier of ornate black cast-iron separated the concourse from the suburban trains.

He strolled along the platform in the fading light, past the dining car and a man sitting on a bench drinking out of a bottle hidden in a brown paper packet, before encountering a worker tapping each wheel with a long-handled hammer.

Almost colliding with a luggage porter, he asked the wheel tapper what he was listening for above the shouts of the Zulus, the voice on the loudspeakers and the general hubbub. He bellowed that each good wheel resonated like the bells of the Durban post office clock while the noise of a cracked one was "like a half-full Durban dustbin."

Outside the window of his compartment his name, mis-spelt as 'Mr. D W Krikwod', was on a card under a spring clip, along with the names of his three other compartment companions for the journey, Reed, Mobely (he learnt later it should have been 'Moberly') and Strafford.

At the tobacconist's kiosk he had time to buy a packet of Boxer's Smoking Mixture and the Natal Advertiser newspaper, the front page of which was smothered in small advertisements for Swan pens, haberdashery 'just landed from the SS Mexican' and American dentistry.

First into the compartment, he made for the window-seat, facing forward (he hated travelling with his back to the engine) and took in the leathery carriage smell.

In between the windows was a heater (no need for that in Zululand, he thought) on top of which was a metal hand basin with brass hot and cold water taps protruding from the wall between the windows. A small oval mirror above the taps rounded the compartment furniture, except for the luggage racks, heavily upholstered seats and wide notched leather straps used to haul the windows and the louvered wooden blinds up and down.

Both compartment windows were down when a face appeared which said in a public school voice, "I believe I'm in the same compartment. I wonder whether you'd mind grabbing my suitcase through the window? The name's Strafford."

Toby Strafford was of medium height, sturdy and with an open face. He was dressed in khaki trousers and shirt, and a linen jacket. His ubiquitous hat was from Natal Hatters (Donald noticed the name inside the brim later).

Strafford had been sweating in the humid heat and only had time to find his way to the compartment, introduce himself properly, and stow his suitcase above the upper bunk before two other faces appeared at the window, almost simultaneously, with the same sort of luggage-handling requests.

Figures began to cluster on the platform to see them off – a robust woman called Maud with titian hair, a large bosom and a frock resembling an overgrown herbaceous border, the wife of Arthur Moberly, the editor of The Zululand Times, their two young daughters, Pitty and Jean, and Judy Eriksson. Judy shared rooms with her older sister Dorothy at the same Berea boarding house called 'Barbican' where Donald was staying.

The suburbs of the Berea sprawl across low-lying hills

on the western outskirts of the city. Donald could never work out why it was named after a biblical village in southern Macedonia.

His friends, Jan-Pierre and wife Caroline, stood at the back of the platform gathering, saying little.

Dorothy was already making eyes at Noel Reed but winced when he laughed like a donkey.

From later conversations as the train clattered, swayed and rumbled its way to Empangeni, he learnt that The Zululand Times was based in Eshowe with modest offices and a staff of three, including Moberly. He had been to see the Durban agent of a new gadget called Linotype and was on his way to Empangeni to drum up circulation and advertising, with the intention of reaching as far as Hluhluwe and Pongola and inland to Ntambanana.

Linotype was an American invention for setting lines of metal type at a speed that promised to sweep aside the laborious way of typesetting by hand, letter by letter; but the cost of the device was too high for a very small rural paper, as was the ancillary equipment of flongs, stereos and rotary presses.

He had taken time off for a few days with his wife and children and had been staying at the Marine Hotel which overlooked the harbour. The rest of the family was staying on for a few more days before returning to Eshowe.

Noel Reed, Donald learned, was the assistant manager of a sugarcane estate beside the Mhlatuzi River, not far from Empangeni, belonging to his brother-in-law James Bell and his wife Edna, with Emily the daughter and their two sons Andrew and Nigel living in the main house.

Noel lived on the farm in a separate cottage, a comfortable walk away, with Lucy his wife and their two very young children.

The train gave a sudden small lurch, a trick of the engine driver to persuade friends who had come on board for last-minute-chats to get off the train in a hurry.

A man's voice bellowed suddenly over the platform speakers a nasal stream of words as incomprehensible as those of the vegetable auctioneers in the Pine Street market. After the guardsman had waved his green flag and rolled it up, tucking it under his arm, the Garratt engine sounded a steam-chord and the coaches began to creak forward, couplings clanking. Clouds of steam and smoke enveloped those left behind to speckle their clothes with soot as the train gathered speed. Some passengers leant out of windows, waving handkerchiefs. The drinking man was now asleep on the platform bench and slid past, as did a weeping woman near the end of the platform.

"Well, that's that for a while," said Moberly. "I wonder what they're going to throw at us for dinner tonight. Shall we sit together?" to which they all agreed.

Clanking along behind the passenger coaches were open trucks with goods cloaked in tarpaulins, and cattle trucks from which came sounds of lowing. Behind all that was the guard's van with its red lights.

Metal footplates and short concertina tunnels made of thick leather served as links between the swaying carriages, the plates sliding backwards and forwards as the train rocked its way up-country, adding to the adventure of reaching the dining car as if negotiating a way along a ship deck during high seas.

The menu was a dither between English and railway Franglaise, and was still offering its 'Victory Menu' celebrating the Armistice. (The chef was planning to baffle

7

Dutch-Afrikaans diners by printing a jumble of Dutch and French on the reverse, the steward confided to Moberly, although such diners might be more ambivalent in celebrating what many of them regarded as a catastrophe.) The options comprised

Victory Menu

Tomato Cocktail
Crème Imperial
Jelly Consommé en Tasse

Fillet of Sole Bonne Femme
Fillet Mignon Béarnaise
Green Peas French Beans
Pommes Chateau
Roast Stuffed Chicken & Cress
French Salad

Cheese Dessert Cafe
Savarin Infaute
Coupe Zululande
Friandises

They left it to Donald to order the wine.

"I'll just stick to whisky," Moberly said. "Wine gives me gout. So why are you going to Empangeni; planning to settle there?" The question was directed at Donald.

He replied that, as an ex-serviceman, he had been allocated fifteen hundred acres to develop a mixed dairy and cotton or sugar farm in the Ntambanana area, about 17 miles northwest of Empangeni and still in its raw state.

He was one of a group of 62 military and naval survivors demobbed towards the end of the war and able to lodge £500 apiece towards the commitment.

"I was one of the survivors – although Spanish flu almost polished me off just before the Armistice. It got many of my friends, but I recovered, thank God. I believe it was far worse on the Continent."

Donald had been part of the British South Africa Police Force (the BSAP) committed to harrying General von Lettow-Vorbeck, the German guerrilla tactician who, with his small army of a few thousand Germans and well-trained Askaris, led more than 100,000 Allied soldiers a merry dance all over East Africa, including parts of Moçambique and Northern Rhodesia.

"It was a pity to give General Smuts his head in that campaign," Donald said. "He was too embedded in the ideas of commando warfare he practised so well against the British during the Boer War. In East Africa, he should have mounted a full frontal attack instead of pussyfooting around. We could have been saved a lot of lives."

"But you don't know what you've let yourself in for, planning to travel to Ntambanana!" said Moberly. "I had a helluva time getting to Tam from Empangeni last year at the beginning of the rainy season and the road – such as it is – had turned into just mud and dongas. Only managed to reach the place by hitching my truck behind a friendly ox wagon and even they had to battle through the quagmire. Got mud somewhere in the engine and I had a struggle to get back along the same route, when the car had been sorted out. The return journey was just one big quagmire too. I had to detour through the veld much of the time."

Reaching for his wallet, he pulled out a sepia snapshot

of a car taken axle-deep in mud with an ox wagon and voorloper in the background. "That's the kind of condition you're likely to encounter – and that was on a sunny day." Donga is the Zulu word for an eroded gully.

Donald had figured that after surviving four years of military life in punishing Tanganyikan and Kenyan terrains, existing on limited rations and often for many days without any food at all, he would be able to live through anything the Zululand bush could throw at him – although he kept these thoughts to himself that evening.

He thought back of sheltering from German bullets that flew past him like bees, the killing and wounding of his comrades and the endless trudging through the disease-ridden East African scrub amidst the smell of rotting corpses, many of them porters who had died from starvation.

On hearing Donald's explanation, Strafford pricked up his ears and said that he too had been demobbed at the end of the European war. He had had to pay his own passage 'home' after serving as Senior Naval Officer aboard HMS Fox before being assigned to the navy's Far East station at Singapore.

The 'Fox', with HMS Goliath, plus a tug and a steam pinnace from the 'Goliath' played pivotal roles in bottling up and eventually destroying the three-funnelled cruiser Konigsberg in the Rufigi River, fifteen miles upstream from Dar es Salaam.

That was after the German raider had sunk HMS Pegasus in Zanzibar harbour on 20th September 1914. 'Dar' was the capital of German East Africa, which stretched from the Rufiji River in the south and Witu in the north, near Lamu on the coast.

Strafford said that he had gone down with a devastating bout of Spanish flu just before the navy demobbed him. His recovery was a close call.

Donald and Toby agreed that they had much in common as they were both heading for the same spot in the African veld.

Toby was Irish (or 'Anglo-Irish' as members of the Ascendancy were often described) and had received a letter written in London from Phoebe, one of his sisters, strongly advising him to stay away from Ireland for the time being. Anti-Anglo-Irish estate-owner sentiments were boiling up after the Easter uprising in 1916 and attempts had been made to set fire to a neighbour's 'Big House' and outbuildings. The family in Ireland had had to let the labour go, of the few who had remained loyal, sell off the cattle and sheep at rock-bottom prices and leave hurriedly for Wales, departing from Kingstown harbour on the ferry, although there was some dithering about whether to depart from Kingstown or Rosslare, the latter being the closer.

Since that event, his father had died in London and left Toby an inheritance in gilts, which he was able to turn into a tidy sum through Somerville, the family solicitor.

His mother had inherited the Irish estate that lay between Wexford and Enniscorthy, although this was not much use for the present, plus a healthy investment; interest from which was more than adequate to provide for her daily needs and his two sisters. It left sufficient capital for his mother to buy and furnish a house in Montpelier Street, Knightsbridge, near their London cousins (and all too near Harrods, Toby had mused, remembering his mother's buying-habits. He was lost once, when very young, in the Ladies Clothing department when she disappeared into a changing room with a cloud of clothes).

Toby had reasoned that it would be best to start afresh in South Africa, 'the new land of promise' and to visit London later, once settled.

He had heard of the proposal by the new South African government from his Durban bank manager (the same bank where Donald worked, although they hadn't come across each other) to allot about 1500 acres each to 62 ex-servicemen.

Toby's application, like Donald's, was successful – bearing in mind that South Africa had no navy at that time and the task of defending its coast was the job of the RN and the 'Wavy Navy', the Royal Naval Voluntary Reserve, thus rewarding an Irish navy man with links to South Africa was not out of order.

The dramatic sinking of the Konigsberg near Dar es Salaam during the war had caused a sensation in South Africa at the time and Toby made sure that his participation in this victory was brought to the attention of the authorities in Durban.

"Anything you miss about Ireland?"

"Ah. That's a cruel question. Yes, of course. It's home and will be forever so. There's a saying in Ireland 'Éirinn go Brágh!' which means 'Ireland is forever!' and it expresses the sense of permanence in the soil of Ireland which I miss here. The difference between the veld and Ireland's green hills is harsh. The messy independence movement going on over there and civil war threatening could have been averted if Tom Kettle hadn't been killed at the Somme three years ago. Now there was a man who could have united the country under All Ireland Home Rule, a great lawyer and friend of that writer, James Joyce.

"Perhaps what I miss most of all is the sound of the pipes and fiddles. As a child, I used to creep in on Saturday nights and hide in the hay when the workers, their wives, sons and daughters would meet in one of our barns and dance to the kind of music you will never hear in Africa. It had a beat and a kind of stumbling quality, as if the music would hit a discord, when a note and the note above it would challenge each other to create a brief pause and then find a way around it, until the next discord was encountered. And I miss the Yola."

"The what?"

"The Yola – or what's left of it in words you don't hear anywhere else. It's as if bits of a ghost-language poke their heads through in conversation every now and then. My father described it as a palimpsest. Yola was Middle English taken over to Ireland with the Normans and spoken in the Bargy and Forth baronies in County Wexford, where our old farm is. Hibernian English took over centuries later but there are still traces left in odd words – like 'saak'- to sit beside the fire, or 'bolsker' meaning an unfriendly person. 'Drazed' means threadbare and so on.

"I know all that because my father used to make a point of writing down such words whenever he heard a new one. He explained that a palimpsest was the resurfacing of some of the old words scraped off a parchment which had been overwritten."

"Well, you'll have to get used to hearing a lot of plumpsists and funny-sounding words here! Dutch, Tamil, Zulu, English, Tswana – and a jumble in between."

"Yola means 'old'. It was a wonderful childhood, growing up with my sisters alongside tenant farmers and labourers who knew more about Irish sheep and cattle husbandry than you can shake a stick at. I think my parents were popular with the workers and they were fair, so I'm appalled to learn of what has happened. I miss our dogs and horses too."

The conversation drifted to the Zulu naming of Empangeni and Hluhluwe, and Moberly, who seemed to understand Zulu quite well, explained that 'Pangeni' meant 'to snatch' because so many Zulu girls had been snatched by crocodiles on the banks of the Nseleni River where they fetched water near the little settlement.

"Frankly, I think that's the explanation for us whites. The truer meaning probably refers to the snatching of the local land from a defeated nation.

"From long experience, the Zulus have always been canny about avoiding malaria areas. Now, of course, by grabbing the richest land we are pushing them into dodgy areas of high malaria and wooded regions of tsetse-fly infestation.

"Just you watch. This will cause more trouble in the years to come. The others will be ill-treatment, low pay and being regarded as third class citizens in their own country.

"One of the few good things that came out of their defeat (other than our getting their land) is the retaining of most of the Zulu place names, all with equally descriptive origins. Look at the map of Natal and you'll find that Zulu place-names predominate to this day, except in Natal's northwest; Dutch names like Utrecht and Vryheid remain in that part as evidence of the old Natal Republic established by the Boers. One of the other regions being opened up to white farmers is at Hluhluwe, named by the Zulus after the vines with viciously long thorns which twine around forest trees in the area. It's a name that could daunt the Welsh.

Schloo-Schloo-we.

"I prefer to think of it as the sound of the wind through the gum trees, though, which an Australian imported and planted because he saw a get-rich-quick solution for producing mine props and extracting tannin from the bark. Now the trees are sucking up the water and lowering the water table in some parts – so when you put down a borehole make sure it's well away from the gums.

"The Zulu word 'Eshowe', which has been accepted as the name for Zululand's capital, does actually refer to the sound of the wind through the Dlinza Forest in the middle of the little town."

"So from where and how does 'The Sausage Wrap' get its news?" asked Toby. "Are you the bloke who writes the reports?"

"The same. I'm the editor – although my assistant sub-edits most of them nowadays – as he has been doing while I've been in Durban. The third member of the team is an extraordinary woman, Ivana Popovic, who's married to the Serbian butcher next door to the newspaper office. We call her 'Poppy'.

"It flies in the face of the typographical union for a girl to set type, but we are not members and for the time being, we can get away with it. She's responsible for all the typesetting and can work at an extraordinary speed, picking out the little metal upper-and-lower-case letters and assembling them into one-line cradles which we call 'sticks'. God knows how the Popovices got here from their part of the world, but get here they did. I think they had trouble accepting the Kingdom of Serbia being rammed together with the Croats and Slovenes.

"She has a few quirks, however, one of the most

pronounced being the tendency to omit the preposition 'the'. I believe that there is no equivalent 'the' in Serbian, so that explains that; but I do wish she would try to avoid clangers – like last week's when she spelt 'public' as 'pubic'. We were in such a hurry to get the paper out that we missed it. She misspelt 'plucking' the other week in an article about plucking the tealeaves on our local estates. And there are several new inventions like 'ant dazzle' instead of 'anti-dazzle' with which she has bewildered Zululand car-drivers – the few that there are; but she's a whizz when it comes to typesetting.

"You may know all this, but for the sake of those who don't and may care to learn, each letter is a separate metal 'piece' which must be plucked with tweezers from a printer's tray and assembled on a 'stick'.

"Capitals are kept in the upper case of type and stored in little open wooden compartments in alphabetical order while the lower case letters are stored in just that – the pull-out lower case, with the letters positioned according to the frequency of use – so the 'e' occupies the central box while the exes and zeds are kept way down among the dead men in the bottom left-hand corner.

"Poppy has to set the lines, often against a tight deadline, from scrawled bits of paper attached to a clipboard in front of her, correcting appalling errors and perhaps rewriting material as she goes, while setting the type at the same time. Marvellous how she can read metal type upside down and left to right – and spot most errors.

"We can run short of 'e's. I don't know what happens to them, perhaps the mice eat them; so it's not unknown for our having to set one page, then break it up and use some of the 'e's for subsequent pages after we have printed that page on the broadsheet.

"The rows of type which have been set are placed in 'galleys' – metal cradles holding the columns of type and run off on a proofing machine – just an inked roller in a frame holding the galley and hand-rolled over the type with a length of newsprint paper flattened firmly on top.

"It's my job to select information and weight the emphasis and direction of what we publish and to proof-read along with my assistant – so the real onus of imperfection rests on my shoulders."

"Where do you get your news from?"

"It just arrives, in many forms and from correspondents – letters, phone calls, telegrams, bumping into someone; it accumulates. At the beginning of the weekly cycle we often wonder how on earth we will be able to fill the pages by deadline, but something always crops up – and of course we keep some 'fillers' on standby. We have correspondents in most parts, and when a new region is developed we appoint someone who is knowledgeable about the area and knows the community well.

"When a report comes in from a remote point it's usually difficult to verify information via other sources before deadline – so, often, we have to make liberal use of useful words and phrases like 'alleged' 'thought to be', 'may' and 'according to', to hedge our bets and stay out of trouble.

"The newspaper acquired its nickname from the Popovic's butchery next door. Leftover back numbers are retrieved by the paper and sold to him for a few pence to wrap up customers' sausages.

"Our commitment is to stick to our last and report as thoroughly as possible on Zululand news. There's enough exciting stuff going on to leave the broader national and international coverage to the big boys in Durban, Cape Town, Johannesburg and other main centres... and we don't have Skibereen Eagle pretensions."

This small Irish paper published in the village of Skibereen caused many a guffaw with an editorial which concluded with the lines, "The Skibereen Eagle has its eye on the Czar of Russia!" at a time when Russia was threatening expansion into parts of Manchurian China.

"Poppy also handles the setting out of advertisements, for which we are ever scrounging, during the slack period of the week."

With unconscious prescience, Donald said, "That's fascinating stuff. Perhaps we'll have some stories for you in the years to come."

Turning to Toby, he said, "We must talk again about the navy and this cotton business, but right now, I'm for bed; so I'll see you all back in the compartment."

Moberly and Reed lingered on but Strafford rose with Donald to lurch back to the compartment, although Donald broke away to the lavatory at the end of the carriage.

He always took a childlike interest in flushing the pan with the foot pedal to watch everything, paper and all, swished down to the rails. During the day, he could see the sleepers whizzing by and wondered how hygienic it was, but assumed that the Railway knew what it was doing. Perhaps ants and the African sun cleaned up the mess.

In their absence, a cabin steward had lowered the bunks and bedding was in place, smelling of railway laundry. The lights had been turned down except for dim blue bulbs left on at the bulkheads – just enough to see by and for those on the upper bunks to clamber up the short ladders; although individual reading lights could be switched on too.

Moberly and Reed, returning to the compartment after several more whiskies, had to settle for the lower bunks converted from the seats.

The daytime backrest photographs of the Western Cape's fertile Hex River Valley cradled by mountains and the Union Buildings in Pretoria had now become the ceilings of the lower bunks. The Pretoria building had been completed in 1913, the two wings symbolising the Dutch and their English-settler counterparts, the central court signifying unity. The Blacks, Coloureds and Indians were not represented architecturally at all.

After much bumping and stumbling about, Moberly and Reed settled down to be rocked to sleep by the clickety-click (and the occasional clackety-clack as the carriage crossed over points) and the swaying of the carriage, which drowned Donald's occasional snoring until they reached Ginginhlovu station during the early hours of the morning.

Here, bright lights casting bands of light through the wooden carriage shutters, which had been closed by the attendant when he prepared the bunks, and the bellowing of Zulu workmen throwing around what seemed to be a world collection of empty milk cans ensured that they were all jolted awake.

"Jesus, why are natives so bloody loud! It's their big mouths for shouting from hill to hill that does it," muttered Moberly. "This is one of the penalties of taking the milk-train" – not quite the expletives to be expected from the editor of a paper started by an Anglican bishop.

From his lower bunk, Noel said that if it were not for the growing threat of nagana further up country, Ginginhlovu wouldn't have become such a nodal-point for milk can exchange. The full cans were swopped at this point between

Durban and Mtunzini for emptied ones.

"The Natal government thought that the ideal place for extending dairy production would be Ntambanana, but the disease is taking hold there and herds are being devastated, without any cure in sight, so I wouldn't touch the idea of keeping cattle with a bargepole. Besides, getting fresh milk to market would be impossible, taking into account the state of what's left of the road."

The deadly disease of nagana in cattle and sleeping sickness in humans, its 'cousin', is spread by the tsetse fly.

"A better option would be to focus on either sugarcane or cotton, and I'd put my money on cotton."

Because much of the line was single-track, the trains into nighttime Zululand enjoyed a life of their own. They stopped for no apparent reason, miles from anywhere, remaining stationary on a siding in the African dark, until a train from the other direction rattled past. They would then start to creak and roll forward, only to shriek to a halt for another long wait while drums of oil and sacks of fertiliser were unloaded at a Halt with more thumps and crashes, before lumbering forward again.

These known Halts served remote farms, most of them not even boasting a platform – merely a signboard bearing the surname of the farmer. It was the penalty of taking the passenger-and-general-goods milk-train.

After the stop at Ginginhlovu station [pronounced –'geen-gen-shlor-voo'] which fell silent after the milk-can workers had completed their tasks and the platform lights were switched off, the train began to clunk forward.

"Wait for it!" said Noel. "Here comes the clang" and clang it did indeed as each carriage smacked against something protruding at wheel level just past the end of the platform.

"That sound makes me homesick, wouldn't miss it for the world. Means we're well back in Zululand over the Tugela River and home is not very far away. Can you smell the molasses? That's from the Entumeni sugar mill, miles inland from the main rail line. The wind must be blowing northeast.

"Next real station is Eshowe – that's where Moberly would have been getting off – after a string of Halts, before you begin to smell the sugar mill at Felixtown – the signal that Empangeni is approaching down the track. G'night. Slaap lekker [sleep well] – or at least for the next few hours or so."

And so, in fits and starts, sleeping passengers, 'post for the rich and post for the poor', electrical generators draped with tarpaulins, ploughs and corsets, boxes of soap and cisterns, horse tack blinkers, chinaware, Bohemian beads, books on bee-keeping and tins of sausages rumbled on through the night to Zululand.

The sound that woke Donald for good was the rattle of a steward's key outside the door of the compartment and the words "Koffie! Coffee!" It was still dark.

The compartment door slid open noisily to reveal a galley trolley, robust SAR/ZAS cups and a stack of saucers, coffee spoons, a coffee tureen, sugar and a bowl of rusks all offered by a navy-blue-uniformed SAR / ZAS steward. He had a row of pens in his waistcoat breast pocket.

SAR and ZAS were the English and Dutch initials of 'South African Railways / Zuid-Afrikaanse Spoorwegen' introduced when the railways of the Cape Colony, the two republics and the Natal colony were united in 1910.

"Jurra, man! There's nothing like this new Spoorwegen

coffee!" said Noel as they all slurped away. "You could build bridges with the rusks until you dunk them. Could use them as pit props on the mines too. Cheaper than gum trees."

Chapter Two

Looking out of the dining car windows while eating breakfast, Donald saw the waxing gibbous moon in the early daylight and remembered Punyane saying, "When moon in sky daytime, no rain." It was usually true, but that night was to prove him wrong.

The milk train was chugging up through hilly countryside towards Empangeni, 450 feet above sea level, and the humidity that made everyone sweat in Durban, even in the early morning, had diminished sufficiently to suggest they would arrive to a sparkling morning.

Bacon and eggs were eaten with heavy EPNS cutlery on still extant 'Natal Government Railways' plates set on a starched white Irish Linen tablecloth, as groves of yellowwood trees slid by. Next to pass were wag-'n-bietjie trees (the Dutch-Afrikaans for 'wait a moment', because the limbs were covered in long thorns which caught up clothes); then Mpange trees swung by. Scrub alternated with field upon field of green sugarcane as the telegraph lines swooped from pole to pole. A remote wood-and-iron farmhouse with wide verandas scooched into view, then a group of young black girls strategically decorated with beads and precious little else, bearing earthen water jars on their heads. The bare-breasted younger girls waved as the train passed. He marvelled at their sense of balance, their beautiful dark skin, their erect bodies and their smiles.

Donald spotted a small herd of impala before his companions did as the train overtook a Tin Lizzy on the rough road parallel to the track, which was throwing up clouds of dust on its bumpy way to Empangeni.

"I'm going to like this place," he thought, thinking back to his days in East Africa.

With a clatter of points crossed and a final steam-chord, the train pulled in slowly to Empangeni Rail. It might have been a normal English country station, with carefully tended geranium and nasturtium beds, if it were not for the loud voices and figures of the natives waiting to offload goods and luggage, the sand-filled fire-buckets hanging from the roof supports, and the view beyond the station of the stockyard of hard earth and the clump of gum trees. Distant mountains floated above a heat haze even at this early hour.

Men and women with a few children, most of them wearing hats, stood on the platform expectantly. Among them were the manager of the general store, waiting with his Indian helpers to unload supplies, and the postmistress and her assistant, waiting for the mailbags.

Reed was welcomed through the compartment windows by a group who turned out to be Edna and James Bell (Noel's in-laws), their sandy-haired daughter, Emily, and Lucy, Noel's wife, a thin woman with stringy hair. Hovering behind them were Gokul, their Hindu assistant, and several black labourers from the farm to help with the manhandling of heavy crated equipment from the rear of the train.

"You almost arrived on time! That's surprising!"

said Lucy up at the train window. Her voice was 'English Colonial'. (The train kept its own timetable and was often delayed by those prolonged loading and unloading at Halts along the way.) "We had just settled down to station coffee when you came around the corner. Thank you for rescuing us. Hello. Durban go well?"

"Hot, humid and busy as ever. Yes, it went well," Noel said. "This is Donald Kirkwood. Planning to make a go of cotton farming, Toby Strafford likewise and George Moberly from the Zululand Times, who you probably know. Be careful what you say in front of George; can't give away all our dirty secrets. Not just yet, anyway!

"I know George plans to stay at the Masonic, and as it's Friday he has lots to do before catching the train back tomorrow lunchtime as far as Eshowe, but I wondered if Toby and Donald might stay with us? We could discuss the snares and pitfalls of farming at Ntambanana over the weekend. Eh Lucy? Nothing much will happen of any consequence over Saturday and Sunday, except tennis and church." This last remark was addressed to the men.

James said that they were both welcome to the farm although they would not have the opportunity of meeting their two sons, because they were away south at a friend's farm in Amatikulu for several weeks. He said they had some idea of grazing eland and cattle on the same land and were studying the effects. Although eland were herbivores they tended to eat tubers, flowering shrubs, seeds and so on – leaving cattle to munch away at the grass. "Who knows? Could be hare-brained. This is daughter Emily. We nearly christened her Miranda because she was born during a furious tempest, but thought better of it."

Emily smiled prettily at them when they said hello and

25

shook hands.

As chairman of the Empangeni Cane Growers Association, he said he would be delighted to go over the general farming ground with them from a sugar-planter,s point of view at early dinner that night, to which his wife Edna agreed warmly. She liked new company. "We'll try to inveigle Arthur Schnurr and his wife Marie down from Ntambanana for dinner and persuade them to stay over for tennis tomorrow afternoon – provided we manage to get through on the party-line and they survive the road from Ntambanana.

"Schnurr represents the Zululand Cooperative Cotton Association to which the League of Returned Soldiers and Sailors is affiliated, and his advice could be very useful. You both play tennis, don't you? We all just stumble around. Best part is Lucy's homemade lemon cordial between sets. Remember to ask our young grandchildren how it's made; and watch out for Marie's returns; petite as she is, she's left-handed and packs a wallop."

Donald thanked heaven for his father's determined tennis coaching during weekends at his house on Kew Gardens Road, before being shunted off to Dulwich College.

Toby, who said he did play tennis of sorts, "despite not having much opportunity aboard a naval vessel," turned out to be far better than he admitted.

He said, "What I haven't got is tennis shoes and I bet neither has Donald," after their exchanging quick glances. "Do Empangeni shops run to such things? Or should I say, does the Empangeni general store run to such things?"

Emily said Loftheim's did indeed, pointing at the general store across the square. "They're like Harrods. Stock everything. Well, almost. No elephants. Somewhat smaller. They've announced their intention to open another store further up Maxwell Street for 'whites Only' but I'll forever prefer this one. I like the smells, the jumble of people. Always reminds me of childhood.

"Pity about this place at the moment is that we are scattered into three communities – Empangeni Rail, The Mill (white sugar mill supervisors and the Indian settlement), and the village-proper."

Pointing as she spoke, she said, "The village is just the station, two small churches – them and us," (by which she meant the Dutch Reformed and the Anglicans. The Catholics had to be content with a Mission, although there was talk of founding a convent on a hill near the mill), "a few offices, some houses further out, the residency, a magistrates court, police camp and a gaol.

"There's a small bank beside the store, Mr. white's chemist shop next door to the doctor's surgery, a minute public library in the Public Hall in Turnbull Street run by volunteers and the office of van der Plank, the solicitor, near the surgery."

All who had greeted them had things to do in the village, not least Donald. They agreed to meet up on the steps of the station at half past twelve and Bell suggested that Donald and Toby should leave their large trunks at the station, which they did.

Donald walked past white's Chemist to the little postal agency, an annex of Loftheim's, to buy and send postcards – one to Judy in Durban: "All well. Met pleasant people on train. One is future neighbour at Ntambanana. Another manages a farm where we are staying over weekend to meet cotton man. Also met local newspaper fellow. Spot of luck.

Look after hot, sticky, humid Durban for me, and see you Tuesday week. Donald."

He tinkered with the idea of adding 'with love' but thought better of it.

The other he wrote to his cousins at Yonder Farm, near Darvel, Scotland: "My Zululand adventure has begun. Arrived Empangeni today. Met some good people. Zulu girls wear just a few beads. white girls here very pretty. Write soon. Love Donald." The Natal stamps he received from the postmistress were overprinted 'Zululand': "We're using up old stock," she said, as she franked the postcards with a muscular thump, thump. We'll work our way around to the 'South Africa' stamps by Christmas."

The post mistress, who liked her meat and brandy when she could get it, had a faint moustache, was short and burly, did not shave her armpits and spoke a guttural English with an out-of-place Malmesbury 'brei'. She was sweating in her little hot office because she had all the windows closed. Sticky fly strips dangled from the ceiling. "Can't stand the flies. Not like the Swartland. Are you here for long or just visiting?"

"I'm here for long. Going farming at Ntambanana. Any advice?"

"Welcome to the 53 Mile – that's what this station used to be called. Don't know why. If you're planning to buy oxen or a horse, watch out for nagana. Talk to the vet, Eben Brink, if you can find him, before you buy anything. Also chat to the wagon maker, Johan Mocke, who's on the level but with him you have to bargain. Offer him lunch to soften him up. Mind you, the only place for any lunch at all is the hotel, where the Indian waiter always serves soup with his thumb in it. I noticed he had a sticking plaster around it the other day.

"Who are you going to see now?" she asked. When he explained it was the manager of the Natal Bank across the square, she said, "Well, make sure you offer your left hand when you shake hands. Good luck!"

Puzzled, he thanked her, noting that the only other person in the post office was a pretty young Indian girl who was the telephone switchboard operator for the party-line system, concluding that, jointly, they would be a goldmine of local gossip.

The girl was barefoot.

Every subscriber to the party line network had their own code of long rings and short ones. Anybody could pick up the phone and listen in; although there was an understanding that this was 'not done', it was a rule broken regularly. Callers would often say "Mabel! Put your phone down. I can hear your clock ticking."

To make a call, subscribers would lift the handset, turn a small handle on the side of the Bakelite telephone which would ring at the village exchange, and give the name of the other party.

Trunk calls to remote destinations (like Durban or Pietermaritzburg) became a reality in 1912 and had to be booked through the village switchboard. The line was never very good and both parties had to howl down the phone to be heard. Although the line improved over the years, older residents could never get used to the idea that they no longer had to bellow, so still did.

Donald stepped down into the square and narrowly escaped a hissing steam water lorry spraying the square to keep down the dust. By the time he got to the other side he had encountered a span of sixteen oxen pulling a wagon out of Loftheim's yard, nearly colliding with the voorloper, avoided a horse and rider before being hooted at by one of Zululand's few car drivers, who shouted something unintelligible at him.

An open shed of wood-and-corrugated-iron near the general store was filled with hay for the horses and mules. Near the entrance of the bank were a hitching post and a water trough.

The man called Jan Mocke operated the ox wagon 'shuttle' between Empangeni and Ntambanana, as well as to-and-from the other cotton estates of Candover at Magudu, Gous and some smaller ones. Product was shuttled to Mtubatuba, the railhead, from where the raw cotton was railed to the cotton gin in Empangeni.

Earlier, the state had promised to provide lorry transports for cotton product but the road was left to deteriorate so badly that farmers had turned back to the ox wagon as a more reliable means of conveyance.

The bulk of periurban ox wagon traffic emerged from Holford's Cartage near the station because the owner had a contract for railway deliveries. A small team of indentured Indians scraping up the dung followed the path of such panjandrums.

Not far from the store was the forge of Arthur Gouws, distinctive for its blackness and smoke and the clinking, hammering noises. He operated as a farrier, and there was a permanent queue of mules and horses in the next-door field tethered to a long hitching rail waiting to be shod. Gouws made the steel rims for the ox wagon wheels too and worked closely with Mocke, as needs be.

The very small branch of the Natal Bank annexed to the general store echoed, on a smaller scale, the red brick and cast-iron 'broekie-lace' decoration of the railway station. 'Broekies' is the Dutch-Afrikaans word for women's knickers. 'Broekielace' not only describes knicker-lace but the cast iron trimmings used to decorate the verandah railings and eaves of many early Natal buildings. These cast iron confections were brought in as ship's ballast, although locally fashioned wooden versions were also in vogue.

Flowerbeds stood beside the entrance, sheltered from the sun by a spreading flamboyant tree and home to shrill Mynah birds.

Entering the gloom of the interior, he asked the only person in the front office, little bespectacled Miss McAlpin, for the manager, explaining that he did have an appointment for 10 o' clock. He remained standing after having been asked to "please do take a seat" because he considered that sitting down implied he was 'unimportant' and would thus be expected to resign himself to wait until 'the Great One', even in this smallest of small branches in remote Zululand, had the time to see him. He had learned to reject the psychology of 'SOV' (Senior Officer Veneration) during his time in East Africa and, pointedly glancing at his pocket watch, his stance implied that he would grow impatient if he were not admitted into The Presence pretty damn soon.

It seemed to work and he was invited into the sanctum sanctorum to join the manager for tea and, remarkably, Baker's Allsorts Biscuits – a rare luxury from Durban – brought in after a few minutes on a tray by a bare-footed Zulu girl. He took a ginger biscuit and a chocolate-coated one wrapped in striped silver paper.

It turned out that the manager was a mild fellow who proceeded to offer his left hand to shake. Remembering the words of the postmistress, he realised that this was not a Boy Scouts' greeting but one of expediency, as his right hand had been stunted by childhood polio. His spine was bent and his breathing was shallow, causing him to take gulps of air every now and then.

"I was expecting you," he said. "I'm Alan Bustros – and yes, I am Lebanese. I suppose I was posted here as a 'neutral' because I speak the Taal as well as English and I don't belong to either the Dutch-Afrikaans or English 'tribes'. I also understand enough isiZulu to get by and can even stumble about with a few words of Tamil."

Bustros was pale, despite the blistering power of the Zululand sun, dark haired and slightly built with a pock-marked face.

"I received the details you sent me from Durban and see that you've transferred a hundred pounds to this branch already. That's quite a bit, so you mean business. It's in a holding account waiting for you to appear. All you have to do is check and sign the usual forms so that I can transfer it into a new Empangeni account. Would you like to discuss how you plan to proceed with the Ntambanana farm or is this too much like early days?"

Bustros had a silver-framed photograph on a small table beside his desk of his wife and three young dark-haired daughters who looked like him. The desk was of stinkwood, a dark and heavy timber found mainly in the Cape's Tsitsikamma forests and favoured by wagon makers, and the calendar was from Manufacturers' Life of Canada.

There were the usual framed banker's certificates on the walls, and an oil painting of an outspanned wagon and oxen among fever trees signed by the artist 'August Hammar'.

Bustros followed his gaze to the painting and said that

the artist had retired near Empangeni.

"He's a remarkable man and I have a few more of his pictures. I particularly like this painting of his with figures camped beneath old gum trees, the smoke from a campfire billowing up. He came from Sweden to work with Pastor Otto Witt at Rorke's Drift but his timing couldn't have been worse. He arrived just a few days before the place was taken over by British troops preparing to defend the mission station against swarms of Zulus coming from the massacre of part of the British Army at Isandhlwana, across the other side of the Buffalo River.

"He survived the attack by being in the Oskarsberg at the time, a kopje overlooking Rorke's Drift, and then walked all the way to Durban, arriving penniless. Eventually he was articled to a surveying firm in Stanger, north of Durban, which led to his triangulating a good part of the coastal region of Natal and Zululand as far as the St Lucia lighthouse, on foot; his colleague Percy Stott doing the rest. This was some time after Hammar and a Dr Schulz surveyed – on foot – substantial parts of Rhodesia, right up to the Victoria Falls.

"He's a good painter, as you can see, as well as an engineer and surveyor, and you might wish to pick his brains at some time. He's a good man to know."

Returning to the subject at hand, Donald said that he did have a draft business plan but details of it would probably change once he had been to Ntambanana and was able to take into account what had to be done.

Then, of course, there was the option of assembling a dairy herd with all the accompanying expenses, although dairy or beef farming had become far less attractive after hearing about the disastrous effects of nagana on cattle herds.

"Nevertheless, bearing all that in mind, here is a draft for your files. From this you'll see I plan to register a private company with limited liability, but that can wait for a bit until I get to know the lie of the land.

"My immediate need is to buy or hire some sort of vehicle tough enough to survive the road to 'Tam. I know I'll have to get hold of a wagon and a span of oxen, sooner or later, but that can wait until I get back from Durban."

"For wagons, you could do worse than introducing yourself to Jan Mocke," Bustros said. "Jan's a bit of a rough diamond but a good fellow and an outstanding carpenter too. His outfit is behind the station near the stockyard. His advice about wagons, oxen and everything else would be worth listening to – that's if you can understand his Dutch-Afrikaans-accented English. Just be careful before committing yourself to oxen. East Coast fever is endemic here too. It kills off horses, mules and other ruminants. If you have to buy oxen, may I suggest that you stick to the local Nguni? The native cattle have built up a centuries-old resistance to the six varieties of ticks you find here. I could go on about this but will leave all that to Eric Schnurr to fill you in properly. He'll caution you to limit your cattle-dipping too. If you start dipping local cattle too much it reduces their resistance to ticks – don't know why. The Pretoria government-wallahs argue differently, but what do they know? Bunch of pen-pushers.

"The Native cattle and the Afrikanders used by the Boers seem to be far more resistant to 'East Coast' than foreign cattle too; although the Nguni are not good for beef. Too narrow at the haunches."

There was a photograph on the wall nearest the door

of a smiling middle-aged couple. "Those are my parents," said Bustros. "We were standing on a huge circular rock overlooking the St George church at Beth-Maroun when I took the picture and that's Mount Lebanon in the distance.

"What's your Dutch-Afrikaans and Zulu like? Any good?"

Donald said that he could get the gist of Dutch from his exposure to German in erstwhile German East Africa, but he would be tongue-tied if he had to speak it; although he confessed he couldn't speak more than a few words of Zulu.

"Well, if you don't do something about learning some more pretty damn quick you'll be cutting yourself off from many of the people you'll be dealing with and often depending on.

"Perhaps a good starting point would be to get a simple Zulu / English manual from Loftheim's. As for Afrikaans, evidence that you are actually trying to pick up the lingo will go down well. Ask for guidance on who would be the best person to teach you. Avoid politics like the plague, but try to learn a bit about their rugged culture.

"Afrikaans is still regarded by most English-speakers here as a kind of 'kitchen-patois', a pastiche of simplified Dutch with a good helping of German, a spot of French, Malay and Hottentot mixed into the pot. It grew out of the need of the Dutch Boers to communicate with their slaves in the kitchen and the farm.

"Although it had become a lingua-franca among Boers by the time of the first Anglo-Boer War, it is not used in official documents and you won't find it being taught in schools. A pity though. How slow we are to accept the inevitable. High Dutch became the other official language after Union in 1910, as you know. Before that, it was English-only in Natal.

"The scorched earth policy of Kitchener, that saw farm dwellings in the interior of northern Natal, the Transvaal and elsewhere set on fire, livestock slaughtered, the rounding up of Boer women and children during the latter part of the second Anglo-Boer War into concentration camps, is something which will never be forgotten or forgiven.

"The death of more than 20,000 women and children in such camps is still very fresh in every Boer's mind, and all those in Natal whose mother tongue is English – no matter whether or not you have ever been to England – are lumped together with the same simmering resentment. Do you blame them? Being even-handed in your business dealings with them will go a long way to getting grudging acceptance, but go to great lengths to ensure you understand the extent of any verbal agreement entered into. A lot can get lost in translation if you don't and that can introduce unnecessary misunderstandings, sooner or later. Don't rely on a handshake. As a banker I don't have to tell you to get agreements written down and signed by both parties.

"Mind you, you never will be completely accepted. Many of them still regard Natal as rightfully theirs, although their eyes glaze over when the whole subject of Zulu presence and ownership crops up.

"It's often argued by those who live in ivory towers that the land really belongs to the Bushmen, who were indigenous before the arrival of various Nguni tribes, including the Zulus who filtered down from areas further north in about 700 AD.

"Nguni is the umbrella term for a grouping of tribes

with similar language roots, including the Swazis, the Tsongas, the Pondos, the Shangaans in Moçambique, the Ndebele and of course the Zulus, plus some smaller tribes. You'll still find a lot of Tsongas living in the far north-east of Natal.

"The Xhosa language is a derivative of predominantly Zulu and some San – hence the frequency and variety of 'clicks', so typical of the Bushman. The Pondos speak a variety of Xhosa."

Donald noticed the ease with which he pronounced the 'Xh' in Xhosa which sounded a bit like the giddyup clicks one makes to a horse. There are other words in Zulu and Xhosa that require one to employ a tocking sound with a fluted tongue that Bustros pronounced with equal ease.

"In other areas of farming, much will depend on the makeup of your work force. You'll probably think that the Zulu men are 'lazy' or might find that they won't work for you at all. You are not alone. Labouring in the fields is traditionally 'women's work' (except when new ground must be tilled), men's work being rather the care of their cattle, the important digging of deep pits in the cattle enclosure in which to store grain for the winter, and the building and repair of the huts.

"Their being suppressed after the 1903 Bambatha Rebellion was put down, well after what seemed to be the final dismemberment of the Zulu nation by Chelmsford at the battle of Ulundi, has helped to smash their self-esteem and build resentment; hence the general refusal to work for white farmers.

"Frankly, I am a great admirer of the Zulu. It troubles me greatly that we are busily destroying their traditional way of life.

"Shangaans from across the border in Moçambique could turn out to be a better bet for labour, as long as tribal animosity can be ironed out. Labourers from other parts of the country – like Basutoland and the Transkei have no resistance to malaria – so avoid employing them unless you enjoy paying for funerals. Other than that, it's almost inevitable that you will wind up with Indians. As you'll have observed, Natal's swarming with 'em.

"Most of them were indentured so you might have to go through the rigmarole of paperwork if they haven't finished their five-year renewed contracts."

He said that Indians had few reservations about working on the land and they worked hard. One or two of the wives could help with cooking and the housework, Bustros suggested. "But do pay them responsibly. Just a thought: With many emigrating from the Madras, there's no doubt the women would be able to cook you damn good curries. You've probably eaten them in Durban.

"I'm told that you get the best curries in the Britannia Hotel at the end of the Umgeni tramline. It's been known for farmers to catch the tram to Umgeni from the Durban post office, eat a legendary curry at the Britannia washed down by more than several lagers, then stagger across to the Umgeni railway station in time to catch the Zululand milk-train.

"People say that coolies are somewhat careless about hygiene, so just make sure that domestics wash their hands in a solution of Condy's Crystals before they prepare food and be in the kitchen to ensure they do it.

"You'll come across a few Dutch-Afrikaans families at Ntambanana and other places in Zululand – such as Hluhluwe and Mkuze further north up the coast, most of them impoverished by the destruction of their farms and livestock during the Anglo-Boer conflicts. Many have not had the opportunity of acquiring much education; but don't on any account underestimate their courage, determination, intelligence, basic farming know-how, tracking skills and marksmanship.

"And take into account that there's resentment at the failure of a further rebellion by the 'bittereinders' just four years ago, who had visions of finally overthrowing the British yoke and creating a 'free and independent republic' embracing Natal, the Orange Free State and the Cape. Only the declaration of martial law in October 1914 by Smuts and Louis Botha (both government leaders despite the fact that they are Dutch Afrikaners) brought about the crushing of the revolt through superior forces of 32,000 at their disposal against the rebels' 12,000.

"So the Northern Natal interior, and even where you are proceeding close to the coast, still simmers in parts with 'bittereinderskap' [bitter-end resentment].

"As for cars, I suggest you find a 'Tin Lizzie' in Durban. Cheap and tough. The man to see there is a Georges Chapard. You can rail it up here instead of enduring a very, very long bone-shaking ride – that is, if you ever managed to get through. The Model T is rugged enough to survive an earthquake, a rhino-charge and even the dongas, corrugations and potholes of such farm roads as there are; not like your Model N, which is more for your fancy tarred Durban streets.

[Donga is the Zulu word used by everyone in Natal for the eroded gullies, some quite deep ones, which existed on the makeshift roads, often rendering passage impossible. They were created by heavy rainfall and poor drainage.

Occasionally, the deeper ones were filled with stones so that vehicles might pass. Corrugations are the washing-board ripples that develop at right angles to the road that are made by the accumulated bouncing up and down of tyres on a sprung suspension. The more inflated the tyre, the more quickly the corrugations form.]

"Meanwhile I'm sure your new acquaintances, the Bells, or one of their farmer-friends, can fix you up with a loan car to reach Ntambanana – if the road is negotiable. Mind you, a horse might get you there quicker, taking into account the state of the road after the recent heavy rains – abnormal for this time of the year. But I guess that you will have quite a lot of basic equipment to take along and store somewhere. Far too much for a horse; and then of course East Coast Fever is making even them harder to find. A thought might be to tag along with Mocke's ox wagon shuttle. You can be certain you will get there; but make sure you know where you are going to leave the stuff at the other end.

"A final observation: We English speakers are working among three defeated peoples – the Indian (albeit of sixty years ago, in India), the Boer and the Zulu. Expect sudden outbursts of resentment."

Emerging into the bright sunlight, he was drawn to Loftheim's General Store beside the bank, thinking he should buy something to present to his hosts.

Above the separate entrance for Blacks was fastened a 'Naturelle / Natives' sign, near which a group of black women was sitting on the edge of the stoep, as close as they were permitted to sit to the 'Blankes / whites' entrance. Many were weaving grass baskets and mats. Some of their bare feet were as wizened as the legs and clawed feet of old tortoises.

When one made to stand up to stretch her legs she got onto her knees and moved her hands about as if to hold on to someone. A young girl went to steady her. Donald saw that the old woman was almost blind. On scrutiny of the other basket makers, he realised that many of them had the opaque eyes of blindness. They stared into the distance as they wove. One of them turned her head towards him and he saw she had advanced cataracts.

Others sat offering homemade utensils for sale – a collection of kraal-fired earthenware pots, brooms made from a bundle of reeds lashed to a bush stick stripped of bark and mats woven from grass. Some of their children, the picannins, had made small sunbaked clay models of Zulu cattle.

Donald thought that chocolates, even if they were available, would be useless as they might melt into a sticky mess on the way out to the farm, so he settled for a large maroon and white striped tin of Baker's Assorted Biscuits.

The store engulfed him with the smell of coffee, leather, mealie-meal in sacks, and sweat. Big glass jars of liquorice allsorts crowded the shelves, along with tins of bully beef, tinned spaghetti, tinned jam, tinned peaches, tinned corned beef, sacks of samp [pounded dehusked corn kernels], tobacco, blankets, umbrellas, clothes on hangars, rope, leather saddles, paraffin and display boxes of small coloured glass beads separated by colour. Over-the-counter medicaments were grouped separately.

Hanging from the rafters were the metal parts of ploughshares and harrows, three-legged cooking pots and a clutch of bicycle tyres and bicycle frames, while deep shelves behind the counter boasted bolts of Tonga Salampore and Striped Salampore cloth, hoes, metal picks separated from their handles, shovels, serge trousers, blankets, shoes, Primus stoves, paraffin lamps, pump action mosquito sprays, torches and much else besides, with more bicycle tyres hung from other beams among swathes of rope, zebra, nyala and wildebeest skins, and a net full of spinning tops.

On the counter were jars of leaf tobacco, packaged tobacco, CTC cigarettes and amorous-motto sweets, some in Zulu for those who could read the Zulu newspaper, Ilange Lase Natal.

Above the shelves of tinned foods (snoek from Cape Town, black Mabela porridge, powdered milk and condensed milk) were tinplate posters advertising bicycles and Assegai Smoking Mixture.

One of the bicycle tinplate posters was of a muscular white man robed in a mixture of Ancient Greek and Zulu chief splendour, brandishing a knobkerrie (a thick stick terminating in a knob, although this one had protruding spikes). He was brandishing a bicycle above his head.

The competing cycle tinplate portrayed a black man hurriedly cycling away from a lion and pointing to an inset drawing of an exhausted beast from which he had escaped.

Donald pondered on the advertisements, wondering what messages might be communicated to an African's gaze. He conjectured that the knobkerrie advertisement was just downright weird and was conceived by the owner of the factory or his daughter, somewhere in Germany and with only the vaguest idea of what went on in Africa.

As part of the Zulu initiation to manhood required a youth to display manly courage and kill a wild beast like a lion (if he found one handy, or some other wild beast if he could not) rather than running away from it, he thought that the tinplate would make any self-respecting Zulu shy away from the idea of actually being associated with such a cowardly bike.

The enamelled Assegai Smoking Mixture advertisement portrayed a large bearded white man seated on a veranda stoep in a rocking chair, his pipe emitting clouds and clouds of grey smoke through which a Zulu warrior in full regalia was leaping, brandishing an assegai.

The heat of the sun beating down on the iron roof caused sudden crackling sounds whenever it came out from behind a cloud.

No matter where Donald entered a country store later on in life – and he was to enter many – that first encounter with Loftheim's Empangeni General Store would surge back to mind.

Emily and her mother were there, accompanied by a French or Italian-looking girl of about the same age as Emily, talking to other farming women examining fabrics. The girls seemed to be talking sotto voce and Donald noticed her friend glancing at him when she thought he wasn't looking. Emily's mother was fanning her face with a grass fan in front of it – as most of the white women were doing. It was not long before he bumped into Toby, both of them with tennis shoes in mind.

"They're jolly good tackies!" the Indian counterhand said as he brought down shoeboxes. "Straight from Durban, 'Runnicans'. Velly, velly good!"

Donald saw how thin his arms were and how drawn his face was and could only conclude that he was not getting enough to eat, even though some of what he had eaten exuded as garlic and curry breath every time he spoke. He was to encounter similar physiques in Zululand and in

Durban in the years to come.

In the 'Natives' part of the store, a scantily-clad teenage native girl was selecting coloured beads with great care, guided by what seemed to be her sister and her mother. The colours and their quantities seemed very important.

Her mother went on to buy sugar in a twist of 'sausage-wrap' before counting out coins fished from a small bunched rag.

Sweat began to trickle down Donald's face and he was glad to make his escape to the shade of the flamboyant tree.

The bottle store, licensed to Gyn & Belcher according to the hand-painted sign, was further down the road in another wood-and-iron structure attached to the hotel, and into which he went to buy two bottles of Cutty Sark whisky, one to present to his weekend hosts and the other to accompany him to Ntambanana.

Indians were allowed to buy spirits – the favourite being cane spirit, distilled from fermented sugarcane molasses – but natives were not, for fear that alcohol, in any quantity, might inflame another uprising. They had to be satisfied with mild 'native beer' brewed from a nutritious wild black corn, and sold in the small native beer hall, well away from the main road and the station. Nevertheless, there was a constant secret brewing of illicit liquor, fortified by cane spirits bribed out of a white man or Indian. Called 'tchwala' or 'skokiaan', this moonshine often had a devastating effect on the imbiber.

It was now approaching the time to meet up with his hosts, and after bumping into Toby yet again, who was plying his own path between the bank, the store and the small office of Broccardo & Co, Accountants, they agreed to leave the rest of commercial operations to the following Monday.

They passed the smell of roasting beef and beer wafting out of the entrance to the Masonic Hotel with its line of tethered horses and long watering trough, and paused to greet Moberly, mentioning that they were off to their host's farm for the weekend. They agreed to meet up again with the journalist at Ntambanana when he next visited, the quagmire of a road permitting.

The town's small bakery exuded the smell of fresh bread. It was attached to the hotel, but was owned and operated independently by Bustros the banker's brother and his wife, Donald learned later.

Emily and her brunette friend, Sonya, were already standing with Noel, Lucy, James and Edna when they crossed the square to the station. Sonya, slim in blouse and riding breeches, was holding the reins of a saddled horse – a hairy thick-legged mix between a hunter and a muddle of other breeds.

Donald noticed the same two barefoot natives he had seen at the station earlier now sitting beside sacks of mealie-meal [ground yellow cornmeal], the metal parts of a plough, big square tins of paraffin and parts for a steam-powered pump on the steps of the station entrance just behind them.

There were two vehicles beside them, one a Chevrolet farm truck with canary yellow wheels though now coated in dust, and the other a dark blue Ford model A with a dickey seat which folded out behind the main cabin, likewise covered in dust.

Emily introduced Sonya to the two men and said to Sonya, "We'll be playing tennis after lunch on Saturday and the Schnurrs might be there. Come along if you can. That's a solemn invitation. I'd love to catch up on your news." As she spoke, Emily flicked her eyes to the two men and back again.

"I'd love to, but may I ask Zeno to drive me there? I can't see myself riding all the way to the farm in this heat. He's very proud of his first car, even though it's decidedly second-hand and in mother's name, so ooh and aah when we arrive. I just hope he can drive as well as he says he can."

"Why not come to lunch as well?" said Edna. "James bagged some guinea fowl yesterday and we'll be having a roast too."

Zeno turned out to be Sonya's twin brother, offspring of the Empangeni accountant whose office Donald had noticed earlier.

Two Rhodesian ridgebacks sat beside James with their tongues hanging out and panting from the heat. As soon as the group made a move towards the vehicles, they scrambled and bumped onto the back of the truck; while James, Noel, Donald and Toby helped the two Blacks heave fuel and equipment in the same direction.

"Emily, you can share the dickey with Donald. Toby, come and tuck yourself into the car between Edna and me. You can't ride with Lucy and Noel because there's limited room for the two of them in the cab, with the gear lever taking up the rest of the space – unless you care to have your teeth shaken out by sitting on the back with Nthembu and his brother.

"Why on earth Edna decided to buy this contraption, I don't know. Mind you, it has an engine roar strong enough to frighten away crocodiles. So be prepared for a very noisy but 'fashionable' ride, before which I had better fill up."

James went to the back of the car and opened out the upholstered dickey seat, which was exposed to the dust and elements but great windy fun to ride in.

Beside another water-trough and hitching bar for horses was a Pegasus petrol pump – pump being the operative word, as petrol had to be drawn up from the subterranean tank by the Indian attendant levering up and down on a long French-curved metal handle, after he had turned a pointer on the dial to the number of gallons needed.

Golden yellow petrol started to bubble up from the bottom of one of two long glass vertical cylinders, the other remaining empty as the liquid accumulated in the first. The cylinders were held in place in a cast iron stand finished in red and higher than a man, with the name 'Pegasus' atop and an icon in red of a winged horse.

Each cylinder held one Imperial gallon.

Donald watched Toby's particular fascination with the procedure and wondered what he was thinking about. He was contemplating the future of oil and petrol distribution throughout Southern Africa, in fact, and about the inevitable mechanisation of tasks requiring engines, petrol, diesel and oil to jostle aside ox, horse, fodder supply and manual labour.

When the one cylinder was full the pump would 'ping' and empty the fuel into the car's petrol tank after the attendant threw a lever, thereby creating a vacuum sufficient to draw up petrol into the adjacent cylinder.

At that point, Sonya brought her horse along to the water trough beside the pump and winking barely perceptibly at Emily said, after spotting Donald sitting with her in the dickey seat, "See you tomorrow!" while her horse sploshed away.

"Well. We're off!" said James, after settling up in the

store, although they weren't; because the fuel system had developed an air bubble and the car refused to start. James slammed out of the car, unscrewed the petrol cap, poked a rubber hose into the tank and began to suck until the petrol rose up the pipe and he had to spit it out. "Ugh! What an awful taste!" he spluttered as he got back into the car, breathing petrol fumes.

"Whatever you do don't smoke," said Edna, as the car commenced its long bumpy ride to the farm. Donald managed to learn that Emily was majoring in English and Social Anthropology in her final year at the new University of Cape Town. It had been elevated to full university status with the power to award degrees, and she was one of the first students to enroll in the discipline of Social Anthropology that had been developed by a Professor Brown.

"Have you read Goddard's 'The Passing of the Great Nordic Race'? No? Well, don't. It's dangerous scientific bigotry. It's a pity that anthropology can become so easily entangled with myths about Nordic superiority and eugenics. My social anthro studies veer well away from all that rubbish and are based on solid fieldwork."

This went well over Donald's head but he looked suitably impressed.

"So can you shimmy yet?" she shouted, changing the subject. "University and the Age have made us girls independent, unfettered, unchaperoned and uncorseted. Do you think that makes us more attractive, or less?"

She was wearing a white cotton blouse sufficiently unbuttoned for Donald to glimpse more than the top of her breasts when she leaned forward, khaki riding britches and well-worn brown farm boots, all topped by a floppy brown hat from which her flaxen hair fell halfway down her neck.

She was slim but looked as if she could handle a horse and a rifle with ease. Her wide-set eyes were blue-grey and intelligent, her nose chiselled and her mouth generous.

Donald thought she was beautiful.

"I'm impressed with your being able to speak Zulu so fluently," Donald shouted, "at least it seems fluent to me. I noticed your talking to your two farmhands."

"Oh, Nthembu and Hlakanyana? [N-tembu and Shla-kan-ya-na]. We grew up together on the farm – not exactly in the same khaya but I learned to speak Zulu almost before I could speak English properly. Having a Zulu nanny helped a lot too; though I'm still battling to speak the other language, Die Taal, in the way sentences should be assembled and pronounced. My vocabulary is sadly limited and I find it difficult to get around all those guttural bits and muddle up where to put the verbs. Sticking a verb at the end of a sentence is disturbing. Mind you, the Krauts do it and throw in a 'het' here and there." This remained a shouted conversation.

"I'm sorry. I don't follow you."

"Well. It's all those tenses. If you say 'the baboons climbed the mountain' in Dutch-Afrikaans you would have to stick the verb at the end of the sentence, introduce a 'het' somewhere and attach a 'ge' to the verb – a strange guttural sound as if you are about to spit. Well almost. You'd have to say (I think) 'Die bobbejane het die berg geklim'. And instead of just sticking an 's' at the end of a noun like 'baboon' to become the plural 'baboons', the word changes from 'bobbejaan' to 'bobbejane' [bawb-ber-yah-nah]."

"So your knowledge of Zulu might explain why you're majoring in Social Anthropology. My guess is your thesis is an aspect of Zulu culture. Right?"

"So very right. It's the variation in the Zulu customs of lobola [bride-price] in the structure of a cattle economy, but now suffering from devastating cattle disease. That's the main thrust, but set in a wider study of the society, still adjusting to the intrusions of the Boers and then defeat by the British. It's difficult because while I may be able to observe from fairly close at hand and evaluate lifestyles through conversations with Zulus, any anthropologist worth her salt should live with the tribe – and that is clearly impossible for me."

"Yes, I can't quite see your living in a mud hut."

"I don't know how much you know about this collection of tribes or how much you care, but I'll give you a potted history and culture lesson back at the farm, if you like. No doubt the Zulu life-style is somewhat remote from the WaHeHe and Swahili you came across in East Africa."

"I'd like that very much indeed. I need a spot of conditioning for what lies ahead."

Donald looked back to see how far behind the other vehicle was, but all he could see were billows of dust kicked up by their car. It became apparent that Noel was hanging back to allow for most of the dust to settle.

Then the car hit a small donga which hadn't been filled with aggregate properly or which had been eroded again by a sudden downpour.

Donald and Emily were thrown together violently and instinctively clutched each other to stay in the dickey-seat. Their eyes met for much longer than entirely necessary and at that point Emily knew; she just knew.

They disentangled themselves as Jim got out of the car to see what damage had been done. But after crawling under the chassis in the dust to see if the suspension was still intact and satisfying himself that all was well, he climbed back into the cab, dusting his clothes, muttering about the Natal administration and its neglect of the farmers' welfare, failing even to repair such rudimentary roads that led out of Empangeni.

Donald was to mutter such observations himself when he made his second journey to Ntambanana by motorcar.

After they had recovered and dusted themselves off, Emily said, "Expect to meet a rather charming Swiss couple with strong German connections at the tennis on Saturday. That is, if it doesn't rain. You don't mind, do you? The war thing behind you as much as possible? What about Toby? Their names are Hubie and Frieda von Weldenburg. (I like the 'von'). Hubie is almost comically formal, but finds it difficult to click his heels when he is wearing tennis shoes. Frieda's a blonde charmer. Wish I had her legs. Don't know where they fit in exactly, they seem more German than what I imagined German-speaking Swiss people would be, but they have bought a rather large chunk of land nearer Richard's Bay. No doubt, all will be revealed.

"Can't help wondering where they managed to get their money from, considering that Germany is in such a mess – reparations and all that, and getting worse. Mind you, the Swiss banking system prospered during the war and I take it that they were in Switzerland for all the war years. So perhaps that explains that. Daddy seems to think they could be a Good Thing. Vaguely titled, and it is a Swiss title after all, or at least it is suggested that Hubie is, so it will raise the tone just a smidgen above 'we ruffians'.

"Yet, I'm not so sure. Something odd. Weird philosophical undertones. I don't like all his talk about eugenics, but I am told that the sabre scar on his face is real and not provided by an obliging surgeon. But that was fashionable in Prussia wasn't it, rather? Officer Class? Not Switzerland. I don't know. Fishy."

Emily had a way of uttering a few essential words every now and then to sum up what others would spend some minutes explaining. Verbs were not always present in these short bursts.

"For a sugar-cane farm, the area is particularly malaria and tsetse fly prone, but they do get a good view of the Bay.

"Don't let Frieda charm you to death. I might just get a little jealous. Can you speak any German from your encounters in the war years? Even though they are officially Swiss-German, a few words of the lingo might help. I imagine they must speak a Swiss dialect version – what's it called – Schweitzer-Deutsch? Or would that be only for the Swiss plebs? Rather like the Russian court only speaking French."

Donald said that he understood "a smattering" of standard German. Emily said, "Well use your smattering. It could go down rather well."

At the steering wheel, James kept to the right of the road for, from long experience, he had learned that this ameliorated the shock of endless 'corrugations' which made the car shudder and everyone's teeth chatter.

Donald resigned himself to keeping his teeth clenched and remaining conversation-less for the rest of the journey, when the car suddenly slid to a halt in a cloud of dust on coming around a corner.

Emily said, "Oh-Oh. Odd-toed Ungulates! We call them Mr. and Mrs. Jones because they're always together. They strayed from the Umfolozi Game Reserve some time ago but we're just letting them be until the rangers turn up to shoo them back."

The two white rhinos were blocking the road.

Zululand is rhino country. There are two subspecies in Africa, the white and the black rhino. The white rhino is bigger than the black and has a marked muscular hump to support its huge head. Its broad flat mouth is also distinctive. The smaller black rhino, being a browser only, has a pointed mouth for grasping tree leaves and twigs. The width of the white rhino's mouth, on the other hand, is ideally suited for grazing grass.

Emily said, "They like this place because there's a watery hollow nearby, a place to wallow when we get some rain, lots of grass and shade from the fever trees."

James leaned out of the cab, thumped his hand several times on the side of the door and hooted, which made the rhinos stroll off into the bush beside the road. Donald noticed a giraffe peering over the trees and then another.

"We're quite close to the game-reserve and these two must have made an opening in the fence some time ago which was mended again before anything else could escape, except for those giraffes.

"You may find a few white rhinos lurking at Ntambanana, although I heard that some fools were taking pot shots at them. Hope not," Emily said, before the car started off again.

"Marvellous to see, until one of them decides to charge you... the big trick is to step behind a tree at the last moment, if that ever happens to you." (She had snatched the opportunity to shout above the travel noise during a stretch when there were few corrugations.)

"Fully grown, they weigh more than 4,000 pounds, but they're not very maneuverable. Tend to gallop at you in a straight line if you get between a mother and her young or if it just decides to charge at you for no apparent reason. In a worst case, the best thing to do is climb up a tree. Rapidly. Not ideal if you have to shimmy up a thorn tree, but worth doing so in the circumstances.

"They've made a helluva mess in one of our fields, just by moving around," Emily said, "but what can you do? We've grown fond of them. Anyhow, if you were mad enough to kill one you'd land up with one bloody big carcass.

"The cane rats do just as much and more damage to the crop. They live near the river and the mud wallow and we'd leave them alone if they stuck to eating aquatic grasses, but they have a particular fondness for sugarcane – cotton too.

"Adults weigh in at about 20 pounds weight. They're voracious herbivores and can breed at six months. If it weren't for their arch-enemies, the snakes, the fields would be overrun with them."

Donald learned that the small band of Shangaans on the farm liked to eat them. They caught them most frequently when the cane was set on fire just before harvest – a way to raise the sucrose content and burn off the foliage so that stripping off the leaves was less arduous and the load for the mill held a minimum of trash.

"The flames drive them out of the fields and that's when the natives have a field day. Cane rat meat is higher in protein than beef and has a lower fat content." Emily shuddered while saying this.

"One could breed them, perhaps. And they don't sicken like cattle."

The car rumbled across the rail tracks of a siding, past a small team of Indians man-handling cut and stripped sugarcane sticks from an ox wagon onto a few open rail trucks.

Emily said that this was cane due to be railed to the sugar mill at Felixtown, near Empangeni. To make the most of each truckload, cane sticks were lined vertically inside the walls of the trucks so that the rest of the cane could be piled horizontally as high as possible.

The road curved left, leaving the corrugations behind, and entered a cool grove of dove-cooing eucalyptus trees and past vegetable patches and a line of wood-and-iron dwellings with mosquito screen doors. A young Indian girl at the entrance of one of the homes waved at Emily. She said, "That's Masheila. She goes to the tiny school for Indian children, St Mary's, near us, started by our minister with the approval of the Natal Department of Education, some distance away from the white children's school."

"It's a so-called Government Aided Indian School but it has only a minimum of resources, the building and desks are rundown and the pupils have to buy their school books. Indian education is not compulsory and it's not free. In Masheila's case and some others from our farm families Daddy pays 75 percent of their fees. Trouble is, they breed like rabbits so he has had to introduce a scale of support in relation to length of service. He managed to locate a white teacher who had headed up a small Indian school in Isipingo, south of Durban.

"Masheila is eleven years old and in standard four. Seems to be doing rather well. Clever little devils these Indians. They'll take over the country one day. Her mother and father, who can't read or write English but can read and write basic Sanskrit, are askance at her advanced views. She's far too young to wear a sari yet but knows how to dress in one by watching her mother, so taught me how to wrap myself sari-style with one of my mother's old curtains. Tricky, because I didn't have a pavadai (that's the blouse for the chest) and we couldn't improvise a petticoat either so when it all came undone I had nothing underneath. Glad her father wasn't around. Much mirth.

"When I'm home from varsity I drive her and some other Indian children to their classes as often as possible. For the rest of the time her father takes them there and back in a mule cart. Sometimes Lucy drives them. It's not unknown for Masheila to have to trudge all the way home when Reddy doesn't get there in time.

"The Indians that live and work on our farm are lucky, as Daddy treats them as decently as he can – unlike those working on some estates I can think of.

"Her parents and the other Indians here weren't aboard that paddle steamer 'Truro' which brought the first lot of coolies from Madras in 1860 to work here as indentured labour. They arrived only in 1910. The father has served his five-year indenture, but signed on for another five years, now almost completed. Soon the family will be free to settle anywhere they like – except the Orange Free State – or they could return to India; but I think many of the Indians on the farm seem quite happy to go on working here for a while.

"The voyage from India took four months when the scheme started and many of them sickened and died from malnutrition, typhoid, smallpox, tuberculosis and syphilis. But steamers are much faster now and the voyage is far less hazardous."

The agreement between the British administration in India and the Natal authorities on the indenture of Indians in Natal required that a percentage of them should be women (a strangely Malthusian ratio of 40 females to 100 men).

The introduction of females was viewed with resigned concern by most estate owners as it suggested a permanent 'invasion' (as in fact it turned out to be). Most planters viewed them as 'dead stock', as all the farmers desired were an adequate supply of healthy Indian men to work the fields.

In time, many planters came to recognise that Indian women could be exploited, as the farmers were not obliged to pay for the two thirds cost of their immigration and could employ them at particularly low wages in the fields, hoeing, weeding, planting beans between the cane lines and planting setts.

The status of Indian women was higher on the Natal tea estates as their dexterity and experience in plucking the top two leaves and the bud from the Camellia sinensis bushes far exceeded the dexterity of other local sources of labour.

Nevertheless, their wages were just more than half of an Indian man's twelve shillings a month, rising to thirteen in the second year.

In most instances, both on sugar and tea estates, Indian families were housed in primitive wood-and-iron or brick–and-iron 'lines' where overcrowding was the norm. Tuberculosis was rife; more so where conditions were at their worst, and deaths were commonplace.

Frequent reports of ill-treatment and employer violations of the terms of the indenture contract eventually reached the ears of the Indian government and for eight years, further immigration was suspended.

The hiatus stimulated the formation of a Natal

Commission of Enquiry and led to the appointment of a Protector of Indian Immigrants, which provided for some minor improvements. Then the floodgates of indentured immigration were once again thrown open until the Indian government in 1911 terminated the scheme permanently. Although indenturing released Indians from contracts five years later. a majority had no option but to sign on for another five years, through poverty.

Emily said that Indian labour helped to rescue the sugarcane, tea and cotton industries in Natal which were suffering from an acute shortage of labour, brought about by the potential Zulu workforce being lured away by the mines and the attractive wages offered, at a time when the introduction of a poll tax had forced them to seek employment.

However, this was not the only reason that Zululand farmers were short of labour. Perceived as lazy and unreliable, the truth was that many of the Zulus near the northern and central Zululand coast were suffering from poor nutrition and malaria or sleeping sickness as well. Scurvy was also present due to the absence of any fruit in the diet.

If an indentured Indian breached his terms of contract, ruthless farmers could and did extract harsh penalties for minor infringements – withholding wages completely. Some were known to flog workers for absence, usually through illness.

If an Indian under contract 'made a run for it', his escape would be reported to the police and he would be located, and, as often as not, flung into gaol.

"This is slavery by another name," said Emily. "The Dutch were the last to abolish slavery in 1863, thirty years after Britain and sixty years after the Danish; but in the Cape, the system of slavery was replaced with former slaves being indentured to the same owners as 'apprentices', a practice which ended only in 1840. See the parallel?

"The idea that all the Dutch Boers upped-sticks and trekked away from British rule because of the abolition of slavery is a myth. Most Trek Boers came from the eastern parts of the Cape and, in the main, didn't own slaves. In fact, when their three republics were established - the Free State, Natal and the Transvaal - the prohibition of slavery was enshrined in their constitutions. But – and this is a big 'But' – racial separation was also enshrined.

"The affluent Dutch in the Western Cape (with slaves) stayed put and just rolled with the punches and demanded money for their pre-abolition investment in slaves, indenturing their ex-slaves without much change except that they had to pay them a very modest wage."

"I see. Just to change the subject for a moment – what purpose do those small red flags on long bamboos serve and that small wattle-and-daub hut, set apart from the lines?" asked Donald.

"Those little flags are called 'jhandi' and are erected in front of Hindu dwellings after a pandit [priest] has performed a 'puja' for a significant household event.

"Such a small hut thatched in straw is actually a tiny temple for communal worship, perhaps providing some sense of security in a very foreign and mostly hostile land. It's where Hindu marriages, births and deaths are celebrated.

"I know of one farmer called Edmond who objected to the development of all this mumbo-jumbo – as he called it – and drove his truck over it. He was discovered dead in one of his cane fields some weeks later but any evidence of the cause of his death was destroyed by the jackals which got at his body first.

"I heard that the corpse of an Indian labourer was also discovered in one of the Edmond cane fields some months ago. The doctor said that he had died of starvation. Edmond was a swine. Just desserts.

"I stumbled across some minimal knowledge of Hindu customs when I met a man and his wife called Moothoosamy up from Durban, Third Class on the train. He is a 'Free Indian' (one who has completed his contract) and was visiting the Reddys and other Indians in the lines on a Sunday.

"He explained to me that most of the Indians on the cane fields were Sanatharist Hindus, their sect concentrating on the reciting of the myths and legends about epic heroes.

"Mentioning Third Class reminds me about that little Indian lawyer called Gandhi who was slung off a train in Pietermaritzburg about twenty-five years ago because he insisted on travelling First Class, and a white had complained.

"And look what that started! All because First and Second Class are reserved for whites. I wonder if he would have caused so much trouble if that white hadn't objected. The little fellow went on to fight for the rights of Indians through what he called Peaceful Resistance until he wore Smuts down – but you know all this."

Donald said, "I saw some strange squiggles that looked like writing on some of the goods trucks. Any ideas on what they are? There was a top line of squiggles in white with one below in red, then below that another in blue."

"I'll have to swear you to secrecy on this before I reply.

All right?"

"All right."

"The squiggles are Hindi, written in Devanagari (from left to right), my little Hindu friend, Masheila told me in the strictest confidence – so I would appreciate your not saying a thing about this"

"Mum's the word."

"They are messages by indentured Indians from one estate to another – the gist being 'My name is (say) Aryan Prabakur on North's Estate near Empangeni and come from Pudupakkam village in Tamil Nadu and my wife Nirani is from Paranur. Contact me by this means if you are from the same part and have news of our families'. It's a neat idea because these trucks travel the length and breadth of the Natal railway system, most of them touching on other tea and sugar estates sooner or later.

"You can identify Devanagari by the broken horizontal line which runs along the tops as part of the letters."

The car pulled up at the Bell's farmhouse, a rambling assembly of interconnected thatched rondavels [circular structures with thatched roofs] and verandahs, with a brick-built portion at the one end roofed with corrugated iron, ubiquitous in Zululand.

A plump ginger-and-white cat was crouched on the low back-verandah roof, watching the Mynah birds swaggering in the yard.

The truck arrived some minutes later and Toby got out. Lucy shouted, "We'll go straight on. Hand us your luggage and James will show you the path to our house. I'm sure you will have things to sort out, so see you later."

Donald and Emily clambered out of the dickey-seat by means of the grab-handle and a vulcanised foothold which protruded from the rear mudguard like a toadstool, while Edna bellowed in Zulu to Joseph, the kitchen boy, to come and help cart provisions into the house.

After going into the house to make a call, James returned and said, "We've invited Eric and Marie Schnurr over for dinner. They are good friends and they are braving the 'road' to Empangeni from Ntambanana for a spot of shopping. They'll be staying with us until Sunday, leaving after tennis.

"The Schnurrs keep spare racquets and some tennis togs in the boot for just such occasions. It makes sense when farms are spread all over the place and such roads that we have are awful. Driving that road back to Tam at night would be a nightmare – especially after a good dinner and a risk of heavy rain. Among other things, Eric is the Secretary of The League of Returned Soldiers and Sailors and is closely connected with developments in Tam. He can guide you through the mangle of dealing with the bureaucrats at the Department of Agriculture's Tobacco and Cotton Division.

"For my sins, I'm this year's chairman of the Empangeni Sugarcane Growers' Association, so I'd be delighted to give any general farming guidance you might care to listen to. There's a lot happening in this neck of the woods and a few tips might be useful."

Donald thanked him on their behalf and felt that this first contact augured well for the years that lay ahead.

"Let me show you the way to Lucy's house."

After showing the path past the tennis court Jim left them saying to Donald, "I see you're getting on quite well with Emily. I'm rather proud of her. Bright girl, even though her head is a trifle full of reformist zeal she picked up at university. She'll continue to bend your ear about the Zulus and indentured Indian labour until the cows come home. See you both at dinner. Don't worry about ties."

Chapter Three

At Noel and Lucy's cottage, Donald was shown to a guest bedroom and left alone to stretch out on the iron bed, creaking with rusty springs. The mattress was slightly hollow in the middle and he found it cradled him comfortingly.

The afternoon heat helped lull him to sleep and dream of snakes twisting up trees. Sounds of milk cans changed into howitzer fire when a girl he knew to be Emily flung herself upon him, naked, breasts dangling, to shelter from the shells that rushed overhead with the familiar sound of linen tearing apart. They put their arms about each other when what seemed to be a large restless cane rat came between them. "Those snakes are really Hluhluwe vines," Emily whispered as she pushed the cane rat aside.

He woke up suddenly to become aware of a large dog jumping off his bed and scuttling out of the door.

Through the window came the drumming sounds of partridge and fork-tailed drongos imitating other bird sounds, making it difficult to determine whether drongos or the bulbuls were making the full-throated bulbul calls.

The Zululand sun had set and the crickets and frogs were starting up. Toby knocked and came into the room to say, "I believe we're expected over at the main house for drinks and dinner in about half an hour."

"Good! It was the heat which made me doze off. I'll be ready soon and we can walk over together. Are Noel and Lucy joining us?"

"They will, but probably later because they're preoccupied with putting their young children to bed at the moment and I gather this takes quite a long time – supper, bed-time stories, briefing the nanny and so on."

When they reached the main house, James was standing outside the yard door listening to the distant rumble of thunder.

"The flying ants are out and the wooden windows have become difficult to open again so we're in for a storm very soon. Even the barometer agrees with me. Very unusual for this time of the year. It just shows you ... you can't farm by the calendar."

"Never mind, it'll be over late tonight and the tennis court will dry out by tomorrow afternoon. The surface is made of termite ant heap, which drains very quickly and provides an excellent surface. Ideal for spectacular slides. We have plenty of tackle, mainly left by absent-minded players, by the way.

"I'll get Felix to roll the court and mark the lines with whitewash just before lunch tomorrow. He's the son of the gardener and for a young Zulu; he's quite good at keeping the lines straight."

And indeed the time between distant lightning and the rumble of thunder was becoming shorter as the Schnurrs' approaching car was heard rattling over the siding lines.

"You've arrived just in time," James said as the first large drops of rain hit the corrugated iron roof noisily while the Schnurrs climbed out of their car. The petite wife was carrying a couple of racquets in their frames with sandshoes tied to them by their laces. The man held an overnight case.

"Welcome! Here let me take your bag. Toby and Donald, I'd like you to meet Eric and Marie Schnurr."

"Hello," they said and shook hands, Marie wincing when Donald gripped her hand a bit too strongly, crushing her fingers against some of the rings she was wearing.

They made their way through to the long front verandah, enclosed with wire mosquito frames and wooden windows which looked out onto the garden. The view of distant cane fields was being swallowed by the dark as the sound of frogs and crickets continued to swell. Sudden whirls of wind sprang up making the foliage of the eucalyptus trees thrash about.

Emily had changed into a simple cotton frock. Edna had dressed for dinner too. She sat in a cane chair with her feet on a pouffe, smoking a Balkan cigarette in a mother of pearl holder. She wore a string of pearls as nonchalantly as a gardener's hat.

Donald became mesmerised by the length of ash that accumulated at the end of her cigarette before she flicked it into the tray. "Keeps the mosquitoes away," she said, when she saw him watching her smoking.

"Awful things, Turkish cigarettes," said Emily who sat well away from the smoke. "Smell like cow dung."

James smiled and advised Toby and Donald to follow the Zululand custom of including a daily measure of quinine powder with their drinks.

He kept the quinine in a small glass jar with a measuring spoonlet on the drinks tray. Edna said, "You'll be glowing in the dark like the rest of us soon," and explained that quinine in solution glowed under ultra-violet light and even – if one looked hard enough – in sunlight.

"Turns us a bit yellow," said Emily. She noticed that Donald had a slight limp. She had draped herself on a kind of wickerwork chaise-lounge.

"Even now we look a spot jaundiced because of the confounded stuff. Isn't that right, Eric?" and the Zululand veterans did indeed appear mildly so under the soft electric light – the farm generator causing the lights to throb.

Donald wondered if Emily glowed in the dark and had a sudden vision of her lying naked like Goya's nude Maja and faintly glowing. He wondered if certain parts might glow more than others.

Schnurr said that he had heard of the newcomers' success in obtaining land at Ntambanana and suggested that the three of them might set aside some time the next day to discuss aspects of what to expect – and some hazards for which they should be prepared.

"I gather you've both landed fifteen hundred acres. You were in luck. Many servicemen were turned down. And then, of course, there were others who changed their minds when the full impact of what they were about to embark on made them quail – either that or they couldn't come up with the £500 deposits."

Donald had been able to cover the deposit with ease as he had inherited more than £3,000, his share of his father's estate. His early days were spent on the Scotland sheep and dairy farm. His father's other interests were in coal merchanting and exporting, while steam was king, expanding to cotton lace manufacture as world demand boomed. The looms produced camouflage nets during the latter part of the war and the family benefited from substantial government compensation in 1918.

Donald's brother, Andrew had lost his life at the Front in 1916, so the family could hardly be accused of 'war-profiteering'.

The Kirkwoods had a second home in Kew, Richmond, and as children, Donald, Andrew and the sisters Winnie and Jean enjoyed the biannual flits by train between Scotland and London via Edinburgh, with all the excitement of packing and bunk beds that went with it. His uncle, who lived nearby in Pagoda Avenue, Kew Gardens, was a banker with Capital & Counties Bank at 39 Threadneedle Street in the City.

Donald mentioned that he and Toby had discovered that the greater part of their Ntambanana lands were adjacent to each other, which might help in the pooling of some resources in the early stages, to which Toby nodded in agreement. Toby's modest wealth was inherited from his Anglo-Irish father. ('Anglo-Irish' was an unfortunate word, encouraged by embittered movements hell-bent on ridding Celtic Ireland of the Cromwellian invaders, although many of these settlers had arrived far earlier with Strongbow and the Normans in the 12th Century. In fact, the entry in Burke's Landed Gentry of Ireland described Toby's family as being 'from great antiquity, long before the usurpation of Cromwell in 1649'.)

"We'll talk before tennis tomorrow," Schnurr said. "It'll prepare you, despite her slender appearance, for Marie's left hand volleys later on. To my mind, left-handed squash and tennis players should be banned from right-handed matches. They have such a devastating advantage."

At dinner, while the late-rain thunderstorm crashed and roared, with Jim muttering "that's going to lower the sucrose content," the talk, interrupted every now and then by the crackle of thunder, drifted to rainfall, sucrose content of the sugarcane, the correct balance of precipitation, temperature and sunlight, the continuing difficulties in obtaining enough reliable labour, nagana, malaria, the noise of milk cans being heaved about in the middle of the night on the train's way to Zululand, crocodiles and the Ntambanana earth tremors.

Edna had switched off the dining room lights in favour of table candles, about which a few moths fluttered. The head houseboy, Joseph, wore white gloves when he waited at table. Kirkwood felt a foot against his and glanced across to see Emily's eyes on his.

"You do realise, do you, that "Tam" has been known to have quite strong earth tremors? Nothing catastrophic, about 3 to 4 on the Richter scale, but enough to frighten the poultry," Eric said.

"The other hazards are a lousy and deteriorating road to the settlement, no railroad anywhere near it, malaria in the low areas, sleeping sickness, fatal nagana in cattle and horses, labour problems, East Coast Fever – and a high risk of flooding on farms near the river.

"Now I've put the wind up both of you I'll tell you tomorrow all about the positives. Tam's a land of promise as long as you have nerves of steel," at which both Toby and Donald smiled.

"Well, let's take our coffee in the drawing room," said Edna. "I like to see that the servants have time to clear up and get home before Jim turns off the generator. Be warned; it will be dark as pitch when he does, because the heavy cloud cover will obliterate any chance of moonlight."

Turkish coffee was served in demitasse cups. Biscuits

from the tin he had presented to Edna were in a bowl on the table. They were already soft from the humidity.

"Things seem to be going from bad to worse in Germany," James said. "I read in the Natal Advertiser, which came up on the same train as you did, that something much like the Russian revolution is breaking out all over the country with soldiers, sailors and workers forming councils based on the Russian model. Ghastly stories of what the Bolsheviks are up to in Russia too. It seems that Lenin is hell-bent on breaking forever the grip of the bourgeoisie and any form of civilised government in favour of the peasants. Over two thousand of the so-called 'possessing class' were executed in a place called Kharkov, according to the paper; and executions by firing squad are going on in other parts of the country at the same pace. Has the world gone utterly mad? Haven't they had enough?

"It's a contagion like the Spanish flu and it's sweeping across borders. Apparently, the latest German upheaval first started in Kiel and the councils are seizing military and civil powers in major cities. The upper middle-classes and what's left of the aristocracy are worried – to put it mildly (after what happened to the Czar and his family last year) and that explains why Hubie and Frieda were frantic to extricate their Swiss relatives in Germany.

"May I read you this short piece I found? 'Karl Liebknecht and Rosa Luxemburg of the communist Spartacist league, joined by supporters of the Russian revolution, have declared a Free Socialist Republic at the Berlin City Hall'. But it all seems very uncertain, because the Spartacists are being opposed by the socialist worker councils, according to the German newspaper, although contradictory reports are still coming out of Germany'.

"Amazing, isn't it, how quickly the papers get the news nowadays by the undersea cables. Mind you, I think the cable operators have a fight on their hands now that wireless telegraphy is operating so well. Soon we'll be living in an electrical fog of wireless signals.

"I've heard that an enthusiast in Durban is tinkering with something called shortwave radio. It can send voices and music around the world. Fancy that! Mind you, I believe the Hungarians in Budapest have been able to get the latest news by telephone into their homes and hotels for years. A 'Stentor' reads news stories every hour. All the listener has to do is don headphones to listen in. They even receive live performances from their opera house. Called 'Telefon' something-or-other."

Returning to talk about the turmoil, Toby said that the Bolsheviks seemed to be merciless. He had heard from a naval friend who had volunteered to clear up the mess at Enzeli when the Bolsheviks entered the town and took them prisoner. They had to watch daily executions of men and women. The brutality of the executions – especially of the women – can't be described in mixed company."

A flash and loud crack of thunder wiped out the rest of that train of thought, and Jim offered a nightcap to the men.

Noel said, "I think it's time we all retired, Jim. There's a break in the rain, which won't last and I can see these two lads are as tired as I am. It's been a long day."

Turning to Toby and Donald, Noel said, "Jim and I have to get up at the usual cock-crow tomorrow. If you two feel inclined you might like to come with us to tour the farm" – an invitation they accepted with alacrity.

"Eric, I'm sure you've seen enough of this place for you

and your good wife to get up later!"

Joseph was seen through the drawing room door placing two oil lamps on the floor inside the back entrance to the house. They were primed and lit and turned down to glimmer level.

Beside them were several umbrellas.

The rain had stopped as suddenly as it had begun, replaced by the sound of water gushing from the drainpipes. The lightning continued, illuminating the gum trees with sudden flashes, accompanied by grumbling thunder.

"It's one of those circular storms," Emily said. "You think it's over and then it comes back again. It'll return in half an hour."

"You'd better hamba ekhaya manje, Joseph. Just pasop for the umyazi. Stay away from the trees," Edna said, in a jumble of English, Zulu and Dutch-Afrikaans which she and Joseph understood perfectly to mean "You'd better go home immediately, Joseph. Just watch out for the lightning."

Jim said that he was going out to turn off the generator in the shed.

The throbbing sound stopped soon afterwards and the electric lights faded out so that the group, including Emily, stood illuminated only by flickering lightning.

Donald felt Emily's hand creeping into his. Their hands squeezed gently then parted.

Toby and Donald had thanked Edna and Jim for a delightful meal and an insightful evening, bade good night to Eric and Marie Schnurr and followed Noel out of the kitchen door to his car. (Noel and Lucy had driven over later, after installing their nanny to stay with the children, and were worried that the thunder had frightened them; so were eager to get back.)

They squeezed in, Lucy sitting bonily on Toby's lap for the short ride to the Reed's house.

Arriving, they all said goodnight and repaired to their bedrooms. Donald attempted to read a few pages by lamplight of 'The Thirty Nine Steps' by John Buchan, a novel he found on the bedside table. He had opened the book at random but got no further than trying to absorb the lines about a Sir Walter waiting for the hero in a dusky dining room before realising he was reading with his eyes closed. He heard noises coming through Toby's bedroom door resembling the grating roar of waves washing up and withdrawing on a pebble beach.

In the greater distance, Noel was snoring too. Donald was just awake enough to hear Lucy say loudly "Noel, you're snoring! Turn over!" and hear Noel mumble that he couldn't be snoring because he was awake, before Donald himself floated into sleep's unfathomable forests.

iKhwezi, the morning star of the Zulus, glittered in the pre-dawn sky. A distant cooing started of red-eyed doves as a breeze sprang up and rustled the shadowy eucalyptus trees, followed by the insistent call of a Diederik Cuckoo and the commencement of a weaverbird colony's twittering in the gum trees.

A dove started with its Morse code ... ... - - / ... ... - -/ and stopped again halfway through its call with a ... ...

Another eosphorean sound of which Donald was only drowsily aware was the creaking, swishing, muffled thudding and grunting of cattle being driven out to pasture; dark moving shapes in the half-light encouraged by whistled commands of an umfaan [young Zulu herd boy] who walked beside them, occasionally cracking a very long whip over their heads.

Donald released a dream where his BSAP sergeant was trying to sell him handfuls of cotton under gunfire in East Africa when a group of hadedas [Ibis birds common to the eastern parts of Africa] took off just outside his window with cries of maniacal laughter.

This seemed to be the signal for Jemima the maid to make loud crashes and bangs with pots and pans in the kitchen, and for a bantam cockerel to start crowing mercilessly.

In Zululand, dawn comes quickly.

Dressing without shaving, he made his way to the kitchen to find Noel and Toby about to spoon down mabela porridge made from black corn. There was bread from the Lebanese baker in Empangeni on the table and a jar of thick cut marmalade. Rotund and barefoot, Jemima was frying eggs, bacon, tomatoes and brinjals on the Aga stove. Coffee added to the bouquet of pleasant morning aromas, the steam from the coffee pot curling in a shaft of early sunlight.

"Good morning. The 'alarm cook' and the 'alarm cock' must have woken you, a wakeup combination that never fails. No need for an alarm clock on this farm!" Noel said.

The party-line phone rang with a short ring followed by two longer ones, the Reed code, whereupon Noel picked up the receiver in the kitchen and said "OK" and put it down again.

"That was Jim. He's driving over to collect us in fifteen minutes. I'm taking a couple of guns, but they're just in case we meet something very big and unfriendly – and that's not very likely."

Donald caught a glimpse of two little girls in nighties

scampering into Lucy and Noel's bedroom followed by the giggling squeak of springs as they jumped into bed with their mother.

Jim appeared with a truck, which back-fired when he switched off the engine, and invited Toby and Donald to clamber onto the back along with the dogs.

As there was little to hang on to, they were thrown all over the place by Jim's driving over the rudimentary road and were glad to get out for a spell to look at his sugarcane.

"Sugarcane is actually indigenous in this area," Jim said. "The Zulus have been cultivating it for centuries, along with millet, mealies [maize], beans, gourds and melons. They called the sugarcane 'Umoba'. The Portuguese discovered this through trading contacts in the 17th century, but the sugarcane we are growing is not the local variety. Ours, 'Bourbon Purple', is a hybrid from Reunion."

Toby spied a strange contraption of hessian and corrugated iron about the size of a cow positioned beneath a clump of trees, and asked what it was.

"That's an idea of a fellow called Harris. He's been trying to work out how the tsetse fly locates its prey and he seems to have discovered that they spot their next meal by sight rather than by smell.

"Several farms in the district are trying out the traps and they actually seem to be working. He's also discovered that the fly is attracted to the colour blue – hence the big blue rag draped on that box over there. We're acting as miniature research stations.

"Harris reasoned that if you positioned something roughly of the same proportions as a cow near a wooded area, the flies would be attracted to it; and they are. They fly under the 'belly' of the trap and then make their way up to that box at the top and can't get out. Funny thing, they don't bite Zebras. Something to do with the stripes confusing them. The tsetse breeds in thickets bordering forests."

He said that tsetse fly spread sleeping sickness [the human form] and the animal form, nagana, was causing deaths among otherwise healthy cattle herds. The Zulus had their own theories about the cause. They believed their cattle had caught 'Umagane' by grazing and ingesting the saliva of big game feeding on infected plants. There was also the belief that the spirits of their ancestors had got the hell in with them for allowing their descendants to be defeated by the white man and were punishing them.

"David Bruce, a microbiologist brought out from Scotland, established some time ago that a relationship existed between game, the tsetse fly and domesticated cattle; and it was Bruce who discovered that the fly acted as the carrier of the parasite found in the blood of wild animals, which are unaffected by it.

"Oddly, it was the rinderpest epidemic in the 1890s which killed off about 90 per cent of all the cattle in southern Africa and most of the game, that resulted in keeping Zululand nagana-free for some time. 'Rinderpest' means 'cattle disease' in German. Crop destruction through locust invasions, followed by a very bad drought which preceded the rinderpest devastation, led accumulatively to near-starvation of the natives, leaving them with no crops and no meat. It was a case of one damn thing after the other.

"Rinderpest, which the Zulus called 'umaqimulana', means something like 'to throw down' and refers to the quick and unpleasant deaths of their cattle and the game upon which they depend.

"After the contagion burnt itself out, no permits were

issued for the shooting by white farmers of kudu and buffalo. They were classed as 'royal game' for the Blacks.

"This was because, after the main Anglo-Zulu war and the second Anglo-Boer war which followed, Zululand was annexed to the Crown. The Chief Magistrate and Civil Commissioner for Zululand, Sir Charles Saunders, recognised that the local natives depended on game for essential protein and that there was precious little game still alive. The natives were starving, so what little game there was left had to be reserved for them."

Noel said that it was established, years later, that those particular beasts – the kudu and the buffalo – were actually the main carriers of nagana – and of course, the Umfolozi Game Reserve [founded in 1895] was close to the sugar estates and settlers' cattle-herds. This permitted the regeneration of a major pool of kudu and buffalo on the doorsteps of the new farms, established when about a third of Zululand was thrown open to white settlers in 1906.

"It was just a matter of time before many of our cattle and those belonging to the natives succumbed to nagana as the game population recovered. When it began to take hold, the game preservation rules were waived so that thousands of head of game could be shot out in an effort to bring the tsetse-fly under control.

"You would weep at the wholesale slaughter of nyala, one of our most beautiful species, along with endless zebras (that skin on your bedroom floor, Toby, is from one of them). It was random, reckless and lacking any scientific control and it didn't work. Bush-clearing and burning was done on a massive scale too.

"Further up north the blue wildebeest suffered the same fate, as it was thought that they had to be wiped out for the sake of the cattle; the current thinking being that they were to blame for the increase in nagana in that region."

Jim said that the wildebeest herds used to cross the Mkuze River to graze on pastures of a few white farmlands, as there was ample grass in the low-lying parts of those farms during the winter months.

A wealthy Mkuze farmer managed to get hold of a biplane from the Paterson Aviation Syndicate in Kimberley and used it to spot the wildebeest herds, until he crashed it and was killed. Once the herds were located he would land on a makeshift strip hacked out of the bush, and along with some friends mow down the wildebeest with hunting rifles when they neared the river.

"Those that were not killed with the first shot were finished off later by some of the African labourers, and then the carcasses were loaded up on an ox wagon, to be skinned and processed at the farm for the workers at a sawmill he owned.

"You can spot a tsetse – looks a bit like a bee and about the same size – by the way its wings fold flat on top of its body and the yellowish band around its abdomen. These critters are completely dependent on blood as their food-source – game and domestic cattle, although game is not susceptible to the disease. The tsetse's proboscis sucks up blood along with the trypanosome (heh! I got the name right!) parasites from game animals.

"When next it settles for a meal – it could be on an ox or cow, or you – the infection takes place. The parasites pass through the blood-brain barrier and penetrate the nervous system, causing changes in behaviour, poor coordination and immense weariness – a desire to sleep all the time, hence the name. Without treatment at an early stage, when the bug is only in the lymph glands, it's tickets."

They moved on to watch the ten-foot high sugarcane being harvested by Indian labourers, who were assigned to this part of the farm away from the few Shangaans working on the estate, to avoid friction.

The cane was cut to about six inches above the ground, leaving protruding stubble. Noel explained that the sugarcane stubble, called a ratoon, would regrow in situ and give a good sucrose yield for the next five to ten years. It would also be well on the way by the time the first heavy spring rains arrived.

"That rain we had last night was, I'm fairly sure, one of the last we are going to see until spring in September. Our cane is never allowed to flower and produce tiny seeds, called fuzz by the way, because the flowering halts sucrose production. So the last six inches is lopped off, well ahead of that time. Planting the fuzz would produce an entirely different variety because our cane is a hybrid developed from about six different strains.

"We set fire to the cane just before harvesting, as otherwise we'd be left with a lot of leaf trash to cope with and it's easier to cut after the leaves have been burnt off. If you had been here a few days ago, you would have seen the fires and all the cane-rats escaping. You have to make sure there is no wind to speak of when you do it and know your onions when it comes to the firebreaks being wide-enough. You get huge fireballs, but the fires die down in a few minutes"

Noel sliced a piece of cane and divided it among them.

"Here, taste. Crush it between your teeth and taste the sucrose juice. Hmm. Just right. Not too much rain and not too little and the burning has helped to improve the sucrose content even further. Chewing it is a bit like operating a sugar mill in miniature. You'll have to spit out the bagasse – that's what's left after the mill crushes the cane.

"In another part of the farm we finished replanting 'setts' in early March, skipping the weeks of super-high humidity in February, and we'll only start planting again in early September; but this style of cultivation is time-consuming and more labour intensive, so we only replace the existing roots every five years with short lengths of seed cane.

"First, most of the trash has to be removed, mainly by ploughing, to throw up the roots for labourers following behind to chuck the trash into an ox wagon. (Can't just be ploughed into the soil). After that, the soil must be harrowed to break up the clods.

"Then comes the furrowing to follow the contours, using ridgers with sharpish points to keep the grooves deep and narrow in width – the distance between furrows depending on rainfall patterns. At this altitude we keep the furrows about five feet apart.

"Seed-cane lengths are laid in the furrows, cut into 'setts' – short lengths leaving a joint towards each end – from which the new cane will sprout. Furrows then have to be covered as quickly as possible to keep in the moisture.

"Before that's done we plant a fallow crop of sunhemp to enhance soil nitrogen. It grows quickly especially after a good rain and can be ploughed in when it flowers and reaches a yard high. Sunhemp tends to block out weeds."

Donald noticed the Indian workers only wore dhotis [loincloths] and although most of them looked wiry, their arms and legs were very thin. Some of them smiled and a few waved. They were using pangas [long sharp steel blades with wooden handles]. Unusually, one of them was a woman in a sari who came over to the group and in broken English said that she was working in place of her husband who was 'very sick'.

Noel asked where he was and she indicated that he was at home. He said he would come to their hut to gauge his condition.

"Oh bloody hell," said Noel, once she was out of earshot. "Here's another one, Dad. Let's hope it's not malaria or sleeping sickness or worse still, Spanish Flu. Arthur Urquhart told me the other day that he was finding that there were a growing number of shirkers on his farm. Probably they're just plain sick. Mind you – I'm not surprised. He flogged one the other day because he thought the Indian was being cheeky. I'll go over to our fellow's hut to see what's wrong. They're not malingerers so this seems serious. That's the second one this week – and it's happening more and more often. It could mean we'll have to call in Dr Lombard – but he's passionate about his fishing on the weekends so he'll have escaped to Richard's Bay until Monday. The tiny bait shop there must celebrate his visits."

Turning to the two guests, he said "He stays there at what's called 'the hotel'. It's really just a few rondavels and getting there and back is not for the faint-hearted.

"Seen enough for the moment?"

Noel whistled to the Ridgebacks which set them bounding into the back of the truck to pant and slobber over Donald and Toby when they climbed aboard.

The day was sparkling after the overnight rain and they returned to find tea and sandwiches laid out on a brass tray beside the tennis court. Schnurr was already sitting there on a bench near the sun shelter, reading through some notes and smoking.

Felix had started to line the court with a mixture of lime and water dispensed from a squeaking marker, which he pushed along the traces of earlier lines.

Jim and Noel left them with Schnurr for an informal briefing.

"Just to fill you in, I know my surname is German (my ancestors came from Baden Württemberg) but we settled in Pennsylvania in the 18th century, so consider me more as an exiled American – that's why you might have had some trouble in placing my accent. I've lived here for about a year and could otherwise have been an odd choice – with my surname and my American background – to represent, among other things, returned servicemen about to start farming here."

Eric was thickset, just under six foot and the kind of person you would like on your side in a fight, as he had a determined glint in his eye and the muscular strength to go with it. His hair seemed to have been combed last time it was cut, and that must have been some time ago. His fingers were thickset and short and he wore a fraternity ring.

Seeing Toby looking at it, Schnurr said, "By accident. I must have been invited to join during a slow day in academia. Still – it's handy in the 'States where students recognise these things. Useful if one ever gets into a fistfight too. Great knuckleduster."

He spoke in a low rumbling mid-Atlantic voice which was guttural – as if a German had learned to speak English from a Scot - and typical of the Pittsburghian English – 'as she is spoke'.

Like most white men living in Zululand, he wore khaki

trousers and a long-sleeved shirt, both of which helped to keep flies, mosquitoes and ticks at bay.

"After university I went back to school – yes literally, at Bolivar Agricultural School – with the realisation that I needed 'hands on' training to prepare myself for what I thought lay ahead. I earned my stripes studying cotton production in the Louisiana Delta before war broke out; but by late 1916, I felt driven to join a voluntary unit while Woodrow Wilson was still dithering. I won't bother you with the details, except to say that I soon found myself on an American merchant ship dodging torpedoes on its way to England. I wound up serving as an ambulance driver for First Field Hospital, 2nd Division AEF – stationed at a farmhouse most of the time at Bezu le Guery. I remember my ambulance registration number to this day – SSU 578 4.

"Fiddled my name, for the duration, to Eric 'Stringer'– Schnurr is 'string' in German, as you, Donald, will probably know. The action I experienced was not better or worse than yours. Most vivid was an appalling shower of shells we had over our heads for three days, bursting quite close at times and blowing men at your elbow to pieces.

"After the war I decided to strike out to Africa when I read about the growing cotton boom, predominantly in Zululand, and with my cotton-knowledge the whole exercise seemed pretty romantic at the time. Elephants, gold, diamonds and all that thrown in.

"There was also another reason for coming to Zululand: Marie Labuschagne, whose family came from Mauritius to develop a sugarcane farm on the Richard's Bay side of Empangeni, but high enough to be out of the worst of the malaria belt. We met in London at a crazy party in a flat in Albert Hall Mansions just after the war. She was very vague (and has been ever since) about what she did do, except to say it was war work in the Registry. She said her knowledge of French proved useful. Marie had been three quarters of the way through her studies in London, majoring in French, when the war started and someone tapped her on the shoulder and invited her to work for them in 'Registry' in a rather mysterious outfit.

"When I met her she was sharing a flat near the top floor just opposite the Albert Hall itself with three other Natal girls. I remember well the elevator that only the eccentric British would have tolerated. It relied on a counterbalanced thick rope which ran through from top to bottom next to the operator who moved the cage up or down by pulling on it. He wore a strong leather glove and slowed the contraption by just treading on a foot pedal. It was not the fastest machine in London and he went home at midnight. Needless to say, I was often there well after pumpkin-hour.

"We were married in Chelsea Old Church quite soon after getting together, although, on reflection, we should have waited until we got to South Africa; but winkling a passage to this part of the world during the post war chaos was almost impossible. Her parents took a long time to accept me, but all that's OK now.

"I guess the combination of knowledge about cotton cultivation, stretchering wounded marines (and enemy) in France plus the fact I was married to a Natal girl qualified me for the job – in the absence of anyone else handy in Zululand at the time with this blend of qualifications that might have come forward.

"In Ntambanana you'll be under my wing until you get bored with my advice; in the sense that I will do my best to help you pick your way through the idiocies of bureaucracy and perhaps open a few doors when needs be (not that there are many doors in this part of the world).

"First, the Department did construct a road to Ntambanana (the one Marie and I struggled through to get here and which after last night's rain will be worse going back until it dries out) along which a motorised transport service was supposed to ply. It was designed to link Tam farmers to the cotton gin at Empangeni and the railway, but the 20-mile route is on its last legs through lack of maintenance. All that fanfare you might have read in the Durban papers about a motor transport service has turned out to be trumpeted hogwash. It'll be another two years before they get their act together – if ever.

"You had better know that the threat of infection in cattle has been greatly underplayed. These government poepgats in Pretoria (I learnt that useful Dutch-Afrikaans word from Jan Mocke, the wagon maker here) had failed to notice that tsetse flies had wiped out most of the native cattle by the time Ntambanana was being heralded as a beef and dairy heaven. Yet the authorities kept on with the idea that 'Tam' was an ideal place for cattle. They stumbled on the thought that cotton production might be an alternative during one of their very rare good days.

"So take my advice, steer away from investing in anything with four legs except, if you must, a sufficient number of Afrikander oxen to pull a plough until tractors become more plentiful, and a Nguni bull and milking cow (both are the hardiest of their kind) – and even then you'll have to work hard simply to keep them alive. Consider cotton farming instead.

"We're lucky that a fellow called Thieler developed

a vaccine for Rinderpest, otherwise we would still be suffering from the horror of that ancient disease brought to the West from Russia. So vaccinate the few cattle you must have.

"Tam is alongside the Umfolozi Game Reserve which is riddled with ticks. The Nguni have been tick-resistant for centuries, so approach dipping only when necessary. The Afrikanders may need more dipping than the Nguni. There is a dipping station on one of the Ntambanana farms so be guided by the advice of the fundis there. More about that later.

"Sorry, but what is a fundi?" asked Donald.

"A wise man, an expert. 'Fundi' is an abbreviation of the Zulu word 'Umfunidizi' – teacher. On the side, you could tinker about with sugarcane on a small patch – just to see what happens and gain experience from that. Try pineapples too – they seem to grow well at Tam.

"But give or take a few things, not least the bollworm and the cotton-seed beetle, the country is ripe for cotton although it could be flatter; but reasonable rainfall, not as heavy as down here near Empangeni, fertile soil, access to Indian labour (if you're lucky) and a growing market for cotton suggest you could do well.

"You'll know that by 1911, the idea of importing even more Indian labourers was abandoned after their number exceeded a hundred thousand, and there was an outcry that Indians were outnumbering the whites in some parts. Although many of them have rejected the idea of returning to India in favour of swopping their return trip passes for cash, some even for property, they remain willing workers when paid adequately and like to build up their savings this way.

"There's a spot of petty cheating here and there but nothing serious. Just watch out for the few who hit the cane-spirit bottle. They're a bit like the Orientals in this regard. They get tight as ticks after a single glass.

"Some of the native men have a liking for dagga [cannabis] and the weed grows here indigenously, all the way up to Swaziland. The women and children aren't allowed to smoke it. You can pick up the tell-tale signs – bloodshot, sleepy eyes, unpredictable mood swings, hunger and thirst. Avoid employing such men like the plague. Sends them off the rails eventually.

"But if you stumble across a patch being cultivated on your turf by men from a neighbourhood kraal, I suggest that you should leave it undisturbed. Just plough around it. A South Coast farmer and a policeman were murdered recently for uprooting and setting fire to a crop on the farmer's land. Many rural Zulu men consider that permanent access to their dagga plot is an inviolable right.

"You are welcome to stay in our Tam house, such as it is, until you get sorted out – and I know Marie would welcome that too."

Donald and Toby thanked Schnurr profusely but said that they had plans to camp on their individual allotments with the means in their trunk luggage to do so, but would value storing the trunks in one of his sheds.

"Well, at least, feel free to come along for the odd visit and meal when things get a bit rough – and sure, we'll stow your luggage.

"OK. Your priorities will be to bore for water, establish field layouts and sites for dwellings and get labour to dig a longdrop or two the moment you get there. I take it that neither of you have had farming experience?"

Smells of the roast began to waft from the kitchen accompanied by the clatter of plates as they confessed that they had not much agricultural exposure, although Toby said he had attended a short agricultural course at Cedara agricultural college (in the Natal midlands) shortly after he arrived in the country.

Donald said that he had gained some experience on a farm owned by his father in Scotland, but that was in sheep and dairy; in addition to which he had acquired four years of bush craft while serving with the BSAP in German East Africa.

"My advice to both of you is to read up on sugar and cotton production pretty damn soon. I've some friendly literature back home in Tam which you're welcome to borrow for as long as you like."

The distant sound of a car rattling over the siding lines heralded the approach of visitors. "We'll talk again later," said Schnurr. "I suspect that's the Broccardo youngsters arriving."

And it was. Sonya stepped out of a rather worse-for-wear little car, wrapped in a light blanket to keep off the dust. When she threw it onto the back seat she revealed a white mid-calf skirt topped by a white long-sleeved cotton jumper, cut sailor-style and ending over her hips. A small sailor's scarf was about her slender neck.

Following the convention of the time, Zeno's tennis togs consisted of a white long-sleeved shirt and long cream summer trousers.

"Eric, you're not frightening the guests with facts about Zululand again, are you?" asked Zeno. "Well? What do you think of my new toy? Mind you, my other car is a Crossley of course, but this is my 'brand new wildly second hand

Ford' and it will do very nicely for the time being. What do you think of her?"

Their parents were of Huguenot stock from Menérbes in the Provence-Alpes-Côte d'Azur region of France. Dark-haired Sonya and Zeno looked alike although Sonya was of a slighter build. Their catgut- strung racquets were of wood and looked as if they had emerged from a furniture factory, the idea reinforced by the square wooden clamps that kept them from warping.

Being twins, Sonya had entered high school in the same year at St Anne's as Zeno had at Hilton College, on the opposite side of the ridge above Pietermaritzburg, which most people called 'Sleepy Hollow'. The single-sex schools were for 'young ladies and young gentlemen' and came with a high cost to the early struggles of the Broccardo parents who scrimped to ensure that their children received what they regarded as the best possible education money could buy at the time.

Both Sonya and Zeno had done well, with Sonya going on to major in English at University College in Pietermaritzburg which she was completing, with the intention of taking a second degree in Law, while Zeno was reading Engineering and Agriculture at the same college.

They, like Emily, were on vacation.

Through their acquisition of a markedly Eurocentric education, they remained insulated from the reality of the conditions from which they received their succour. In fact, they were – through no fault of their own – transplants from another and remote society. While their relationship with natives and Indians was cordial, the lack of equal opportunities for the latter races to better themselves was regarded merely as a fact of life. They were apart; as were, in a sense, another defeated nation, the Dutch-Afrikaners.

Eric, Donald and Toby gathered about Zeno's car, a well-worn example of what Zululand roads would do to a vehicle over a few years.

"Wonderful! When did you learn to drive?" Eric was thinking of his friend Oom Scheepers who had at last bought a car (one of the few in Empangeni), had refused all offers of driving lessons and promptly reversed it into one of his ox wagons. After several incidents like this in the village, where he managed to run over a dog, bash into a fence and a tree, and then declared his intention to drive to Durban, Constable Jacobz of the Natal Mounted Police went out to his house and exclaimed in exasperation, "Ag nee, Oom. Dis te gevaarlik. Neem die trein en ry in Durban rond met die trem en huurmotors" [Ag no, Uncle. It's too dangerous. Take the train and ride around Durban in the tram and taxis].

"Dad polished up my skills but I had learnt the basics in Pietermaritzburg at varsity," Zeno said. "A friend of mine had a car – of sorts. Frightened the admiring schoolboys when it backfired. It so happens we use the same facilities as the school and visitors have difficulty in knowing where school ends and varsity begins. The lecturers alternated between being teachers at the school and lecturing us. We started off in a spare two-roomed building on Maritzburg College grounds feeling frightfully studious and important but sweltering under the tin roof – one room for BAs and the other for Intermediates, although the Science students managed to escape the heat by spending much of their time in the 'stinks' at the school. The Law students beat the heat by attending special lectures in the Supper Room of the

Town Hall. We've all moved to town now, but the sound of traction engines and some mad taxi driver who drives with his hooter is distracting."

Joseph beating a brass shell casing interrupted the discussion. A friend's son who had survived Delville Wood had retrieved it. The gong now hung from a back verandah rafter. The son had fought with the 2nd South African Infantry Regiment and had come through the carnage of Bernafay.

"Well, it seems we're being summoned to lunch."

Sonja and Zeno knew the Bell family well, including the native kitchen staff, and greeted them warmly as they passed through the kitchen with 'Sanibonani. Ninjani?' [Hello! How are you?]

The conversation at lunch came around to 'Zulu bush telegraph' and how quickly news spread without the aid of radiotelegraphy, telephone or heliograph.

Emily drew the visitors' attention to the way Zulus, particularly umfaans [young boys], could shout messages across valleys from one hilltop to another.

Another way was for a traveller to greet, converse and pass on messages to a walker coming the other way and to go on talking until the person was quite distant, both repeating the process upon the next occasion; thus carrying messages quite quickly to distant parts.

She pointed out the significance of Zulu beadwork, done only by the women. "You noticed how carefully that Zulu girl, guided by her older sister, was selecting beads in the store yesterday?

"I do know that beads manufactured in Jablonec – part of the Austria-Hungarian Empire – were so prized by some tribes that they were traded for gold and slaves. Some people call them Trade Wind Beads.

"The glass bead code is based on a triangle and limited to a maximum of seven colours, although that number is usually less.

"The triangle corners represent the father, mother and child. With the apex pointing down it means 'unmarried man'. Upwards means 'unmarried woman'. Another overlaid smaller triangle pointing down to form a simple diamond shape symbolises 'married woman' and when both apexes meet downwards it means 'married man.'"

She said that this geometry embraced a subtle interplay of coloured beads with inherent positive and negative connotations indicating if the person was engaged, married or unmarried and whether a man might identify a female in a crowd whom he could 'chat up' without reproach.

"But the language of the beads is far more subtle than that," Emily said, "and I am only now beginning to grasp the significance of one colour of bead placed in a pattern alongside another, as each colour, other than white, carries a double meaning.

"Blue, for example, can mean Fidelity or a Request, but on the other hand 'Hostility'. In the 'Ibheqe', a communication of love, black next to the white signifies Marriage; red, next to the black signifies a Longing Heart. The inclusion of yellow implies 'Pining' and the introduction of blue following yellow, red and black requires a reply or response to a wife whose husband is far away – most usually working in a goldmine on the Witwatersrand or on the railways somewhere.

"These are love letters and can be carried by a friend going to the husband's same place of work. There is much yet to understand and I am ashamed by my ignorance of a culture that we seem to be hell-bent on destroying."

There was a pause and all at the table were left silent and staring at their plates.

"Well! Suddenly we are all very quiet. You'd think a ghost had entered the room," Edna said cheerfully. "It's time for cheese and biscuits. Joseph, letha ushiza [bring the cheese]."

Tennis started up about half an hour later after a humorous fuss about the correct height of the net. James would wind the cable up and down with Zeno holding a vertical racquet against the centre of the net in one hand and another racquet topping it held sideways in the other and shouting. "Up a little" and "Down a little." James' deliberately over-wound each way until the joke played itself out. Much racquet spinning followed to establish the order of play among shouts of "Rough or smooth?"

"I'll do the ladder and keep the scores," said Edna. "It's just too hot for me to play this afternoon."

The two little girls arrived ahead of Lucy and Noel bearing jugs of Lucy's lemon cordial as the von Weldenburgs arrived in a Horch car which must have been one of the very few in the country. It was covered in dust.

Donald saw what Emily meant about Frieda's legs.

"Well. How are the Ubermenschen doing today?" Hubie asked, after the introductions were complete and looking about him observing growing signs of farming prosperity. He said it as a jest to compliment his hosts, but the Bell's response was muted and Emily froze, her face reddening.

Donald recognised the influence of an English school education in Switzerland underlying the development of an 'officer-class' German. He had encountered one when he was captured in German East Africa during 1916 and later escaped.

That officer spoke almost impeccable, clipped English, with a few mispronunciations, and he remembered him very well indeed from his unremitting attempts to winkle out gems of enemy information. Donald escaped one night when the guards fell asleep and spent the next five days starving in the African bush to the point where he ate grass to stave off hunger, while fearing encounters with snakes and other wild animals. Miraculously, he found his way back to his unit without being eaten himself.

"What do you mean by 'Ubermenschen'?" asked Toby.

"The overlords; those who rule over the Untermenschen, the 'sub-humans, the under people'. I was referring to the philosophy of Friedrich Nietzsche who expressed this in his 'Thus Spake Zarathrustra'. You will remember that he thought that ordinary people were born 'bungled and botched' and worth little more than being good for aiding the 'Ubermenschen' to achieve their ambitions. They were expendable. You could call it Social Darwinism.

"One of your countrymen, Toby, George Bernard Shaw, had the same view. I was so fascinated by an article of his observations which appeared in 'Blick', a Swiss paper, that I cut it out and have kept it ever since.

"Shaw is a member of the Eugenics Education Society in London and called for the development of a humane but deadly gas for the mass-killing of 'the botched'. Even the natives have a way of dealing with the 'ultra-botched' – you know this, Ja?"

"Go on."

"Well, you may have come across earthen pots in a

kraal with a very wide neck?"

"I can't say I have noticed them."

"They are for the botched, even among the Untermenschen. They are for unwelcome new-born twins that are put into such a pot and killed with boiling water."

Zeno and Sonya exchanged glances silently acknowledging that Hubie was too crass to recognise his faux pas.

"Ja. And this is done to malformed new-borns too. But if you look impartially, we of the Nordic races are far more advanced; are superior to what we find around us in Africa, yet we should take a lesson even from the primitive races and eliminate the botched at birth – and breed a superior Nordic tribe to take over Africa."

"Your observations are disturbing," Jim said. "As for Shaw, such remarks by him rather contradict the philosophy implicit in his play, Pygmalion, don't you think? I read a précis of it recently. Not even an Eliza Doolittle?"

"I think not," said Hubie. "I saw the play produced in German at the Hofburg Theatre while visiting Vienna during the summer of 1913. It was shown in Austria even before London. I was very impressed."

"Yes, I saw the first English production in London at the His Majesty's Theatre," said Toby. That must have been only in April 1914, just before the war."

"Ach! How things have changed since then, ne? …Not even Eliza?" Hubie said, repeating Jim's question. No. Not Pygmalion likely! Not in the long run. Did not the milk-white Galatea (called Eliza in Shaw's play) go back to her Untermenschen roots?" he asked. In Zululand, 'bloody' had not entered the vocabulary of conversation when there were ladies about, so 'Pygmalion' was substituted to aid emphasis. They all laughed.

"Do you believe that the labourers of this world have no hope of rising to exceptional heights?" asked Jim.

"I believe they don't – with a few exceptions, although I cannot think of any exceptions at the moment."

"I think that they are 'botched' because they have not had the advantages of advanced hygiene, nutrition and education – and it is our job to bring that about," Jim said. "Many of the natives suffer from chronic malaria too, and some from bilharzia, and display all the symptoms with no means to prevent contracting them. From what I can recall of the play, Pygmalion's Eliza rises above her roots and does not return to them. From the fresh sense of worth extended to her by Colonel Pickering courteously addressing her as 'Miss' Doolittle, the phonetic lessons given by Professor Higgins, probably a better diet and regular exposure to higher class society, she is enabled to join their ranks and – possibly – marry Freddy.

"Thus Shaw dramatises that with exposure to opportunity, a member of the 'Untermenschen' can rise – within the limits of their ability, their absorption of higher class graces and fortuitous opportunities thrown their way. I think one of Shaw's intentions was to ridicule the superficial standards of 'Society'. At heart he is a socialist."

"Vielleicht [perhaps]. But my wife Frieda does not agree with my views anyway. She teaches Braille. It requires much patience. They should make an ivory statue of her."

Donald smiled when he spotted the oblique reference to what he could remember of his school days, when his Latin master discussed Ovid's interpretation of the legend of the Cypriot Pygmalion falling in love with an ivory statue he had carved of a woman which came to life.

"Teaching Braille? That is impressive. Verily, a Swiss-

Boche succouring the botched," said Jim quickly. "I think that Shaw, from what I can recall of one of his essays, was speaking ironically about gas-ovens and the botched, reducing to the absurd the opinions of the extremists. He does that a lot.

"However, eugenics has become disturbingly fashionable in certain circles – even H G Wells talks of getting rid of the unfit and in that group he includes the 'swarms of black, brown, dirty white and yellow people'. Thank God, no one has put into action such thoughts in this century – but there will always be a danger of some monster, like Lenin, doing so. It happened in the recent past, after all. Look what we did to the aborigines in Tasmania, for example, and the Bushmen here. Shot out like vermin. Actions in the last war were close cousins. Where did you teach Braille, Frieda?"

"Many, many German soldiers, those that survived, were blinded by mustard gas. Some of the lucky ones were brought to a Swiss convalescent home where I worked and Braille was the breath of life for them. They could read again."

"It's a long way from that kind of praiseworthy activity to roughing it out here in the African bush. Not much chance of teaching blind Zulus Braille, unfortunately. Blinding cataracts and glaucoma are quite common among our 'Untermenschen' but most cannot read or write at all."

"Teaching Braille to a blind soldier requires determination from the teacher and the pupil, and so does developing a farm. I am sure I can apply my determination to helping Hubie."

"Do you have any contact with other Braille teachers in Natal?" asked Donald.

"No. I have heard that there is a small group in Durban; but theirs is 'English Braille' and mine is German and Swiss-German. Maybe one day I will make contact."

Tennis went on pleasantly enough for the rest of the afternoon with Marie Schnurr devilling all comers by her left handed serves, recoveries and positioning shots when playing both mixed doubles and an 'all-girls' match.

The twins were best when playing together, with Zeno and Sonya seeming to know the moves of the other without calling them out, so that they made a formidable pair to beat.

They also joked with each other in a secret shouted subtext, which was disarming. Emily called them 'Les Enfants Terrible' as, when interacting, there was something Cocteauesque and entangled in their telepathic closeness, even though it was merely an innocent game of tennis.

"Where did the name 'Zeno' come from I wonder?" said Donald. "Sounds Greek."

"His father likes mathematics and philosophy – particularly the Greeks and I gather that Zeno was best known for his development of paradoxes to reduce an argument to the absurd. I gather paradox means 'against the usual odds' or something like that and Zeno, born second, came as a bit of a surprise. A gift from God."

Donald and Emily were exposed to the twins' 'secret language' when playing against them in the last game of the day. After that game, Edna, lighting a Turkish cigarette, said, "Well, its mosquito time and we must go indoors and you, Hubie and Frieda, much as we enjoy your company and the enlightenment about Nietzsche's crazy ideas, should be going before we are attacked by squadrons of mozzies. I can hear them warming up their engines as we speak. I read somewhere that an Irish scientist claimed that the whine of the malaria mosquito was in a different key to less harmful varieties, but I wouldn't like to be the one to test the theory."

While gathering up his things, Hubie mentioned that a young nephew, Luitpold, was coming out from Germany via Switzerland "to visit us in darkest Africa, and perhaps to stay. He is nine years old. We are expecting him in a month's time with Frieda's sister, Anna; anything to get the remaining members of the Wertz family out of that country's chaos, with the currency collapsing about their ears.

"Well it's time for auf wiedersehen." Smilingly, he said, "I can see that you do not agree with my ideas about Uber and Untermenschen. Perhaps we should fight a duel over it – say, with flyswatters at dawn."

After they had left, Emily said, "His reference to Untermenschen made me shudder. He seemed oblivious to the obliteration for which their kin under General Lothar von Trotha was responsible in German South West Africa.

"The Kaiser charged him with exterminating the Hereros in 1904 which he described as Unmenshen [subhuman]. What is it in the Teuton character that makes it believe it has the right to be merciless and superior?"

Chapter Four

In Zululand, it was assumed that one went to church on Sundays, and the Bell guests fell in with the general idea although both Donald and Toby had attended only occasional Highdays-and-Holidays after returning from active service.

It was hot and humid again by the time the party set off in several farm cars and Noel's truck for the Holy Cross church in Maxwell Street. Lucy and the children were crammed into the one-and-only front seat.

The church was on the Bell side of the village and adjacent to the one-roomed junior school, both built of wood and corrugated iron.

Donald saw that all buildings (and there weren't many), other than the railway station and the bank, the undertaker's, the police station-cum-magistrates' court, the new community hall and the solicitor's, were built on short brick stilts, partly to keep the wood away from termites and partly to allow for cooling airflow. Building on stilts also sidestepped the need to cast a more costly concrete slab foundation.

The stilts supported wooden floor beams upon which the wide and creaking boards were laid. Thus the sound of anyone walking on the church floor was magnified by the hollow beneath, making those who had arrived earlier wrench their heads around to see who was late.

Toby's mind drifted back to a moment of looking up at the church pennant flown above the ensign, a mixture of St George and Dutch icons, on HMS Pegasus during the church service. This had preceded, by only a few hours, the lurking submarine presence which could have culminated in his ship being sent to Davy Jones Locker had it not been for the arrival and depth-charging of the sub by HMS Implacable and Underwing. Both ships looked macabre in their naval dazzle camouflage. The sub surfaced as a result and was rammed.

Once inside the church, Donald remembered that one had to pretend not to recognise anyone, giving the impression that one was so immersed in spiritual matters that other beings were not noticed.

Thus the Lebanese banker family and that pretty Italian-looking girl Sonya who had come to tennis and lunch the day before had to be ignored completely until the congregation emerged into the daylight after the service.

This was ridiculous, he thought, as he traced Emily's breasts beneath her dress and smelt the tobacco on the breath of the man who sat behind him accompanied by two restless children (where was the mother?). The father made no effort to prevent his young daughter bumping the back of his pew right through the service, when she was not climbing through the backrest to stare up at him. He watched the woman across the nave blow her nose quietly then look in her handkerchief, and saw that James' eyebrow hairs were more than an inch long.

The sun beat down on the iron roof and although all the windows were open it was stifling.

Donald groaned inwardly when he caught sight of the list of five hymns and by the sounds slurring from the harmonium, whose aged player seemed to have a poor grasp of Bach while fingering the keys before the service began.

When it started, conducted by a young clergyman with a stammer, the congregation was thrown into a flurry of page-rustling and turning in the Book of Common Prayer, desperately trying to find appropriate pages in time. The cleric was too occupied by his stammer to instruct the faithful on which page they would find the next section of the service.

Some of the pages of Toby's book were torn and others missing. Donald turned a page of his to discover a note scrawled in the margin, which read 'see page 333'. He turned to the page only to find something about weddings rather than the beginning of a mysterious and exciting message, before being brought up with a jolt when everyone stood up to mumble their way tunelessly through another hymn.

When it came to the sermon, Donald began to fumble about in his pocket for some change. The Reverend Robert Short (he was unusually tall, thin, dark-haired and wore horn-rimmed glasses) always kept his congregation spellbound. It was not for the content of the Collects for Peace and Grace and his sermon, which seemed to have something to do with rain, locusts and God's mercy, including a quotation from Ecclesiastes about the burden of the grasshopper, the hour being late and the labourers few; what kept them attentive was his inevitable stammering over the next word starting with a 'p'.

When he did and gasped there like a fish out of water several members of the congregation shouted "praise!"

which relieved the tension until the next build-up. It became clear that the worshippers made allowances for their Reverend's shortcomings and were prepared to help him along.

The references to locusts and a biblical labour shortage were unsettling to the ears of many farmers in the congregation, as locusts had invaded and repeatedly devoured much of their crop every year between 1905 and 1908 and there was no saying when the swarms might return.

Labour shortages had increased savagely when the land under sugarcane had expanded from about 800 hectares in 1908 to more than 4,500 hectares by 1918, while the labour reservoir of the few Zulus who would agree to work for them had shrunk and available Indian labour had not increased. Now there would be more pressure from ex-servicemen, like Toby and Donald, who would require labour, although admittedly some miles away.

The Communion 'Body' was a small square of not absolutely fresh brown bread and the 'Blood' tasted like Passover muscatel which Donald had savoured in a girlfriend's parents' house some years back.

He was half listening to the service and half pondering on his own thoughts about religion. He realised that the service gave comfort because he had listened to and spoken the same order of tribal words from childhood; but he had great difficulty in coming to terms with reciting the Nicene Creed, Christian principles and the Sermon on the Mount: yes, but God's producing a son by incarnating Mary, the rising up three days after crucifixion and later ascending into heaven again under the general heading of 'I believe': no, he thought, while making his way back to the pew to settle dutifully for the conventional number of minutes. Miracles were last year's language.

What about the Hindus, Muslims, Janes, Zulus, Trobian Islanders and everyone else, each with their own paradigms of heaven and hell, all kitted out with their own golden calves or sacred cows of mystics, daemons, wizards, ancestors, gods and divines, all convinced that theirs was the one true faith?

He remembered the remark of Leora, an early Jewish girlfriend (whose parents had invited him to attend their Passover Seder). When the discussion came around to Christianity, she said, "Donald, you don't really believe all that rubbish, do you?" They were naked at the time and smoking a cigarette between them lying on the bed in her flat.

Donald's thoughts wandered to the philosophy of Herbert Spenser's 'First Principles' and felt that he was closer to that belief in the all-encompassing Absolute Beyond Human Knowledge than finding comfort in the tribal trappings of religious ceremony.

After the service, when everyone had snapped back into their usual chattery selves outside the church, Toby and Donald learned that Short and his wife were popular as a young couple. Toby was pleased to hear that the minister had served as ship's padre aboard HMS Argus, the first Royal Navy aircraft carrier converted from a liner under construction when war broke out.

His wife was talkative, slim, painted her nails and generous mouth scarlet even on a Sunday, and was Australian, whom Short had met in the Far East.

Sonya and her twin brother Zeno joined the party, as it was agreed that Sonya, her brother and Emily should introduce Donald and Toby to the Mhlatuzi Lagoon at Richard's Bay. Jim and Edna were to go back to the farm for the Sunday roast.

"Hello again," said Zeno. "I'm the raspberry, planted by our parents to make sure you don't get up to mischief. Besides, it's my car and I'm the driver – so you can't really do without me."

"Be careful crossing the river!" shouted Zeno's father and Zeno waved an acknowledgement without turning as he started his car. "Check the height of the river before you cross! And remember to bring back some oysters and fish!"

The bay, which was swarming with fish and bountiful with oysters, was only 17 miles away as the crow flies, but a poor yardstick of measurement which did not take into account the hazards of driving on what was only an ox wagon track, through one drift and then another. It wound through sandy patches deep enough to make the wheels spin uselessly and small dongas that turned driving into an art form.

At Double Drift near Nsezi Lake, the Mhlatuzi River was swift-flowing and swollen from the recent rains, making both crossings hazardous.

Zeno said, "Well, we haven't the luxury of expecting an ox-span to pull us through. Mind you, we do have a block and tackle to sling around a tree, and a sledge hammer, if the worst happens and we really do get stuck mid-stream; so here goes, everybody!"

And away they went, with the coffee-coloured water swirling about them. After plunging through the first drift there was little time for rejoicing before being confronted by the second and more challenging river crossing.

High ground was reached with the sound of water

rushing off the car.

"The water level will have gone down a bit by the time we go back home," said Zeno.

Reeds grew close to the track on both sides and Toby wondered what animals might present themselves at any moment. There was a '.45' rifle, a standard precaution, wedged between the seat and Zeno's door, and a handful of cartridges in the open glovebox..

After the drifts came another stream that had to be inched across on wooden planks supported by wobbly poles. "This is Rickety Bridge," said Zeno, "and you can gather how it got its name. One day it'll collapse, but hopefully, not just yet.

"Now comes the last tricky bit. I'll have to drive like hell to get through the worst sandy stretch because we have to get to the top of the ridge without stopping. If we stop we'll sink into the sand and vanish without a trace.

"Here goes again. Let's hope Tommy still has a few Castles left in that tin bath of his," and the car slithered upwards between lots of pampas grass to a small rock at the summit. The track then turned right to present, suddenly, the vista of the Mhlatuzi Lagoon and the Richard's Bay 'Hotel'. The latter consisted of a few free-standing thatched rooms surrounded by rudimentary verandahs and a wood-and-iron summerhouse / bar attached to a minute store for the local natives and which sold bait for the anglers.

The hotel overlooked the lagoon and a beach that stretched from the hotel over seasand to the shore, give or take a few tufts of grass.

Due to the heavy inland rain of the night before, the river had broken through the sandbank that normally separated the lagoon from the sea, bringing with it pebbles and small stones that washed back onto the beach.

Tommy turned out to be the tubby Indian cook and general factotum who lived with his family in even more modest quarters behind the hotel. Strings of fish drying in the sun hung outside several of the rooms.

Bottled beers for guests were kept in a tin bath placed in the shade and filled with water, to which was added the remains of a large ice-block. This had come up all the way by train from Durban, packed with others in a box of straw, and then transported by 'nagmaal' ox wagon to the hotel. (The smaller 'nagmaal' ox wagon was sent to Empangeni every now and then for fresh bread and meat.)

Toby remarked that Natal surf thundered and crashed, unlike the placid surf of the Irish Sea of home which sounded more like the wind blowing through trees.

As the group wandered down to the beach Zeno stooped and drew a crumpled piece of paper out of the sand. "Look!" he said. "It's an old five rupee note! How on earth did that land up here. It does look really old."

"Get rid of it, Zeno. Throw it away! It's said to bring really bad luck," said Emily.

"You don't really believe all that rubbish, do you?"

"No, I don't, but get rid of it anyway. There are some nasty stories about finding these notes and what happened to the people later. Take what happened to Andrew Furlong, for example.

"He discovered hundreds of these notes churned up by the incoming tide when he was down here with his brother several years ago. They came from the wreck of the Newark Castle which was on its way to Mauritius ten years before the war.

"He took them home and was found dead in a paddock

the next day. He had been strangled when his horse galloped around a gum tree in the field while he was trying to harness it and the halter caught him around his neck.

"His daughter found the rupees in one of Andrew's bedroom drawers several weeks after the funeral, and gave them to their Indian kitchen servant as a memento of India and to get them out of the house. They had no worth as they had been demonetised by the Bank of England when the news reached London.

"A day later the servant was killed by a puffadder when she stepped out of the back kitchen door. Three people had been drowned in the surf when their boat capsized here – a woman passenger, a steward and a cabin boy. The woman's body was buried temporarily on this beach very near where you are standing. Most of the rupees were collected, but notes occasionally turn up years later."

She said, "Come on, it's low tide and it's so hot. Let's just go for a quick cool-off, then we can borrow Mr Grantham's boat from the hotel (I asked his permission just now) and go to Hippo Island on the lake; though we won't be able to land. Lots of crocs and hippos, even the odd Zambi shark," said Emily.

Only the girls and Zeno had costumes, so the other two had to make do with their shorts in the hope that they would dry out on the way home – despite the humidity that kept all clothes feeling damp at the coast.

"Look! There's a point over there where a channel has opened to the sea. We can wade across to the other side."

The two girls disappeared into the hotel and Zeno went to change behind the car.

A few Indian anglers were standing in the shallows south of the hotel, slightly away from the channel, their

18-foot rods anchored in leather sockets strapped to their waists. A little Indian girl with long black hair was near them, absorbed with collecting pebbles and shells at the water's edge. She had built a sandcastle and was finishing it off with a shell-covered dome and a defensive perimeter of sand and pebbles, knowing that it would be swept away by the incoming tide, as children always do, no matter wherever they live near a sea shore.

"She come when she not in school. Every day she build sand houses." Toby realised that a little Indian girl on the east coast of Africa would not have been exposed to Eurocentric stories of knights, chivalry and 'castles'.

Every now and then one of the men would reel in; check the lures, barbs and floats, and re-bait the hooks from a stock of 'sea lice' in a bucket of sea water. Donald never did find out their actual name, but they looked like shrimp and had been dug from the sand as the wave receded, leaving tell-tale streams of small bubbles in the wet sand. The fishermen had to be watchful and dig into the sand immediately the wave had gone or the bait would burrow too deeply to be recovered.

While waiting for the girls, the men strolled over to watch the fishermen casting. They were standing in the shallows at a point where the beach was steeper than the rest of the strand, making the backwash faster and collision with incoming waves more violent. It was here that the waves broke first, sweeping up the incline of the beach carrying a lace of foam, before hesitating and rushing back in time to reinforce another wave as it curved, teetered and crashed. Spume had accumulated at the water's edge in patches and wobbled with the occasional gust of wind.

Donald asked the fishermen how they made their

weights, and one of them explained that they melted down the lead seals off cane-spirit bottles before pouring the molten metal into little moulds with hooks held in place by pliers until the lead cooled.

"Best place for fish is after third small wave and main breaker – see water where is flat. Most fish come to see what food waves dig up from bottom," one of the Indians said. "Best time for fish before sun come up. Getting too late now.

"I change bait plenty times because fish get clever. If I get good bite, I let fish run away long time then pull hard and walk backwards. Makes hook go deep."

The girls emerged from the hotel's primitive summer-house in a cloud of beach towels, lifted and swirled by the seashore breeze to flaunt the latest thing in figure-hugging woollen tank suits which stopped at mid-thigh, covered by short modesty skirts.

When they got into the water up to their waists, the black and red skirts floated on the surface.

The Indian Ocean, swirling warmly about them, was brown with silt swept down after the recent rain and Emily shouted to the others to be careful. "This is just the kind of water that Zambi sharks like! They come right into the shallows when it's like this; on second thoughts, I think we had better get out!"

One of the last moments experienced by Zeno was of being furiously bumped by a large underwater creature, throwing him off-balance.

Donald was only a few yards away when the female shark bit into Zeno's chest with such force that it lifted him out of the water. As the predator dropped back into the foam, Toby raced against the backwash and grabbed both Zeno's right arm and the remains of the left upper arm to pull him clear; but the shark had already taken a huge chunk out of Zeno's side, and moments later he was dead, blood gushing out of the enormous hole in his chest.

The shark had gouged away most of the left side of Zeno's rib cage, heart, left lung, pancreas, left kidney, stomach entrails and arm. For a frozen moment they caught sight of the creature's full jaws dripping with blood and flesh before it disappeared into the murk. There was no knowing whether it would return for the rest of the body.

Emily and Sonya froze waist-deep in the wash in a tableau, unable to move. Donald screamed "Get out! Shark! Get out of the water! Get out!" while both Toby and Donald dragged Zeno's body to the beach, his face set in a rictus of pain.

Toby, filled with horror, gestured desperately to the fishermen with frantic arm signals. One of them rushed to pull his young daughter away from the water's edge, much to her fury.

Doctor Lombard, who had been ogling the two girls through his binoculars from the verandah of the summerhouse, saw what was happening and shouted to Tommy to come and help.

"Bring plenty towels!"

They both raced down to the distraught group on the beach, to be joined by Grantham, the hotel owner. Sonya had thrown her bloodied body over Zeno. "Oh my God. Oh my God!" she cried repeatedly, shuddering and weeping. "We've all been such bloody fools! What can we do to save him?"

"Sonya, all I can say is that he died very quickly, almost instantly, because the beast got at his heart and other organs. There was just no hope. We tried our best to get him away but you can see that it was just hopeless."

Mrs Grantham and two natives came running down the beach with a wood and canvas bed frame. Zeno's body was covered in blood to which the sand was sticking. Several curious seagulls fluttered down at a safe distance.

Toby and Donald had both witnessed the effects of naval guns and army howitzers during the war, with soldiers and ratings blown to bits in their midst, but this was different as there was no anticipation, no warning of battle to come. Donald could think of no death worse than being eaten alive. It was even worse than being burnt to death, worse than mustard gas tearing at the lungs and far worse than drowning.

He and the other men lifted the body so that they could get a tarpaulin between him and the stretcher to meet up on the other side and wrap him. As they lifted him, there was a sigh from his remaining lung.

The beach sand was hot underfoot and rough going, as the group struggled their way up to the hotel with the stretcher. A sudden gust of hot wind swept rivulets of sand along the beach, stinging their ankles.

The body was carried to one of the rondavels, after Dr Lombard had formally pronounced him dead. In the hotel he wrote out a certificate to that effect, including a brief summary of what had happened.

"I will have to report this to the police in Empangeni. May I use your phone?" The party line phone was on the wall near the front entrance of wood and corrugated iron and they could hear him calling for Captain Smit. On hearing he had gone home for the day he called him at his house and asked him to visit the parents, but to wait for an hour until Emily had called them.

He also called the Empangeni undertaker at home.

Lombard came back and asked, "Do you want to call Reverend Short, or shall I?"

Emily said, "I think I had better, and Sonya is in no state to make calls." She went to the phone, noticing that the paint on the wall inside the entrance was beginning to flake and couldn't resist flicking off pieces while she waited for Short to come to the phone. The line was bad and she had to shout.

She was quivering as if she had a fever though able to think clearly enough through a fog of numbed emotions.

Slumped on a scruffy sofa, Sonya continued to weep helplessly and Doctor Lombard asked Grantham for blankets to cover her, as she was shivering uncontrollably, despite the heat of the afternoon. Her legs, costume and arms remained coated with particles of beach sand and blood from Zeno.

"Are you sure that was Zeno?" she croaked suddenly. "I'm sure I saw someone else on the beach at the time. One of the fishermen. He just can't, can't be dead. It's all wrong."

No one answered, but Emily threw her arms about her and drew her to her body.

Dr Lombard, a large man who in another life could have been a vet and spoke English flavoured with a heavy Dutch-Afrikaans accent, came into the lounge and said, "I am taking your brother back to Empangeni in my truck. You three must drive back ahead of me in Zeno's car. Emily, you know the way best, so you should drive the tricky part from the bay, then perhaps let one of the men take over from there. If you are not up to it at the moment, let one of the men drive the whole way."

Out of earshot of Sonya, he murmured that he would be taking the body directly to the Empangeni undertaker, who had been alerted. He said that there would be a need for the identification of the body to be made again at the undertakers, in the presence of the police, but that this could be done later.

"After I leave the undertakers I will come along to see Zeno and Sonya's parents, Paolo and Bianca. One of them might need a sedative; certainly Sonya will. I would also like to check up on her too as she is taking this very badly indeed. Emily, you might find it a good idea to stay there for a couple of nights."

Grantham came in with a bottle of whisky and glasses and poured all present a generous slug.

Mrs Grantham followed him into the room with a plate of sandwiches and insisted that they all ate, including Sonya, despite her reluctance, confusion, trembling and numbness.

They drank in a silent libation, glad of the distraction and the internal warmth it brought.

As they went to Zeno's car Toby looked towards the beach and saw that the little girl had returned to gathering shells and repairing her sandcastle, which had been swiped by a particularly big wave.

"The tide must be coming in," Toby thought. One of their bloodstained beach towels was left on the sand, but he said nothing.

He took the five-rupee note, crushed it into a ball and threw it into the bushes.

And so it was that the sad party started their drive home, away from sight of the bay, curving left then skidding down through the sandy stretch, over Rickety Bridge, over the Mzingazi River again and along the uncertain road to Empangeni, Donald swopping with Emily once they reached the level part of the road.

Toby sat in the back with Sonya swaddled and cradled against him. She must have developed the habit of sucking her thumb as a very young child and this she did now, shivering with spasmodic sighs. He caught sight of the unreliable fuel gauge over Donald's shoulder, pointing to near empty, and suggested to him that they should free-wheel down inclines to save whatever fuel there was.

Zeno had been quixotic, dashing out of the house without much preparation, and he had neglected to check the level of petrol in the tank before departing.

As they entered the village, Dr Lombard drove off to the undertakers without Sonya noticing. Shortly afterwards, Zeno's car ran out of petrol as they reached the far end of Maxwell Street. Donald undertook to walk past the new Public Hall to the petrol pump in the hope that a container would be available at the store, only to realise as he reached the pump that, because it was Sunday, the store was closed.

Returning to the car, he said, "Well, we will just have to hoof it and leave the car here until Monday, or get petrol from the house."

They were so absorbed in the tragedy that they were oblivious to the darkening skies and sudden whirl of wind heralding flashes of lightning and crashes of thunder, bringing the last heavy downpour of the season.

Wet through, cold and filled with dread, they walked the muddy distance to the squeaking gate and up the drive to the Broccardo house. They found Paolo and Bianca Broccardo slumped in deckchairs on the front granolithic-floored verandah, along with their 12-year-old daughter,

Joy, who sat on a skin-covered pouffe, leaning comfortingly against her mother's legs. Dr Lombard was already there, sitting in a cane chair that strained to contain his large frame. The raffia on the chair arms was beginning to unravel.

Lombard was able to describe what he had witnessed through binoculars, and said that he was present at the death. He was sparing of the gruesome details and assured them that Zeno could not have suffered as the death was immediate, although privately, he felt that he must have died only after experiencing terror, anguish and great pain.

Wire mosquito-mesh enclosed the verandah, and careworn zebra-skins were scattered on the red granolithic floor. There was a mounted buffalo head and several other beasts on the corrugated iron wall, which was pierced by several windows. Riding boots, a knobkerrie, sticks and a long rhino hide whip were stacked in a far corner. The mosquito-wire door squeaked open and clattered shut every time someone arrived.

A strange terracotta flowerpot stood on a stand near the entrance, in the shape of a dwarfed goggle-eyed dolphin with ferns growing out of it.

As the doctor and Emily had made phone calls from Richard's Bay on an open party line, the news had spread and several friends of the parents had arrived, including Jim and Edna Bell, to sit on an array of cane-chairs and awkward deckchairs. Even with their back supports ratcheted up as vertically as possible, the impression was given of passengers about to nod off to sleep on the deck of a mailship after sipping beef tea, rather than as friends 'paying their respects' in the twilight.

Seeing that Bianca was well distracted for the moment,

Paolo stole away with the doctor and asked, his face an unhealthy pallor, "So what do we have to do next?" Lombard replied that the body was at the undertakers because the refrigeration plant at the police morgue had run out of paraffin. He believed there would be no need for a post mortem because he, the doctor, had witnessed the accident. However, it would be necessary to identify the body formally, for the satisfaction of the local police, and it would be better for Paolo to do so, to which he agreed. He arranged to be at the undertakers reasonably early on the Monday morning accompanied by Dr. Lombard, who said that he would notify the police.

An inquest might have to be called, Lombard warned, but a 'death by misadventure' could be expected. He had no doubt that Toby, Donald and Emily would have to be present, along with one of the parents, if an inquest were held.

Toby rose to discuss the recovery of Zeno's car with the doctor, stuck as it was with no petrol in Maxwell Street. Lombard offered to rescue it with some fuel siphoned from his vehicle, then park the vehicle beside the mango trees, well out of sight of the front verandah, leaving the keys with Mario.

Emily had meanwhile prepared sandwiches, which she brought in on trays, with Sonya trailing behind as Lombard, Paolo and Toby rejoined the verandah group.

Paolo went in to the sitting room to bring out whisky and brandy in cut-glass decanters, with a soda siphon and a muddle of glasses.

It remained humid although the temperature had dropped slightly. Summer temperatures in Empangeni can go up to 112 degrees Fahrenheit, so the present autumn warmth was regarded as 'cool'.

Bianca felt that a part of her body had been torn from her, and a great sense of forlorn isolation descended, with not even Paolo being able to reach the intensity of her agony. Zeno's death was so unexpected that she had difficulty in accepting that he was truly gone forever. She wondered how she would be able to endure the rest of her life. She sensed years of investment in love hopelessly lost, washed away as if by a flood, and began to question the reason for her existence. Paolo was close to Sonya and while he felt Zeno's death desperately, it was not the same as a mother's, Bianca knew.

The evening wore on, Paolo filling in the silences with offers of yet further rounds of drinks, until Edna said, picking up her Balkan Sobranie cigarettes, "We must go home, Jim. Emily, I know you will want to stay here with Sonya for the time being. We'll take our young guests home with us and I will phone you about arrangements tomorrow," upon which Edna, Jim, Toby and Donald rose with a scraping of cane chairs on the granolithic.

The bone-shaking drive home in the dark to the farm was a silent one, except for the rattles of the car and Edna saying once, "Such a bloody waste," and a near collision, just before crossing the siding rails near the entrance to the farm-proper with a kudu standing in the road, dazzled by the car's headlights. "It's seldom we see a kudu so close to the farmhouse," Jim said, as they turned into the yard. "They like acacia and there isn't any near here."

Bush telegraph had reached the farm by the time they arrived, with Joseph, Gorkil, Masheila and Jemima waiting for them, sitting in the dark on the kitchen steps. Jim said, "It was a Zambi. There was nothing anyone could do to save him, although Toby and Donald braved the water to get Zeno out as quickly as possible. Thank you for waiting here."

Gorkil said, "Master Zeno was good man, like sister. He talk kindly and do good deeds when come to farm. We think good Karmas help him find moksha; his good spirit will return."

Jim raised his right hand as if in a benediction while he turned away and said, "You have waited for us a long time. Go home now. Good night."

Donald went to sleep in his creaking bed, thinking about life after death, Karma and reincarnation, wondering if there was anything more to it than faith sweeping aside reason. The sight of the kudu had disturbed him and the dark tableau of waiting servants he would remember forever.

He dreamt of monsters and the thumping crash of Indian Ocean breakers.

Toby tried to turn his thoughts away from the tragedy by opening a well-thumbed journal on sugarcane cultivation he found in his room, but large brown moths fluttering around the light, over his magazine and against his face, disturbed his reading. When he turned to dowse the lamp, he was startled by several pairs of bush-baby eyes staring at the moths through the window's mosquito netting.

On his way home Dr. Lombard had to pass the police station and saw that a light was still burning in the front office, so knocked on the door and found Captain Smit rummaging through the drawers of his desk, muttering "waar in die hel is dit!" [Where in the hell is it].

"Waarvoor soek jy?" [What are you looking for?]

Breaking into a muddle of Dutch-Afrikaans and

English he said "Ek soek the regulations. Agh. Op die blarry desk in front of me. You read. It's not in Dutch, only in English."

Dr. Lombard studied the pages Smit thrust at him then said that page fifty was all about pawnbrokers. "No, man! Page fifty one!" Smit said. "Act Number Ten dated 22nd May, 1897."

"Well it covers regulations to be followed by town councils of a borough; but we're not anything like a borough. And we're not a town; we're not even a dorp. But I'll read it. Number Five: 'Whenever any dead body shall be found, or any case of sudden death wurra, wurra, wurra … well, it says clearly 'sudden death' and being bitten to death by an unfriendly shark is just somaar that. It says that any police officer … and then it goes on and on and on 'any police officer' etcetera 'at once give or cause to be given to the Coroner of such borough notice of the same – wurra, wurra, wurra concerning such death.'"

"Item Six says that 'The coroner may direct a post-mortem examination of any body by any medical practitioner' and – wurra, wurra, wurra – 'The medical and other witnesses should be summoned by the messenger to attend an inquest.'

"So there we have it. We must go and talk to Colonel Tanner, the magistrate, and leave it to him. He may decide that it isn't necessary to call an inquest and just accept an external post-mortem report from you, but – you know what he's like; he's a stickler, so my bet is that he will."

"Wat 'n gemors!" [What a mess].

"Well, at least we're still following the old Natal regulations. The Union regulations become law only next year. Look at this!" he said, showing him another much thicker document titled 'Union Gazette Extraordinary', dated 14th April 1919 in parallel Dutch and English text. "This Dutch is in such 'High Dutch' legalese that I find it difficult to follow. And me a Dutchman, nogal!"

Before dawn, distant drums from the kraal far beyond the cane fields mingled with the chorus of early bird calls. Perhaps the drums were talking to Zulu ancestors of the death of a young white man who had done the Zulus no wrong.

Chapter Five

"We should move into Empangeni today," Donald said, while waiting for breakfast as they took a turn in Lucy's garden.

"I don't think we've overstayed our welcome, but it might be more practical if we moved back to the Masonic Hotel, assemble all the other bits and pieces we still have to gather, attend the funeral on Tuesday and then move off to Ntambanana, coming back for the inquest if one is called. Otherwise I, for one, will overshoot my leave at the bank in Durban, with all hell to pay."

The subject was broached at breakfast with Noel and Lucy while the children were cutting stamping patterns into half-potatoes at the other end of the yellowwood kitchen table, having breakfasted some time earlier. Their printing ink was beetroot juice squeezed into a saucer, and the patterns soon covered pages of the 'Sausage Wrap' that Noel had taken from the sideboard.

"Jemima, please take the children ukubona izinkukhu ezintsha [to see the chickens]. They hatched this morning," which Jemima did, after knowing glances were exchanged between them.

"Look," said Lucy, "I realise that this whole catastrophe has put you in a difficult situation, not of your making, but we need to plan how to cope with the Broccardos.

"Noel's got all sorts of things to attend to today, not least these possible malaria cases among the Indian workers, so I suggest I take you into town, see you booked in at the Masonic Hotel and then we three can visit Mr. and Mrs. Broccardo and the daughters. I'll clear that by calling them after breakfast, if the phone works. Otherwise we'll just have to pitch up unannounced."

"This leaves the problem of finding you some sort of transport to and from 'Tam', as borrowing Zeno's car would be out of the question.

"The most practical is for you to take the 'Slowcoach' which is what we call the ox wagon shuttle that departs on Wednesdays and usually arrives at Ntambanana the same night, all being well, returning on Thursdays. Jan Mocke operates it. This means you can load your trunks and other bits and pieces onto the wagon and walk beside it some of the way. It'll give you a good idea of the terrain. You'll have the opportunity of getting to know an Afrikaner with an extensive knowledge of the veld."

They located Edna near the mango trees from the whiff of the Turkish cigarette she was smoking. She was wearing a shapeless cotton hat and equally shapeless gardening dress, and was feeding her hens. She had a cigarette in her mouth with the ash hanging on pendulously. Jim had already left with Noel to see the ailing Indian workers. Lucy explained their visitors' decision to transfer to town.

Both thanked Edna profusely for the family's hospitality to which she replied, "Well. Life must go on and you have your own challenges to meet in the days to come, and challenges there will be. However, do continue to keep in touch and come and visit us. I know that Jim and Noel would like to keep track of you – and you must meet our sons.

"Remember, write to Jim for advice whenever you want to and he'll respond as soon as he can. Schnurr is a good man too. Meanwhile we'll see you at the funeral on Tuesday. Ghastly business."

'The Masonic' was double storeyed with a brick facade echoing a modest version of the railway station, although the rest of the structure was of wood-and-corrugated iron with wide verandahs on both the ground and first floors.

The first floor verandah overlooking the daytime business of Maxwell Street served guest rooms that opened onto it through French windows.

A few of the rivets securing the verandah roof had come adrift during summer storms and had not been secured, allowing sheets of corrugated iron to rattle whenever a late night wind sprang up, alarming guests out of their slumbers.

Monkeys were another source of disturbance for, at that time of the year when mangoes, paw paws and loquats were abundant, they would jump from nearby trees and race the length of the hotel's roof, clattering, thumping and jabbering just before sunrise.

One of the back rooms downstairs was used as a general meeting room for the Empangeni Farmers' Association, the Women's Institute, and the Masons whose paraphernalia was kept in two padlocked tin bins near the double doors leading to the kitchen. The second bin held their supply of wine and liquor.

Masons' meetings were the noisiest. Strange thumps during their assemblies preceded members emerging to partake in equally boisterous and thumping dinners and speeches, half-heard through closed doors in an antechamber to the main dining room before noisy dispersal; some walking home, others clambering onto their tethered horses and the rest scrambling into one of the few cars in Empangeni, for those living furthest away.

Donald and Toby registered at Reception, and left their luggage to be taken up to their rooms before re-joining Lucy.

Toby glimpsed the main dining room beyond, which was smelly from years of beer and overcooked cabbage. The walls were a pale shiny green, mottled and depressing, decorated on three sides by a house painter's idea of pyramids, palms and camels. On the remaining wall were the stuffed head of a kudu and several lesser antelopes, their bulging eyes glaring at the diners.

Some of the tables were already being set for lunch, the Indian waiter taking pride in folding the napkins into starched white cones on each bread plate.

They found Joy, Sonya's younger sister, on the verandah searching for Paolo's spectacles. "Daddy's becoming ever more absent-minded," she said, "and since the accident (Donald noticed that she could not bear saying 'Zeno's death') he has got worse. He doesn't concentrate on what he's doing, so puts his spectacles down on a chair and wanders off and then gets distressed because he can't find them. It's happening more and more.

"I still can't believe Zeno's gone. Not really. None of us can. I went in to his bedroom to look for something and felt sure I heard his laugh outside the window – you know the way he used to chuckle" – and Joy started weeping.

"He was untidy like me, and his room is just like it was when he rushed out of the house yesterday."

Zeno's mother was sitting on a bench in the shade of a syringa tree at the far end of the garden. Her knitting was lying neglected in her lap while she stared fixedly at a row of hydrangeas.

Paolo had gone off to his study to write letters to their many relatives and friends, advising them of the turn of events, but subsequently wandered the house, looking for his spectacles. Sonya did not put in an appearance.

Bianca looked up when the three appeared, but did not say anything. Lucy sat down beside her, gently took her hand and, speaking for the two men, said, "Donald and Toby have moved to the hotel and of course will be at the funeral tomorrow. They are committed to leaving for Ntambanana early on Wednesday and so will have to buy final essentials in town today and consult various people.

"Being new to the area, I am going to suggest that Emily goes with them to show them where to go for various items and then walk back to be with you."

Bianca nodded her head dully, but otherwise showed no other reaction.

Before arriving, Donald and Toby had agreed to avoid muttering platitudinous 'condolences', but rather express shared distress and sorrow, answering any questions put to them as fully as seemed appropriate. In the event, Bianca didn't ask them anything and just said "Goodbye. We will see you tomorrow."

She fluttered a farewell as they moved off through the house, passing Paolo on the way. "I see Joy has found your spectacles," Donald said, to which Paolo replied, "Yes. I am beginning to wonder how I will manage when all our children have gone, those that are spared. We will see you tomorrow."

The garden gate to the street groaned. Sonya said, "I wish Daddy would oil it. It's been like that ever since I remember. Zeno said he would but, once again, he didn't do it," and trembling into tears, she stumbled back to the house.

The small party walked towards the general store, passing a Sunlight Soap hoarding depicting a black washerwoman, a large white bundle of washing on her head, and a legend reading 'No matter whether your clothes are washed in the river, in well or town's water, there is nothing so good as Sunlight Soap. Remember that!' Driving home the point was a small caption to the illustration on the hoarding, which read 'Returning from the river with the laundry, after washing with Sunlight Soap'.

Donald said that he wondered to whom the main billboard message was directed – indirectly to the white English-speaking housewife who might be obliged to buy the soap for the Zulu washerwoman or the washerwoman herself. If the latter were the case, he asked whether such a long and cumbersome message in English would hit home – although the visual message might.

"How literate is the average Zulu woman in these parts?" he asked.

"In English? Not very and for most, not at all," Emily said, abandoning her style of unfinished sentences whenever the subject turned close to her anthropological heart. "The first Bishop of Natal, Bishop Colenso, did develop an English / Zulu dictionary with a Zulu colleague called William Ngidi more than fifty years ago, but there are still not so many literate Zulus in Zululand to make use of it. Nevertheless, the times they are a-changing.

"An isiZulu language newspaper called 'Ilange Lase Natal' (meaning 'The Sun of Natal') was started about fifteen years ago by a John Dube, but it cannot be assumed that a reader in Zulu would be able to read or write English as well, although half the paper is in the latter.

"I haven't seen many copies floating around this neck of the woods. Most would be sold in Durban and Pietermaritzburg and the rest to migrant Zulu workers on the Transvaal mines and the railways, for those who could read a newspaper well enough.

"Worth looking at a copy. Especially the somewhat Hogarthian cartoons about the effects of Skokiaan – illicit liquor – and other social perils."

Emily said that efforts were continuing to standardise Zulu spelling – and an important conference was held in Pietermaritzburg in 1905 with that end in view.

"But whoever developed that soap advertisement must have been slightly cuckoo, because the average Zululand native woman would not be able to read the words. This has led to the 'illiterati' remaining fiercely loyal to a brand in which they can trust, like Sunlight; the combined group of letter-shapes being recognised as an icon for the soap.

"Last year while in Durban, I saw a native tacking an advertisement tinplate outside a store, upside down. But believe me, I am not being disparaging – just suggesting that there is a very long way to go. One can only hope that the steady evolution of indigenous literacy does not develop into indigenous revolution.

"I promised to give you a potted overview of Zulu culture at some time, what I know of it – so here goes. It'll keep our mind off things. But first, bear in mind that the various tribes under the general heading of 'Zulu' are part of the Nguni who originated a long way away – from the Congo delta – or so the current thinking goes, based on linguistic traces.

"A people of the Iron Age, they came into contact with the more ancient Stone Age dwellers, the Bushmen, otherwise known as the San, who were indigenous to Natal and other areas as far away as the Karoo.

"The Zulus brought with them a culture based on cattle accumulation, storage of corn underground, polygamy and lobola – the latter being a payment in cattle for brides (always from outside the immediate clan).

"It seems that the Iron Age and Stone Age people dwelt amicably, in the main, in the same region for centuries and that inter-breeding was fairly commonplace. This could explain why the Natal Zulus utilise some of the 'click' sounds which are far more plentiful in San speech and are not so evident in Nguni speech further north.

"As I said, the Zulus are a cattle-based culture. Before the coming of the white man, they would migrate seasonally with their beasts between the summer grasses covering the foothills of the Drakensberg and the midlands, to the coast during the winter months, where grazing remains the sweetest for much of the colder season.

"The San, being hunter-gatherers, persisted in poaching Zulu cattle over the centuries and this led to their being chased into the Drakensberg Mountains and their partial annihilation, although it is thought that the Boers bumped off the rest for the same reason.

"That's the background on an odd thousand years or so. So much has been written about the recent history of the Zulus, the Anglo-Zulu wars and the Bambatha rebellion that followed in 1906 (a concerted effort to throw off the yoke of the white man) that I'm not going to bore you with that prolonged and ghastly business all over again – except to say that we invaded their territory and the Zulus resisted. We overcame, and now we have to live among them with the consequences of our rapaciousness. We are, in fact, an occupying force, armed with all sorts of tricks and regulations not required of the whites to keep the Zulus in their place.

"This is not to say that we, the English-speakers, did not usurp the Boers in a similar manner in Natal, particularly the northern interior in such places as Ladysmith and even early Durban, well before Zululand began to be opened up. Long before that, the Boers had come over the Drakensberg Mountains into what must have seemed a Promised Land to do their own spot of usurping. It led to disastrous clashes with Zulu tribes on many occasions, as well as the English settlers in early Durban.

"Always remember that the Zulus are comprised of smaller tribes united (except for the Matabele who escaped to Rhodesia with Chief Mzilikazi) only by the force of dictator-chieftain Shaka during the early part of the 19th Century.

"The Zulus do not believe (or at least didn't think otherwise until the white man missionaries tried to alter that) in a unifying 'Sky God' or 'Unkulunkulu'; although it is thought that there is a Being which controls the thunder and lightning. Other than that, the idea of an 'all-seeing creator of the universe' to whom one could appeal through an intermediary was an import of the early missionaries, who introduced Christ as that very being, empowered to communicate with and regularly appeal to a unified

European God. Of course, the Catholics offer a few more specialist envoys in the form of the various saints. Perhaps an undue simplification, but let it rest at that. This neatly contrived to push aside the power of the sangomas though not with much success.

"Although many Zulus will give the impression that they go along with Western Christianity – even going to missionary church meetings and singing hymns, I contend that those practices mask their deeply held belief in the powerful presence of the ancestor-spirits, who live underground and who really influence for good or ill the daily life of their descendants.

"We Europeans are not so very far from parallel beliefs, after all. A belief in incorporeal witches and their daemonic servants was still alive and well in England during the mid-seventeenth century and only in the early 18th century were the Witchcraft Acts repealed. Now all those notions of a spirit world outside the main religions have transmogrified into spiritualism, psychic mediums communicating with the dead, planchette, ectoplasm and all that Madam Blavatsky hocus-pocus.

"I must qualify all that by mentioning the growing importance of a kind of quasi-Christianity called the Nazarite Church, founded by Isaiah Shembe about nine years ago and which now has an untold number of followers. It's a blend of Zulu beliefs and Christianity. Shembe is the African Messiah who said that the Holy Spirit appeared at Nhlangagazi and instructed him to start a church which followed the Ten Commandments.

"But most Zulus in this part of the world – especially in the north east– learnt at their mother's knee that the Great Earth Mother arrived centuries ago in a big canoe made of reeds near the lakes of the St Lucia estuary, on the north east coast. The place is still riddled with crocodiles and hippo.

"The theoretical Zululand is bounded by rivers – the Thukela in the south, the Phongolo to the north, the uMzinyathi to the west and the Indian ocean itself in the east.

"This Earth Mother was said to be enormously fat and was accompanied in other reed canoes by her fat son and two wives. It was she who imparted the mysteries of the nation, the Zulu legal system, the culture and religious practices.

"The Zulu belief in the continued existence of ancestors demonstrates a tenet in the spirit life after death – not so very far, in this sense, from Christian teaching, Hinduism and Confucianism – and heaven knows what else. Mind you, the Hindus believe you return in other forms, don't they, and life and death are circular and repetitive, unless you are excessively good enough to reach Nirvana.

"For most Zulus, the Amatongo – the ancestor spirits (some call them the Amadhlozi) – still hold strongest sway. They have the power to influence the lives of the living for good or ill and it's up to the living descendants to keep them content."

She explained that sangomas, that is, diviners, had to be utilised by the living as intermediaries to communicate with and appeal to the ancestor-spirits.

"The Zulus call the body's life force the umoya which accompanies the 'shadow', representing the personality of the individual. When a person dies the umoya leaves the body while the spirit may live on as an idlozi only if certain conditions are practised in life."

Emily suddenly sobbed.

"Look, for obvious reasons I am not in the mood to go on just now, although it helped to get my mind off Zeno for a while; but if you are at all interested we can go on exploring the nature of the Zulus when you return from Ntambanana.

"The Broccardos forgot to serve breakfast and I am absolutely starving. I suggest we brave a railways rusk and coffee at the station, before I fall down. It opens ahead of the Durban train's arrival."

The small cafe on the platform was quite full with the all-pervasive smell of railway coffee and people waiting for the train. The moment they entered they realised that this had been a mistake, as friends and strangers crowded around them asking for a first-hand account of the shark attack, even though the Natal Mercury had not yet arrived from Durban (the incident would be revisited by the weekly Zululand Times, published that coming Friday).

Emily said loudly to everyone in the room, "Look, this is awful enough. We are still in a state of shock and would appreciate it if you would leave us alone; but thank you for your concern."

Whereupon she muttered to Donald and Toby, "Come on, we're getting out of here. I really can't stand this! I'd rather starve," and marched out of the cafe, along the platform, down the steps and into the street again.

"Goddamit! Will we never be left alone? Awful, awful, awful! I've got a good mind to come with you to Ntambanana – just to get away from this."

The Mercury did arrive with the Durban train. Bundles of copies were collected by several Indian store employees, one of whom left some copies on the station cafe counter.

The billboards splashed

FATAL ZULULAND SHARK ATTACK

Donald said, "I'll walk you back to the Broccardo's gate then join Toby. OK, Toby? Let's meet in about half an hour in the store."

As they walked, Emily said, "Thank you for that. I don't think I'm in a fit state to meet any of those people and besides, Sonya needs my companionship. She's a good friend. Absolutely devastated about losing Zeno. Like peas in a pod. Inseparable twins."

"Well, here we are," he said.

As they stopped out of sight of the house beside a flowering frangipani tree, Emily turned to Donald. She wrapped her body against his and kissing him, said, "Thank you. I don't know what it is but I can't help being fatally drawn to you. Better know that. Don't think there will be any other opportunity to say anything more before you two toddle off to Ntambanana. I suspect you feel the same way. I know that by the way you look at me. Sonya noticed that too. I know this must strike you as awfully forward, but university life makes one cut to the chase and be less inhibited. The funeral is going to be absolutely ghastly and we will all have to be on our best public behaviour."

The adrenalin rushed through his body before Donald was able to stammer, "I-I do feel the s-same way," then muttered that someone was coming when he heard a twig break and broke away reluctantly.

It turned out to be an umfaan [young Zulu boy] wearing nothing but a moochie, but by that time the spell was broken. Donald said, "I had better get back to Toby," his thoughts in a turmoil.

[A moochie is a piece of leather or cloth that covers the loins, suspended from a leather thong around the waist.]

Donald started out for the store then turned. They stood looking at each other for a long while, before he slowly waved. Emily was plucking some blossom and as he gazed she put a flower in her hair. The rotund frangipani tree was cloaked in waxy white flowers with yellow centres issuing an ambrosial fragrance. The scent would always be with him when he thought of Emily and that moment and those that followed.

Toby had bought a copy of the Mercury and was leaning against a verandah wall at the store, studying the report when Donald found him.

The article was fairly accurate and read:

Richard's Bay. Monday 21st April 1919

The son of a respected Empangeni family, Zeno Broccardo, was fatally attacked yesterday in shallow water at Richard's Bay by what is thought to have been a female Zambi shark.

Close witnesses to the attack were three friends and Zeno's twin sister who were in the water with him: Donald Kirkwood, Toby Strafford, Sonya Broccardo (Zeno's sister) and Emily Bell.

Empangeni's Dr. Japie Lombard saw the attack from the Richard's Bay Hotel verandah. A group of Indian fishermen standing in the wash nearby also witnessed the attack.

According to Mr. Fred Grantham, the proprietor of the hotel, who joined in the attempt to resuscitate Mr. Broccardo, the young man was attacked in about four feet of water, which had been muddied by the river silt brought down by the overnight rains.

The flooding had forced open a channel to the sea from the lagoon. As the channel was only waist deep, the friends had decided to wade across to the sand dunes on the other side.

An angler who witnessed the incident, Ramsamy Mukherjee, said that the shark he saw was massive and that there was a desperate attempt by everyone to get out of the water as quickly as possible.

His immediate concern was for his seven-year-old daughter, who was playing at the water's edge when the attack occurred.

Dr. John Stranack, a Durban marine biologist, told the paper that the bull shark (often called the 'Zambi') was known for its aggressive nature, especially at new moon when most attacks take place, and its predilection for warm shallow coastal waters.

He said that the female of the species could grow to more than 12 feet in length, and the majority of near-shore shark attacks in shallow waters close to estuaries were attributed to this predator.

Bull sharks would often bump a victim before launching an attack. The technique was to disorientate the prey.

The Broccardo family could not be reached for comment before deadline but Reverend Robert

Short told the paper that the funeral would take place at 11 o'clock on Tuesday 13th April in Holy Cross Church, Empangeni. He understood that donations in memory of Zeno Broccardo were to be sent to the Colenso Education Fund, through his office.

Donald drew a fold of paper from his pocket and said, "It might be a good idea to build up a Tam 'war chest'. I've no idea of what we're going to find there (or even what we won't find) so I'm assuming that access to anything will be very limited indeed. As we'll be neighbours (though some distance removed), would you care to share your thoughts on what might be needed?"

"Good idea. I've drawn up a list too, believe it or not. Let's see if Loftheim's lives up to its reputation as being a miniature Harrods. Bit small for elephants."

They wound up buying matches, candles, paraffin lamps, cans of paraffin – complete with tinplate hand pumps which squeaked – tin-openers, three-legged cast iron pots and plates, knives, forks and spoons, small tins of butter and jam, sugar, salt, pepper, powdered mustard, flour, tea, coffee, bully beef (a kind of tinned brisket), powdered milk, quinine, tins of fruit, bandages, Condy's Crystals, aspirin, and bread from the Lebanese bakery.

The store arranged to pack their purchases in separate tea chests and send them up to the hotel later. "Are you going to store all that stuff in your tent?"

"Not likely. The ants would get at the sugar, the cane rats would gnaw the candles and the termites would destroy the tea chest. I'm going to hope I stumble across a solution once we get there. There must be someone nearby with a spare corner in a shed."

* * *

"Curry?" suggested Toby as they repaired to the crowded hotel verandah. Donald asked if they could share a table with what turned out to be two Durban land surveyors who had been serendipitously engaged in staking out the last few farm allotments in Ntambanana.

"Name's Murray," said one holding out his hand. "And thisz Wilson." Murray was slurring his words. "We've come for curry, but that bloody churrah's taking his time. Hey! Churrah!" he shouted to the passing Indian waiter, "Where's bloody curry?"

"Scoming sir. Now-now."

Donald had come to realise that 'now-now' meant 'now immediately' while all other applications of 'now' – like 'now' and 'just now' – could mean, in this part of the world, anything between 'now' and next Christmas.

Murray's nose was bulbous and he was tanned to leather by much outdoor exposure, as was that of his co-diner Wilson. His wide oblong mouth resembled a post box opening. His eyes were rheumy, evidence of a hard-drinking lifestyle, and his upper lip supported a wispy moustache, yellowed in the centre by cigarette smoking. Hardened by years of walking over rough ground, his frame was wiry though slight, compared with his companion's, the burlier of the two. The second and third fingers of his bony left hand were yellowed by nicotine. Wilson, on the other hand, was thickset; his hairy arms, face and neck were tanned like his colleague's and he was still wearing his wide-brimmed leather hat.

True to the waiter's word, Murray's and Wilson's curries

arrived with rice, sambals (diced banana, onion and tomato), coconut to sprinkle on the top, papadums and slices of white bread on side plates to help contain the after-bite within bearable limits of the hot Madras curry.

Natal whites, particularly the English-speakers, had encountered and taken a liking to this hot curry when it was introduced into the country by the indentured Indians from 1860, most of whom had been recruited from Madras and Calcutta. Curry in Madras seldom contained meat, but the Natal version often did, usually mutton but never beef.

Donald hastily ordered the same plus two lagers "now-now" with the nodded agreement of Toby, before the waiter could escape. He pondered how everything would fit on such a small table once their order had arrived.

Soon after Wilson had started eating, his nose began to stream from the heat of the curry, whereupon he yanked a handkerchief out of his pocket and blew his nose loudly, then asked where the two men were from.

It was humid and everyone was sweating through their shirts. The few women on the verandah looked uniformly bedraggled.

On hearing that Donald had fought in German East Africa, he said quietly, after looking around him to ensure that neighbouring diners could not hear him, "We were in the 2nd Mounted Rifles (Natal Carbineers) in 1914, in German South West Africa. Our job was to put down the Afrikaner rebellion. It was messy and we lost two men at the Gibeon Station fight in April, 1915.

"I don't think we'd be very popular here with the Afrikaner 'bittereinders' – and there are still some of them about in this part of the world, and inland even more so – so keep it under your hat."

"An appropriate phrase that," said Donald, pointing at the man's hat.

"What? Oh," he said and burst out laughing. "Good word that, 'bittereinders'. They were going to fight on to the bitter end even though the second Anglo-Boer War had ended twelve years ago – and they might have succeeded when Britain's focus turned to Germany and the start of war in Europe. The Irish had the same idea in 1916 and it looks as if they are succeeding in kicking out the Brits.

"Germany played a big part in providing a lot of help to the Boers, remember – Mauser 'broom-handle' guns and Krupp artillery. The bittereinders envisaged a general uprising of resentful Afrikaners in this country linking up with the Germans in South West. So we might have been living in a Boer republic with a lot of Kraut influence by this time if it had worked."

"What's your story, Toby?"

"Well, I'm Irish."

"Woops!" Wilson muttered. He had sobered up with the curry and Toby saw he was about to order another plateful. "Hey, churrah! Some more!"

"Don't worry. My family are or were Southern Unionists, so on the 'wrong' side. The indigenous anti-treaty 'underground' started calling us 'Anglo-Irish' ever more vociferously, although the family had arrived with the Norman conquest and centuries before Cromwell started burning priests – and probably much earlier than that – yet things were beginning to turn nasty by the time my family managed to reach London. They'd heard (incorrectly, as it turned out) that our estate in County Wexford was under threat and that it might be set to the torch, even though there was never any suggestion that the family would be killed.

"All the labour had left them, notwithstanding my ancestors treating them well and providing employment during the potato famine; I assume that the workers were coerced into doing so and I don't blame them, but it did leave the family in a bit of a pickle.

"Actually, the rumours came to naught and the house still stands but remains vacant, I have learnt. The brambles and ivy have begun to smother the place, including the walled garden, and the fields must be in a terrible mess, as they have remained untilled for years. I believe the stable doors were removed. That's about all the physical damage that has been done. The family managed to sell off the cattle and horses at knock-down prices before they left.

"Our family is far from being alone. There seems to be an orchestrated wave of animosity stirred up by the Anti-treaty forces and lots more families like ours have or were talking about bowing to the inevitable and leaving the country of their birth, despite the risk of being torpedoed.

"Now there's the threat of a civil war breaking out even if Ireland does gain independence, to make things worse, between the moderates and the bitter-enders who are likely to want the whole of Ireland set free from the British yoke. It's a mess.

"God knows what will happen to all those abandoned estates – I suppose the provisional government will cut up the farms into smaller units and turn the rest into hotels and golf-courses. There'll be more golf courses than golf balls. I just hope that things will die down again, although there is no sign of anything getting any better. Just worse.

"A sister of mine wrote of a family near Limerick and heard of what happened to the owner who was confined to a wheel chair. When the Fenians came and told him to evacuate his family from the Big House before they burnt it down, he refused to leave and said that they would have to burn the house down with him in it – so they repaired to the nearest pub and never came back...He used the petrol that they had abandoned as fuel for his tractor. I'll give it to them, although there have been some nasty exceptions, they aren't out to kill people, just to destroy emblems of British association.

"The terrible thing is that all these hotheads are decent lads really and the turmoil is tearing families apart, rich and poor, and splitting the entire fabric of Irish society as we know it. During the last year of the European war, the tidal wave of anti-Anglo-Irish sentiment was going on at the same time as German submarines were torpedoing British merchant vessels and passenger ships off the Wexford coast. It was horrific.

"Britain even had patrol airships based at nearby Johnstown Castle, not far from our estate, in an effort to spot and depth charge the U-boats – and uncounted numbers of County Wexford men were dying at the Front in France while serving in the British Army. A dichotomy if ever there was one.

"With hindsight, I realise that the 'Anglo-Irish' landed gentry and particularly the absentee llandlords had, without even reflecting upon it, suppressed an intelligent indigenous race for more than 600 years, just as we white settlers are about to continue to do to the natives and Indians and to a great extent the Boers. It's a sure bet that the Boers will continue to get a lousy deal for years to come, no matter what the Act of Union implies. The whole idea of teaching Dutch-Afrikaans in schools, for example, is rejected. However, when one is born into a privileged lifestyle one just accepts things as they are, Empire, Pax Britannica and all that.

"I was in the Royal Navy Volunteer Reserve – the 'Wavy Navy' – when all this Irish business started, and involved in the German East African campaign in its naval form. We – that is us on HMS Chatham, HMS Goliath and a steam pinnace – combined to blockade the Konigsberg on the Rufiji River near Mombasa in 1915.

"Before that occurred, the Konigsberg had managed to torpedo HMS Pegasus in Dar-es-Salaam.

"The German captain, Max Looff, was a very clever man indeed. He managed to camouflage the upper parts of the Konigsberg by felling trees and strapping them to the aerials and three funnels, and then lie low around a bend in the river, out of range and fifteen miles upstream.

"Eventually it was spotted by a Durban man, Denis Cutler, who had been persuaded to scan the area in his Curtiss seaplane. Konigsberg was attacked by two naval monitors able to get up the river due to their shallow drafts. When the captain realised that the game was up he scuttled the ship to put out a devastating coal fire. But while all that was going on the Konigsberg's fifteen heavy guns were being dismantled by the crew and landed out of sight, in preparation for being taken overland to join von Lettow-Vorbeck's lot who were being chased all around East Africa by Donald and thousands of his mates."

Donald smiled at this. He remarked, "My mates and I suffered as much from starvation, disease and the smell of dead animals, dead soldiers and rats as actually getting killed by the Krauts. It's awkward to think of anything else when your toes are full of jigger fleas and your body is being invaded by guinea-worm. That German was a ruthless guerrilla warrior (and there was not much pity for the local Africans when it came to ransacking their villages for food) and we seemed to have ever-mounting odds to battle against. To cap it all our hearts sank when we heard by the usual grapevine that a German Zeppelin was making its way down Africa to deliver supplies to von Lettow. Never arrived though. That's a lot of effort – to travel 4,000 miles then fail to deliver the goods.

"We never really defeated him. In fact, his forces were still fighting until 14th November 1918, after the Armistice on the 11th. He only stopped when the local District Officer – name of Croad - appeared with a bearer waving a very large white flag on a rather long bamboo. Croad had to explain that an Armistice had been declared, confirming what the German had learned from a captured dispatch rider.

"After agreeing to a ceasefire, Von-Lettow marched his men to Abercorn and arrived late in the same month. Well, that's far too much about us. Tell us about Ntambanana."

"Well, what do you want to know? How can a naval man who probably can't ride a horse tackle farming in Africa? With difficulty, I would say. There's a lot to learn even for anyone who grew up here.

"We can describe which the best allotments are and which are so close to the river that when the river was last in flood we had to wade waist-high in swamps to stake out territories. Would have made excellent crocodile meat," said Wilson.

"From what you said you seem to have got the best upland sites. Generally, you get less rain than here around Empangeni and, although the estates in the south are

144

fairly good for sugar, where you will be I suggest you stick to cotton. Forget beef and dairy. Your stock would all get nagana and die.

"And cotton's fetching good prices – depending on fibre grade, it can reach well over £11 a bale at the moment; but watch out for the manager of the gin mill. There are rumours of his paying low-grade prices for top grade bales.

"Harvesting takes place in May and planting for the new crop is in September – spring. If you get plenty of sunshine in September, fertile soil and good rains, the cottonseed will begin to sprout seedling leaves within five to ten days. Then between a fortnight and a month, the important leaves appear. But you know all this?"

"Go on."

"In about seven weeks small buds show, swell and open to flower. They pollinate and then die away to reveal small green 'bolls' which swell and eventually open to reveal the cotton fibre.

"It all sounds so easy, except you'll probably walk into a permanent labour shortage, cotton seed beetle, two kinds of bollworm, drought, floods, mild earthquakes and machinery breaking down, with no mechanic other than yourself for miles and miles. I forgot to mention 'reticence' between the Boers and the English speakers, wild animals – and snakes. There's more danger from being bitten by a snake than being attacked by a wild animal.

"Hey, aren't you the two guys who witnessed that shark attack? Ag man. Ghastly eh? What happened, shallow water, eh?"

Toby said that the event was too close to be relived and that the funeral was the next day, so they preferred to leave the description to the papers.

"We were just friends in the wrong place and the wrong time."

Wilson's enquiring voice had risen and by this time diners from neighbouring tables were turning their heads, with three preparing to come to the table to question the survivors.

Hastily, Toby and Donald signed their hotel verandah chits and made their excuses. They agreed to meet up again at the wagoner's.

Donald went to the post office and prepared a telegram to Judy in Durban: "WITNESSED TRAGIC SHARK ATTACK + ATTENDING FUNERAL TUESDAY BEFORE TRAVELLING NTAMBANANA + DETAILS MERCURY + MORE LATER + DONALD."

Once again, he decided to omit the word 'love'. He also pondered on how to reduce the number of words even further, as telegrams were costly and were charged by the number of words including spelt out punctuation marks. He deleted the words 'tragic' and 'more later' and then all the stops and handed the form over to the girl for transmission. It now read WITNESSED SHARK ATTACK DETAILS MERCURY FUNERAL TUESDAY BEFORE NTAMBANANA DONALD.

He deleted the 'stops' after being told that the operator would have been obliged to spell out the stops and charge for them, ever since an American telegraph operator had omitted a comma and his company lost a costly lawsuit as a result.

Chapter Six

Mocke's hot wood-and-iron shed smelt of wood shavings and simmering casein glue. Pencils of sunlight shone through holes where nuts and bolts had rusted out of the corrugated iron walls so that anyone walking in the shed would be alternately illuminated and dropped into shadow, much like the flickering images of very early cinema or those sequential photographs of animal locomotion. Mocke's young grandchildren loved to run up and down watching each other's Muybridgean images.

Toby was already there when Donald arrived and Jan Mocke was remarking about a wagon that had been brought in for repair.

"This wagon-man has had to make do with the wrong materials to repair these wheels – and it shows. That's why two of the steel tyres have come off – he used the only kind of wood he could find – a hardwood instead of the soft wood from the weeping willow.

"If a hardwood is used the brakes heat up and the steel bands expand and come off; and that's exactly what happened here.

"Many kinds of wood are used to make up a wagon and you can tell if that carpenter knew his craft properly. See, the builder used lemonwood for the wheel-segments, wild peach for the spokes and ironwood for the axles. That is completely correct.

"And look. He's used a different kind of wood, knobthorn, for the disselboom [the draft pole protruding from the front of the wagon and attached to the separate front wheel array] and that is correct too. But you can tell that this wagon has travelled far and the owner has had to improvise as he went along.

"Indeed, the wagon was well built. Such wagons can be taken apart so broken pieces can be swopped for new ones, because all wagon parts are made to the same measurements; and the whole wagon can be dismantled for another reason too – so that the pieces can be loaded onto the oxen when some rivers must be forded.

"Their proportions dictate the width of roads (but not the track we will travel along to Ntambanana) so that a full span of oxen can do a U-turn, and it also dictates the dimensions of public squares. Man! Die ossewa is 'n wonderlike ding" [The ox wagon is a wonderful thing.]

They heard that Jan had learned his craft just before the second Anglo-Boer War as a young apprentice at King's Wagon Works in faraway Pampoenkraal, a Cape hinterland town on the main route to the Transvaal goldfields. (It later changed its name to Durbanville.) In its heyday, King's had produced a variety of more than 300 wagons a month.

Despite King's strenuous lobbying for the railway to pass through the town, thus ensuring continuing easy access to supplies, it was not to be and led indirectly to the steady decline in the company's fortunes.

During the second Anglo-Boer war, Mocke fought under General Lucas Meyer, his most memorable occasion being the first major battle of the conflict at Dundee close to Isandhlwana and Rorke's Drift. Over 250 British soldiers were wounded or killed there against 97 Boers slaughtered or wounded.

He encountered MacBride's Irish Brigade, many of them explosive experts from the Transvaal goldmines, fighting with the Boers and was startled to realise that they were facing Irish soldiers serving under the British. It was a case of 'Fitzgerald fighting Fitzpatrick and Brannigan shooting Burke at the Battle of Dundee'.

Returning after the conflict, he found that he had been replaced by Scottish artisans recruited by the owners, so on hearing that areas of Crown Land in distant Zululand were being opened up to white settlers and familiar with Natal, Mocke decided to make his way there again and set up a modest wagon construction and repair shop in the expanding village of Empangeni. He was confident in his expertise and knew that most of the woods required to build wagons were in plentiful supply in the Zululand forests.

Mocke foresaw that he could build up a useful parallel trade in hiring or selling oxen-spans and wagons for pioneers heading further north into Zululand, towards Moçambique and the interior.

His decision was reinforced by the arrival of the railway; the discovery of gold in Natal and Zululand (the first of 32 sites in 1867 by one Fred Markham) and the recognition that the wagon would be an essential component of supplementary transport and agricultural life for many years to come.

Before the advent of steam, electricity and the petrol engine, the ox wagon was ubiquitous throughout southern Africa and retained its position long after these new forms of power began to appear.

Teamed with the Afrikander trek ox, its transport capabilities played a pivotal role in the Great Trek by Boers (mainly Dutch farmers but with a fair sprinkling of French Huguenot descendants and northern Germans) moving away from British rule in the Cape Colony. In the early part of the nineteenth century, ox wagons carried them into lands north of the mighty Orange River, even further north past the Vaal River and east over the barrier of the Drakensberg Mountains into fertile Natal. 'Trek' means 'pull', and it was indeed a huge and mighty pull of wagons by teams of oxen over African terrain that had never seen a wheeled vehicle before.

Wagons drawn together in a circle made a formidable laager against attacks by black tribes encountered on the way, and upturned wagons and stacked mealiebags helped to provide a makeshift laager against a Zulu attack on British troops defending the mission station at Rorke's Drift in Natal during the Anglo-Zulu war.

The ox wagon even made possible the supply chain between Barberton and the port of Lourenço Marques in Portuguese East Africa, a way without roads, during the gold rush of the 1880s.

"My price for transport and luggage between Loftheim's at Empangeni and Piet van Jaarsveld's store at Ntambanana is three shillings per hundredweight. From how you described your luggage I guess that your loads together will work out to about five, so that will be fifteen shillings each, one pound three bob. That's for one way. You must see that your luggage is here on time and know that we depart at six o' clock on Wednesday morning, op die kop [sharp]. There can't be any guarantee that you will reach 'Tam on the same day – the wagon travels at about three miles an hour and we have to water and feed the oxen on the way – but the weather looks calm so it is probable you will get there on the same day. Make sure that your luggage and belongings are waterproof, and understand that I will expect you to walk beside the wagon most of the time because the wagon will be full. Besides, it's more comfortable op pad [along the way].

"We outspan every few hours or so and rest until the oxen have grazed and digested enough. It's a good time to eat some padkos [food for the road] and make coffee."

Toby and Donald agreed and set out to make arrangements to get their trunks from the station to Mocke's shed the same afternoon, although nonplussed as how to do so because they were too heavy to carry a long distance. The hotel manager came to the rescue by offering a few labourers to load them onto the hotel handcart then pushing it across to the shed.

Dali-esque shadows were lengthening; the sun, low on the horizon, picked out small stones, pebbles and leaves in the dust. The Mynahs were setting up their usual sunset racket by the time they reached the hotel verandah and ordered sundowners. Hadedas were strutting on a patch of grass nearby, ignoring the hotel cat and the small three-legged hotel dog called 'Rommel' – the Boer word for 'rubbish'. The dog had lost its back left leg from a mule-kick. The Indian waiter was still wearing what seemed to be the same thumb plaster, now grubbier.

"We had better drink up before mosquito-time. There are our two surveyors again. They must have been there the whole afternoon. Who's that codger, I wonder, on the next table? Don't we know him?" Toby asked, as soon as they sat down. "Yes. That's von Weldenburg!"

Donald looked across and waved but he didn't seem to notice him, continuing to talk to his companions in what sounded like Dutch-Afrikaans, though mangled by a person more at ease with German.

He was able to recognise the meaning of the word 'broeders' by this time (von Weldenburg uttered it), but the repetition of a word which sounded like 'bont' puzzled him. He made up his mind at that moment to learn as much Dutch-Afrikaans as quickly as he could and cursed himself for being so ill-prepared for life at Ntambanana.

Suddenly pretending to recognise Toby and Donald for the first time the Swiss turned to them, smiling and shouted, "Hello! Awful about Zeno, huh? You will be at the funeral tomorrow? Of course. Then we will speak more," and turned back to his Afrikaans companions, who exchanged glances among themselves.

His party got up from their seats soon afterwards and headed for the dining room, von Weldenburg nodding to Donald and Toby as they left.

There were few women in the dining room and those that were, were mostly middle aged and in the company of their husbands. One or two had vaguely noticed that the Edwardian era was over, though not yet evidenced by hemlines. Short skirts, bobbed hair and flattened breasts were not for them, although some had succumbed to cigarette smoking in public.

One woman had tightly waved short hair, evidence of a recent trip to a hairdresser in Durban. Like miniature corrugated iron, Donald thought.

Von Weldenburg's party was at the other end of the dining room with brandy helping to increase the volume of their chatter as the evening wore on.

The only table available (the room was not large and the pressed-steel ceiling made it noisy) was occupied by the two surveyors who motioned to them to join them, which they rather reluctantly did, Wilson knocking over a glass of beer.

Their table was beneath the wall of antelopes. A beetle of some sort dropped from one of the animal heads as they sat down and scurried over the tablecloth until Wilson squashed it under the glass ashtray, and called an over-worked and sweating Indian waiter to clean up the beer-spill and to bring a clean cloth. Donald noticed the slogan on the ashtray read 'Men of the World Smoke Max'. A loud slamming noise in the hotel later that night startled him from sleep and the words 'men of the world squash max' went round and round in his head.

The meal was what was to be expected: soup, which the menu claimed to have been made from peas, accompanied by tired bread rolls and scalloped butter, kept relatively unmolten by small dollops of ice. (The management had the only refrigerator within a hundred miles, other than ones in the police morgue and the undertakers. It was powered by paraffin). Fine slices of grey leathery meat accompanied by cabbage and potatoes concealed by thick brown gravy were served on cold plates. Sponge cake smothered with syrup completed the main part of the no-alternative menu – it was, after all, sugarcane country.

The cheese and aged water biscuits that finished the meal were pounced upon eagerly as the highlight of a singularly awful dinner that could not have been ruined any further by appalling cooking. The port was passed around anti-clockwise and occasionally absent-mindedly clockwise or across the table when the biscuits arrived.

"Zfrench serve cheese before pudding," said Wilson. "Typical. No manners. No bread plates either." Donald and Toby were getting almost as befuddled as their companions were, although Toby wondered what was particularly despicable about the French eating cheese before desert.

"Well ... I don't know. Serves 'em right," Donald said. The conversation had slurred steadily into bursts of inconsequential comments and longer and longer alcohol-induced pauses.

He thought that a Frenchman would have left the dining room in horror at first taste of the potage. Mind you, he thought, Frenchmen don't eat with their mouths closed; at least his Durban friend Jean-Pierre didn't.

However, what he did glean from the conversation, which continued to sputter like the final moments of an expiring candle, while diners not far away were beginning to disappear behind clouds of cigarette and pipe smoke – everyone was smoking by this time of the evening – was that there was a lively illegal trade in liquor between Indians and the natives. He learnt that ritually, some Zulu men smoked dagga, though their women and children did not and their men forbade them to do so. Another snippet that came his way was that elephant and rhino were being slaughtered for their tusks and horns. These were shipped out of Durban to the Far East and that von Weldenburg was a man to be watched – whatever that meant.

"Well, I'm off," Donald said, rising. "Early night. Sad day tomorrow. Dreading it. G'night."

He found his way up the stairs, thanking heaven for the handrail, leaving Toby to his own devices and then realising on reaching the landing that he had not collected his room key from the reception desk, so had to make his way down to collect it, clutching the handrail again.

He almost collided with Wilson, who was crawling on all fours up the stairs, clutching a bottle and giggling.

Negotiating the dimly-lit corridor serving the bedrooms was now rendered hazardous by food trays left outside doors with shoes for polishing by praecoxian drudges. He stumbled over a beer bottle and glass on a tray with a crash before reaching his door.

The rest of the night was a slowly revolving oblivion until he awoke to the noise of monkeys thundering up and down the roof, his sleep interrupted only once by the slamming sound in the middle of the night which had led him to mutter about squashing Max.

In response to a rattle on the door, he opened it to find a barefooted Zulu girl in 'nanny' clothes, with a smile like an open piano, bearing his tea and biscuits.

A dead cockroach came out of the spout when he poured the second cup.

Coming down to breakfast he noticed, for the first time, a small cabinet in the foyer beside the reception desk. It displayed a curious collection of labelled items including a set of false teeth, a wooden foot, several handbags, a railway ticket, a man's hat, a half-empty bottle of Sloan's Liniment, hair clippers and several books, the top one titled Natürliche Schöpfungsgeschichte by Ernest Haeckel.

Still with a sticking-plastered thumb, the Indian waiter who had served them curry the day before, now behind the desk at reception, explained that the cabinet housed left-property items, each one labelled with the room number and the date when it was found in guests' bedrooms after

155

departure. Some had been there for several years.

Donald wondered how the people with the missing foot and teeth were getting on and who would be reading about The Missing Link and the history of creation in a remote hotel in the Zululand bush and then leaving it unclaimed – and why in German, rather than the English translation. He thought for a moment about von Weldenburg and his fascination for Nietzsche's theories, and asked if he might look at the flyleaf.

Producing a small key from a string of others, the Indian complied. On the flyleaf was von Weldenburg's name below which was enscribed: 'Um Hubie. Glückwünsche aus! Mit viel Liebe von Frieda'.

The find was labelled with a date from several months back, so Donald said, "What a surprise! I'll be seeing the owner of this book later today. May I take it and hand it to him? He must have been worried about mislaying it as his wife gave it to him."

The Indian said, "Please wait," and disappeared into the kitchen to return a few moments later to say that that would be in order and handed over the Haeckel, saying "Please give me a receipt," to which Donald agreed.

Chapter Seven

The hot wood-and-iron church, which crackled with expansion noises every time the sun came out from behind a cloud, was packed with friends of the family and full of the noise of clumping and shuffling feet. More and more sympathisers arrived until the vergers ran out of Books of Common Prayer and Hymnals, requiring strangers to share – some of the books with substantial numbers of pages missing.

Toby turned the pages of his, hoping in vain to come across another mysterious 'See page 333' type of message.

The same harmonium-player of the previous Sunday service was struggling away with Bach while a huge spider was crawling up the wall behind her. The Reverend Short walked to the door to meet the flower-decked coffin and lead the bearers with the principle mourners to the body of the church, after which the Broccardos and some others took their seats.

Donald spotted the young Indian girl from the Bell's farm, Masheila, who had crept in to sit in the back row. She wore a dark sari, sandals and unusually, a black floppy hat. He couldn't help thinking how beautiful and demure she was.

The coffin was bedecked with sweet-smelling

frangipani blossoms and other flowers gathered in the Broccardo garden by Joy, Sonya and Emily, and a nosegay from a small wood brought by the Broccardo's 'garden boy'. It included a switch of Nqutu [wild willow], signifying bravery.

He learned later that, as young children, Zeno and Sonya would love to sneak outside just after dark to watch the moths fluttering about the flowering frangipani tree at the end of the Broccardo garden.

Their parents were horrified when they discovered them, as dusk is the time when malaria mosquitoes are most active. Their father gave them a strong talking-to and made them take a daily dose of powdered quinine – without any sweetener to cover the bitter taste.

Emily took her seat with the Broccardos between Joy and Sonya. The rest of the Bells were in the same row.

Their aged Zulu nanny and stubbly-haired 'garden boy', who must have been at least sixty years old, sat immediately behind them in the same row as Donald and Toby, dressed in the best they could manage and restless with awkwardness.

Short said: "Grief is the price we pay for loving. We are here to celebrate the short earthly life of Zeno Broccardo, beloved son of Mario and Bianca, brother of Joy and his twin sister Sonya and to commit him to God's care.

"From the number here I can see that Zeno and his family are well-loved by so many. You are all most welcome.

"While most of us may regard our 'here and now' as the earthly reality and that Christ's future is ephemeral I am reminded of (here the stumbling block of pronouncing a word starting with a 'P' aided again by shouted options from the congregation) P-P-Paul's sudden realisation that our present experience is rather the one which is insubstantial. For now, we see only through a glass darkly. Bow your heads as we pray for Zeno and his family."

With that completed, he said, "I have asked Zeno's father to read the final paragraph of First Corinthians where Paul addresses our future hope."

At that moment Zeno's Dalmatian padded into the church, tongue hanging out and panting. After sniffing into various pews, he recognised the smell of the Broccardo family's shoes and wriggled into the row to sit, as best he could, thumping his tail. Sonya bent down, stroked his head and tickled him behind the ears.

It was difficult to gauge Mario's state of mind for his face was set. Clumping up to the lectern, he paused, polished his spectacles which had misted up and read, "Charity never faileth: but where there be prophesies, they shall fail; whether there be tongues, they shall cease: whether there be knowledge, they shall vanish away. For we know in part, and we prophesy in part.

"But when that which is perfect to come, then that which is in part shall be done away.

"When I was a child, I spake as a child, I understood as a child, I thought as a child; but when I became a man, I put away childish things. For now we see through a glass, darkly; but then face to face; now I know in part; but then shall I know even as also I am known."

He stumbled on returning to his seat and farted as he sat down.

After a hymn was struggled through not only by the worshippers but the organist as well, Short said "Zeno, so full of promise, was snatched from us by a cruel act of marine nature. I know the Broccardo family well and could see that Zeno was poised to play an important part in the future of Zululand.

"He displayed a love of nature with which Zululand is blessed in such great abundance and his family – not least Sonya, his twin sister, shared his vision for the future. He saw that it lay in reconciliation and went out of his way to form friendships not only with his kith and kin but with Dutch-Afrikaans farmers, the Zulus of the area and the Indians who labour in our cane fields. He realised very well, while attending the University of Natal in Pietermaritzburg, that education for all (though not only education) was a key to unlocking this country's greatest potential, its people. It explains his family's wish that, instead of flowers, gestures of sympathy should take the form of donations to the Colenso Education Trust, knowing that this would further his dream."

At this point, many farmers in the congregation stirred in their seats, mindful of the Bambatha rebellion by the Zulus and farming's endless labour problems. One whispered to his wife: "I think that's going a bit far." Another muttered, "Dis nie reg nie. Nie aanvaarbaar" [It's not right. Not acceptable].

"Turning to his passion for nature, you will see that his coffin is covered with flowers. They are from the Broccardo garden that he loved so well and wildflowers gathered by Dumisane from a little forest near the village this morning. I was asked by the family to single out and thank their servant for gathering these. From early childhood, Zeno and Dumisane were good friends. Ngiyabonga [Thank you] Dumisane!

"This is one reason why the second hymn is 'The Flowers of the Forest', an ancient song indeed. The other reason is that the melody and the words are often performed for navy personnel who have been snatched from us by the sea when the service is conducted on land.

"As most of us will be unfamiliar with the words and the melody, I decided to leave it to my wife Mary to sing it for us, supported by a small chorus from Dumisane's village (there they are at the door of the church). They have spent many hours rehearsing the melody.

"So that's what all those natives were doing outside the church," Farmer Meiring murmured to his wife. "They'll be sitting beside us next. Just look at that couple next to the Bells."

"These are what are thought to be the original English words, although (Short smiled) Robert Burns might have begged to differ."

She sang as the choir hummed the air:

I've seen the smiling of fortune beguiling I've tasted
her pleasures and felt her decay
Sweet is her blessing and kind her caressing but Now
they are fled and fled far away
I've seen the forest adorned the foremost Wi' Flowers
o' the fairest baith pleasant and gay
Sae bonnie was their blooming their scent a'
perfuming But now they are withered away.

Toby found the melody and voices moved him unexpectedly, with the memory of the torpedoing of HMS Triumph by a German submarine off the Gallipoli peninsula in May 1915 and the dismally few ensign-draped coffins of the bodies recovered which lined the nave of the draughty little church on the Greek island of Samos. The hymn had been sung by what was left of the crew. The ceremony had been on land because traditional burial at sea was out of the question in such embattled waters. Although still neutral, the Greeks 'looked the other way', rather than arresting the crew for the duration of the war.

Short's mentioning of Bishop Colenso rekindled in many farmers the memory of his unpopular defence of the Zulus at a time when Chelmsford was hell-bent on invading Zululand by crossing the Buffalo River (marking the official border between Natal and Zululand) on trumped up claims about marauding bands of Zulus threatening the future of Natal.

Chelmsford's covert motive was to occupy Zululand and expand the grip of the British Empire, to suppress the indigenous occupants of the coastal lands north of the Buffalo River, and in the process open it up for white settlement.

Colenso was the first Anglican Bishop of Natal. Born in Cornwall, he distinguished himself at Cambridge before taking up his Natal post by invitation of the then Bishop of Cape Town, a Robert Gray.

He established good relations with the Zulu king of the time, King Cetshwayo, translated the New Testament into the Zulu language 'isiZulu' and produced the first English-Zulu dictionary, the written language being based on Latin script and set down by early missionaries.

Colenso shocked the conservative establishment with the 1855 publication of his 'Remarks on the Proper Treatment of Polygamy', exhorting tolerance of the practise by the Zulus.

In addition, he spoke out against the unjust treatment of the Zulus by the colonial regime and took up their cause

against the colonialists, figure-headed by the Secretary for
Native Affairs at that time, Theophilus Shepstone, who – as
Colonial Secretary – persisted in sending largely unfounded
reports to London about Zulu intentions to invade Natal.

Colenso found himself estranged from colonial society,
yet persisted in championing the cause of the natives
against English and Boer oppression.

His intrepid defence of the Zulus exposed the racialist
foundation of the colonial regime and earned him as
many enemies among the clergy as among the colonists
themselves.

He had been deposed as Bishop in 1865, bringing about
a split in the Natal Anglican Church, though the properties
vested in his name permitted him to continue as Bishop of
Natal until his death in 1883.

Baynes, a successor, had contrived to bring about a
reconciliation of the two groups by 1901, yet the
reverberations of Colenso's defence of the Zulus continued
to pass through Natal society like a gravity wave, long after
his death; hence the displeasure among farmers and their
wives during Zeno's funeral service, when Colenso's name
was mentioned.

On Short's referring to 'frangipani', Emily half-turned
and threw Donald a glance.

Various readings, a eulogy by Zeno's good friend from
varsity and Short's brief but stammering sermon followed,
after which the psalm 'The Lord is My Shepherd' was
read by Sonya. The final hymn 'God be at mine end and
at my departing' sung by Mary and accompanied by the
humming of the little Zulu choir was enough to reduce
many to tears. Meiring managed to stifle his emotions with
a bout of coughing and nose-blowing. Short wound up

with the Lord's Prayer and the final Blessing.

"We are now going to move out of the church and follow Zeno's coffin to his eternal resting-place in our little graveyard," Short said; whereupon the harmonium slurred into more barely recognisable Bach. Donald wondered if the Indian responsible for pumping the air cylinder behind the church had fallen asleep.

"I have something of yours," Donald said when he found that he was walking beside von Weldenburg on the way to the grave.

"Ja?" asked von Weldenburg and gasped when Donald handed over his book.

"Ach, Mein Gott!" Hubie said. "I thought it was gone forever! Where did you find it?"

"In a cabinet of mislaid items at the Masonic Hotel."

"Sie haben mir das Leben gerettet! Herzlichen Dank!" he exclaimed, lapsing into Swiss-German. "Please. When you return from Durban and before you go on to Ntambanana, Frieda and I would be very pleased if you would visit us on our new farm for a few days. I really am immensely grateful."

"Herzlichen Dank für die Einladung und ich werde ganz sicher versuchen die Zeit zu finden für einen Besuch. Wir könnten Ansichten austauschen über unsere Erfahrungen während des Krieges und unsere Hoffnungen für die Zukunft unserer Landwirtschaft."

"Sie sprechen Deutsch bemerkenswert gut. Wie kommt das?"

"I think that we had better revert to English as I am reaching the border of my imperfect German," Donald said. Emily was walking beside him now and their hands brushed, clasped longingly and reluctantly released.

"I learnt a smattering of German as a 'guest' of von Lettow in German East Africa – that is, before I managed to escape again."

They had reached the graveside by this time, with people clustering as near to the grave as possible. Little Joy had some difficulty in pushing through to where her parents stood. It was just in time to grab her father's hand and watch the coffin being lowered with Short declaiming, "We now commit Zeno's body to the ground; earth to earth, ashes to ashes, dust to dust: in the sure and certain hope of the resurrection to eternal life."

Sonya put her arms about her mother's shoulder then dropped flowers onto the coffin with Joy following her example. Neither had ever been to a funeral and burial before.

Both of them were churning with misery.

The Broccardos had invited everyone who attended the funeral to refreshments at their house.

Frieda glanced at Hubie, Donald and Emily and said, "I tink ve could do mit a trink" and they followed the rest of the party (mostly on foot, but some on horseback) to the Broccardo household. It was not far to go.

Toby followed suit, thinking how primitive the whole thing was. "We just dig a hole; bury the body, then surround the act with all sorts of pious words muttered by the clergy. Burial at sea is at least more practical. The body is recycled almost immediately and the fish have a good meal."

"Look Frieda!" said Hubie, showing her the book by Haeckel.

"Where did you find it?"

"No, Mr. Kirkwood found it at the hotel. I am so very pleased. I have asked him and his friend to visit us when they return from Durban."

"Yes, yes, you must!" Frieda said. Donald thought that even dressed in black for a funeral and despite the Zululand heat, Frieda managed to look exotically foreign and chic.

The Broccardo verandah with its terracotta dolphin, out of which swordfish ferns were growing, quickly became crowded.

The consumption of liquor loosened tongues and farmers did what farmers do everywhere – they talked about farming matters, with Meiring voicing his concerns to the Bells, out of earshot of the Broccardos, about the impact of Spanish Flu on production, labourers and the settler families.

"You heard about Rentia? Beautiful girl. Man – so pragtig. Fair hair, blue eyes, a real Dutch beauty. Twenty-three. Apple of her old man's eye. Poor old Labuschagne, with his wife dead from dysentery and all. The girl died from the 'Spanish' last October on their farm near Ginginhlovu.

"I was visiting the place when it happened. He said it was the pneumonia that killed her, but even when I was there she had a very high temperature and was having problems with her lungs – making a crackling sound every time she breathed.

"Labuschagne told me that she started to bleed from the nose, and then the mouth and her skin went darker. Her breath smelt like old straw. Ja, man. It took just three days – three! – for a beautiful girl to get sick and die. And they say the 'Spanish' is back and it will be worse this time.

"Man! It's those bloody Churrahs, I'm sure. They are

so dirty. How can they live like that? All that betel nut and spitting. They say that one of them had the Spanish from one of the last boatloads from Madras. He was under contract to be put on the train as far as Ginginhlovu to work for Meiring, but he died soon after he arrived at the farm. Now look what's happening. What are the Health people doing about it? And what are we going to do if the Indian workers die off – and a lot of us too for that matter?"

His concerns were not unfounded, although misdirected. The pandemic of Spanish Flu had swept through South Africa and the rest of the world during 1918 and again in 1919. It was first identified in American military training camps in 1918 and was spread by the movement of thousands of troops to the theatres of war. Conflicting reports suggested that it had originated at a staging post of British troops in Étaples, France during the same year.

Both warring sides concealed the seriousness and general statistics relating to the disease during the last year of the conflict. Spain was not a combatant, however, and allowed the reporting of the pandemic to reach the media, leading to the disease being branded 'The Spanish Flu' as Spain was thought, in the popular mind, to be the source of the disease.

There were whisperings that Germany was actually to blame, introducing the virus to devastate Allied troops towards the end of the war.

Some 'Bittereindes' suggested that it stemmed from those Dutch-Afrikaans 'hansoppers' [those who surrendered to the British by raising their hands] who now served in the new South African government and had unleashed the virus to wipe out their opponents.

The first wave in 1918 was comparatively mild, causing only two or three recorded deaths, although prostrating the many that contracted the condition. The tail end of the initial appearance of the pandemic entered Natal through the port of Durban, carried by troops, both black and white, returning from Europe and German East Africa at the end of the war.

The incidence of the disease was one that radiated from the route traced by the new railways – along the new Zululand line as well as the inland route through Pietermaritzburg, the Natal Midlands and on to Johannesburg.

Homecoming African soldiers carried the contagion to their rural kraals so the pattern of distribution resembled that of the stem and veins of a leaf.

The first wave confined whites and Indians to their beds and the Zulus to their earthen floors. It benefited those who fell ill and – in the main – recovered – as it appeared to render them immune to the second wave that would prove to be far more vicious.

A sailor who came off a ship in Cape Town introduced the second and more virulent wave in 1919. It swept through the port and the Cape interior and became known as the 'Driedagsiekte', the three-day sickness. The condition progressed rapidly from early symptoms to death within three days.

Although Rentia's death was a straw in the wind, Zululanders regarded it as an isolated incident at the time, believing that Zululand was too far away to be affected. They would be proved wrong.

"I'm off to the hotel," Donald told Emily. "We'll need an early night to keep our six o' clock meeting with Jan Mocke and his oxen tomorrow morning. As you pointed out, we're on our best behaviour tonight, but I would dearly love to meet up with you when we get back on Friday. I know the Schnurrs are on the party line phone and so, if it suits you and you would like to meet up, I could phone from their house; although might it be indiscreet for me to call you at your parents' farm?"

Emily didn't answer.

"I'll be taking the Saturday afternoon train back to Durban, so I'll be staying overnight at the Masonic – and I expect Toby will be doing the same. Do you feel like meeting up for a Friday evening dinner? If so, could you telephone through a message for me to be left at Reception? Provided the line from Tam is working, I could phone the hotel for your answer. But it wouldn't do for us to be seen dining alone in Empangeni, so it would mean asking Sonya if she could come along too; that is, if she will be up to it by that time?"

Emily burst out laughing and said, "That's the wordiest invitation I have ever had for dinner! It would be fun but might be difficult, being stuck out at the farm. I'll ask Sonya if I might stay with her. We'll see. It's a matter of my getting back to Empangeni on the Friday as well. We could be doomed from meeting, y'know."

After bidding farewell to the family, Emily accompanied them as far as the frangipani tree, with Donald's arm around her waist for the first time, making his pulse race. He felt her hands on his arm behind her back. There were white moths fluttering around the blossoms in the moonlight. Then Emily said, "I must go back to Sonya," and kissed him softly and lingeringly on the mouth and Toby on the cheek. They left her there at the complaining gate and turned left for the Masonic at the other end of Maxwell Road.

Toby said, "I think you've made a conquest there."

The moon sat yellow and large on the horizon and the evening star burned brightly.

They encountered a mumbling figure staggering towards them out of the gloom, as if dancing to a secret rhythm – first several steps to the right, a pause, then a drunken run forward to a halt and a swaying, anchored by a step back.

Closer to the side entrance of the hotel bar were some others engrossed in an ataxic brawl accompanied by grunts and curses.

The friends entered the hotel without waiting to see the outcome.

Mocke grunted to Donald and Toby a "Dag sê!" [Good Day] then introduced their travelling companions Joop and Herina Myburgh and their three little girls aged five, six and eight, Angelien, Katrien and Susannah.

"Joop is my cousin and I am coming along on this trip to help them settle in at Tam. Joop, like you, Donald, fought under General Smuts in the 9th South African Infantry in German East Africa and even Moçambique, so he too was allotted land at Ntambanana."

Pleasantries were exchanged and Donald noticed that the wagon was piled high under the canvas canopy stretched over an arched framework, not only with provisions and equipment ordered by farmer-families and the small Tam store, but the Myburgh's household furniture, which included several brass bed end-pieces and stinkwood chairs. Toby and Donald's trunks, they discovered, were buried under this pile, which left little room for sitting.

They all turned to watch the driver inspan his animals. Every big-horned Afrikander in the 12-oxen span was familiar with its place and responded to its name being called by the driver – names like 'Sataan', 'Bliksim' (the two strongest), 'Vatjougoed' and 'Wonderlik'.

The yokes [the 'jukke'] and chains were positioned on the ground, ahead of the call to inspan.

Once in place, the yokes were dropped over their necks and secured by prongs ['skei'] dropped from the yoke on either side of the ox's neck and bound by strong leather thongs.

The ox hump is used to exert its formidable pulling power, unlike the horse that relies on its shoulders.

The two strongest oxen, massive beasts, were positioned at the back of the span so that they might be called upon to manoeuvre the wagon when the rest of the team could not be used; also to exert their substantial braking-power when descending, passing on the signal 'exert braking' to the rest of the beasts in the train.

Mocke's wagon team was of three coloured [mixed-race] folk he had brought with him from the Cape. The most junior of the team was the young voorloper [the 'ahead-walker' – the one who walks ahead of the animals and leads them].

The most senior was the driver who, when he is not walking beside his animals and talking to them in 'oxpraat' ['ox-speak'], sits at the front of the wagon atop a 'wa kis' [a wagon-chest]. He is the wielder of the very long whip made of hide, which he cracks over the heads of appropriate animals to encourage their exertions, though never touching them.

Last is the brake man, whose skill comes into play

when the wagon descends.

"Daar is my driver 'Witbooi' en dis 'Maandag' die voorloper, en daardie skelm is 'Donderdag' my brake man," he said in a mangle of Afrikaans and English in order to be fully understood by his ox wagon team.

'Skelm' means rascal, but Mocke applied the word playfully. Such folk were often named after the days of the week or months of the year.

The driver was the most skilled of the three and could be considered a master of his craft. Through his years of experience, it not only led him to understand the character of each animal and to establish trust by it, but to be able to react to terrain irregularities, flash floods, the encountering of other vehicles and much else besides.

He would understand the ability of each quadruped, and would be able to 'fine tune' them by positioning each ox to best support the efforts of its yoked mate and the greater whole of the span itself.

One of these skills was to detect when the oxen needed to outspan and refresh with grass or fodder (if the veld grass had died off in the winter) and water, allowing them sufficient time to chew the cud before inspanning again, in all about two hours per outspan.

With the advent of barbed wire late in the 19th century, farmers were able to fence off their land bordering the road to Ntambanana, which meant that access to farmland grass had become patchy. Thus, the Natal administration was obliged to provide fodder at certain outspanning posts along the way.

Witbooi was required to know where these outspan points were and to reach them before his team of oxen tired. He also had to ensure that there was adequate autumn or winter fodder there for his animals by exchanging reports with oncoming drivers.

Donald and Toby saw that Mocke had a rifle and that the wooden butt was scarred with cut marks.

Seeing them examining it, Mocke said "I used to slice biltong [strips of dried and salted meat] on it during the War of Independence which you call the Boer War." At 56 years of age, Jan still used the same rifle, a Westley-Richard's falling-block, single action, breech-loading gun.

Such a rifle was not superior to the Martini-Henry employed by the British, but the Boers were better shots, resulting from learning to shoot on their farms from an early age – and that included shooting from horseback.

They were brought up to kill for the pot and to defend their remote homesteads against marauding natives. For the same reason, their horsemanship was generally superb.

Joop possessed a hunting rifle too, as did Donald who had managed to hang on to one from his German East Africa days, but it was inaccessible in his trunk. Only Toby carried no weapon, except a hunting knife.

Mocke mentioned that he was taking along his horse so that he could ride ahead to survey the road and look out for oncoming wagons. He hoped to do a spot of hunting for the pot as well.

Then came the driver's cry, "Trek, Jumloot! Trek, Ferreira!" The drag chains tightened between the yokes as the oxen took the strain, exhorted by the whistles and shouts of the driver and the crack of his long whip over their heads. Slowly, Mocke's wagon began to trundle and bump along at three miles an hour.

Mrs. Myburgh chose to ride on the wagon, sitting on one of her stinkwood chairs lashed in place, which occupied much of the remaining sitting area, along with her two youngest children.

Young Susannah, the oldest, walked ahead for a while with the voorloper 'Maandag', while Donald and Toby strolled behind the wagon followed by Joop, deep in conversation with Mocke and conducted in Afrikaans.

Donald and Toby might have been disturbed if they had been able to follow the substance of the sotto voce discussion, for it was an exemplar of the resentment felt by the Boers.

Jan was saying to Joop, "Look, I cannot resent the existence of these two rooineks and their desire to go farming. Let them be, but it's time we gave thought to throwing off the British yoke in the long run and reinstating our rightful place. We have to admit that we are now looked down upon, no matter what is written in the Act of Union about equal rights among all whites. The only way left for us to reassert ourselves is to form a society that will make a start to bringing this about.

"I know that there were some strong efforts back in the Cape to give a voice to our aspirations like the Society for Real Afrikaners [Genootskap vir Regte Afrikaners] but these didn't foresee a time when we could regain the whip hand! The Cape Bond was different. It included everyone born in Africa and was open to all races. What is now forming is exclusive to us Dutch-Afrikaners.

"As you know, many of us tried and failed in 1914 to overthrow British domination by force, which preceded your fighting the Germans in East Africa. That uprising was a disastrous failure. This next time it will be by stealth, influence and eventually the ballot box.

"You fought with General Smuts, like Donald in front

of us, but soon will come the time to see that the only way we, as a Boer race, can gain our supremacy again is in the way I am describing."

Mocke was alluding to the 1914 'Boer Revolt' when a swathe of Afrikaners who fought with Maritz in the Second Boer War attempted to form a Dutch-Afrikaans South African Republic – only four years after the founding of the Union in 1910, which was intended to unite both Dutch-Afrikaans and English-speaking interests to exploit the labour of the indigenous people.

"This new idea of a bond (he pronounced it 'bont') will help us to be strong and be brothers in our determination to regain equality and eventually supremacy – not through the use of arms this time but through control of administration and the vote.

"I must tell you that I met a man called Henning Klopper in Empangeni a few days ago. He is a railway man and had come down from Johannesburg to inspect the condition of the rail line here and listen to arguments promoting the idea of extending the line from Mtubatuba to Pongola.

"We had lunch at the Masonic with a few other Afrikaner farmers and a German called von Weldenburg (although he is pretending to be Swiss) who has invested heavily recently in land to rehabilitate a sugar estate on the Richard's Bay side of Empangeni.

"When the subject was raised, von Weldenburg said that he would support the idea 'behind the scenes'. He seems to have considerable influence within the German diplomatic corps, despite the turmoil going on in Germany at the moment, and this contact with such an anti-British element could be very useful in the years ahead, as it was during the War of Independence fourteen years ago, you will remember.

"But we must be careful. There are others like General Jan Smuts and Prime Minister Louis Botha who head up the South Africa Party which remains polluted by British Imperialism.

"Klopper said that he, a man called van der Merwe and another by the name of du Plessis, plus eleven more leading Afrikaners whose names I cannot recall immediately, pledged at a meeting in June last year to form an organisation called Jong Suid Afrika [Young South Africa] although the name was changed to the 'Afrikaner Broederbond' some weeks later.

"It is not a secret society. Not yet, although the thinking is that Afrikaners who become members could be penalised within English-speaking organisations if their affiliation to the Broederbond became known. So there are plans to go secret.

"The movement is not for the average citizen – only for those Afrikaners who have managed to rise to prominence, so that they can be in the position to penetrate important farming, industrial and commercial organisations at executive level and influence decisions in favour of our interests. They will be able to help Afrikaans employees climb the ladder too, or prosper in farming and be favoured if a contract is to be awarded.

"We believe that we were planted in this country by the Hand of God, to survive as a separate volk [race or people] with our unique calling. Membership will be restricted to Dutch Afrikaans men only, of high standing and by invitation. I am letting you know all this because you are my cousin. You are not a 'man of means' yet, so it is not likely that you will be invited to join; but your time will come.

"A symbol has been chosen, of a triangle through which a rope is threaded, symbolising unity; and the Bond already has a motto – 'Wees Sterk' [Be Strong].

"However, the uniting symbol for all Afrikaners, not just the high and mighty among us, is the ox wagon. Without it we would never have been able to escape English rule in the Cape. Without it we would never have been able to form laagers in our defence against the black tribes that attacked us on our treks away from English rule; and without it we would never have been able to carry the produce of our farms to market or transport our families to Nagmaal at the nearest dorp."

(Before annexure of Natal by the British in 1840 it is sometimes forgotten that the dominant white influence was that of the Boers who settled in dorps [a Dutch word for village], the most important of which was Pietermaritzburg. This left a legacy of Dutch village planning which included a church beside the main market square, water furrows and neat little houses in line, facing each other along well-treed roads, wide enough to turn a wagon and span of oxen, and an out-of-town graveyard, unlike the English custom of locating graveyard and church on a shared piece of land.

Families would travel by ox wagon every quarter year to celebrate Nagmaal [religious communion 'time of the night meal'] with the ox wagons pulled up in the square near the church. Not only were these gatherings of important religious significance to a God-fearing people but attractive opportunities for families to exchange gossip, often eating together and to trade.)

"Every time you see an ox wagon like this one and

watch its turning wheels, think of us the Dutch people and our overwhelming need to roll together and form a mental laager to keep outsiders at bay.

"We must never forget how our women and children died in the British concentration camps and how they destroyed our farms, and our humiliation by the British when we surrendered at Vereeniging."

"But what about all these Blacks – and the coloured ones like your ox wagon team?" interjected Myburgh.

"The Black people will never be anything but servants, cutters of wood and drawers of water for us, The Chosen People. They have their place and must remain apart. They are just lucky that they are no longer slaves. The brown people, the Kleurlinge, are often good artisans when they don't drink too much, and artisans they will remain."

"And the Indians?"

"They are good labourers in the fields and we will never be able to do without them because most native men refuse field work; but we will keep them in their place as 'underfolk'. Whatever rights they now have will be steadily reduced. One of these is to prevent their ownership of land – as has happened with the Zulus in the present government. Access to higher education will be restricted and the idea of equal rights put forward by that little churrah, Gandhi, who is causing so much trouble, will be suppressed.

"The Bond will encourage all sorts of new organisations to further our cause – the right to have Afrikaans in schools, Afrikaans women's societies, business institutions, political parties, newspapers, banks and cultural organisations which will glorify and encourage the endeavours of Afrikaans artists, musicians and architects. Just you see. It will come to pass so that one day we will, as a volk, rise in stature above our English counterparts to the degree that they will be the ones looked down upon and their works disparaged. And when that time comes we will saddle up [opsaal] for a new South African Republic and throw out the poisonous connection with England forever.

"You, as an Afrikaner, are one of the lucky ones to receive an allotment of land at Ntambanana and there are a few other Afrikaans families there already. But the batch of new Tam settlers will be English-speakers with English names like Shepstone, Thompson, Maxwell and Brook – I've seen the latest list of sixty-five names for 1919 and there are only two Dutchmen among them. Make a point of assisting Afrikaners generously and Englishmen reluctantly so that, slowly, the wheel will turn in your favour.

"We will talk about all this later in Tam when we have more privacy."

Mocke's horse was tethered at the back of the wagon with plenty of slack and was clearly at ease with this arrangement. When the wagon was about to descend steeply – usually to a drift, Jan would take back its halter.

Both the older children were barefoot and knew very little English. Herina's English was clearly a 'second language' – and very much a stumbling and hesitant second best. This did not inhibit the children from chattering away in mangled English-Dutch-Afrikaans to Donald and Toby as well as the other two.

Falling back to talk to them for a while, Susannah asked them, "Why don't praat die Taal?"

Toby explained that he came from Ireland and Donald from Scotland. "Not praat die Taal there?" she asked.

"No, but if you like you can teach us some Taal. We would like to learn very much," Donald said, loudly enough for Joop to hear clearly.

"Do you agree, Joop?" Donald asked and Joop smiled his approval and waved. And so a friendship began.

Susannah started immediately by pointing at her head and said, "Dit is my [pronounced 'may'] kop," at her foot, saying, "dis [a portmanteau word for 'dit is'] my voet en altwee," (pointing at both feet) "my voete."

[V is pronounced as an F in Afrikaans and the W as a hard V. The 'is' is pronounced as 'uss'.] Her mother, perched on the wagon, was listening proudly and intently.

Jan joined the group and said, "I am going to ride a little ahead and make sure there are no wagons coming the other way – this route can get busy with oxen and meeting a wagon coming around a corner is a real nagmerrie [nightmare]. Perhaps I will see something for the pot too."

The older children soon tired of walking beside the wagon and were helped up to sit and lean against their mother. After a few more miles they were asleep, lulled by the rocking of the wagon as the wheels passed over the uneven terrain.

Toby was amused to watch the torsos and heads of the children and their mother sway in unison, although he noticed that the mother and Susannah were coughing a lot in their sleep and Susannah was growing increasingly restless.

It was nearly three hours before the big-horned Afrikander oxen indicated by their slowing motion that they needed a rest and this was sensed by the driver, who called for the need to outspan. He instructed the voorloper to lead the wagon train off the rough road onto the veld, which was still sweet and green at this time of the year.

There was a stream [a 'spruit' as it is called in Dutch-Afrikaans, pronounced something like 'sprrate'] that widened at that point into a shallow pool, making it an ideal halting place for the beasts to slake their thirst.

The oxen were unyoked and set free to tear away at the grass and shake off the tickbirds, which had pestered them by riding on their rumps and pecking the ticks clustered around their ears and eyes.

Herina stepped down from the wagon with the children to join Joop, Donald and Toby while the ox wagon team gathered tinder and small branches for Herina and their own fire some distance away. The mother was coughing badly but made little of it, although she was perturbed when Susannah lay down curled up in the grass, muttering "Ek voel siek, Ma, en ek het 'n hoofpyn" [I feel sick, Ma, and I have a headache].

Speaking in Afrikaans, Herina said, "Just rest there, my darling, and I will brew something to make it better."

Herina had been quick to locate the bare ground which had been used many times before as a picnic spot, evidenced by the blackened earth and scraps of charred sticks.

She lit a fire under a triangle of short branches Joop had tied together from which a 'poetjie' [small pot] was hung by a hook and chain. Next, she threw in potato and pumpkin pieces she had been preparing as the wagon rolled along, beans, the dismembered carcass of a chicken, a handful of spices from a small Joko Tea box, and water drawn well upstream, away from the oxen.

Some of the water she had saved for another small pot which she nestled in the fire to leave to boil and into which she put what seemed to be tree bark wrapped in a handkerchief.

"What are those pieces in the handerkerchief?" asked Toby. Struggling to reply she called for Joop to come and explain.

"It's for Susannah's hoofpyn. They are pieces from the wilgerboom – I think you call it the veld willow. See, there's one over there. They're all over the place near water. We cut a small square of bark and lever it off – it's the pink part we want. She has put the pink parts into the hankie and tied a knot. After leaving it to boil for some time the water will go reddish, so she'll know it's ready. Then she will squeeze the juice into a cup through another hankie."

Meanwhile Joop brewed up coffee on a primus stove and soon the site was aromatic with coffee, cooking food and wood smoke.

On the brow of the hill stood a clump of small native children, admiring the oxen and wondering at the umlungu scene of domesticity.

Jan had returned with a dead impala slumped behind his saddle and busied himself with bleeding the animal by securing it about its hocks and suspending it from a short horizontal pole supported by wooden frames stored in the wagon for that purpose. He then slit its throat at the vee of the neck. Some of the blood he collected in a bowl and poured into the pot, sharing the rest with his driver team, to their evident pleasure.

"Blood stops the giddy spells," Mocke said. "I don't know why, but we are healthiest if we add blood from animals and some milk to our stews, even if the milk has gone sour. Even our eyesight is improved.

That's one of the reasons we could shoot straighter than the rooineks. It has always been like this on the farms and during our war with you."

He was right about the blood. Blood is rich in salt, vitamins and minerals that were otherwise absent from pioneer diets.

"If you don't bleed the game after slaughter the taste stays very strong and the meat 'goes off' quickly. This meat will be just right by the time we spend a few days in Tam," Mocke said.

A few boulders proved convenient seats for the adults while the children sat cross-legged on the ground, except for Susannah who remained curled up on the grass.

The wagon crew crouched on their haunches some distance away, and the oxen, having grazed their fill, settled down in the grass to chew the cud with tickbirds settling on their rumps again.

"Where are your farms?" Joop asked and Donald explained that they were on the higher ground and that it turned out that his was next to Toby's.

"Are either of you married?"

"Not yet. Neither of us has been lucky enough to find such a good wife as your Herina. Like you, we have been rather busy for the last four years. Toby told me that he was in the navy during the war. We bumped into each other for the first time on the train to 'Pangeni last Friday only to discover that we were both taking up farms in Ntambanana. So here we are, on the same ox wagon. You and I shared the war in East Africa but it's difficult to talk about it to anyone who wasn't there. It's good to meet someone who knows how very bad it was."

When everyone else was out of earshot Joop said quietly to Donald, "Do you ever see horrible things from the war? In the middle of an ordinary conversation, I suddenly see a face of someone I had to shoot. It's impossible for me to talk about it with anyone including Herina or even Jan who wasn't in the last fight; but sometimes I think I am going mad. They're like ghosts. I found I nearly shot someone in the middle of one of these delusions. With war you are ordered to do all the things you were brought up to consider evil and criminal, but which our officers were telling us to do. A friend has vomiting fits when he gets these visions of the young enemy he bayoneted. I have seen another who has developed a violent twitch of his face and he looks drunk when he walks.

"During these moments I am not myself and when I recover it leaves me with a sense of doom. I carry with me always that something terrible is going to happen to me or my family even though I know that this is irrational."

"Yes," said Donald, "there has been a lot of talk of the fight in East Africa as the 'last of the gentlemen's war' but the killing remains the same. I got nightmares when I saw the soldiers I had killed, in the middle of the everyday while I was talking to someone long after the war. For a long time afterwards, I had difficulties eating and sleeping; I heard a ringing in my ears too and dizziness sometimes. And that was before I got Spanish Flu. There was one man in our unit who was struck dumb."

(The First World War produced more than eighty thousand cases of varying degrees of 'shellshock', mainly in Europe but in other theatres of war too. The percentage of officers suffering from it was greater than in the men under their command.

The condition challenged the weak and the strong equally. It was not one brought on by cowardice but rather by officialdom abrogating civilised standards. Returning to the framework of social rules governing civilian life after the war often triggered such attacks.

Susannah, who startled Joop by shaking her father's arm, interrupted their discussion. "What's the matter, Pa? You looked frightened."

"Nee, my skat, ek is nie bang nie." [No, my darling I am not frightened]. Toby went over to watch Jan preparing to skin the impala.

"I've never seen this done before," Toby said. He hesitated and then said, "And the children, so young, are they used to seeing dead animals being skinned?"

"Ag. Joop will tell you that they have seen it before and they must understand this is really what life is like. They eat meat so they must know where it comes from. Joop's family and mine have seen hardship but it toughens you and seeing an animal being skinned is part of that process."

"Please explain what you are doing as you go along."

"OK. The flesh must still be warm so you must skin it straight after bleeding. First, remove the scent glands here, just behind the knees of the back legs. Then cut the skin just above them and do the same. Cut around the genitals in a circle. You must cut slowly and with the knife-edge outwards; like so, lifting the skin as you go with the fingers of your other hand.

"Do the forelegs in the same way then cut down the centre of the body. Slowly. So. Next, I cut off the tail for soup then cut the inside of the forelegs.

"Now you can help me roll the skin back on either sides of the cut and do the same for the body. How strong are you? Look, our arms and hands are full of blood but this can't be helped. We must now separate the head and neck; so we will give a strong twist of the head. That way, to the right. OK? Here goes." There was a crunch of the vertebrae separating. "Good. Now all we have to do is cut the parts that still cling.

"Next, we take out the guts. Cut up to the backside and down as far as the breastbone. Then we will let the guts spill out. Let it hang down – so we can inspect it. Ja. The liver is healthy. It's not mottled. No white spots."

Toby's thoughts flew to that day in class when his Latin master discussed the Etruscan and later Roman custom of employing soothsayers who based their divinations on the state of livers in ritually slaughtered goats. The liver was regarded as the base of life itself, so revealing the will of the gods. If this were so, it would seem that the future portent for growing cotton in Tam just might be very good indeed.

"So we can take out the kidneys and the liver. Now the heart, the lungs and the windpipe."

He yelled to Witbooi, "Kom hiersoe!" and followed this up by offering his men the offal (which they would have to eat at the next outspan, as it was best when it was freshest), one of the kidneys, the tail and the head, after he had extracted the animal's brain. The cheeks of the head were considered a delicacy by his wagon team.

"We will cut up the meat into joints next time we stop, but meanwhile Herina will cover it with cloth and keep it hanging inside the wagon at the back, away from the sun and the flies. It could still drip a bit with blood."

He said that he would keep the skin rolled up in a large bucket with a mixture of the buck's brain and water, and tan it only when he got to Tam.

"Kom, kom!" Jan shouted to his wagon team, "Ons moet trek!" [Come, come! We must get going!] Witbooi walked to where the oxen were resting and called them by name. "Kom Sataan. Kom Bliksim! Kom Vatjougoed! Kom

Ferreira!" until the whole team rose out of the veld and lumbered over to their places.

He and Toby went to the stream to wash their hands and arms and half-fill a bucket of water before returning to the wagon train now assembling.

At that moment a black Tin Lizzie truck, which was heard approaching a mile off, clattered around the corner and slid to a halt. On the doors was the legend 'Candover Cotton'. A hairy, sweating, sandy-haired man of about 35 and medium stature climbed out stiffly and introduced himself as Lourens Theron. The skin around his intelligent eyes was creased from squinting against the sun.

He said that he had journeyed down from the Candover Cotton Estates near Magudu much farther north, first by post cart to the railhead at Mtubatuba, then by train to Empangeni, and was now driving the rest of the way to Ntambanana in a battered company Model T truck kept at Empangeni for just such purposes.

"I had no idea that this road was so bad. It's even worse than the track to the railhead at Mtubatuba. The only alternative to get our cotton to the Empangeni gin is through the veld and over the mountains by ox-wagon inland to Vryheid eighty-five miles away. We've started building a road but it will be at least a year before we reach the town.

"What we really need is an extension of the railway line from Mtubatuba to Golela. That's what my boss Richard Rouillard extolled to some high-falutin' government officials who had their eyes opened when they did their best to tour the area recently. They were stuck in the mud more times than I can relate. Yes, real 'stick-in-the-muds'; they nearly wrote themselves off completely when they skidded off the 'road' near Louwsburg. I'm told they missed tumbling into the valley by inches. We learned later that we didn't have a hope in hell of seeing the railway extended for the next eight years.

"How the hell our 'stick-in-the-mud' government expects us to export our cotton through Durban efficiently and compete with overseas markets despite this shambles of a road system puzzles me to the extreme."

Jan said that while out hunting he had come across a deep donga ahead just after a sharp downhill bend which – like all the others along the way – had not been repaired. The donga had developed after the heavy rain some days ago and he doubted that Theroux's car would get through unless he made another long detour through the veld. The wagon would be able to stay on the road simply by means of its weight, ox muscle power and strategically placed rocks.

He said that the only car which had dared this route for several weeks past had managed to skirt this and many similar hazards only by detouring through the veld, leaving meandering tyre tracks of flattened grass.

."That must have been the Schnurrs. He must know the route backwards," Donald mused. "They make regular journeys."

"If I get stuck will you come to the rescue?" he asked Jan, who replied, "You will probably get stuck and yes, we will rescue you. Remember to take the detours or you'll land up with a broken axle."

And off he went, after mentioning to Toby and Donald that he might bump into them at the Schnurrs.

Herina climbed up onto the wagon again and helped her three children to sit beside her. Susannah whimpered and had to be helped to her place by both parents, while

Herina began to look tired and was coughing too. After they settled, Jan signalled to Witbooi to start again

"Trek Vatjougoed! Trek Ferreira!" Witbooi shouted followed by, "Trek! Trek! Trek!" cracking his long whip in the air above the team. The voorloper walked ahead, the drag chains tightened and the wheels began to turn, with Witbooi walking beside his animals again, talking to them in the secret language that only he and his oxen understood.

Chapter Eight

The wagon reached Tam close to sunset and creaked to a stop at a small wood-and-corrugated-iron store on brick stilts, which stood in isolation beside the rudimentary road. The setting sun shone yellow through the door and windows, picking out tins of Klim on a shelf and half of the shopkeeper's figure leaning forward with large hands on the wooden counter, his face in shadow. It cast fluttering patterns from a gum tree over the cracked veranda granolithic and the few tufts of kikuyu grass at the foot of the steps that had escaped the trample of many feet. Meandering footpaths radiated from the store through the veld towards the kraals near the forest and on the other side of the Ntambana River, which flows north into the Umfolozi. There was no sign of Theron or the Candover Cotton truck.

Some of the Myburgh possessions along with boxes and sacks of shop provisions had to be unloaded by the Indian storekeeper assistant to release Donald and Toby's trunks which were then left on the store verandah while Witbooi and the voorloper were busying themselves with the oxen.

The children, curled about their mother's feet on blankets, half-awoke at the ceasing of the wagon's rhythm and during the unloading, but snuggled back to sleep as soon as that had stopped, although Susannah was coughing severely in her sleep and twisting and turning, while Herina had grown lethargic and was likewise coughing, at moments, uncontrollably.

Mocke said that he was carrying on a little way to take the Myburghs to their new home over the hill, after establishing that Eric Schnurr would come to the store presently to collect Toby and Donald.

"I'll be staying tonight and the next night with Piet and Hannah van Jaarsveld, as I usually do when I ride up this way. Piet was waiting for us to arrive so let me introduce you. It's a good idea to make friends with him right away. He has sent a runner to the Schnurrs to let them know that you've arrived and are waiting at the store.

"Please accept a portion of impala Herina has prepared for you to give to Mr. and Mrs. Schnurr, and I expect to see you again at 6 o' clock on Friday morning – yes, not Thursday this week – for the return journey. Although the wagon will be loaded down, there will be more room for sitting. Moenie laat wees nie [Don't be late].

"You had better cover up while you wait. This is the worst time of the evening for mosquitoes. Do you have quinine? If not, you'd better get some from Piet before he closes up and take some immediately. Ask him for some water to wash it down."

After which, van Jaarsveld padlocked the door of the store, waved his hat as a farewell and climbed aboard the wagon with the rest of them, except for Mocke who chose to ride.

"Totsiens!" [until we see each other again] shouted van Jaarsveld as he, Joop and Herina Myburgh and the children aboard the wagon creaked into the gloaming.

Night falls quickly in Africa and the moon, hidden by cloud, made the night seem suddenly pitch-dark. They were left with only the sound of the crickets and the frogs in the darkness.

"Well, at least there aren't lion in this part of the world," Donald said. "Less hazardous than East Africa in that respect, but I wouldn't enjoy meeting a cheetah or leopard right now. Mind you, there's plenty of game about again so they are unlikely to bother us."

"Just very privately, what do you think of the setup and our prospects?" Toby asked. "I feel that I know so very little about farming and am going through that stage of wondering whether I have bitten off more than I can chew. I like the Dutch-Afrikaners that we have met but I sense an exclusion from their clan. Probably because I can't speak the lingo."

"Well, I think it's early days and we should just handle things as they come along," said Donald. "I'm exhilarated about owning a stretch of land in Africa and I can see that we could do very well by ourselves if everything comes together – by that I mean good weather, good crops, adequate labour and ready markets.

"I was impressed with that Myburgh woman. Quite used to the idea of taking the rough with the smooth, producing three rugged children and sticking to her man, no matter which way the wind blows.

"It's too early for me to expect any woman to put up with the kind of life we will have to lead in the early days, but as soon as the worst is past I'll be one for getting married. Someone from farming stock – and I have my eye on someone in particular."

Toby grunted, although his smile was lost to Donald in the dark, for Toby had seen how Emily and he had grown together – even in the very short while that they had known each other.

He didn't raise the question of whether the Bells might not be too pleased that a daughter with an expensive education from a well-to-do sugar farming family should throw in her lot with a greenhorn cotton farmer.

He was attracted to Sonya and thoughts of her drifted into his consciousness very often, but wondered if he would ever be able to cross the first bridge of declaration or even how Sonya felt. He thought of those ghastly moments at Richard's Bay and how she had sought comfort in his arms in the back of Zeno's car, on the return to Empangeni.

"Do twins marry twins?" he wondered, among more carnal thoughts. "And do non-twins stand a chance?" He was floating into the unfamiliar territory of the heart. "Can I replace in some way the closeness shared by her and Zeno? Moreover, how would she feel stuck out here in the bundu? Perhaps," he thought, "if Emily were mad enough to marry Donald it might work out rather well."

His line of thinking was interrupted by the rattling approach of Schnurr's lorry.

"Halloo and welcome to Tam! How was the journey by ox wagon? Quite an experience, eh? I guess that in a few years you'll look back and realise that you were experiencing the end of an era. That is – if they ever fix the roads. A disgrace. I think Marie and I are the only few drivers crazy enough to get here by car."

He left the engine running.

"Now look here, Marie has prepared a light supper and she will not brook argument about your eating with us. If you're desperate to pitch tents afterwards that's your choice. If you are determined to do that, I suggest you camp in our grounds and that way you will have access to fresh water. But ideally, consider 'camping out' tonight in the spare rondavel. You'll have the whole day tomorrow to explore your farm sites, meet people and so on – there's little sense in stumbling about in the dark. Agreed?"

"Let's lumber your trunks onto the lorry. We plan to store them in the pantry – once you've seen the size of it you will understand. It'll keep your belongings dry and generally out of harm's way," at which point he slapped his face and arms vigorously. "Bloody mozzies!" he exclaimed.

"Better get going quickly. You will have to get into the cab. Bit cramped and this long gear lever doesn't make it less so. Pull down the flaps to keep the insects out. Sorry for the bumps."

And indeed the ride, smelly with petrol, was bumpier than the ox wagon journey.

After driving around the side of the house and shouting for the servants to unload the trunks, Eric drove on to the front entrance where Marie was waiting for them, standing behind the mosquito screen. A diesel generator, the latest thing, was chugging away in the background. She switched on the external light over the steps of the verandah and almost immediately, a cloud of moths and other night-flying insects formed a fluttering halo. Some had been temporarily attracted away from the night-flowering cereus covered in white lily-like blooms a short distance away.

"Hello again," she said, "and welcome to 'Pamplemousse'. All that white blossom will have wilted by dawn so your arrival is doubly auspicious. It's the 'Queen of the Night' and blooms for only one night in the year. Marvellous, isn't it. We get less night-flying insects when clouds aren't hiding the moon. Clever of them to fly on moonless nights to reduce the risk of being eaten," she said. "Lourens Theron, who you met on the way up, was here a little while ago and said that he would meet up with you tomorrow. How was the ox wagon ride? Was it rather like a long, very slow sea voyage and occasionally as rough?"

"Hello, and thank you for your kindness," said Toby. "Much has passed since that tennis afternoon at the Bells and a great deal of it sad. We'll talk about them later and when you wish but meanwhile Jan Mocke asked me to present you with a quarter of impala which he shot and Mrs. Myburgh prepared for you this afternoon. Jan says hang it for a day or so." Toby said, handing over the meat, Donald proffering the whisky he had bought in Empangeni.

Marie spoke with a Mauritian-French curl to her words and displayed the Frenchwoman's gift of making fashionable anything she wore, even in this remote part of Zululand – in this case, a flimsy white cotton dress and a few gold bangles on her wrist. She had luminous dark eyes and was clearly in love with her husband as he was with her. There were no children to be seen.

The house was a series of interlinked thatched rondavels interrupted by an oblong sitting room hung about by several paintings set in Mauritius – one of her parents' sugar estate dwelling at the end of a twin line of very tall coconut palms. Another was of pamplemousse water lilies [Victoria amazonica] by Xavier Le Juge and another of a Sega dancer. Yet another was an engraved copy of a painting by Pierre August Cot of 'Paul et Virginie'.

Seeing Toby looking at the engraving of a distressed maiden clinging to a shipwreck during a gale, Marie said,

"The girl features in Mauritian folktales and de Saint-Pierre wrote a famous novel about Paul and Virginie on the eve of the French Revolution. He lived in Mauritius for a time and argued for the emancipation of slaves and criticised French class snobbery. He echoed the thoughts of Rousseau. I bought the picture in Floréal – the place where it always rains. I'd just ducked out of a deluge into what was claimed to be an antiques shop (really it was chock full of cast-off junk, in the main) and spied this of Virginie who was drowned during a shipwreck because she refused to take off her clothes. She was dragged down by them when she attempted to swim ashore with her lover Paul, who had swum out to save her from the shipwreck."

On the pantry shelves was an extensive clutter of tinned food, enough to feed a small army, and Marie said, "Yes, it's true. We really do live out of tins and dry-goods in the bundu, and you will find yourselves doing the same in due course.

"In all these joined-up rondavels which make up most of the rest of the house, it's difficult to know where to put cupboards and things because all the walls except for the sitting room are curved. For the dining room, we hit on the idea of an oval table and keeping the sideboard in the flat passage wall joining the kitchen to the dining room.

"The mud-and-straw walls covering a woven wicker frame are so thick that the window ledges are deep enough to provide great opportunities to display things. I have a passion for silver snuffboxes– see, over there – so every time I visit 'civilisation' I disappear on a scrounging expedition. Eric keeps on buying clay models of cattle from the picannins and finding other indigenous things – clay pots, knobkerries and so on. I often wonder what he's going to bring home next.

"Common things that have been in use for a long time attract us as they have so many stories to tell. Take this table, for instance. The legs and frame are of stinkwood and the top is yellowwood. We love it simply because it wasn't new when we bought it. Far from it, in fact, it must be at least a hundred and fifty years old and I often wonder what history there is behind these scratches and indentations. That, for example, is a serious burn mark and there are a series of dents that suggest that the table was used as a surface for repairing things."

This was not quite what the two men were expecting in the depths of Zululand, including the arrival of apéritifs during the nightly chorus of nightjars, frogs and insects.

The roofs were of thatch with wide eaves all around. There were no ceilings, so that the earthy smell of thatch and mud-and-straw walls was ever present.

"Igawe has been told to put together stretchers in our guest rondavels and we insist that you stay the night here," Marie said, for which the men thanked her.

The term 'stretcher-bed' was highly descriptive of the battle with wood and canvas these assemblages demanded. Although the initial rigging of canvas and long sidepieces was simple, to final stretching and securing of the second canvas end-piece threaded through a notched wooden rod, it was a tussle to stretch the canvas sufficiently to clip it into the end of the opposite sidepiece.

"Oh look! There's Baby Bush! It got its name from Igawe in an inspired moment. He (the bushbaby, a kind of nocturnal primate, this one with a white patch on his nose) and his mates arrive after meals to lick clean the pans and plates we leave on the outside kitchen window ledge.

(They're washed hygienically afterwards!")

"Shoo! We haven't started eating yet! Shoo!

"Not so long ago some baboons got into the kitchen during the day while we were away and ransacked it so we have to keep all the cupboards padlocked and even wedge a table against them at bedtime, just as a precaution. They can gnaw their way through practically anything to reach food, including light padlocks and door hinges. Monkeys are almost as bad."

Supper was light. The conversation, lit by paraffin lamps hanging from the roof trusses after Eric switched off the generator, turned to the remote Zulu kraals on both sides of the river after discussing at some length the horror of Zeno's death.

"The last elephants were shot out by poachers about twelve years ago," Eric said. "Before that they always crossed the river at a certain point near here. This had gone on for centuries and their weight had hardened an underwater path on the riverbed. Nowadays the natives living in kraals on the far side make use of this underwater 'elephant highway' to get to Van Jaarsveld's store, a trek in itself.

"Crocs lurk in the reeds on both banks, so to frighten them away, the natives stick together and cross in a tightly knit group, shouting and splashing the water with their hands and sticks. It sure adds another dimension to the shopping experience.

"I suggest that it would be a good idea to 'present your credentials' to the local Zulu chief when you return to Tam permanently. And when you do, there are certain protocols that are worth observing.

"You will need to take along a trusty interpreter (and I will find you one and help you negotiate a fee of some sort).

"It would be a bad idea to just walk into the kraal. Bear in mind that the arrangement of the huts follows a rigid pattern. The entrance to the kraal is usually between the huts of the unmarried girls on the left and the unmarried boys on the right.

"The cattle enclosure for overnight stockading is in the middle of the settlement. Corn is also stored there, underground. The hut of the chief's mother is the largest and the most important, directly opposite the entrance. Looking from the entrance, the chief's hut is on the right of that.

"His First Wife has a hut on the other side of his mother's while his Third Wife lives in a hut next to her. His Second Wife has a hut to the right of him: that is on his left.

"And so it goes with the wives, depending on how wealthy in cattle the chief is, for you need a lot of lobola to have several wives – lobola being the word for 'bride-price' and always paid in cattle, never in cash.

"Zulu polygamy has its ups and downs and I don't envy the average chief if he gets caught in the middle of an interwife squabble, but hey! It does bypass divorcing one woman for another.

"The chief's pride and joy will be his cattle as it has been ever so for the Zulus. That's one of the reasons why they're kept in the centre of the kraal overnight. The other reason is protection from predators. In the daytime, they graze in the veld under the watchful eyes of his older sons. Without appearing to give the impression that you were covetous, you could praise the quality and their number, adjudged from the ones you have seen grazing. This will be a sensitive issue at present as the cattle are dying like flies from nagana. So tread carefully. This chief takes great pride in several almost white beasts, suggesting that they are descendant cousins of the Royal Herd – the Inyonikayiphumuli. You could praise those particularly.

"When you go to visit, don't assume you're going to meet him on the first occasion, although one of his umfaans will have reported your approach. He would have spotted you from one of several watchtowers. With substantially lessened stature since the Zulu defeats, he is likely to keep you waiting – just to make the point that you, as a white, are not God Almighty in his domain. Added to that, a native's sense of time and days is not that of the European. white Man Punctuality is not the watchword.

"The best strategy is to wait near the entrance, at a respectful but visible distance, until someone comes to ask you what you want. Some sort of offering would be handy at that point – a slaughtered animal would be appropriate. Once you get through the rigmarole and are invited into the kraal near the chief's hut, make sure you drink the native beer that will be offered in a clay vessel by one of the wives. It's an insult to refuse.

"Approach the main purpose of your visit circuitously. It is considered extremely rude to just blurt out what you want. Discuss anything you like – for example why you are in this neighbourhood, his cattle, his children, the weather, the harvest – before you get to the nub of your visit.

"If all goes well you will find the path smoothed when it comes to supplying labour – but I doubt any help will ever be arranged for cultivation work. That is for women; but you might be able to arrange for a voorloper when ploughing with oxen and some sort of heavy manual lifting, where a display of strength or knowledge of cattle would be necessary. Roof thatching is man's work too and they're pretty damned good at it."

"What do you think of this Spanish Flu business? Has it affected the locals?" asked Donald.

"Yes, on top of the spreading disease natives here are in a bad way. Three of the local induna's milking cows have died from nagana with more sickening. I predict he's going to lose the lot. Now his oldest son has sickened and died from Spanish Flu. He had served behind the lines on the Western Front in the South African Native Labour Corps, Fifth Battalion.

"He came back to the kraal only a few months ago and was dead soon after. There's no telling what will happen next – who will be infected.

"Well, that oldest son was very unlucky," Toby said. "Both Donald and I contracted the first round of the 'Spanish' when Donald was returning from the East African war and I from Singapore. It turns out that both of us are now supposed to be immune against the second wave, which is said to be more vicious."

"I can only hope that the spread misses us, being remote from the main source. Going back to this cotton business, may I give you some extra insights on how all this came about? You may know much of this but perhaps there are details you won't – and it's useful to know," Schnurr asked, to which they nodded, only to be interrupted by Marie emerging from the kitchen with a silver tray and tea set.

"Vanilla tea anyone?" she asked. "It's from Mauritius and delicious." All accepted then settled down to hear out Eric.

He said that since the defeat of the Zulus at the battle of Ulundi in 1879 by Lord Chelmsford's men and the crushing of the Zulu Bambatha rebellion in 1906, the Zulus had remained understandably embittered and resentful at their land being 'stolen by the white wizards'. During the rebellion, white families on remote farms had to flee for their lives.

"After things were brought under control again, a Zululand Delimitation Commission was established to set aside Reserves for the Zulus and appropriate the rest as Crown Land. You can guess who was given the most fertile ground.

"King Dinizulu kaCetswayo had been banished to the island of St Helena in 1890 after his defeat at Ulundi, followed by 25 aMakhosi and Izinduna who were exiled there after the Bambatha rebellion. So you can imagine how popular Ulundi and the crushing of the rebellion has made the white man in these parts. The fact that five thousand Boer prisoners were also banished there after the second Boer War has helped to spread embitterment about St Helena and imprisonment in the Boer camp as well. St Helena's a bit of a swear word and you can understand why.

"Since the end of the second Anglo-Boer War in 1902, there was mounting pressure by English-speaking farmers elsewhere in Natal for the authorities to release parts of the Crown Lands in Zululand for white agriculture. And so it came to pass that more than two and a half million acres were circumscribed for this purpose near Eshowe, St Lucia and Richard's Bay.

"Occupancy was controlled by the Natal Land Board and allotments were released very slowly, with the Ntambanana valley having only twenty farms by 1909.

"The push to release further allotments came much later, in 1919 as you know, to satisfy the needs of returning warriors like you two after the War. Be alert then, to deep bitterness and resentment at the way things have turned out among both the Dutch-Afrikaners and the Zulus.

"Well, for us farmers it's early to bed and early to rise. Here are paraffin lamps to light your way.. The longdrop is around the back in a shed. I had better show you how to get there. Hit the lavatory seat with the knobkerrie you'll find there just to frighten away any scorpions or other goggas before you sit down and you won't have to be reminded to take a lamp. There's a candle and matches in the shed as well.

"Iqawe will heat up water for you to wash and shave tomorrow morning and will hammer the gong (actually it's bit of rail) to wake you, then another to call you to breakfast.

"I've arranged for you to meet Lourens Theron again – the man from Candover you met 'op pad' [on the road] today. He's coming over for breakfast but he will leave straight afterwards because he has many things to do..

"Then I'll be showing you your lands. Be prepared for a bit of a shock, as it's just bare veld. You've got a lot of work ahead before you can plant! I'll introduce you to the borehole man and arrange for some temporary labour to dig long-drops. Both are top priority.

"You'll need a borehole until you manage to build and supplement this from roof runoff into water tanks. Relying on river water is not a good idea … pollution, drought, bilharzia, crocs and all that, but particularly crocs.

"From your prolonged bush experience, Donald, I know that you'll ignore any attempt by a well-known straggler who hangs about when he sees a couple of greenhorns (if you will pardon the expression) and claims to be a water-diviner. Lot of nonsense. There's plenty of underground water in this area and all you have to do is drill down to the right depth, testing as you go. The big trick is to know when to stop drilling so as not to whistle past the source.

"Pumping the water out and storage will be the real challenge. My choice would be by windpump into a storage tank, giving you the chance to irrigate a vegetable patch, water the cattle and even have a shower when you need one. However, that would all cost money, though it's geld well spent. Meanwhile the drilling fella will lend you hand-pumps for a small consideration. They look a bit Heath Robinson but they work well. The metal rod and valve down the hole is connected to a large mounted wheel and a longish lever. He'll recover the hand-pump when you decide to erect a wind-pump.

"When you do build your houses, remember that the greater the roof span you create the more rainwater you will be able to collect.

"If you roof with corrugated iron – and that's pretty inevitable – make sure you put up a well-earthed lightning conductor. They're a wise precaution anyway because Zululand attracts an abnormal number of lightning strikes. In Nongoma, for instance, I heard that nine natives were killed by lightning at the end of the rainy season. They were sheltering in a rondavel with a metal roof. That brought the count up to eighteen killed by lightning in one month. The other strikes were on the usual beehive huts.

"The natives put pieces of shaped dolerite and magic pegs on ridges near their huts in the hope of warding off lightning, but haven't gotten around to the idea of lightning conductors.

"Marie and I have asked André Steenkamp and his wife Marijke to join us – and that includes you two – for a braaivleis [barbecue] tomorrow at about 5 o' clock and we insist that you stay the second night with us too."

After a nod from Toby, Donald said, "That is very kind of you. Thank you."

He had picked up a piece of curiously shaped stone from one of Eric's window-shelf collections and Eric said, "That's actually one of those Zulu lightning stones I was telling you about. André will be able to tell you more about them, lightning birds and thunder trees. Fascinating stuff.

"City-folk are fairly insulated against lightning by all that underground piping – far more so than us out in the bundu, so are far less conscious of the dangers. It's forgivable that the natives have formed all these unscientific myths and fancies around lightning.

"Tomorrow, we'll put Jan's leg of impala to good use and Marie will be introducing you to a sensational braaivleis sauce made to her own secret recipe. She calls it her 'Floréal Special' and claims to have learnt the recipe from a Chinese smuggler. Mauritian sugar-barons – and I am thinking of a Louis du Buisson in particular – have been known to offer marriage to get hold of the recipe! But she is as good at keeping secrets as selecting the best suitor, even though she's dropped hints from time to time about pineapple, vanilla, rum from sugarcane and chili powder being hidden in there somewhere.

"We're high up here on this hill so are relatively malaria free and will be able to sit around the fire for a while as the meat sizzles to give us enough time to test the purity of our brandy.

"André is one of our pioneer farmers. He settled here with his wife in 1909 – just after the Bambatha Rebellion – and he has some interesting stories to tell."

* * *

While it was still dark, the sound of bats fluttering into roost in the wattle rafters the next morning woke Donald, who stole out to the longdrop, remembering to smite the lavatory seat with the knobkerrie before sitting down.

A clutch of cut-up pages on a protruding nail of month-old Zululand Times served as toilet paper.

In the light of a sputtering candle and while beating off a persistent moth, he was able to piece together a report about the fate of an attacker of an indentured Indian farmhand whose employer had come to his rescue. The assailant had fled to the Nseleni River and was snatched by a crocodile.

The remains of his body were found by members of the Natal Mounted Police beside the riverbank, being guarded by several reptiles.

The new day's half-light was bringing colour to a mysterious world as he emerged from the lavatory, a day full of dew on spider webs and promise.

He made his way past an ancient cycad to his rondavel and mused that there were many common-usage words in English for the half-light after sunset – dusk, twilight, gloaming – but none, that he could recall, for the silvern half-light before dawn. Aurora wouldn't do.

"Any wives in tow yet?" asked Theroux at breakfast while Marie was in the kitchen. "Not yet," said Toby, "and that applies to both of us."

"It can get lonely on a farm and a wife and children soften that feeling of being cut off. But you'll have to find the right kind and that usually turns out to be a girl who's grown up on a farm."

"I don't think Eric realises how lucky he is."

"Oh yes, he does! I gather you've decided to focus on cotton and that seems a wise thing to do. There's a growing world demand for it coming and we can compete; it'll be boom times in Zululand – although, as you'll have discovered over the last 24 hours, transport to the nearest cotton gin is a major score unsettled with the province, as is labour. The other factors are drought and disease – human and animal.

"But nothing equals cotton ... although I've heard some mutterings about a new-fangled 'artificial silk' that the Americans are touting. Probably just a flash in the pan!" he shouted in jest. "You know what the Americans are like. Full of bull and bunkum."

"Hey!" Schnurr said, "I'm American, remember! And without an American, you wouldn't have a cotton industry in Natal at all. Right now we have that expert Scherffius bringing all his experience of cotton production in Louisiana to 'liddl ol' Zululand' to power the industry along."

"I say that Natal cotton will be king," Theroux went on, "especially now that sugarcane sales are falling off their perch. Prices are dropping because of over-production by places like Java, Mauritius and Cuba, so they say.

"Well, I really came around to wish you well and say that if you ever need some extra voice-power to agitate about the transport and labour situations, I'm your man. Here's my card, sorry it's a bit grubby, and I know where to find you. Ask Scherffius about crop rotation. I predict that if we go on flogging the soil to death by planting cotton every year we'll go from boom to crash in five years – or less.

"I heard there's some codger at a university in Alabama

who has been rotating cotton with a soybean crop in the winter. Fixes the nitrogen in the soil, he says. He started the experiment at the turn of the century and his field is still producing a maximum yield of cotton, year after year. I think they call it the 'Old Rotation.' Worth remembering. Well, cheerio. Eric's lent me one of his horses to make some visits."

"Right," said Eric, easing out of his chair. "Let's go see 'dem farms' of yours. Be prepared for a let-down. Just bare undulating veld, lots of rocks and quite a few trees dotted about; but there are many other farms adjacent to yours in the same scheme so you won't feel completely isolated. I've arranged for 'Tiny' van Rensburg to be there along with his steam-powered borer. You can't miss him – he's the tallest fella in Ntambanana and wears the widest cowhide hat I've ever seen.

"Although he has the monopoly for water boring simply because there isn't anyone else, he won't try to take you for a ride because part of the cost will be carried by the province – one of the few good things those momparahs in Pretoria have come up with; also meaning that the Pretoria bean-counters are monitoring charges.

"You also get – but you know this – free ploughing by steam tractor the first time around after you've got all the rocks and trees removed. As for the rest – you're on your own."

They rode in Eric's truck over veld so rough that the three men assumed weightlessness every time a particularly large bump or aardvark hole was hit, until they drew towards a man standing on the skyline who dwarfed his African helpers. They were grouped beside a growling machine emitting smoke and steam.

"Dag sê, Jannie!" (The natives were ignored.)

"Wragtig! Ons het vroeg in die môre gesê, Eric, not half past bloody lunchtime," said Jannie. "We have been waiting for you for at least an hour! Ja, well. Meantime I've been working out the best place to find water and this is why we're stationed here. This is on the farm of Toby, né? Is that you? If it turns out to be a dry well you and the government still have to pay for the machine time and my services. If we strike drinkable water you pay me a premium of fifteen percent on top of the basic costs."

"Well, it depends on what costs you are talking about."

"I charge three Pounds a day. My guess is that we'll find drinkable water at about 350 feet, so that would work out at about a day and a half at an all-in cost to you of about £4.60s – voetstoets. That includes the fifteen percent premium. It would cost far more but Pretoria picks up some of the bill. Part of my job is to leave you with a hand-pump. For that you pay a deposit of £3 but get that back when you replace it with a wind or motor pump."

"Well. It seems reasonable and it's a permanent investment in the value of the land," Toby said, after turning to Eric Schnurr for his reaction. "All right, thanks, and go ahead. But when do you expect payment?"

"I will tell Eric when we hit water and ask him to telephone a message through for you to collect at the Masonic Hotel reception desk – and the same applies to Donald. So double-check when you come back from Durban and before you journey to 'Tam'. I have an account in my name at the Natal Bank in Empangeni and you can pay into that."

He turned to one of his men standing beside the steam engine and said something that sounded like, "Shaya steamehla!" which galvanised them into action, the drill screw commencing to turn and splattering everyone with soil as it began its journey down to the chthonic streams of the Zulu spirit world.

"And what about my operation?" asked Donald

"I looked it over before you arrived and tied a red flag on a stick way over there where I think there's water," Tiny shouted.

"Let's drive over. Just watch out for stones and dongas," Jannie said, clambering into the truck and leaving the Zulus to stare after them, the wizard-plunderers of subterranean waters.

"Where are you going to build your house?" Schnurr asked Donald, after the same borehole rigmarole was completed and Tiny van Rensburg had been driven back bumpily and noisily to his machinery.

"It's a critical question because I'll have to know where to get the longdrops dug – as close to the houses as possible. Bear in mind that the prevailing winds here are north-easterly. Look; you can see how the tree-foliage is bent away from the prevailing wind (always a useful way to orient yourself if you get lost on an overcast day) so the 'whiff' can be carried away from the precinct of the house and be positioned as far as possible from the borehole.

"Ideally, your houses should be north-facing in the Southern Hemisphere to reap the most sunlight, but you might have to compromise between that and taking in the best view.

"A good decision is to build as high up as possible, away from the river valley mists and malaria. Over there, for example, far away from clusters of trees too. Lessens the risk of tsetse-fly."

They ate sandwiches, prepared by Marie, under a spreading Pangeni tree with a view high over the river valley, and watched a black and white fish eagle swoop down with claws outstretched to snatch a wriggling fish before winging away westwards.

"The Zulu name for them is Inkwazi," said Eric. "They even go after croc hatchlings."

That evening, as Eric was being helped to build up the fire for the braaivleis (it is subdued with water to very hot embers before cooking starts on a griddle that is placed over it) he said, "Look. Why are you fellows taking the trek back to 'Pangeni with Jan Mocke? He's an excellent bloke, but you have no need to walk that distance again. I had a word with Pretorius from Candover and he said that he'd be delighted to share the car journey back to 'Pangeni with you. What say you? If yes, I can ride over to the van Schalkwyks to let Jan know there's a change of plan while you two fellows help Marie get the other bits and pieces together for the braai."

And so it was agreed.

"The van Schalkwyks are in a bad way!" Eric reported after a hurried return. "He's staring at me like a madman. His wife and little Susannah, the eldest child, have been taken badly ill. This is terrible, terrible. They obviously have the Driedae and he seems to have retreated into a mental hovel of horror, staring at me as if I am about to kill him. We must help. Mocke has appealed to me to help them, as best we can.

"Marie, grab whatever medicine for flu you can for me and call the Mission Station nurse. If you can't get through

I'll have to ride over. No point in waiting for Dr Lombard to arrive from Empangeni tomorrow. I'll bring the truck around to the front and we'll see what can be done. As for poor van Schalkwyk, I just don't know. Mocke is restraining him as he has his gun and it looks as if he wants to kill everyone. He thinks he's still in the war. This is a tragedy for such a fine family. No, Marie, you stay here, my darling. You must not be exposed to the virus, please, please! I already have had the Spanish at the end of the war – and so have Donald and Toby. We're immune now. I'll take along a bottle of dilute TCP for us to gargle and wash our hands with before we come home. You'll just have to excuse the stink."

They arrived to find Mocke and several farmers with their wives in the house, all with their own ideas of what should be done. Some counselled heavy slugs of brandy; others did not, though there was consensus that their bedroom windows and door were to be thrown open.

Herina Myburgh and Susannah had already acquired the telltale mauve skin hue of the stricken, accompanied by rasping breathing and extensive nose-bleeds.

The two youngest children, Angelien and three-year-old Katrien were being kept out of harm's way by a farmer's wife, little Mrs. Potgieter, who was better known for supplying eggs to neighbouring farms in a Heath Robinson wire crate she had made herself. She would wrap each egg in a square of very old issues of the Zululand Times, which she insisted had to be ironed flat and returned to her.

Her mother had died in one of Kitchener's concentration camps at Louwsburg while her father was fighting in the guerrilla war. Their home had been burnt to the ground, their livestock slaughtered and their labourers put in a concentration camp for natives. She was a bitter woman and did not conceal her intense dislike of anything English-speaking. She never read the English language Zululand Times she used to wrap her eggs in, even though she understood the language well enough.

Nurse Schwitter arrived on horseback from the Mission, greeted Eric and immediately shooed everyone out of the house. "These people are suffering from a highly contagious sickness and what you are doing by staying here is risking the spread of it further, to your homes, your families and your labourers.

"Go home, change and wash your clothes and what's even more important, wash your hands and gargle with dilute TCP. Make nose and mouth masks with these rolls of muslin like mine. Use three layers." And she showed them how to make them. "And that includes you three," she said pointing at Eric, Toby and Donald. "You too, Jan Mocke!"

Jan explained the present condition of van Schalkwyk and said that he could not let him be alone; he would just move him away from the house to a friend's.

"Nurse, we'll move away too," Toby said, "but, before we leave, you should know that my friend Donald and I both had the first form of the Spanish Flu late last year and as you can see, we have recovered. So has Jannie, the husband.

"When we were still in uniform at the end of the war we learnt from others that a blood transfusion from someone who had recovered from the mild form of Spanish gave the patient a sporting chance of survival. Donald and I have discussed this and we are pleased to offer a pint or two of our blood for these poor people."

Schwitter said that it made sense but it was a 'kill or cure' option. After deep thought, she said, "Well, we will try

213

but I will need to share the decision with a member of the family or the closest relative."

Donald said, "Joop van Schalkwyk's opinion is out of the question at the moment as he is crazed by his own demons; however, Jan Mocke is a close relative and seems to be well thought of. Ask him."

Speaking softly, she said, "I will. There is nothing to lose as these people are dying in front of our eyes. If Mocke accepts the responsibility of agreeing, I will take separate syringes of blood from you both and give the daughter ("What's her name?") a small and very slow transfusion of one of them first, watch her response minute-by-minute and stop immediately if I notice a bad reaction. Susannah will be the priority. I think that the mother has less chance of survival but I will treat her as quickly as I can after Susannah."

Blood transfusion had come into its own during the second battle of the Marne in 1918, although the discovery that different blood groups existed came well after the war and with it the realisation that administration of an incompatible blood group could be disastrous. Before that, catastrophic reactions to blood transfusions were common. However, the only treatment for Spanish Flu that was known to work was a transfusion from a patient who had recovered from the affliction. There was no vaccine for any type of influenza.

Herina and Susannah were in a hot little corrugated-iron bedroom – albeit with the window open. A blanket hung from the door lintel and no one but the nurse was allowed to enter the chamber of rasping breathing and unwholesome cadaver smell.

The nurse said, "We must separate the mother and the

daughter. I will tell them that this is to reduce the risk of re-infection, but the real reason is to avoid the daughter watching her mother die, as I most surely think she will, unless my prayers are heard. It's a warm enough evening for Herina to be on the verandah, and we can rig up a mosquito net. Susannah's window has mosquito mesh so it can be left open and we'll leave the blanket covering the doorway. Men, seeing you're probably immune, please help me shift Mrs van Schalkwyk. I will stay with them until I can establish how they're doing."

Herina's bed was too big to be carried through the door horizontally so her almost lifeless body was lifted out of the bed and put in a wicker chair on the stoep while the two men up-ended the bed and walked it through the door.

Schwitter was a practical Lutheran, but in her preparations and drawing of blood, she muttered what seemed to be a prayer in Norwegian, over and over again.

The mother was barely conscious of the preparations. Donald and Toby sat on the verandah in deckchairs ratcheted up as far they would go to upright, elbows cleaned with surgical spirit and what looked like vets' horse-syringes used to draw off blood; after which Nurse Schwitter went into the sickroom to treat Susannah. She could be heard speaking in broken Dutch-Afrikaans, gently explaining what she was about to do and coaxing her patient to remain as still as possible. There was then silence for a long while, except for Herina's pathetic wheezing on the verandah and Susannah's gasping breath. Mrs. Potgieter stood watching procedures from a distance after handing over the care of Angelien and little Katrien to a close friend who led them away. It was difficult to gauge what she was thinking.

The transfusions were received by both mother and

daughter without disastrous rejections.

By this time, Donald and Toby had rejoined Schnurr, who was leaning against the trunk of a cashew tree. Eric said, "I don't think we can serve any further useful purpose by staying. I'll have a word with Mocke and say as such, but offer any other help if needed. We should ask the nurse for some surgical spirit to disinfect our hands before we go home and some TCP if she can spare it. I've got some brandy in the truck. We'd better gargle with it too. We'll arrive home stinking like a disinfected brewery, but to hell with it. Better say totsiens to Jan?

"When we get home I'll phone the Empangeni switchboard if I can get through and see if she can get through to alert Dr. Lombaard and the chemist to prepare. I believe there's an anti-flu mixture on offer but there are strong doubts about its effectiveness.

"If this second wave is as serious as I think it is there will be many orphans. What you did today was good and will not go unnoticed among the Dutch. Well done.

"The natives will need help with whatever cattle they have which survive nagana if they're too sick to care for them. Do either of you know how to milk a cow yet? Nurse Schwitter's going to have the hell's own job persuading a native to give and accept blood – if she is even considering the idea … more of all this later."

Little Susannah did manage to cling to life. The neighbours reported to Schnurr later that her desperate efforts to breathe, battling against the threat of drowning in her own blood, were successful, so that her condition began to improve perceptibly by the morning.

Herina died during the night.

Later, Mocke was to curse himself for his negligence in leaving a loaded hunting rifle on the verandah as, on hearing the news of Herina's death, Joop had grabbed it and ran out into the veld in despair, threatening to shoot anyone who came near him... or perhaps it was the ghosts of his shellshock demons he was seeing.

It was little Mrs. Potgieter who overheard his shouts and managed to calm him sufficiently by appealing to him to consider how much Susannah and the other two children would need him now, and how Herina was depending on him to care for them for her sake as she looked down from heaven.

(Worldwide, an estimated 50 million people died of Spanish Flu and 2,616,805 cases of the flu occurred in South Africa, leading to 139,471 deaths, of which 13,962 were in Natal.

The deadly second wave of the pandemic made landfall in Cape Town then raced inland, unlike the first wave, which had reached Durban in September 1918, introduced by soldiers returning from the Western Front, the Middle East and German East Africa.

Most, but not all, Spanish flu fatalities were among healthy adults aged between about 20 and 40 years old, unlike 'normal' flu, which attacked the very young and the elderly.)

The emergence of the second wave was so swift that it took some time before Zululand communities came to recognise the true seriousness of the outbreak, as it was assumed that this would resemble the first wave and that the majority of victims would recover.

Eric, Donald and Toby arrived back at the Schnurr household in the short-lived African gloaming to find

André Steenkamp in the garden under the thorn tree. He was clutching a tumbler of brandy and soda, and a curved pipe in the one hand while poking the braaivleis fire with a stick in the other, after splashing water from a small jug over the logs. He was an overweight, dark haired man with a gravelly Dutch-accented voice and thinning slicked-down hair.

"Ja, hello. Why does the bloody smoke from a braaivleis always blow into your face? Marijke and son Piet are in the kitchen helping Marie with the food. They just left me to bring out some chairs and watch the fire," he said. "Marie told me about the van Schalkwyks, by the way."

Eric related the most recent events and said, "It looks very serious indeed and old Mocke's got his hands so full I don't think he'll be able to take his usual cargo down to Empangeni on time.

"Just to add to his woes, I heard him say that he thought that Sataan, one of his strongest oxen, was sickening with nagana and he feared the worst. Apparently, there are discharges from its eyes and nose and its hind legs are beginning to show signs of paralysis. Finding an ox up here to replace such a strong animal will be nearly impossible. His driver, Witbooi, is as upset as he is.

"They're trying a remedy but I have no doubt that it will have to be shot. The next difficulty will be to prevent the natives eating the meat."

The spring-loaded mosquito-screen door squeaked and clattered. Led by the younger Steenkamp lighting the way with a paraffin lantern, Marie and Marijke emerged from the kitchen carrying trays of prepared impala meat, cooked vegetables, Marie's secret sauce and homemade bread.

As sparkles from the fire flew up towards the thorn tree canopy, accompanied by the sound and aroma of sizzling impala, the conversation dwelt on the plight of the van Schalkwyks for a while, then turned to the unreliability of local labour.

"It's hopeless to rely on Zulus for labour! One of the reasons is we can't afford to pay as much as the bloody goldmines," Steenkamp said, "but the other reason is that they regard working in the fields as women's work.

"And it was a big mistake of the bloody Natal Parliament to try to levy a £1 poll tax on every native over 18 years – except for those who were already paying a 'hut tax' – as a way of forcing them to work in the fields. To add further insult, parliament introduced a dog-tax too.

"Marijke and I nearly lost our lives as a result when a magistrate tried to collect it from Chief Bambatha and his men."

Turning to Toby and Donald he said, "You may not know the background so I'll explain. After the Anglo-Boer War, Boer War, South African War – call it what you will – the Natal Government was broke and was unable to pass various tax bills through parliament, and there was a post-Boer war depression.

"This was at a time when deep-bedded Zulu resentment was mounting as a result of growing white and Indian immigration into Zululand, the seizing of Zulu lands for white's sugarcane farms, the introduction of birth and death registration (completely foreign to the Zulu) and their being barred from buying European liquor. It was a powder keg.

"Ahead of the Bambatha confrontation, at a place called Kranskop, a magistrate called Leslie ran into real trouble when he went out to collect the tax from the Hlongwe and Cele tribes. Picture the scene – there was the magistrate sitting behind a table with a few assistants out in a field in the middle of nowhere-in-particular and the natives refusing to pay. To emphasise their refusal, some of the natives hit his table with their sticks. He had to hotfoot it back to town. There was much shouting and angriness, in fact he was lucky to escape alive.

"The upshot was that he contrived to get them to be presented at Kranskop court by their indunas [chiefs] charged with impudence, where they were imprisoned and received twenty-five lashes with a cat-o'-nine-tails.

"The next attempt to collect the tax from a tribe headed by Chief Bambatha (head of the Zondi faction living in the Greytown district) resulted in the inevitable refusal. Shots were fired and the magistrate had to high-tail it again for safety, firstly to Marshall's Hotel in the middle of the veld and then the police station at Keate's Drift on the Mooi River.

"By this time the Zulus' blood was really up and they ransacked the hotel and drank all the booze. Things just got worse – as they always do in such clashes – to the point where loads of troops had to be sent up from Durban after a mighty quarrel with lots of people – natives and troops – being killed near the Umvoti River quite near here. At this point, we decided to get the hell out of our farm and hide in the forest nearby. It was not 'fun', as you English might say. It rained and rained and it rained for days – as hard as the late rain we had the other day, but this was at the height of the rainy season."

Although Toby was Irish and Donald Scottish, they let the reference to 'English' pass without comment.

"The climax of the revolt was after the magistrate for Mhlabatini, a Mr Steynbank, was shot at a drift while watering his horse. This caused troops and horses to be sent by train to the railhead at Mtubatuba, after which they had to ride north to Nongoma to surround King Dinizulu's kraal, the chief being seen as the main agitator during this end game.

"The story is more complicated than that but Bambatha was eventually arrested, stood trial in Greytown and was banished to the Transvaal where he died.

"I think what I am trying to say in all this is that the Zulu seems to be a lazy, polite and smiling man in skins and feathers until something happens (such as a perceived gross injustice) that infuriates him and tips him over the edge. So tread carefully."

At this point Donald asked Marie if he could phone through to the Masonic Hotel reception desk during the course of the evening for a message he was expecting. From the note read out in stumbling fashion by the Indian stationed there, he learnt that Emily had contrived with Sonya to be in Empangeni and that they would be at the Masonic reception desk at five o' clock the next evening. His heart leapt, but another short message was read out to him from a Kim Logan in Durban, which left him puzzled.

It read, "Please call Kim Logan. Logan Imports & Exports, Pickering Street. Phone 45-6983."

He had no idea who this Logan was and how he managed to locate him at the Masonic Hotel in Empangeni, but assumed it concerned the purchase and export of the region's future cotton crop.

He returned to hear Steenkamp talking about the Ethiopianists – who had broken away from the Wesleyan

Methodist Mission, which had many native members, to found the Ethiopian Church. The breakaway rejected all things white and European, calling for 'Africa for the Africans.'

"This was all part of the stew of revolt which led to the rebellion. There was a kind of 'verbal order' given at that time which more and more Zulus accepted – that much of what was white had to be destroyed, including pigs and white fowls. Also included were white utensils for holding food or eating out of. The implication was that it included the destruction of whites. Any Zulu who disobeyed this order would have his hut struck by lightning.

"The construction of a 'Steamela' into the heart of Zululand exacerbated Zulu fury even further as the steam train represented yet another symbol of white colonisation and witchcraft."

Toby said, "You mentioned lightning, and Eric said you were very knowledgeable about how the locals protected themselves from it."

"Well, I can't claim to be 'knowledgeable', but I have learnt that the Zulus here pursue all sorts of practices to ward off lightning. I don't know what there is in the ground in these parts but we do get an abnormal number of lightning strikes compared with other regions of the country. Perhaps it's the magnetite. What I have learned was from an old Kehla. He had a serious sore on his hand which I treated with disinfectant, so he came to trust me.

"A Zulu storm-and-lightning specialist is called 'umelusi wezulu', a 'herd-boy of the sky'. Some close encounter with lightning from which he escaped unharmed will suggest that he has 'the calling'. Lightning could have struck a rock close by, for instance, or passed through his hut without it catching fire ... that sort of thing.

"He will go through a complicated initiation by a qualified 'inyanga yezulu' with lessons on 'muti' [medicine] preparation. The muti will include the fat from the 'bird of the sky', the flesh of a tortoise, the crushed stem of the umzunka tree and the ifafa lily – and about six other ingredients. During his training he is given black horns for holding muti and a stick of black cattle's tails.

"One of his jobs is to doctor pegs with the muti and position them around the hut or kraal. Specially shaped dolerite stones are also used. When thunderstorms are gathering, anything light like lightning is covered up – shiny tools, white cloths, reflecting water and containers. Our weather boy must also go up on a hill above the kraal and wave his thunder-stick in the direction of the oncoming storm to drive it away from the settlement.

"Look, I could go on for hours but, in passing, it's worth listening out for the cries of the ground hornbill and Burchell's coucal. When the spring or summer days are sultry and you hear either of these birds the Zulus will know that rain, thunder and lightning will follow. I think that the sound of Burchell's coucal – the 'rainbird' – is one of the most beautiful in Africa; once heard it's never forgotten – a long bubbling cooing on a descending scale."

Before serving up, Marie asked Marijke to go with her to watch the moonflowers in the hedge. "They're about to open. The moon has come out behind the clouds and will light our way over there. I love to watch them open after dark."

And sure enough, as they reached the hedge, the delicate white trumpet flowers began to open.

"I think I'm pregnant," Marie told Marijke when they

were alone watching the blooms unfold. "All the usual signs, headaches, lower back pain, tingly breasts with nipples tender and darker, and the rest. I had to read up about it to make sure."

"That's wonderful!" said Marijke.

"I haven't told him yet until I can get down to see the doctor in Empangeni. Keep it to yourself but I had to tell someone, and as you're my very good friend I decided to tell you. I will probably need all the advice you can give in the months ahead."

Chapter Nine

The Candover truck swept round to the front of the house next morning as they were finishing breakfast and Theron called "Ready to depart? I don't want to switch this contraption off."

The Schnurr visitors had packed and left their belongings at the front of the house before breakfast and thanked Eric and Marie for their kindness.

Eric had undertaken to monitor the borehole drilling and digging of the longdrops while they were away.

"Don't delay your return. Lots to do. I mentioned that there is a move to establish a farmers' cooperative here and I will put your names forward as future members, as we agreed. A cooperative will give us a collective bargaining power for dealing with the cotton-gin management – and suppliers and agents."

Marie came down the steps and handed the group a hamper of 'padkos' [food for the road].

"We'll all have to cram into the front of the truck. It'll be a squeeze in amongst the levers but so be it. We'll stop every so often for a breather."

"Right! We're off!" said Theron. "Just watch this. Driving such a beast is an art form. I release the handbrake and open the throttle lever on the dashboard a bit and press the left pedal."

The Lizzie moved off with a shrill whine as they waved goodbye to the Schnurrs, who were standing close together and holding hands.

"Now that we are going at more than ten miles an hour I'm going to release the left pedal and the car will probably jerk a bit."

And it did jerk more than a bit.

"Yippee! We're in high gear. Let's see what's left of the road to 'Pangeni'. The first bit is even more rudimentary until we get past van Jaarsveld's store. That clanging at the back is the cans of extra fuel. I've wedged bundles of post in between to hand in at the agency in 'Pangeni'," he shouted. "I'm told that we should be prepared to see some pretty unpleasant nagana stuff here and there on the way along."

And they did. On one occasion, they encountered several emaciated cows dying in a field close to the road. All were very thin, their ribs protruding and they were half-paralysed, seemingly abandoned by their native owners who might have been too sick to tend them. Vultures surrounded them.

"Nagana," Donald muttered.

The party stopped and he shot them out of their misery while Theron kept the engine running. A little distance down the road they caught sight of the remains of twelve beasts which had been dead for several days. Their carcasses were being picked bare by what Emily had called 'aerial dustbins', the vultures – which the Creator must have conceived to clean up the mess left by death. The hides had collapsed onto the skeletons, from which most of the flesh had been torn. Flies swarmed and ants crawled over them.

They stopped the car again beside a huge old Eucalyptus

tree in flower, attracting squadrons of bees, bumblebees and small wasps. Marie's padkos turned out to be tinned sardines on bread topped with lettuce plucked from her garden.

"Seeing all those bees reminds me of an attack in East Africa," Donald said. "We were under fire when we were attacked by a swarm from behind. Not pleasant."

"What happened?"

"I was sufficiently distracted to be captured but I managed to escape some days later."

They washed down the sandwiches with boiled water drawn from the canvas evaporator-bag hanging from the front of the bumper. Evaporation cooled the water.

"Well. Now's the moment I most dread; cranking old Lizzie to life. If it backfires, the crank handle can spin the other way so quickly a lot of people land up with a 'Ford Fracture'. Now you know why I always prefer to keep the engine running rather than having to start the dang thing. I just have to be bloody careful how I set the choke.

"Donald, would you check that the hand brake is pulled up tight? I'll wait until you can tell me that it is. If it isn't, old Lizzie could run me over."

"I've pulled it up tight as she goes."

"OK. Here goes. Once it fires I have to withdraw the crank handle immediately."

Following the tracks for the rest of the journey made by Eric Schnurr' repeated journeys and reinforced by his own drive to 'Tam, Theron shouted to them the story of Zululand gold.

He said that the frenzy for finding deposits and nuggets of gold went back well before the metal was found on the Reef, and that the first gold in Zululand was discovered by a Fred Markham on the Mfongosi, a tributary of the Thukela river.

It started a gold rush.

Soon a shantytown had sprung up to house more than three hundred people, a diggers' committee was formed and one enterprising soul started a passenger coach mule-service to Greytown.

The gold reefs boasted exotic names like Molly's Luck, The Sunrise, New Sheba, with two wood-and-iron hotels. It was said that the Gum Tree Hotel boasted Indian waiters, sold gin at four shillings a bottle and stocked all the latest newspapers.

Chapter Ten

As they chugged, whined and bumped their way into Empangeni they were aware that the atmosphere in the village had changed. Maxwell and Turnbull Streets stank of disinfectant, the water troughs were empty and it was evident that the many tethered horses and mules at the blacksmiths had not been fed; there was no sign of the smithy.

Loftheim's was one of the few places open with Loftheim himself and his wife, assisted by an Indian counter hand, distributing tins of food and mealie meal over the counter. The Masonic Hotel beer garden was empty of swillers and the chairs remained upended on the tables. For a weekday, there was an unusual movement of many people in the church grounds, with stretchers being carried into the schoolhouse next door by farmers, helped by natives. Many of the workers wore masks.

There was a large notice outside the station to the effect that only passengers bearing a medical clearance certificate would be permitted to travel.

Queues outside the doctor's surgery were being controlled by the Natal Mounted Police.

"Well, well, well," said Theron. "That's messed up my plans somewhat – and no doubt yours. I wonder what conditions will be like at Candover if I can get there. I'm going to return the truck, find a drink if there are any, then join the queue at the doctor's for a travel certificate. I did go down with the Spanish late last year and have recovered so – from what I have heard about the disease – I must assume that I'll get a Spanish flu clearance card. I've no doubt you will be doing the same, so I'll see you in due course. Keep a place for me in the queue, if you can."

Donald and Toby repaired to the hotel to find the reception desk unattended, so Donald rang the bell on the counter. The manager came through from the kitchen to say that no bookings could be taken.

"But we booked two rooms several days ago!" said Toby.

"So you did," said the manager after getting their details and checking the records. "These are still available, but I'm afraid that the dining room is closed and there is no room service. I can offer you clean bed sheets if you don't mind making up your beds (just chuck the dirty ones in the bath at the end of the corridor) and I can knock you up a couple of sandwiches. I may even be able to find you a beer or two if you would care to join me in the kitchen – but that's it. All my staff is down with this awful flu and the chef has died from it."

Donald watched him clasping, rubbing and unclasping his hands and thought: "I suppose that's what's meant by the 'wringing of hands'.

"This is a disaster," the manager said, under the baleful glare of a buffalo trophy high on the wall behind him, "Not only for his family but for the hotel and everyone in Empangeni. I believe the flu is even worse down the line and in Durban. There has been an almost complete collapse of the usual services because most people are just too sick to work. It's like last year's epidemic all over again, but far worse. We can just hope that the doctor and the nurse don't go down with the bug as well. What has the world brought on us? The town's phone service is still working, though, but I don't know for how long, if the girls fall ill. That could be another catastrophe."

"I believe I have two messages left for me at Reception. Mind if I take a look behind the counter?" Donald asked.

He found three. The first was from the mysterious Durban importer and exporter, Kim Logan, and the other two were from Emily.

He read Emily's in reverse order and looked at the latest first, which read: "Sorry, we are all confined to barracks by Daddy down at the farm. Spanish Flu. I have to help out. Can't make it but please, please write to me when you reach Durban! Address your letter to me at the farm and later letters when I go back to varsity to 'Women's Res., UCT, 6 Hope Mill, Cape Town'. You can phone me at the farm, meanwhile. I go back to varsity by train on the fifteenth via Durban before catching the train through Bloemfontein to the Cape. What a dreary long journey it will be, but we could meet up in Durban if you like; I could stay overnight in Durban ... With love, Emily"

The "pleases" were heavily underlined as was "love" and the reference to staying overnight.

The second note was handwritten and must have been left by Sonya on Emily's behalf. "So the plot is out," Donald mused. "Sonya's a brick"

The other message was the one he had received at the Schnurr's.

"Well, that's it for the moment. Dammit," Donald

thought, among dashed hopes of a more romantic evening in Empangeni and said out loud, "As we're supposed to be immune, perhaps we should kill some time this evening by volunteering to help. Agreed? Let's go and offer our services at the surgery. Lombard must be worked off his feet."

Lombard and his assistant, a Nurse Jenkins, were indeed being besieged, to the point that he had dragged a heavy table across the entrance to his surgery in order to block sick intruders, and was attending to patients from behind this barrier.

After indicating that they were not trying to jump the queue, Donald said to the doctor, "We've recovered from last year's Spanish so are probably immune. What can we do to help? All we will ask for are travel passes, as we have to travel to Durban early tomorrow. The same applies to Theron in the queue over there, who has to return to Candover in the morning. He's recovered from last year's flu."

"But I know you two from that shark attack at Richard's Bay! I hope that next time we meet there won't be another catastrophe. Thank you for offering to help. As a first step, can you top up the fodder for the animals at the smithy's and Loftheim's and see that there is adequate trough water?

"Most people are so sick that it's almost impossible to get anything done and our animals are suffering from neglect too. Staggering how quickly this second wave has struck. Days ago things seemed fine again after last year's wave died down.

"Get the police to break up the queues here and at the chemist's. Tell them I am ordering that they should be scattered away from the surgery. Stop them forming groups again. Ask the police to explain that it reduces the risk of the contagion spreading through sneezing; then I will be able to attend to them one by one when the policeman beckons them. The police must hand out these numbered raffle tickets and facemasks and Nurse Jenkins will keep the duplicates. She will jumble up the ticket sequences to reduce the risk of arguments about priority breaking out. Forbid anyone to spit and threaten them with expulsion from the vicinity if they do. Say I will never treat them ever again if they do.

"The chemist has a big stock of paper cups and will give anyone who presents themselves a dose of hydrogen peroxide in weak solution. Ask the police to tell everyone to go off and rinse their mouths and moisten the rim of their nostrils with it and to spit into that paraffin tin way over there. We will get rid of the contents later on. We've poured a lot of Jeyes Fluid into it to kill the bugs. Nurse is giving out enough aspirin to go on with, and quinine if they don't have any at home, and codeine for coughs.

"The worst hit are the natives, followed by the Indians, and the town hall has been set aside as a hospital. There are no beds; they just have to lie on the floor, not that that is unusual for them – and a lot are dying there.

"I am afraid there is a great need to get bodies removed – the white deaths from the school and Blacks and Indians from the hall – and buried as soon as possible. This kind of climate is not kind to infection and dead bodies. You can help by transporting the white deaths in the hotel mule cart. There are some natives here who have recovered from last year's Spanish and have been ordered to help load. Make sure they wear face masks.

"Reverend Short and his Dutch counterpart Pastor

Louw are stationed at the graveyard for whites next to the Anglican Church. The burial ground for the Dutch is too far away from town and Louw has accepted that members of his congregation may be buried in the nearest cemetery, being the Anglican. They are sharing giving short 'last rites' services in batches of twenty-five as bodies are brought in. Burial is in a communal grave (we've run out of coffins) after their names are registered by Miss Tatham the librarian who will pass them on to the police and the Coroner. Lime is being chucked over them and some spades of earth before the next batch are presented.

"The natives and Indians are to be buried apart from each other in the other graveyard to hell-and-gone near the sugar mill, and it's good luck that the Mohammedans don't believe in coffins, so they're just wrapped in cloth – provided by the hotel for those families who don't have any – it's the hotel's old linen, but it has been laundered. Getting the bodies there is a mission in itself and I am lost as to what minimal funeral rites are required – but I think they must be buried facing Mecca. No idea what point of the compass that is. Northeast might just have to do. As for the Hindus – the majority – their burning and burial ceremonies are beyond me too. See what you can do to find out and mobilise whatever forces are needed – or at least any of them who are not too sick. We'll just have to bury them with the rest. I realise that this is going to cause problems later on but we'll just have to cope with that when the confrontation arises. This is no time to go around burning corpses on funeral pyres. Takes too long; increases the risk of further infection. The most they can do is to keep the Mahomedan and the Hindu bodies separate. Getting the names of the dead is critical of course so ask the police what is being done on that score."

And so began a bizarre night, not unlike the collecting up of the fearful and torn cadavers of war. Toby thought back to the horizon flash followed by the sound of a great explosion when a torpedo sent HMS Stanger to her grave. Aboard HMS Galloway, he watched the winking of the signalling light while his Leading Signalman read out the messages as they came in: 'Following from Renown. Stanger magazine blew up and sank in two minutes. Searching for survivors. Raise steam and report when ready.' Below him, the Parts of Ship squad was slamming watertight doors and the gun crews were racing to clear their gun-mountings.

When Galloway reached the site of the sinking, only seventeen survivors out of a crew of over a hundred could be picked out by the crewmen. The rest were an oily soup of dead floating bodies, body parts and general flotsam. Those still alive were brought aboard by members of the crew who had to clamber down the nets and, black with oil, help them out of the water – all too weak to climb the ropes by themselves. Some had to be roped up. They were shivering as much from shock as the cold, and most of them were unable to speak, their staring eyes reflecting the ordeal through which they had come.

On the advice of the Indian phone exchange girl, Donald managed to make contact with Marie, the wife of Knud Skaar at the Norwegian Mission Station. He explained that he and his friend had their hands full, attending to the whites, but from what Dr Lombard had told him, the doctor was concerned that conditions down at the Community Hall among the natives and Indians could be desperate.

Donald said Lombard believed that leaders from the

local Hindu, Mohammedan and Zulu communities should be involved in the administering of minimal last rites, record keeping and burials. He predicted a hullabaloo would break out concerning the washing of Mahomedan bodies and the demand for a private tent or hut in which this could be done.

Marie Skaar said that they were aware of the situation and were in contact with and mobilising the appropriate people.

"I'm afraid that there will be an urgent need to build a lot of orphanages after this curse has lifted!" she said.

Relieved of their obligations to Dr Lombard, Toby and Donald made their way to Loftheim's yard to fill the water troughs and replenish the fodder, moving on to the smithy for the same purpose, after which they corralled the hotel delivery cart and its brace of mules to present themselves at the school hall to remove bodies.

Most of the night was filled with loading stiffening corpses onto the hotel cart and depositing them at the graveyard. On most of these last, short journeys distressed and exhausted relatives walked beside the cart. The biblical phrase "weeping and wailing and gnashing of teeth" popped into his head, and he instinctively looked at the wailing relatives to see if any of them were gnashing their teeth, but found none.

There was the corpse of one girl of about eighteen who seemed out of place among the rest. There was also a young boy. Most of the dead were adult men and women in their prime of life.

All displayed the signs of Spanish Flu and the pneumonia or acute cytokine storm that killed them, of bloodied noses, staring eyes and mouths open as if gasping for air.

Donald was reminded of witnessing wartime deaths all over again and the sight of exhausted soldiers staggering along with their mouths always open, as if gasping for air. It was past five o' clock in the morning before he said, "I think we have done our bit for the moment. There's that train to catch. I spoke to Tienie Steyn – that plump fellow in a red shirt with black hair and a moustache over there holding that lantern – and he has agreed to take over with his son. He'll return the cart and mules to the hotel when it's all over. The whole caboodle will need several dowsings with Jeyes before it goes back into service.

"I'm going to raid the hotel's larder and booze cabinet when we get back, whether the hotel manager objects or not. We can always leave money on his desk in an envelope with a note if he's nowhere to be found."

The front door of the hotel was locked so they went around to the delivery yard and found the kitchen door unlatched. It squeaked when pushed open. Tom Legge, the manager, was sitting at the kitchen table in the early dawn light. With the aid of a torch, he was reading the latest copy of the Sausage Wrap, a beer and a sandwich at his side.

"Mind if we join you?" Toby asked, to which he responded, while his mouth was full, by gesturing to draw up chairs to the vast and careworn kitchen table and help themselves to bread and cheese.

"You could call this breakfast – it's so late."

"Anything to drink?"

"Help yourselves to beer. Everything else locked away, but I can get whatever you want if you prefer something stronger."

"I'd like to make a local call later. May I?"

"By all means, if the phone is working," replied the manager. Toby said that he too wished to make a local call.

"Well, what a night!"

It was Edna who answered the phone on the farm at six o'clock in the morning. He could hear a bantam cock crowing in the background and the dogs barking.

"Good morning, Mrs Bell," Donald said. "Donald here. I hope I haven't phoned too early?"

"Hello, Donald," came the practical voice of Edna. "No, we've been up since five. We're farmers! Jim and Noel have been up most of the night trying to help his Indians with this Spanish flu mess. Awful. Emily was up much of the night as well, doing her best to help. Are you all right?"

"Yes, and thank you. We're about to return to Durban on this morning's train and I wondered if I might have a quick word with Emily – just to say good bye?"

"Of course. She might sound a bit groggy as she got to bed only in the wee hours, but I know that she'll be pleased to hear from you and she has to get up anyway. The men had to supervise digging an emergency grave a distance away from that little Hindu temple on the farm. Emily took along some sandwiches and coffee to keep everyone going. Difficult to see what they were doing at night. They had to use the car headlights and then the battery went flat so eventually they had to leg it back in the dark. Hang on. Emily!"

"Hello," Emily said, after a long wait, much like someone who had woken from a deep sleep.

"I called to say that things didn't work out quite as we had planned, did they, because of the Spanish, but I really would like to see you in Durban when you pass through on the way back to varsity. Agreed?"

A mumbled "yes" came out of the earphone.

"I think the post will be delayed, so please, would you mind, sending me a telegram to let me know your plans? My number in Durban where I stay is 23-832 and at the bank is 31-3304. You may need them once you're in town. I live at the Barbican on Musgrave Road, on the Berea. Can you write that down?"

A half-asleep "Yes. Got it," came from Emily.

"I am in love with you, Emily," Donald said, with his heart in his mouth.

There was a long pause and then, "Me too. Goodbye till then," came from the other end of the line..

The phone remained unanswered when Toby called Sonya's house.

"If I scrawled a note to the Broccardos could someone from the hotel drop it into their post box? I have to get to the station," he asked the manager.

"Of course. If I can't find anyone, I'll take it down there myself."

Toby wrote 'Dear Sonya. I have been thinking of you constantly and I hope that the family and you especially have managed to escape the Spanish. Donald and I were up most of the night helping at the school. Grisly business. Was so looking forward to last night but now must return to Durban on this morning's train. Tried to call this morning but no answer, so writing from Durban. I will try to put in a trunk call when I get there. My postal address is c/o Mr & Mrs Grenfell, 'Broadstairs', 71 Stone Road, Berea, Durban."

It so happened that the Broccardo household had plunged further into grief, exacerbated by Sonya's inability to reconcile the rest of her life without her twin brother and still being haunted by the sight of his last agonising moments. Her mother's blackening depression made things even worse. The family had stopped answering the party line and they had instructed the garden boy to turn away visitors.

Gaining the platform after showing their Medical Pass Cards to a policeman (who clipped their return tickets too, because the stationmaster was too sick to work) they encountered a solitary white porter, sitting on a two-wheeled luggage cradle.

He said that the train for Durban would be very late (not that it ever was on time) and he told them that his name was Andries Willem Geldenhuys.

"Kyk na my," he said bitterly [Look at me]. He was over-clad in a dark blue porter's uniform and cap and was already beginning to sweat in the morning's humidity. He had lost several front teeth, which gave him an odd whistling manner of speech.

Despite his broken English made worse by his absent teeth, they gathered that his present status was the result of 'what the English had done to him, his parents and his grandparents'.

He was commandeered, they learned, at the age of seventeen by agents of the Boer Wakkerstroom Commando, mindful that civil war was brewing. He received intensive guerrilla training so that, by the age of eighteen, he could be equipped with a Mauser rifle, thirty rounds of ammunition, a horse and food for two weeks and join their ranks with his comrade and childhood friend, Frans Marais.

During the second Anglo-Boer War an incident occurred which would haunt him for the rest of his life.

He said that they were surrounded by the enemy as

the result of their position being betrayed by two of his relations who had joined the British.

To avoid capture, Hendrik and Frans had to stay submerged in a dam like hippos. There they stood in the slushy cold water with just their eyes and noses showing for fifty-six hours before they could make their escape.

He alleged that this exposure had affected his health and he developed rheumatoid arthritis. The turmoil leading up to the war blocked his chances of much education (and he had been a late starter anyway) so he had no option but to take unskilled work on farms as a labourer after the war ("working like one of those coolies"). His friend Frans Marais, who was already working as a signalman ("Daarsy in die signal box, daarop"), had explained his plight to the railway management. As a result, it offered him a job as a general handyman and porter at a modest but secure wage.

"What happened to the relations who betrayed you?" asked Donald.

"Ja, well." He paused and looked at Robert and Toby steadily and said, "They vanished."

He married a Susana du Preez in 1912 and his first son, Petrus, was born in 1913. Two more sons followed and the burden was heavy for him to support his immediate family and his mother after his father's death, from his meagre railway earnings.

"Why is that fellow waving a red flag out of the signal box? Seems pretty agitated."

Dis my vriend Hans," he said and explained that Hans was alone in the signal box because his assistant had died from the Driedae the previous Thursday.

"We'd better go across and find out what's wrong; it's unlikely that the train will arrive before we get back," Toby said.

241

The double-storey signal box stood on the Durban side of the station on the opposite side of the tracks and beside a large mango-tree with branches that would brush the roof during gusts of wind. It was a few yards after the end of the platform and alongside the leaky water tank on its metal tower and the coal bunkers.

As they got within earshot, Hans shouted, "Groot slang hierop!"

"What is he saying?"

The gist was that there was a big snake in the signal box. He was in danger and he could not reach the levers. He needed to change the points before the Durban train arrived; otherwise the train would be shunted onto an old disused siding – and it would be in danger of falling over because subsidence had developed on parts of the rail after the last rains.

"I still have my service revolver in the suitcase," said Donald. "Tell him I'll come up the outside stairs to the door as quietly as possible and watch you, Hendrik, for a sign to enter. If he can leave the room, better still, then he can tell me exactly where the snake is. If this isn't possible without alerting the snake, ask him to keep close to the door side so when I shoot he is out of the way. The walls are of wood framing big glass windows so there's less chance of a ricochet hitting him unless it strikes a lever. Ask him where the snake is now. Is it on the lever side and what does it look like? Is it long and scaly-grey-green, or is it fat and short like a puffadder? I need to know so that I can spot it immediately."

As an aside to Toby, he said, "Now would be the time to possess a handy bronze icon of a snake on a staff."

Seeing Toby looking mystified, he said "Moses. Explain

later."

He learnt that it was a long thin green snake that had slid down among the levers from an opening in the rafters brushed by the mango tree.

Donald crept up the metal steps to the signal box door, conscious that the external metal framework's slight quivering from his steps might alert the snake. Then he crouched, waiting for Hendrik's signal. When Hendrik dropped his hand, Toby pushed the door open gently and saw a long thin green snake threaded between the levers on the opposite side of the signal room. It was a green mamba and must have associated the levers with tree branches. Its mouth was wide open – a sign threatening a strike.

The green mamba is one of the most venomous arboreal snakes in Natal (and indeed the world), grows to about ten feet in length and is one of the fastest. Most snakes, including black and green mambas, attempt to flee humans, but strike when cornered at 12 miles an hour. A bite in a human can be fatal as it cripples lung and heart function. Fortunately for Donald and the signalman, the snake was in the process of digesting a rat or some other small mammal, indicated by a swelling of the first part of its stomach, thus rendering it much more slow moving.

The end was swift. Donald shot it several times in the head and neck. It made a mess of the woodwork behind it and smashed glass panes, which fell to the ground with a crash. Lashing and writhing continued for several minutes afterwards, giving the impression that it was still alive and dangerous. Hans catapulted out of the room onto the metal landing, shaking and muttering repeatedly "Nee wat, nee wat" and fumbling for his tobacco pouch with trembling fingers. [W is sounded as V. Nee is pronounced like 'near'.]

The commotion brought some Zulu rail-workers to the station platform. Hendrik shouted "Nyorko!" and dropped the dead snake out of the door to their feet, where it lay, still twitching, making them yell and scatter.

"Hau! Msolinyorko wena!" one of them shouted – more from fright than anger. 'Msolinyorko' is a Zulu insult meaning 'descendant of a snake'.

At that moment several steam-chords heralded the approach of the Durban-bound train from Mtubatuba, making Hans thump up the stairs to the signal box in time to throw the points with a crash of levers.

The train was almost empty and the compartments smelt of hot old leather and wood after standing in the Zululand sun.

They chose the cleanest compartment, which happened to be occupied by a large untidy white man sitting at the window munching an onion sandwich from a greaseproof packet and occasionally swigging from an Opsaal Brandy bottle..

"It's said that onions and brandy help stave off the flu. Would you like some? There's no catering on the train," he said and introduced himself as John Cuby. "I got on the train at Mtubatuba."

He told them that he was an engineer and had been looking over what was left of the mill, which had been wrecked after a terrific storm on 16 February the previous year, bringing the Umfolozi River down in flood.

"Drowned a lot of people. They say the water came down the valley like a wall. Smashed the railway bridge. The hotel and station simply disappeared along with the whites and Indians who were sheltering on the roofs and at the mill. Terrible, eh?

"Over three hundred people drowned near Somkele, natives, whites and Indians – along with cattle and game – the lot. Even drowned all the snakes. Wiped out most of the cane fields too.

"The Africans had been warning the mill manager for days that a very big storm was brewing. When asked how they could tell, a khehla [old and respected Zulu man] said he was watching the dogs. They were making holes in the ground and eating grass in the morning. Another sign, the khehla said, was of cattle repeatedly stretching their necks and sniffing the air. They were all clustering together, on high ground, sensing danger. He was so bloody right.

"Some workers who'd managed to hang on to big branches of submerged trees in the river were saved, thanks to local farmers who organised lifelines and used their fishing canoes with two in a boat to row across while hanging on to the lines to reach them. Brave. They could have been swept away in the torrent themselves – in fact two were. They found their bodies miles downstream along with many others – that is, those parts that the crocodiles didn't like. Crocs always survive. And the khehla survived too."

Cuby said that the mill company had spent so much money on repairing storm damage that it had gone under, and he had been sent up to see if it was worth buying and getting going again.

"Well. It's going to be a long ride back to Durban so I'm going to snooze. Talk again later," and he stretched out full length on the seat and closed his eyes.

"Explain that Moses and snake reference," Toby said.

"Oh, that! I remembered a story from Sunday school. The Israelites were punished for their lack of faith by being sent to wander in the desert that was full of snakes. Moses was instructed by the Almighty to make a serpent out of brass and fix it on the end of his staff. The lives of the Israelites who looked at the brass snake were saved. Weird story, that one, like so many others.

"We could do with a few brass serpents. Zululand is full of snakes, I'm told."

After the near-sleepless night in Empangeni, Donald and Toby decided to turn in, like the Opsaal drinker. So, as the telegraph wires swooped from pole to pole, the motion sometimes slowing, Toby pulled down one of the bunks and clambered up, after raising the wooden blinds to keep out the sun (and much of the smut that was splattering in through the windows).

Donald lay down on his seat too and stared up at the picture of the Union Buildings that had once again become the roof of his bunk.

As the movement of the carriage began to sway him to sleep he thought about Emily, his bank balance, Greek at school and that he could not think of any Ancient Greek names of 'daymare' gods. There seemed to be plenty for those who stalked the dreams of darkness. Perhaps Oneiroi would have to do, and the name drifted around and around in his head along with thoughts of the nymphs of the Hesperides; one with oxen eyes staring into his.

Chapter Eleven

It was almost nine o' clock by the time the train pulled into Durban station. The usual hubbub of Zulus unloading and shouting in isiZulu to each other at the end of the platform was absent. There were no porters and the station was deserted, with only the essential lights burning.

The only 'official' was a native night watchman in an old army coat that was too large for him, sitting huddled on a fruitbox at the entrance. Beside him, a coal fire flickered in a ten-gallon drum punched with holes. On the pavement the cafe-de-moveon was one of the very few food outlets which had managed to stay open.

"What have you got?" Toby asked the cook.

"No bread. Deliveries stopped yesterday because of the flu, same for meat and fish. I can make you fried eggs on a flapjack"

"Fried eggs on a flapjack it is then. Use some salt. Any bananas? OK, Donald?"

As they ate, a portly, middle-aged couple were being helped with their luggage into a rickshaw. Donald wondered how on earth the rickshaw man was going to manage any gradients with that load and what would happen when they arrived at their destination. Durban rickshaws were comfortable because the axle sat on generous leaf springs, and the two wheels were large and rubber-rimmed – unlike the cruder 'Jinrikisha' invented by the Japanese. By 1919, there were about two thousand registered rickshaws in Durban. Other than the electric tram, the rickshaws and a few petrol-powered taxis, citizens relied on two-wheeled mule and horse-carts for general transport.

To board a rickshaw, you had to step between the handles and then reach the 'couch' by swinging into it via the footrest. You were pressed back into the couch when the rickshaw man lifted the two handles in preparation for setting off. Sometimes the porter would swing it up so vigorously that the tail wheel (there to stop the rickshaw toppling backwards) would scrape the road.

The men had agreed to go their separate ways but to stay in touch. "Where, baas?"

"The Barbican, Musgrave Road. You know the way?"

"Yes, baas."

"You not sick?"

"No, baas. Last year very sick."

"Malene? [How much?]

"Shilling, baas."

"Longele" ['Kitchen-Zulu' for 'all right / agreed'.]

The soft, regular squeaking of the springs, the pad of the man's feet along the tar, the regular clink of the rear lantern which swung gently back and forth during the cool of the Durban evening, drew him back to wartime East Africa when he took a rickshaw back to camp after dallying with a half-caste prostitute.

Where the path turned from Alice Street into Railway Road, figures were pushing a prostrate woman in a wheelbarrow; from what he could see in the dim light her black hair had come undone. Arms dangled on either side of the barrow.

As the rickshaw passed a flashing 'Jesus Red, Jesus Saves' sign on the roof of the wood-and-iron Full Gospel Tabernacle on Cartwrights Square, other figures were lifting bodies into a pony cart. At Greyville, the rickshaw passed a dead body in the gutter.

Judy and Dorothy were in bed when the rickshaw reached the boarding house. He could hear them coughing through their closed bedroom door and suddenly he felt worn out and eager for bed.

"Is that you, Donald?"

"Yes. Hello. Are you all right?"

"We're both badly sick. How did it go?" Judy shouted croakingly through the closed door.

"It went well, but some experiences were more than hairy. I'll tell you about it when you're up and about. Sorry to hear you're sick. You're not alone. Half the population of Natal seems to be struck by the beastly bug. I thought it was all over by the end of last year. Anything I can get you?"

"No, thank you. You needn't go to work tomorrow. The banks are closed. It's in the papers and just about everything else except the library and the municipal offices. The banks and shops will only open next week ... or when things improve."

"Sleep well."

Donald opened the door of his bedroom but didn't bother to turn on the light. He drew open the curtains, raised the sash windows and flopped down on the bed. All was so hushed that he was able to hear the chimes of the Post Office clock in town striking eleven.

"Well, that's that," he thought, while searching for the

half packet's worth of Marie biscuits he had left in a tin beside his bed, and decided to phone his manager at his home first thing in the morning just to establish that he really would not be needed. The bank might want those staff that were able to come in and work behind closed doors – there was always catching up to do.

The Marie biscuits had gone soft in the Durban humidity.

Mosquitoes kept him awake half the night. When he turned on the light he saw that the wall behind his bed was speckled with them – most of which he annihilated with a pillow, although some escaped to return minutes after he switched off the light again.

He got up and slammed shut the windows, and covered his head with the sheet.

These mosquitoes had horizontally striped black and white legs and a particularly loud whine before they struck. They emerged from the watery reservoirs of the billbergia plants outside his windows. Donald reminded himself to find and pour paraffin over the pupae to suffocate them before going into town the next day. Calling on the mysterious Logan was something to do, that is, if his office was open.

Chapter Twelve

Durban's early morning odours wafted up to the Berea from the harbour, the ocean, the whale-flensing station across the bay, shunting yard smoke, its mules, its factories – those that had opened, one distinctly smelling of cooking jam; and there was no better place to experience the descent through its layers than riding upstairs in the Musgrave Road tram on a still morning. Today he could smell Lysol on some of the main roads as well.

On the occasions when he was early he would take the long route heading northwards, for the sheer pleasure of sitting in the tram as it wound through a tight pirouette at Mitchell Park before its bucking plunge southwards again towards Greyville. On most mornings, a particularly pretty girl with Irish-red hair would wait for its arrival at the canopied Mitchell Park tram stop.

She had a peach-coloured birthmark on the left of her neck which she took pains to conceal but which somehow made her even more attractive to him. "After all," he thought, "the wabi-sabi bowls of the tea ceremony are deliberately flawed and greatly prized."

Once, he managed to talk to her when she took the seat beside him upstairs a few rows from the front because there was none other available. The first encounter was followed by several more occasions when they sat together.

He learnt that her name was Prudence Jardine and that she was the chief librarian at the Children's Library in the City Hall.

When he had no time to spare, he would catch the tram southwards, along Musgrave Road, passing the grand houses and the Durban Girls College. Prue said that during this epidemic the pupils were obliged to gargle their throats with salty warm water every morning, and at lunchtime to stand for ten minutes in sunshine in the school's garden facing Musgrave Road.

The track turned left near the less fashionable part of Musgrave Road into Florida Road and town-wards, where he could peer into the second storeys of houses with white-painted wooden verandas under the flamboyant trees.

Judy often rode with him into town too (she always arrived at the tram stop at the last minute) and he enjoyed her company. The last stop was in Gardiner Street beside the General Post Office, from where they would walk to the bank.

Dorothy sometimes caught the same tram and got off in Florida Road near the chemist shop where she worked.

On this occasion, he was alone, with the girls sick in bed. He had called his manager at home who confirmed that the bank was still closed so he phoned the mysterious Kim Logan to see what he wanted and learned that his office was open. He agreed to ride down to town to meet him in his Pickering Street office.

When the tram arrived, he saw that the driver was wearing a mask, as was the conductor. "Well, that's a first," he thought, boarding the tram heading towards Mitchell Park, barely admitting to himself that he hoped he would catch sight of the librarian.

Only three Indians were allowed to board at the next stop from a small group of waiting Indians and natives. The rest were prevented from climbing aboard by the agitated conductor shouting at them through his face mask. One well-dressed Indian again attempted to board and a struggle broke out, causing the driver to come to the conductor's assistance.

"Full up! Full up!" shouted the conductor.

"You lie! We can see! Tram empty! Abelungu ['white skins'] voetsak!" shouted one of the natives.

In 1919, only a few rows of seats upstairs at the back were reserved for Indians and natives, at a time when the Natal Advertiser was leading a campaign for separate trams for whites, rendered even more tumultuous by fears of Spanish Flu contagion. Letters to the editor abounded in objecting to the 'loud, assertive, insolent and ill-mannered blacks with fears that their uncleanliness and their uninhibited spitting, coughing and sneezing helped spread illnesses.'

There was no better example of white intolerance than the two separate occasions reported by a solicitor, George Brett, in a letter to the Mayor, concerning three Indian ex-servicemen, each with an amputated leg, who had been ordered to 'sit upstairs at the back', forcing them to struggle up the narrow winding stairs.

Seeing the dangers of allowing the rumpus to develop further, Donald got out of the tram, took the driver aside and said, "Look. Let them all go upstairs and tell them to keep quiet, not spit on any account and that they must get off at the stop before the terminus. These are difficult times and the town is empty, so no-one will see them and it will calm a difficult situation."

"All right! Only this time. Go upstairs, sit at the back, keep quiet and get off at the stop before Gardiner Street. No spitting. We will wait for all of you to get off there."

The tram smelt of Jeyes Fluid and had only a few white passengers downstairs, of which the librarian was one. She too wore a flu mask.

It was rather like an early Sunday morning when they reached the terminus, there were so few pedestrians about, except for the queue at the side of the City Hall; but the presence of the girl suggested that at least the library was open.

The trunk of the Dead Man's Tree on the corner of West Street fluttered with black-bordered funeral notices. A flu-masked Indian was tacking up more as the tram passed.

"I'm going to walk down Smith Street to get to Pickering Street from the Point Road fork. May I accompany you as far as the library?" Donald asked Prue, as she was about to step off the tram.

"Of course," she said. "I find the sight of sick people queuing at the City Hall depressing, so your company will cheer me up. These days are awful, aren't they? I don't know why the library has to stay open. Some municipal regulation. Only two children came in yesterday with their mother; any person who brings her child into the city while half the town is down with flu is mad, in my opinion. I've had the flu already, so I'm immune, I'm told... I approved of your action to calm an ugly situation developing back there, by the way."

Outside the Hall was a queue of natives, Indians and whites waiting for dry biscuits, soup and a bottle of useless anti-flu mixture.

Smith Street was deserted save for an ambulance

outside a food shop near Point Road, where a counterhand was being helped into it by two stretcher bearers and a nurse.

The offices of Logan's Import & Exports were on the first floor of a nondescript building, shared with a press-clipping agency into which he walked by mistake.

There were a few young Indian and 'Mauritian' [mixed race] women poring over newspapers at tables and clipping out reports. Some wore flu masks. Piles of dismembered newspapers lay heaped in overflowing wire waste-paper baskets and large cardboard boxes. The air was stuffy and smelt of cheap scent, olive oil and curry.

Apologising and finding his way back into Logan's offices across the landing, he stumbled over a cast-iron doorstop in the form of a rhino, before seeing two men, one seated at a desk, the other in a leather-upholstered chair that squeaked.

"Mr. Kirkwood?" said the one, rising to shake his hand. "I'm Kim Logan and this is my colleague Howard Creighton, who's in Durban for a few days. It was kind of you to come to see us in the circumstances and I'm glad that all three of us have shared an escape from the flu this time around."

He noticed that Creighton was wiry and blinked a lot, while Logan would not have been out of place propping up the Durban Club bar.

"Hello. I'm surprised you're still open."

"The port is still working, except where there are quarantined ships, so we have to be. Tea?"

"Thank you. I didn't escape the first round of flu last year but I believe that this makes one resistant to its return. I can see that Durban has been badly hit again and Empangeni is sharing the same fate, and I think this is true of towns all the way down the line. Lots of deaths reported – especially among the natives and Indians."

"Things have been pretty dreadful here too," Logan said. "Odd. It doesn't seem to attack children or the elderly."

"I gather you have something of interest to discuss concerning future exports of cotton and perhaps sugar?"

"Oh yes. Your bank manager gave you rousing references. Knowing that you would be leaving the bank to embark on the hazards of farming, he felt that any help we could provide would go down rather well."

"Someone remarked once that starting a farm was like digging a deep pit and throwing money into it. Bit like starting a mine."

"Well, Logan's has been in the export business for a long time. We've established a good track record, with excellent warehouses here and important cotton-spinner customers in Birmingham and Bremen (back in business, I'm told, but now in the hands of a Scottish company). Prices offered are fair. Our warehouses at the docks are second to none and you're welcome to inspect them. I've kept open our set of books for the last five years for you to have a look at and your bank knows us well. We have trading accounts with it that go back to the beginning of the company."

"Yes. I've stumbled across your accounts and there has never been anything untoward. A healthy operation, it seems."

"We've heard that there are moves afoot for the Ntambanana cotton growers to form a cooperative – perhaps with the other cotton farmers further north, to enhance their trading position and purchase a controlling interest in the Empangeni Cotton Gin Company," Logan said. "That makes sense, but it suggests that export agents and brokers like us and some less experienced traders will be tussling with each other to maintain their share."

"Logan's already facilitates the buying of most of Empangeni's lint as well as its seed-oil, for which there is an ever-growing market."

"But why make a point of contacting me? After all, I'm just starting out, a greenhorn – like my farming neighbour, Toby, and all the others at Tam. Surely it would make far better sense to concentrate on the older hands?"

"Well, Eric Schnurr has spoken to a colleague of mine about you. Schnurr is, of course, the main mover and shaker who can influence which way the cat jumps; but he seems to think highly of you and your friend and suggests that you will soon be in a good position to further influence any decisions the future cooperative makes.

"Ah! Tea," he said, when it was brought in by the ubiquitous barefoot native woman; Baker's biscuits, once again, making an appearance. Donald took a gingernut from a plate of them.

"Well, I'll take a look at your figures and make some general enquiries through the bank, but I can't promise anything more at this stage. I will also have a chat to Schnurr to get the lie of the land."

He noticed that Creighton nodded to Logan, who said, "There's another reason for inviting you down and my friend here would like to discuss this now. However, I am afraid that it has to be kept absolutely secret. Is that in order?"

"I don't know. If you are up to some sort of jiggery pokery I must tell you that I will not become involved and will terminate any further discussion forthwith," Donald said, rising from his chair.

"It concerns the defence of the realm. It has nothing whatsoever to do with farming." Donald sat down again and said, "What on earth do you mean?"

"I will hand over to Lieutenant Creighton. I'm just a commercial agent dealing with cotton, sugar and pineapples."

"Lieutenant? But you're not in uniform."

"Nevertheless it's true. Naval."

"I can't give any more details until I have your assurance that you will not reveal what I have to tell you, except to say that what I do is on behalf of what is known as Room 40 at the Admiralty in London, although it's less and less 'navy' nowadays."

"Provided your operation is honourable, I will give you my word, although I can't see what on earth this is to do with me and farming."

"It'll fall into place. May I give you some background (not secret) – much of which you know – to set the perspective?"

"Go ahead," Donald said. "The bank is closed for a few days and my girlfriend's got flu so I can't say I am preoccupied."

"Well, the cessation of hostilities in 1918 was, effectively, only a pause in the fighting between the Central Powers (Germany, Austria and Hungary) and two out of the three countries in the Triple-Alliance: that is, Britain and France, backed by the United States' 1917 entry. It was not, technically, a surrender, even though Germany was on its knees in the West and its leaders knew that a final breakthrough of the Western lines by the Alliance would be catastrophic.

"The collapse of the third member of the Triple-Alliance, Russia, as a result of the Bolshevik revolution, is another story, of course.

"The armistice would be declared null and void if Germany restarted the war, yet there remained lots of Prussian firebrands who wanted to do just that. It took another six months to conclude a peace treaty at Versailles with all its punitive reparations.

"The German Military spread the rumour that they had been stabbed in the back by the political parties and their parliament and were capable of prolonging hostilities, a belief underscored by the claims of Quartermaster General Erich von Ludendorff.

"He was duly replaced by a General Wilhelm Groener with whom the Entente agreed to enter negotiations for the truce.

"The upshot was a burning resentment by the German Military and – well behind the scenes – the intention of trying again when the opportunity presented itself in years to come, despite the fact that they were being undermined by a sailor's revolt which started in Wilhelmshaven, triggering similar turmoil and army collapse elsewhere in the country. The abdication of Kaiser Wilhelm II was the last straw along with the creation of the Weimar Republic, which the Military regards as illegal.

"Now this is where the Boers come in. Germany was heartily against Britain during the preceding Anglo-Boer war, aiding the Boers with financing (backed by Boer gold) and very good military equipment, following on from the Kaiser writing a letter of support to the Boer, President Paul Kruger.

"At the moment, the eyes of the West have shifted away from Germany, which it regards as a spent force. They are now trained on the rise of Bolshevism in Russia and Germany and the penetration of the trade unions – even here in South Africa – by Bolshevist-tainted elements."

Logan interrupted Creighton by saying, "You might ask what all this has to do with the company. Well, while Logan Import & Export is a sound commercial enterprise focused on capturing the cotton trade and maintaining its sugar business, it also provides a discreet 'home' for Britain's Special Intelligence Service in South Africa. The latter also monitors the growth of Boer political recovery and its developing contact with elements of post-war Germany, notwithstanding the present chaos. Creighton makes occasional use of the spare office here. His cover is trade expansion, representing our overseas principles, which can explain his frequent and prolonged disappearances overseas."

"What does Cole, my bank manager, know about all this?"

"Not much, but enough to keep his mouth shut.

"You must appreciate that we will deny anything we might tell you later if anything ever comes to light and suggest that it's all twaddle cooked up by you to inflate your ego. In fact, at this point, I must ask you to sign this document agreeing to secrecy before going on."

"What happens if I don't?"

"Nothing. We won't arrange to have your throat slit in Point Road or anything, but certain doors will remain closed to you. You will remain an outsider and obtaining credit might become difficult, even though you are presently part of the banking industry."

"That's blackmail."

"Yes, it is, effective but polite blackmail. All I can say is that spying is the oldest profession in the world and has substantially less morals than Kipling's suggestion that the 'oldest profession' is prostitution."

"Go on. I can see where this is going and it disturbs me. The Boers I have encountered are a rugged bunch and have earned my respect; I fought with many. You know and I know that the real reason that Britain crushed the Zulus in Natal was to grab their fertile land, and the only reason Britain destroyed the Boer Republics of Northern Natal, the Transvaal and the Orange Free State was for Rhodes' gang to grasp control of most of the world's production of gold and diamonds."

"That may be a great over-simplification," Creighton said, "but I tend to agree that your summary has a lot of merit. However …the status quo is that the Union of South Africa is only nine years old and remains fragile, and if it got into the wrong hands (which it very nearly did just before the war) it could steadily slide into being another Germanic state in Africa with cracked ideas about racial purity. Cranky, considering that the Boers (in the main) were essentially responsible in centuries past for creating the Brown People in the Cape, the half-castes, including many of the ladies across the landing. Their ancestors didn't get here by ship after all. They were created by white men fucking black women."

"But how do you reconcile Britain's 'Defence of the Realm' with Kitchener's Scorched Earth Policy and the creation of concentration camps where so many Boer women and children died? What dirty kind of 'morality' are you defending?"

"I can't. I think twenty thousand women and children died in those camps during the second Boer War and please God that will never ever happen again. It was appalling; likewise we never want another World War, but our job here (that is, of the Special Intelligence Service – and ultimately for the well-being of South Africa) is to find out, post-war, what the hell is going on now. We are certainly not opposed to today's Boers, only a few individuals. There are many brilliant Boers in government – like Smuts."

"I'll sign the document agreeing to keep my mouth shut although I would have thought that giving you my word was sufficient, but I am not going to spy on the Boers."

"It's only two individuals that we are concerned about here – and one of them is German, not Boer. The other is and an active spy, we believe, for Germany."

"All right. Hand me a pen, but I'll read through it first and strike out whatever I find unacceptable."

"Before you sign, I must warn you that there is a caveat. You may never reveal future secret knowledge to anyone with the exception of your cut-out – about whom more later – not even to your future wife. The maximum penalty of betrayal to enemy powers during hostilities is death."

There was a long pause while Donald read through the short one-page document, printed on one side only of watermarked paper and which was curiously tinted from top to bottom from pale orange to pale green. Creighton and Logan drank their tea, the silence broken only by the crunching of ginger biscuits.

There was a space for Creighton's signature but not Logan's.

"But you, Creighton, said that you were 'Navy'. Now you are talking about 'Special Intelligence Service' which does not seem to have much smack of the sea."

"Absolutely correct. It started out in London during the war as a naval intelligence unit with most information coming from Russia and neutral country networks, but after the war the fellow in charge, Smith-Cumming, created a passport control department and the post of Passport Control Officer to give diplomatic immunity for agents. This facilitated the spread of the British intelligence network in many countries.

"It's now known as the SIS and sometimes as 'C's Organisation' after Smith-Cumming moved away from just naval stuff, even though it is still housed in the Admiralty, one of those oddities.

"We have reason to believe that the recently-formed Afrikanerbond, which has now renamed itself the Broederbond, is about to be turned into a secret society, and among other things is establishing strong ties with the Freikorps para-militarists in Germany. The Freikorps is growing in influence during that country's turmoil – turmoil, yes, inspired by the goings-on in Russia but precipitated, initially, by the Italian socialist movement in Switzerland and that man Benito Mussolini. Extraordinary how Benito then did a complete somersault and rejected 'failed' egalitarian Marxism to adopt Nietzsche's misinterpreted Blond Beast ideas instead; but I digress…

"The ideology driving the German Freikorp movement combines the nationalism of the right and the socialism of the left in an effort to draw workers away from post-war Bolshevik-inspired turmoil. It is portrayed as a 'Conservative Revolutionary Movement'. A prominent member has called it Prussian Socialism and dubbed it The Third Reich.

"At the moment the movement is plain anti-everything – anti-capitalist, anti-middle class and anti-big business – but there are whispers that this might be inconvenient, because it will need big-business to back the movement with the ultimate goal of seizing power. So its focus is expected to shift to 'racial purity' and the cleaning of the stables of Jews, Eastern Europeans, mentally retarded individuals, freemasons, cripples, sundry opponents of their cause, even the Jehovah's Witnesses, all in the name of Eugenics, which they call Social Darwinism and 'Ubermenschdom'. To my mind, it's a load of very dangerous rubbish – but it suits the thinking of the growing number of people who follow it. One of them is an ex-German Army corporal called Adolf Hitler – or Huedler – who is rising rapidly through the ranks of the movement"

"Yes, I've read of him through reports in the Natal Advertiser."

"It seems that he's a charismatic speaker, a real rabble-rouser, and we're watching him rather closely. He was militaristic even in lower secondary school, the Realschule in Linz, Austria, and recruited his schoolmates during playtime to re-enact the Boer War battles. For several years, that philosopher fellow, Ludwig Wittgenstein, was in the same class, although later Hitler was kept down to repeat a year and Wittgenstein was 'jumped up'. Wittgenstein is Jewish by birth but Catholic by upbringing. Perhaps Hitler resents Jews because of that humiliation.

"The 'little corporal' [Hitler] claimed that he was temporarily blinded in a mustard gas attack and was laid up in hospital when the clauses of the Versailles Treaty were announced, but our other sources suggest that he was suffering from a psychiatric disorder called hysterical amblyopia, whatever that is. The implication is that he never saw any action at all.

"Whether that is true or not, the conditions imposed by Britain and France have turned out to be so punitive and have brought about so much economic catastrophe that the little corporal, like so many others in Germany, hates Britain, France, the United States and the rest of us with a white heat.

"At the moment, this is not too ominous for South Africa, but it could be, in time to come, if the objectives of the Broederbond are fulfilled – the final overthrowing of the yoke of British influence and control, and the declaration of an independent republic aided and abetted by Germany.

"While Britain abolished slavery forever in 1833, some senior Boers still like the idea of the permanent suppression of the Blacks and separation from them so as to keep a permanent labour pool. So that's the background. OK so far?"

"Go on, although some of your references to Blond Beasts and suchlike go way over my head. In my opinion indentured Indian labour dreamed up by Britain was legalised slavery – taking into account that I hear that their treatment here on many farms has been wholly unacceptable, for which the Indians had little recourse."

"I can't argue with that, though surely indentured Indians who wish to stay at the end of their contract are able to carve out a better life here than in the rural villages of southern India? Look at the way that many have started up in Durban and elsewhere as market gardeners and fishermen instead of taking the option of returning to their homeland. Many Hindu widows, for instance, customarily prevented from remarrying in India, have been able to find a new beginning in Natal, where caste rules are more relaxed; and there are reports that many Indians who did go back found they no longer fitted in, and conditions were worse there. Natal can be an attractive place for Indians to put down roots – look at the wealthy Indians, mainly Mohammedans who have come to Natal to make their fortune independently."

"You omitted to mention that most of the indentured Indians, the Hindus – the major part of the local Asian population – wound up with so little money at the end of their first contract that they are obliged to sign up for another five years to stay alive. A return to India would be bleak, and they have no capital to start up here."

Glancing at his pocket watch, Creighton said, "I think we are digressing. May I go back to the core of our discussion?" Donald nodded.

"We have scotched the snake, not killed it. It is inevitable that Germany will rise again – despite the ferocious Western reparations, which, in my view, will only stir up more unmanageable resentment, notwithstanding that the Treaty of Brest-Litovsk forced by Germany on the Russians was far harsher. That the Germans started the war will be clouded by later issues.

"One could call the current situation a new version of The Great Game – not in the Caucasus played out at arms' length between Russia and Britain this time, but between Germany and the Allies including Russia. In highly effective efforts to weaken us during the war, it stirred up trouble in major regions ripe for rebellion – Russia, Ireland, India and South Africa. They smuggled Lenin, Trotsky and a group of other revolutionaries from Switzerland through Germany and into Petrograd via Finland even during hostilities, leading ultimately to the collapse of the Russian Army's will to fight and plunging the country into turmoil. Although Lenin will forever deny it, we have good reason to believe that his power-grab is bankrolled by German counter-intelligence through a double agent in Sweden called Israel Parvus.

"Germany assisted the Irish uprising by attempting to provide arms in 1916 (25,000 captured Russian rifles, although these were intercepted through our fore-knowledge. Another shipment got through). They rekindled Boer hatred of British dominance just before the war and helped to spark yet another serious revolt; and they nearly managed to trigger a Holy War and a Pan-Indian rebellion in the British Indian Army in February 1915. Fortunately, we intercepted the plotters and stopped that, but you can see how this might affect the Natal Indian community. It will continue to bubble up in many forms.

"One last example ...look what Germany attempted to do in Mexico in 1917 – secretly offering generous financial support if the Mexicans would declare war on America, guaranteeing that they could retrieve the lost territories of Texas, New Mexico and Arizona after the return to a peace mediated by Japan.

"These describe a pattern of plotting that seems to be part of the Germanic psyche.

"I need not tell you that the Krauts are a dogged bunch – as are the Boers. All I will ask you to do is keep a weather eye on two people and their Boer contacts, not your Boer friends in general. Be assured."

"Go on."

"In appropriate company you can drop a few hints that you sympathise with the current lot of the Boers (which I can understand that you do). You have played tennis with one of their secret sympathisers, a 'notional Swiss' called von Weldenburg. The other is someone called Fritz du Quesne.

"Von Weldenburg is German, and all that Swiss nonsense is just a smoke screen, although most of his war years were indeed spent in Switzerland, accumulating wealth. That is true.

"His performance is somewhat cumbersome in concealing where his deep political inclinations lie and is only dangerous by his being a conduit for German messages to the Broederbonders in your area of Zululand. Are they by word of mouth only? And how does von Weldenburg receive his messages to pass on to the 'bittereinders? Is his wife involved? If not, can she be compromised? If she is involved, does she receive messages in code? Might these be by post? In coded Braille, perhaps? Or could they be by telegram? Is the Empangeni postmistress involved in some way, although this I doubt? Are messages conveyed via a 'cut-out' in another part of the country – or world? And so on. We don't know yet and we need to know.

"Our guess is that messages, in some form of code, are taken to and from Germany by a cook or steward aboard one of the Dutch liners now able, since July, to ply again between Hamburg, Durban and the Far East, and then conveyed by train to Empangeni – probably by a sympathetic steward.

"However, the other man in our sights, Fritz du Quesne, is really the one to watch. He goes under many aliases, one of them being 'Captain Claude Stoughton' and that's the one he's using at the moment. We have an unverified report that he was in the Vryheid area of northwest Natal recently, which makes sense, although we don't know how he managed to get there. Vryheid has many 'bittereinders' left over from the old northern Natal Republic with whom he could make contact. We have heard that he was intending to come through Nongoma to the Empangeni and Ntambanana area."

"That's quite an excursion," Donald said. "What tracks there are would make a rhinoceros weep, I'm told; they're so bad. Only an ox wagon could pull through – with great difficulty, or a horse."

"He's a very good horseman, so I guess horse will be his answer. Du Quesne is an educated man and works for the Germans under the code name of Dunn. He's bright and comes from a solid Boer Huguenot farming stock in Nylstroom with influence in Boer circles.

"At the age of 17, well before the Boer War, when there was less animosity between the English and Boers, he won a scholarship to study History and Politics at the University of London. After graduation he extended his studies at the Royal Military Academy in Brussels before returning to South Africa to serve here in the British Army.

"What turned him violently against all things British was the discovery that his family farm in Nylstroom had been destroyed during General Kitchener's Scorched Earth offensive.

"His sister was killed during the attack, the farm ransacked and set alight and the cattle slaughtered and carried away. His mother was sent to one of Kitchener's concentration camps where she died. We have found no record of his father at all.

"His is a sad, regrettable and fascinating story yet far too long to recall now – but that's the gist of it. It's unfortunate that he is not on our side – but he is not, and that's that.

"By the time of the second Anglo-Boer War he had switched allegiances secretly to become the best scout the Boers ever had, according to his key opponent and chief of scouts, Frederick Burnham.

"He is charming and the ladies like him, while remaining a 'man's man'; but he is absolutely ruthless. We believe his cover is as a sales representative for Opsaal Brandy. He might well be a visitor at the von Weldenburg farm from time to time."

"Right! Now you've dragged me into your net, how am I to communicate with you – that is, if there is ever any reason to do so?"

"All very simple. Never contact me directly at all."

"Then, how on earth do I send messages to your organisation?"

"Well, you already are in touch with your case officer. You simply send coded messages in letter-form through the post. Your occasional letters to a girl in Durban should be short and contain mostly innocuous stuff plus local gossip, farm progress, etcetera."

"Your cut-out is a girl that you rather fancy – Prudence, or Prue rather, who works at the Children's Library in town. Her father just happens to be the harbour-master, but hasn't a clue about her other activity."

"Good heavens!" said Donald. The revelation sent his mind retracing any actions of hers that might have given him a clue about her 'other activity', but could find none.

"I won't explain – for the moment – why she works for us – but the cause is a bloody good one. Next, I will provide you with a devastatingly simple yet reasonably uncrackable code system.

"You and she will possess duplicate copies of a popular novel. I have suggested John Buchan's 'Thirty-Nine Steps' merely because of its popularity and both the Children's Library and the Adult Library have frequently borrowed copies, meaning that it won't 'stand out' as something unusual.

"Also, it's topical. The book was only published in 1915. Read at The Front, I believe. Easy to read and a bit of a shocker. The public don't know that it was part of plan to stimulate anti-German patriotic ardour. Buchan headed up the War Propaganda Bureau set up by Lloyd George in 1914. Thomas Hardy and Rudyard Kipling were also part of the same gang.

"Your letter containing some 'statistics' will in fact start with the page number, the line number and the starting point, always in the same order please. You simply select a starting point and use the next 26 characters that follow. Therefore, the last number you give is the number of characters inwards, counting from the beginning of the line. Avoid lines with commas.

"Here's a copy I brought along just to show you. On page 69, 7 lines down, which starts "and then my own boots placed neatly ..." Got it? The fourth character – as the starting point – is the start of the second word. It is "then." Now replace each character (from left to right) with a consecutive letter of the alphabet"

"So T becomes A, H becomes B, E becomes C, N becomes D and so on. Skip repeated letters. Keep messages very short – like a telegram. The signal that disguised information follows immediately thereafter is a word underlined. Start a new paragraph after the end of the coded message.

"We could get even more secure by enciphering with numerals but I don't think that will be necessary. Instead, we have turned you and Prudence into amateur bird observers. You are recording the number and frequency of various birds that visit your bird feeder at the farm every day for a short period, and Prudence will reply whenever appropriate with similar observations. You can embroider your observations. Here's a list of Natal birds you will be able to observe on your farm and which can also be seen in Durban. You will notice that each bird was assigned a consecutive letter of the alphabet and there are 26 birds listed. So the Red-Eyed Turtle Dove is 'A', the Cape Turtle Dove is 'B', the Diederick Cuckoo 'C' and so on. Prue has the same list. The birds are just a red herring in the unlikely event anyone should question you.

"The string of letters in the coded message supposedly records the frequency of each visit by a bird on the list, notionally within a week, but because a new code is created each time you prepare a message the string will alter each time.

"But remember, you must choose a different page and different line every time you send Prue a letter, or when she writes to you."

"This is fascinating! I don't expect I will ever be able to pass on anything at all useful, but I'll give it a whirl."

"I can't emphasise more strongly when I say on no account ever mark your book. Any scribbles you have to do should be done on separate paper and used as kindling to light the next fire, or thrown down the longdrop.

"You can casually mention here and there your interest in Natal birdlife. Make sure you make or acquire some sort of flat bird tray (pigeons and doves peck food that way) and keep the tray topped up with nuts or porridge-oats or seeds. Have a pair of binoculars in view for sundry visitors. Perhaps Prue can provide a battered manual on Zululand birds, just to add 'colour'.

"Prue will soon bump into you on one of your tram journeys and you will sit together. She will be carrying a copy of 'The Thirty-Nine Steps' and you will express an interest in it. She will mention a talk on the formation of the League of Nations to be given in the Arthur Smith Hall at the Durban Technical College on the second Saturday afternoon from today under the 'flag' of the Workers' Educational Association, by someone called Mabel Palmer.

"Recognising your interest in Prue and perhaps nurturing a growing friendship (with our approval), do agree to meet up and go along. She will bring an identical copy of 'The Thirty-Nine Steps' to lend you. Although it won't be a copy from the library it will appear to be so.

"It'll be well-thumbed, with the usual rows of return dates stamped on the Durban Library sticker. A fudged library catalogue number will be marked on the spine, but some of the pages will be discoloured markedly by stains and on the inside 'library' page will be stamped in large capitals DAMAGED. REMOVED FROM STOCK, so if it's lost and returned by some well-meaning soul it will simply go into the damaged books bin and disappear."

"From all this I realise that not only have you been digging intrusively into my private affairs but following me around. I don't like this at all – to the point that I am about to tell you to go to hell. Furthermore it interferes with other romantic intentions."

"I am sorry. Our only motive was to make sure that you were 'clean', as the jargon goes. Yes, you were followed

– mostly from the Barbican to boarding the tram and riding on the same vehicle into town. I must remind you that you have signed our document freely and without equivocation."

"All right, then; for the time being I'll play along with you until I do get engaged. Then it will have to stop. But you have to cover any expenses incurred in the performance of such duties – travel and so on."

"That goes without saying. Within reason. Just itemise amounts in code and include the details in letters to Prudence. You and she can work out how you get paid so that amounts can't be traced. The usual option is cash, when you meet up."

He noticed that Creighton had managed to munch his way through all the biscuits left on the plate.

Gingernuts left open for a while become soft in Durban's humidity, but these biscuits were still crisp.

The man stood up and said, "We think that you're a good man by all accounts as your war record demonstrates, so we value your efforts in helping us all to block conditions that could deliver the fledgling Union into the hands of the old enemy. Goodbye."

They shook hands and Donald left shortly afterwards, not before saying, "We seem to be living in a very strange society, don't you think? We've just come out of the worst war man has ever experienced and are already preparing for the next. Haven't we all had enough? I came out to Africa as a banker, but the war intervened. I nearly got killed – several times in Tanganyika – and here I am, as a fledgling farmer, being sucked up into yet another plot to stop the old enemy having another go at us."

There was irony in his voice when he said, "Well, all I

can say is that after that little chat I had with your colleague this morning, I must expect tiptop service from your agency. Agreed?"

Logan rose and, extending his hand, said "Agreed."

"But there's one final thought which is bothering me."

"What's that?"

"There is much talk of the Broederbond becoming a secret society. Well, what about Freemasonry – all those secret handshakes and passwords and things?"

"I suggest there is a marked difference. Many Boers were and are Freemasons, not least Commandant Sarel Theron and General Piet Cronje who fought with distinction on the Boer side during their war (I made it my business to know this) and I am told that any Boer of good standing is free to become a Mason."

"And where does that put an Indian or Coloured or native?"

"You have me there. I think they're not yet ready for it in South Africa, although lodges have been in existence in India with Hindu members from the late nineteenth century, and I believe masonry started in Nigeria in 1913; but my rejoinder to your first point is – try to join the Broederbond. You wouldn't be allowed to reach its front door – wherever that might be."

There was a telephone booth on the corner of Point Road and Pickering Street, of cream-painted asbestos cement with a coned vermillion red roof. It was a refuge for decades of Point Road citizens to shelter from sudden ferocious subtropical winds and rains.

Its interior was smothered in crude words and cruder pictures of the genitalia, associated copulations and pencilled messages and phone numbers, but what made it stand out from many other phone booths of the era was the Durban cockroach.

Lift the bakelite handset, mounted vertically on a wooden base, and as often as not you would discover a blanched version of the large Indian *Blatta orientalis*. Cockroaches such as these liked eating phone books, which rather put off callers.

The phone directory hung from a sturdy chain. The first page was devoted to moth-eaten drawings (done in pointillist dot fashion as if the illustrator admired Seurat) and strangely worded instructions (in between the scatological scrawls) – the introductory paragraph being "First ascertain the name and number of the person with whom you wish to be connected." Further down the page were directions on how to dial a number: "Insert the index finger in the dial hole opposite the first numeral of the number with which you wish to be connected and turn the dial to the right until it can go no further" – and so on. It seemed that the author had only recently discovered this wonder of science himself and was eager to communicate such new knowledge to the ignorant.

Armed with a few shillings and silver tickeys (small thrupenny pieces that had recently been introduced) Donald lifted the handset with his left hand, his right hand raised with a rolled Natal Advertiser to strike down any cockroaches.

As none appeared, he put down his paper truncheon and dialled zero to connect to the exchange. "Number please nummer alsjeblief," asked the voice in guttural English and High Dutch.

"Empangeni 32 please."

"Do you wish to make a personal trunk call?"

"Yes."

"It will take a little time and I cannot guarantee that we can get through, so you will have to wait outside the callbox to let others use the phone. Is that in order?"

"Yes, that's in order."

"Who do you want to speak to?"

"Emily Bell."

"What is your name, please?"

"Donald Kirkwood."

"When the call comes through you will have to insert a one shilling coin or four tickeys. Will you have the money ready?"

"Yes, I have it now."

"If you wish to go on talking after the three minutes is up you will have to put in another four tickeys. I will interrupt your call to ask you. Is that in order?"

"Yes, that's fine"

"I will try to call. The line is not good and you will have to speak loudly. Please wait outside the box and I will call this number when I get through."

Donald stood outside the callbox with his heart in his mouth.

A woman, with lips like a bent pen, a shorter than usual skirt, no stockings and loud pink sandals went into the phone booth while he waited, and stared at him as she made a call. 'All fancy hat and no knickers' as his mother used to describe tarts. Oddly, her dress was a shorter version of the herbaceous border dress worn by George Moberly's wife at Durban station so many days ago. After the call, she came out of the phone box and said, "Hello. I'm Luna. Can I help you with something?"

277

"No. I'm just waiting for a call."

"OK. I can wait until you've finished. I've a flat just up the road."

"Luna. No thanks for today, but thanks. Maybe another day."

"OK, My China. Here's my card. Just call me anytime. I can see you're a juntlemun."

"Thanks, Luna."

"Have you some change? I must buy bread and milk for my kid."

"You're lucky to find the food shop open. That's all I've got, Luna. I need to keep the rest for the telephone call. Here you are."

"You're a star, My China. Give me a call soon, eh? I'll see you right. You c'n see I'm a sugar girl, eh? Point Road girly."

"Well, maybe."

"Problemsis clubzclosed. Bloody police say it's coz Spanish."

"Explain?"

"We can't meet in the Firefly Club down the road coz of germs. Germs, Germans, what the fock I care? Need money to live. So's my child."

"How old? Girl?"

"Seven. Seen it all. But I jus' want more for my Elsabé."

"Where do you come from, Luna? Where were you born? Are your parents alive?"

"Whatz your name?"

"Fred."

"Fred. My Ma het gesterf [died] in a concentrasie camp in Irene. My Pa het in die oorlog [war] gesterf [died]. We just had nothing left. Heeltemaal niks [completely nothing].

Onse plaas [farm] was heeltemaal destroyed and I wiz focked by three English soldiers wen I was jus' thirteen. So I came yeer to find some way to make money."

"Why don't you like the club manager?"

"We must stay in the club 'til two in the morning so sailors can drink themselves dilly or the fockin' manager says we have to pay him five pounds every day if we leave early."

"But the clubz closed," she said, "so where do I go? We only fock foreigners from the ships usually and they all know where we hang out. Now it's closed. Even most fockin' ships are closed. So where do they go? Where do I get money? Do you like dancing?"

"Depends on the girl."

Then the phone rang. "Is that her?"

"Yes."

"I can tell you're juntlemun. She's a lucky cow. Tell her that."

He signed goodbye to Luna and smiled, the door banging behind him as he reached for the phone.

"Mr. Kirkwood?"

"Yes."

"You are connected to Emily Bell."

"Hello!"

"You sound so far away. Where are you?"

"I'm in Durban. Just been to a meeting with an agent about cotton exporting. Have you got over the flu drama on the farm?"

"It seems to be burning itself out, thank God, but it's not over. Lots of deaths, especially the natives. I got flu last year so I believe I'm immunised."

"When are you going back to varsity?"

"I'm travelling down by train next Tuesday." Emily cleared her throat and said, "I was going to catch the train from Durban to Cape Town via Bloemfontein but Daddy is making enquiries about my taking the ship to Cape Town. Some say it's not safe on the trains now and it's not certain that the train to the Cape will be running, anyway.

"I need to buy some things in town and do a spot of research in the reference library and Killie Campbell's on the Berea. It'll take more than half a day, so I'll have to stay Tuesday and Wednesday nights somewhere, but the hotels are closed. Any ideas? Could you arrange something and meet me at the station? I'll confirm details by telegram."

"Yes," he said, then the operator interrupted with: "Your time is up. If you want to go on you must put in another shilling"

"No. Let's just say goodbye," Emily said. See you next Tuesday. I hate long-distance. Too public," and she was gone.

Figtree leaves were whirling about the call box when Donald dialled his friend Jean-Pierre Mayer on the off-chance he would find him at home.

"Jean-Pierre?"

"Oui?"

"C'est moi! Any chance of sailing today? I see the tide is in. Everything is closed in town so I wondered if you'd be sailing."

"Ah, hello! I thought you were digging up Zululand! Yes, I was just about to leave ... anything to get away from all this sickness and death. Are you in town? Come along! The weather looks good now, but I think we're in for a good three-day blow, so I need some idiot to sit with me close to the transom on a run. You know what the BRA is like; it always wants to dig its nose into the water. Shall I bring your togs? Yes?"

"Yes. I'll see you at the slipway."

As there wasn't a rickshaw in sight, he elected to hoof it to the yacht club. He saw Luna drifting out of the food shop holding her young daughter's hand and waved, and she waved back.

He was hurried along to the yacht club on the Esplanade by the gathering wind, still thinking of Emily, Luna and her daughter Phoebe.

Jean-Pierre was there before him and was already lacing the sail to the gaff. Around him the halyards and stays of other dinghies in their wheeled cradles were pinging and slapping their masts.

"We won't have to whistle for a wind, eh? This is mad weather for this time of the year. See, the storm ball is half way up on the Bluff and the wind's switching from north east to south west, so we'd better get a move on. Oh, and hello!" Jean-Pierre shouted, shaking hands. Donald had become so accustomed to shaking hands with this Frenchman every time they met and parted that he would often absent-mindedly offer his hand to shake with puzzled staff members when he arrived at the office on a Monday morning after a weekend of sailing.

"Meet any pretty girls?"

"Yes, but I'll tell you about a ghastly shark attack later. I'll just go and change. It's your turn to skipper."

Donald found the clubhouse closed and had to change behind some boats. He wondered how hungry the bay's sharks might be.

The slipway was just that – slippery, and they had to watch their step in the wind as they let the boat on its cradle down to the water and far enough in to allow the boat to float free.

Some British officers had imported two of these clinker-built Boat Racing Association (BRA) dinghies before the war, and sold them to club members for a song when the men had to leave for other postings.

The boats were only twelve foot long and had been designed in 1913 as small sailing and rowing dinghies. The single sail area was abnormally large for a small dinghy. While BRAs were not designed to plane (ride on their own prow waves) they could, frighteningly, do so when running downwind in a strong blow, giving them an abnormal burst of speed. Because the mast is so far forward the BRA will tend to dig its nose into the water at such speeds, unless the crew sits well aft to counterweight it.

"Are there many sharks in the bay, do you think?"

"Of course, but they are far too busy swarming around the whaling station on the Bluff side to worry about us. Why?"

"Nothing. I must remember not to fall out of the boat."

Jean-Pierre dragged the wheeled cradle up the slipway again to park it while Donald stood in the shallows holding the boat steady. Then they clambered in with Jean-Pierre taking the tiller while Donald hoisted the burgee and the sail. These boats had no genoa ahead of the mast.

The horizontal boom controlled the sail, in the hands of the skipper's mate, hauling on or easing the sheets, a seaman's name for ropes, which were threaded through a block attached to the boom. The latter was always a hazard when going about, as it could swing across and hit an unwary sailor on the head.

With the sound of water beginning to plop against the hull Jean-Pierre shouted "Centreboard!" to remind Donald to lower the retractable keel once they had cleared the shallows.

The full force of the wind caught them when they reached the end of the Mole. Then what was merely a stubby structure of wood topped out with canvas and stays turned into a wild horse, calling on all their wits to keep it under control.

"We'll broad-reach heading for the Bluff, then close haul into the wind to tack our way past Salisbury Island towards the mangroves at the head of the bay – or at least as far as we want to go – and go about on the homeward run. Most exciting bit for last. Okay?"

"Okay."

There are moments in sailing when there is perfect harmony between wind, water and boat, the strumming of the wind on tight sail, the lap and splash of water parted by the hull thrusting forward, when troubling concerns are blown away; and this day was one of them. He forgot about Zeno and the shark attack, the disturbing meeting in the Pickering Street office and the deaths from Spanish Flu at Ntambanana and Empangeni; he almost forgot about Emily.

The next few hours called for little further communication except when Jean Pierre shouted "Okay. Going about. Lee ho!" and the boat chasing home before the gathering storm.

Donald allowed the exceptionally large sail to balloon and run out before cleating the sheet and clambering aft hurriedly to join Jean-Pierre close to the transom.

The slap of water increased as the hull rose and planed on its bow wave, accelerating to an abnormal speed while rushing homeward past Cato Creek.

"Lower the centreboard three quarter way! We don't want to broach!" shouted Jean-Pierre. If the sail dragged in the water without the centreboard down there would be the risk of the boat turning turtle.

Swinging to port to enter the protected waters of the Mole, Jean Pierre said "Peace again," as the sail sighed and fluttered and the boat slowed. "That was good. Centreboard up! A beer, huh?"

"And some curry – but there's nowhere to go. Everything's closed."

"My house is certainly not closed. Caroline and the children can't stand the stuff so this is my chance while they are away. Our maid Aysha makes a wicked curry. She always prepares mountains of the stuff when Caroline's not here. Yes?"

"Okay. I'll buy the beer. A place that sells booze is likely to be open."

They brought down the sail, stowed the gear and wheeled down the cradle to capture the boat and haul it up the slipway to its parking place.

"There's this girl."

"Aha! I knew it! They're like bees around a honey pot."

"No. It is different. Wait. I'll tell you over curry."

Jean-Pierre's parents were sugarcane-farmers in Madagascar who also owned a small wine estate on the island. He exported soap, oats, machinery and other goods not easily obtainable there to a wholesale outlet they owned in Tananarive's Upper Town. The business was thriving, allowing him to buy a three-tiered colonial house near Mitchell Park, high up in Durban's Berea where he lived with his wife, two very young children, a boy and a girl, and several servants.

By the time they reached his house the wind was roaring and wuthering about it, shaking and thundering the heavy front door and whistling outside the windows, as if some invisible and angry daemon were attempting to uproot the whole building, along with its occupants.

Large colonial houses in Durban were built at a time when fireplaces were common; despite the subtropical humidity and warmth, it can get quite cold on winter nights.

"It's gone cold. There must be snow on the Berg," said Jean-Pierre.

He lit a fire in the study and there they sat on either side of it, along with the family's Dalmatian dogs Dot and Ditto, while the wind tore at the trees. Shelves overflowed with Madagascan artefacts from the country's pre-French rule: fetishes used in black magic, tribal masks, woodcarvings and relics. A stuffed lemur, its striped tail hanging down, topped a bookcase of exciting books of study and romance.

"Okay. Aysha is heating up the curry and cooking rice and poppadum. Tell me about Zululand and the girl. What about your current girl Judy?"

"I've kissed Judy occasionally but that's as far as it goes. She works at the bank so I keep our relationship at cuddle length. She is a good person, but brought up in a family that knows as much about the rigours of farming as one might learn at an Edwardian tea party.

"She's a pretty town girl who the bank puts near the window to please the eye of customers, but life in Zululand is rough. You have to deal with rough diamonds, make tough decisions and be prepared to get your hands dirty. Day after day. Ntambanana is remote and can be lonely. Sooner or later I'll be looking for a girl to share life with me up there who understands the demands of farming, and I don't think Judy is the one for that."

"À cœur vaillant rien d'impossible," Jean-Pierre murmured.

"What's that? I don't understand."

"I said 'Nothing is impossible to the willing heart' or words to that effect. Perhaps you are underestimating Judy's ability to adapt?"

Donald then explained that he had met an attractive farmer's daughter who understood farming, could speak Zulu and might be willing to help carve out a farm with him in the African veld, if he asked her to.

He told Jean-Pierre about Zeno's shark attack at Richard's Bay and said that Emily was still in her final year at university in Cape Town. He said that he realised that her parents might find it unacceptable for her to marry a man seven years her senior. "Their attitude might be that after all the investment in education and upbringing she would be stuck in the remote veld seventeen miles away from her farming parents, rather than pursuing a professional career and winding up marrying a lawyer or doctor in the big city."

The gale-force winds rattled the windows again and the lights dipped and recovered, which seemed to be the signal for Aysha to wheel in the curry on a dumb-waiter.

She was middle-aged and had come to the family from Jean-Pierre's parents' wine estate in Madagascar. With broad Malay cheeks, liquid eyes and long brown hair she was pretty but of a girth that reflected the many hours spent in her employer's kitchen.

Aysha was barefoot, and Donald wondered why so many servants he had encountered in neo-colonial Natal padded about barefoot. After she left the room, Donald asked why she didn't wear shoes on such a chilly night.

"She doesn't like them," said Jean-Pierre. "She says they make her feel clumsy. We've tried to convert her, but have only managed to convince her to wear them if she has to go shopping.

"Where is your Emily staying overnight in Durban? The hotels are likely to remain closed until this awful flu is over. Are there family friends where she can stay?"

"I've no idea until I hear from her."

"Well," said Jean-Pierre, "If she is stuck, you could arrange for her to stay in my office-cum-guest apartment in Cavendish Chambers. It's on the third floor and overlooks the Esplanade. I use it to keep samples to send to Madagascar for trade and put up business guests, as it's a convenient walk to the centre of town. There's a small kitchen complete with icebox. The iceman comes early on Wednesday mornings and delivers a new block of ice through a flap in the corridor. I just hope he hasn't been written off by Spanish Flu.

"The bedroom has a good wardrobe and a bathroom. My samples and brochures for Madagascar are kept in a separate room along with the filing cabinets and a desk. There's even a phone.

"It is not for me to say that she may not wish to stay there alone," he said, smiling and clearing his throat. "Anyway, there are provisions – not least a few bottles of our wine. I'll let you have the keys."

"That's very kind of you, Jean-Pierre," Donald said. I'll

keep the keys for the moment and keep you informed."

"By the way," Jean-Pierre said, "I've been invited to attend a séance, of all things, tomorrow evening and I need some moral support. Would you help me by coming along? I know that séances are very frequent now, because so many people are drawn into the trap of believing that their children, killed in the war, can be contacted by this means. There are a lot of – how you say – charlatans about, but I have good friends on the Berea who not only lost their son Adam at Delville Wood on Bastille Day in 1916, but a daughter called Chou-Chou. She died from Spanish Flu here last year. She was recently returned from London (somehow Ivan her father wangled a ticket for her) and had been married here for just a week when she and her husband collapsed and died from the 'Spanish'. The parents are still devastated, and are at that stage when it is too early to reconcile themselves with the fact that their children will never come back and that all contact is gone forever.

"They are like so many people here now, trying to come to terms with the war's slaughter followed by Spanish Flu deaths. It's creating even more orphans and a great business opportunity for undertakers. The natives are being hardest hit, I'm told.

"I don't believe all this spiritualistic rubbish but they are my friends so I intend to go along to display support. There will only be a few of us there, including two piano-teacher sisters and another couple, plus the parents. Joelle, the wife, was a close friend of Chou-Chou Debussy in Paris, the composer's daughter. My friends nicknamed their daughter Chou-Chou after her. What makes it particularly poignant is that Chou-Chou Debussy died only a year after the composer and not so very long after the German bombardment began on Paris.

"The host is Jewish and she isn't, but I think she must have converted. They're a lovely couple. Anyway, that's the background. So if you agree to come along and arrive while someone is playing Debussy, you will understand what it's all about."

"I see. Yes. Well, I'll come along as long as no Red Indians materialise, but I need transport there and back."

"Of course. We have an old DKW motorbike in the yard and you are welcome to use it for as long as you're in Durban. Like all Germans, it's noisy, but between backfires, it will get you there. It's called 'Das Kleine Wunder'. Wait. I'll fish around for those keys too. I take it you can ride a motorbike? Take the keys now. It will save my having to drive you home tonight. We had better test the headlight before you start out, though."

"That's kind of you," Donald said, then realised that it was planned for him to bump into Prue the librarian on the tram. "Tell you what, I'll take you up on your offer for the evening but I'm not totally happy on a motorbike so I'll get it back to you somehow. I'm hoping to buy a Model T from a fellow called Georges Chapard tomorrow – if his offices are open."

"George! Now that's a wily Frenchman if ever there was. I know him quite well. Let me know how you get on and we'll plan accordingly. I hope you're not contemplating driving a Tin Lizzy all the way to Ntambanana? The road north, even when passable, is either a quagmire after rain or a bone-breaker in the dry season."

"No. I'm going to send it up by goods-train to Empangeni-Rail then drive it to Tam when the road is passable."

"I didn't understand your reference to Red Indians?"

"You and I know, in our heart of hearts, that all this 'spiritualistic' stuff's probably dangerous bunkum – but at most of these séances I am told that the medium seems to have a particular liking for working through a long-dead Red Indian chief. Or at least in America they do."

"No, I hadn't heard of that; so let's see what happens tomorrow evening. Perhaps we will witness the appearance of an Eskimo or something closer to home."

"Maybe a Zulu!"

Chapter Thirteen

Donald arrived back at The Barbican less than sober. Familiarisation with the temperamental workings of the DKW had taken all his fuddled concentration. He found he had to keep one eye closed, as the alcohol in his system had reduced eye coordination, and with both eyes open the road and lines seemed to fork making him wonder which line to follow. He had narrowly missed a dog crossing the road and slowed down to a crawl, whereupon the motor had cut out.

He shut the front door noisily after parking the bike at the back and clumped up the stairs towards his room.

"Is that you, Donald?" shouted Judy behind their closed door. "Yes. Hullo. Are you two better?"

"No. We don't want to show our faces but we could both do with some tea and sandwiches. We haven't eaten anything for days."

"I'll see what I can rake up in the kitchen. Windy, eh?"

Donald did just that, leaving the ham and onion sandwiches and tea on a tray outside their door after knocking and shouting it was there for collection.

"Thank you. Have you been drinking? Was that you arriving on a motorbike? What a racket!"

"Yes."

"I thought so. We both look and feel dreadful. I'll open the door when you've gone."

The wind had returned by the time Donald found the Cohen's house next evening. He pressed the doorbell in a swirl of mango-tree leaves, at first mistaking the mezuzah on the doorframe for the bell push.

Ivan Cohen opened the door and Donald explained that he was a friend of Jean-Pierre's who suggested he should attend.

"Yes," said Cohen, "we were expecting you, but Jean-Pierre hasn't arrived yet. Come in, come in. Welcome," which he did while some mango leaves danced in ahead of him.

Ivan was a dark-haired, balding and late-middle-aged man with a slight paunch. "My, what a wind! Will it never end! It's been blowing for days."

A tuner was seated at the grand piano in the sitting room, holding an ear trumpet to the piano-frame each time he struck a note repeatedly. It seemed an awkward thing to do, and Donald said as such to his host a few moments later, after accepting a sherry.

"Yes, it must be difficult, but Mr. Goldblatt is going deaf, you see. Nevertheless, his skill is undiminished. He's always been our piano tuner so we wouldn't consider using anybody else. Besides, he used to tune the piano when Chou-Chou was alive and often played Debussy's 'The Snow Is Dancing' to her. It's a difficult piece.

"We called him in hurriedly this afternoon after this strange weather knocked the piano a bit out of tune. Grands are even more susceptible to humidity changes than uprights, especially in the upper ranges."

The man played a few chords that sounded rather like 'Three Blind Mice' then, satisfied, he wrapped the tuning fork and mute in a small cloth before popping them into his linen jacket.

"I see; a deaf piano tuner in a dying profession soon to be replaced by the wind-up gramophone?" Suddenly Donald wondered if he had been crass in using the word 'dying'.

"Dying? I think not. I can't bear listening to the nasal crackles and screeching masquerading as music emitted by those confounded gadgets, despite the fact that we have one which Chou-Chou insisted we got. She had a recording of Gertrude Lawrence singing 'Someone to Watch over Me' which she played too many times for my old-fashioned tastes." He paused and his face looked haunted.

"Besides, a piano tuner would have been employed back at the factory where those music-substitutes masquerade. It would be interesting to hear what an out-of-tune piano would sound like on a gramophone; the normal sound is so distorted it might be difficult to tell the difference.

"But for us, tonight is brought on by desperation. We are not spiritualists, we don't believe that the Angel of Mons was more than a successful propaganda story and we have never dabbled in this kind of thing before. You will understand that we need, desperately, to try to reach out to our son and daughter, if such things are possible, among a few friends who have suffered similar tragedies..

"Donald, you were on active service in German East Africa and the Congo, Jean-Pierre told me, and you will have witnessed so many deaths, and I believe that you also lost your brother at The Front. Jean-Pierre will be the only one tonight who has not experienced tragedy directly, although I believe a cousin of his lost his life from phosgene gas near Fleury, during Verdun. Our connection with him is through Joelle, who knows his family very well.

"What has given us a glimmering of hope is that it is said that even Arthur Conan Doyle communicated with lost loved ones after his son and so many close relatives died on active service. And then there's Sir Oliver Lodge who lost his son at Ypres, suggesting that such experimentation is similar to new work on radio waves."

"If only we had said and done all the things we would have wished to say and do when Chou-Chou and Adam were alive. Adam was our son."

"Yes, I was told."

"Joelle feels there is a chance. I am dubious."

Mrs. Joelle Cohen joined them. With a figure that provided only slight evidence of having born children, she remained an attractive 47. She was a Madagascan Frenchwoman who had already adopted the post-war fashion for cocktail wear of flattened breasts and dropped waists. Her hair was bobbed and she spoke charming colonial French–accented English.

Joelle's husband owned a musical instrument shop in town near the post office, which specialised in Blüthner pianos from Leipzig. Despite an intense dislike of anything German after the war, sales were beginning to recover. "A musical instrument has no country. It adopts the nationality of the person playing it," Ivan had remarked. "One cannot say the same thing about composers, however. Composers like Wagner, for instance. Strange, for a man born in the Jewish Quarter of Leipzig, to turn so anti-Jewish. His extreme nationalism made even his friend Nietzsche despair."

Ivan's narrow but deep store, with its high pressed-steel ceiling, was so cluttered with pianos and other musical instruments, including a harp, that it was difficult to pick a way to the counter at the back of the shop. Loitering customers from the Durban Symphony Society and sundry music teachers and pupils made access even more difficult.

"Mr. Goldblatt will be playing Debussy during the séance. As a pianist he was once considered a rising star."

Jeanne-Pierre arrived and immediately shook hands with the men and kissed Joelle.

Then more guests were let in through the windy front door, as if being admitted through an airlock, including two middle-aged music-teacher sisters, one plump, with a doughy appearance, the other bony with wire-framed spectacles, and an attractive young Jewish couple, the Cantors. It was the husband, a doctor, who insisted that everyone should don the masks he had brought, so the host and hostess fitted masks obligingly, as did everyone else.

Jean-Pierre muttered that the Cantors had lost a stillborn some months ago, while a 'late-lamb' sister of the music teachers, long-term customers of Cohen's shop, died by falling from a rusty old windpump tower that stood in their vast garden. She had liked to climb the structure to catch sight of the sea. Both women were dressed in black and smelt of mothballs.

The Drapers and the elderly Ferrers were next to be let through the airlock with their two grown-up sons, Alexander and Leo. Ferrer had a limp. Donald recognised him from his tram rides and the man's progress with uneven steps up West Street to the jewelry shop. He seemed to be wearing the same suit.

The Ackermans were the last to ring the doorbell,

accompanied by Mrs. Ackerman's father, Saul.

"My God," whispered Donald to Jean-Pierre, "do you realise that we are the only two gentiles here? Feel a bit out of it."

"We could be called the Mensheviks, the minority. I understand these are all friends who live on the Berea and attend the Reform Synagogue in Ridge Road where women participate fully in their ceremonies. That's all I know."

With snacks and sherry on offer, Donald watched with interest how guests managed to eat, drink and converse accompanied by a continuing brushing aside and replacing of face masks and a self-conscious turning away while biting or swallowing. Donald began to wonder whether the medium and spirits would be wearing masks too.

A cello stood on its stand near the grand piano in the sitting room, where the household's preoccupation with music was evidenced by shelves and shelves of sheet music and books on the works of the great and minor masters.

On a papered wall was a cluster of sepia line and wash drawings by Bill Beekes including portraits, Donald assumed, of Adam and Chou-Chou as children. Silver-framed photographs of ancestors clustered on an Adam table. Elsewhere in the room and beside a large Constable-like oil titled 'The Gathering Storm' in an ornate gilt frame was a watercolour sketch of 'Wreckers Coast Northumberland'. A menorah stood on a window ledge.

"I'm told that our medium is a woman who lives near Point Road, so don't be surprised to find her a little 'rough around the edges' but they say she is very good. Our driver has been sent to fetch her.

"You could almost say that we have a minyan here!" Cohen said, at which remark Jean Pierre and Donald looked blank. "Oh, that means a minimum gathering of ten Jewish adults thus able to celebrate various ceremonies. You must have ten – and because we follow Reform practices, we allow women to take part in them. That reform took place in the early 19th Century.

"Friends, before you move to the 'séance room' I have to ask you to remove your money and jewelry, and leave them in the basket with Hymie Ferrer, our jeweler friend, who I know will take good care of them until the session is over. You'll find envelopes labelled with your names."

In due course, the group moved through to a large old dining room where they took their seats around an extended stinkwood table smelling of furniture polish.

Donald found himself seated between the two music teachers.

A large candle was lit. Just before Cohen switched off the electric lights, Donald was startled to see that Luna was the medium. She had been ushered in through a door from the kitchen and winked unobtrusively when Donald caught her eye. Unlike her first appearance in Point Road, she wore a black dress that had seen better days. The doctor smiled and handed her a mask, completing the circle of ghoulish, masked figures.

She was introduced by Ivan as Luna de Villiers. "This is an experiment. We are all logical people, more or less, and that logic tells us that there cannot be an afterlife, but our hearts suggest differently, and some of us believe that all souls return at the End of Days. Tonight's experience could be seen as a prophesy or vision. This is the night we might or might not have to revise our ideas. But whatever the result may be, we all know that our love for those departed this life is eternal, so they will live on in our thoughts, no matter what our individual conclusions might be."

He whispered something to Joelle, who went through to the sitting room to ask the tuner to play, but softly, just so long as the séance continued, and then returned to her seat. Soon, the calm sounds of La Cathédrale Engloutie drifted in from the drawing room.

Luna asked all present to hold hands and concentrate their thoughts. Donald thought of his father. He wished so deeply that he had asked him about his upbringing and early life. Nothing much happened for some minutes although he was conscious of someone breathing heavily. It was Joelle.

Luna then incanted with a stridently Afrikaans accent, "We are calling on you to return for these people around the table who have lost you. Come to us now, you who have gone to the other place."

Suddenly she spoke with a surprisingly clear Colonial-English woman's voice: "What are you all doing in my dining room! This is my house!"

"Who are you?"

"I'm Agatha Goodricke of course. What do you want?"

"When did you die?"

"Aaah! An elephant crushed me against a fig tree when I was walking in the garden. So much pain. Blood everywhere. My body died."

"Are you buried close by?"

"My grave's in the garden behind the bougainvillea. So many elephants."

"Is this place called the Berea?"

"Berea? Don't be stupid. Everyone knows it's called Patahoogte. All those sweet-potatoes they grow.

The elephants steal them."

"What year is it?"

"It's 1850 of course. Everyone knows that."

"You must go back now. We want to talk to others."

The voice faded as she said, "Watch out for the lions!" and then Luna said, as if in a renewed trance and a remarkably different young child-girl's voice: "Maman! Papa! Where's my squeakee mouse? It's gone! Gone!" upon which, Joelle said "No my Chou-Chou; it's here, in your room."

"Keep it safe." the voice said.

"I will, I will," Joelle said and turned a radiant face to Ivan. "You see? You see?" she said.

Ivan could hardly speak; he was so overcome at hearing what seemed to be his dead daughter's voice of twenty years ago that he shouted suddenly: "Stop this! We must stop this before it is too late. Stop!"

Outside, the wind had gathered force again and a large branch, which must have been riddled with white ants, crashed to the ground outside the window as he turned on the lights.

"I am sorry," he said. "We are meddling with things that are not rightfully ours. I am sorry to bring you all this way. Permit me to say instead the Kaddish. We have enough adults here of the faith. We are all mourners and I know you will forgive my saying it in Yiddish. Turning to Toby and Donald, he said, "Please join in. You are welcome to say Amen when those among us who know the prayer do."

He began immediately after Luna had been led from the room.

"Yisgaddal v'yiskaddash sh'may rabboh. Be'olmoh deevroh chirussay, V'yamlich malchussay, Be'chah-yaychon

299

*uv'yo-meychon Uv'cha-yay de-chol bays yisro-ayl, Ba-agoloh
uvizman koriv, Ve'imru omeyn."*

On reaching the word 'Omeyn' Joelle caught the eyes of
Donald and Jean-Pierre and said loudly 'Amen' and Donald
impulsively squeezed the hands of the sisters.

*"Ye'hey sh'mey rabboh m'vorach Le'olam ul'olmey olmah-
yoh Yisborach, ve'yishtabach, Ve'yispo- ar ve'yisromam,
Ve'yisnassay ve'yis-haddar Ve'yis-alleh ve'yis-haIlol, Sh'mey
de-kudshoh, b'rich hu Le'ayloh min kol birchosoh v'shirosoh
Tush'bechosoh v'nechemosoh, Daa-amiron be'olmoh V'imru
omeyn."*

Another 'Amen' and another squeeze. And so the prayer
continued. The young couple who had lost their stillborn
child remained speechless, overwhelmed by sadness and
tears.

*"O-seh sholom bimromov Hu ya-aseh sholom Oleynu
ve'al kol yisro-eyl V'imru omeyn."*

After the last 'Amen' a great silence descended on the
room until Ivan said, "Friends, I am very sorry that I had to
stop the experiment. Forgive me. I ask you to stay on and
listen awhile to our pianist. Hans has exceptional talent –
something that you, my two teacher friends, will I know
recognise. Excuse me for a moment while I settle up with
the medium lady and arrange for Joseph to drive her home."

He whispered hurriedly to Joelle, "We must see to it
that she takes some food too. I heard that she has a young
child and that they have very little money. I know, I know!

But we must give charity. Can you spare one of Chou-Chou's little clothes too?"

The evening dribbled away with the teachers saying that they had to leave early enough to get a good night's rest and the young couple making their excuses to leave early in preparation for the husband's hectic medical practice the next day, eventually leaving only Donald and Jean-Pierre to accept substantial glasses of whisky from their host, with a distressed Joelle retiring upstairs.

"Well. I am sorry. That did not go well and – oh goodness! Hans!" whereupon he went over to the pianist who was still sitting at the piano, not knowing quite what to do.

"Was it my playing that frightened them away?" Hans asked, rising from his seat.

"Ach no, no!" Ivan said, drawing him into the room with the others. "Come, please," he said in a raised voice. "Your playing was magnificent. As usual. It was I who stopped the séance caused by my sadness. Please come. Please. Perhaps you can play something to cheer us up? We are all very sad indeed."

Hans sat down again and launched into Chopin's Fantaisie-Impromptu in C Sharp Minor ending the piece by sliding into its popular adaption, 'I'm always chasing rainbows'.

Ivan clapped and shouted "Encore! Encore!" to which Hans responded with, 'The moon shines on the moonshine," and, "You ain't heard nothin yet" in rapid succession; after which he said "I must now go home or I'll miss the last tram." He replaced the felt (embroidered in gold script on green with 'Ivan Cohen & Co. Limited) on the keys, shut the keyboard with a clunk, bowed to the three men and wished them a good night. Ivan got up from his seat and showed him to the door, thanking him gratefully.

A flurry of mango leaves swirled into the hall when he held the door open for the departing pianist.

After he had gone Cohen said, "One for the road. Joelle has gone to bed, so we can drink whisky until the cows come home – or should I say the elephants. Yes?"

"Yes, thank you," said Jean-Pierre. Turning to Donald Jean-Pierre said, "How's the bike?" to which the latter replied "A bit like the curate's egg – good in parts, but I'm afraid that it might not get me home. It keeps on cutting out and I had quite a struggle to get here."

"Then leave the bike here, with Ivan's permission, and I'll give you a lift back to The Barbican."

Driving home, Jean-Pierre said: "Curious to think that less than 150 years ago the Berea was not the place to linger because of the elephants, buffalo, lion and leopard. Now we have sherry and séances where elephants used to roam. That was a very strange evening, wasn't it? If it were not so sad, I would have found the sight of a group of masked people sitting in candlelight around a table and holding hands very funny indeed. We looked like a secret society preparing for some strange operation. All that was needed was a patient lying on the table – perhaps a Red Indian."

They glanced at each other and burst into guffaws of laughter, which lasted until the car pulled up at The Barbican.

The day dawned bright and Donald went back to his routine of catching the Musgrave Road tram into town after calling Percy Cole, his manager, to find out if the bank was to open.

Although the doors would not be opening for the public, he learnt, Cole asked that he should come in and catch up on Securities.

"I'm worried about one of our accounts, the Umbilo Iron & Steel Works. Something's wrong. We'll discuss it when you come in."

The white driver and conductor were both wearing flu masks on the almost-empty tram.

Advertising banners on the external panels proclaimed that 'Bovril Prevents That Sinking Feeling', illustrated by a fair-haired and rosy-cheeked man in green and white striped pajamas astride a large Bovril bottle floating on a rough sea.

He spotted Prue, the librarian, sans mask this time, and said "May I sit beside you?"

"Of course!" she said, moving several books out of the way.

A group of uniformed schoolchildren boarded at the next stop, thumping up the narrow winding stair in the race to get to the front row; the tram suddenly becoming full of chatter. Many of the children wore flu-masks. The schoolgirls acquired a hint of Bedouin modesty but the sight of boys wearing masks while sporting straw bashers hinted at the macabre.

Some natives and Indians, likewise masked, were allowed to sit upstairs at the back.

In the main, the return of the Spanish Flu in its most lethal form during 1919 passed over those under eighteen and the elderly, attacking men and women – predominantly men – aged between about 19 and 45, explaining why most children were only half aware of the ghastly pandemic which was threatening their parents; although a few children had already lost a father or mother.

The conductor sold Donald a ninepenny ticket 'single' from a selection of fares in a wooden holder held to his waist by a leather strap.

"What are you reading?" Donald asked, knowing full well what the answer would be. Prue said, "The Thirty-Nine Steps by someone called John Buchan. It's a l-load of old rubbish but – frankly – it's quite exciting. Full-full of German spies disguised as English gentlemen and p-planning to bring down the Empire."

Her slight stammer was more pronounced that day. "I've heard about it, but it all seemed a bit far-fetched."

"I have a copy discarded by the Library because it was d-damaged by too many readers. Would you like to have it?"

"Yes, thank you. Why not?"

"Look, because of the obligations of l-librarianship I am required to attend a lecture at the Tech on what could be a dreary afternoon on the Saturday weekend-after-next concerning the formation of the L-League of Nations, and I could do with a spot of company to keep me awake.. Apparently our Prime Minister General Smuts has been charged with drafting much of the Constitution. Care to come along and protect me from the town's vagrants?" – at which point she turned her beautiful blue eyes upon Donald and he heard himself saying, "Yes. I would like to hear about such ideas, just as long as I can hold your hand if the lecture gets too boring."

"You may if you ask me in Esperanto!" (There was a move afoot for the League to adopt Esperanto as its official international language. Only the French were opposing the idea.)

Prue knew that they were playing to a well-rehearsed script, but another part of her mind was saying: "Could this be the one? Am I destined to spend the rest of my life with this man? Is my stammer so off-putting? What are the clues I should be sensing? Why am I blushing and oh, God, why must this birthmark flare up to give away the attraction I am feeling? And what is he thinking about my stammer? Damaged goods?

"It's all about a chase in Scotland where the h-hero turns-turns into the h-hunted man," she said, "after a murder in the hero's London flat by mysterious spies. I tell you what, I'll-I'll bring along an 'expired' copy of the book when we meet at the lecture."

"That's very kind of you, and I look forward to seeing you. Would you like me to give you a lift? I'm about to buy a Tin Lizzie and I'll have to test it out for a few days before I rail it to Zululand. In fact, it's a good opportunity to show off," he said, with disarming candour.

"That sounds exciting," she said. "I'd better give you my address and phone number so that you can call ahead and know where to pick me up. I still live with my p-parents, the Jardines, in Nimmo Road. Daddy is the H-harbour Master. Would you like to write down m-my telephone number?"

The ride to town was always interesting as each stop would introduce new characters. Some of those who boarded were overweight and carried too many parcels; others would bury themselves in a book and leave their belongings on the seat beside them indicating that new passengers were less than welcome to sit there. Then there was the clattering down the narrow winding stairs by a top-floor load of schoolchildren as they reached their school stop. The men who boarded were usually alone and slotted into two classes – hatted businessmen in sub-tropical suits and ties and, less often, workmen in dungarees who usually boarded the tram at Greyville. The married ones had lunch tins. "Why are most lunch-tins curved at the top?" he wondered. One of the suited passengers limped and always boarded the tram carrying two small black cases. Donald recognised him from the séance.

Between stops, Donald asked: "What does a librarian do all day? Just date-stamp outgoing books and file returned books in the shelves?"

"That's rather disparaging. Stamping and tracking books are the least important things we do. I'm the development l-librarian so have to s-specify and monitor what books are acceptable from publishers and h-have a reasonable budget for this. Much of my time is spent in correspondence.

"We teach literacy skills and I operate an outreach programme to satellite libraries in deprived areas. My responsibility is to p-plant the s-seed of enquiry in children's minds – any child's mind, despite discouragement from the state when it comes to natives and Indians ... helping them to have fun while 'finding out things' in addition to just reading for pleasure. The library used to be called the Durban Mechanics Institution, by the way, and was established for the betterment of its members."

"I was jesting and provoking you. I apologise and I do realise that librarianship is an admirable profession."

"That's all right," she said, turning to look out of the window. Donald noticed her nose was sweetly retroussé and her cheeks had flushed.

When they reached town, Donald said, "Well, I'm off to George Chapard's 'Tin Lizzie Emporium' before going to the bank. Shall we part at the corner?" – to which Prue nodded her head, rather too full of her own thoughts to answer with a spoken "Yes."

Her shortish pale blue dress sported a bow on the left hip, he noticed. The notional waist was down below her tummy. Her breasts still established their presence satisfactorily despite efforts to appear flat-chested, a la mode.

"Well, here we must part – you to the library, me up West Street. If I don't see you on the tram again soon (although I hope I do), I'll most certainly telephone you to arrange to meet up for the League of Nations lecture. I hope you get more children in today."

Donald watched her with growing fondness as she walked away to the Children's Library in the City Hall before setting out for George Chapard's showroom. The limping man was ahead of him, still shuffling along with his black cases, before halting and resting them close to his feet at 'Benjamin Caney, Jewellers' to fumble with several keys before letting himself in.

Questions trailed each other through his mind about how on earth the daughter of the harbour master could become entangled with an intelligence service and knowing that it was unlikely that any answers would be forthcoming.

His thoughts were brought up short by the most awful smells of ammonia sulfite emerging from 'Coiffeur', the ladies hair salon which prided itself in 'providing the very best in permanent waves to ladies of fashion'.

Even at this early hour, two women wearing flu masks were seated in special 'dentist chairs' beneath metal racks from which dangling wires were attached to curlers in their hair.

The pavement was divided by a blue line interrupted by alternating slogans of 'Keep Left', 'Links Aanhouden'. Don't Spit', 'Spit Niet!' – the admonishments about spitting reflecting an effort to curb Indians, in particular, from spitting on pavements after chewing betel nut. The sputum stained the pavement with red blobs. It was known that spitting aided the spread of colds, flu, meningitis, polio and tuberculosis, but the habit was commonplace by many workers of all population groups in Durban, exacerbated by boozing, inhaling snuff and chewing tobacco.

Donald mused that if saliva was so suspect why kissing was not discouraged, and whether most Indian and native pedestrians could read English and Dutch.

A slowly revolving wine-red Model T dominated the window of Chapard's showroom, with more conservatively coloured vehicles lurking at the back of the display area. Placards read 'Proudly Ford Canada'.

Chapard was the only one in the shop.

"Yes, I know Ford said 'you can have any colour as long as it's black' but this is not absolutely true. You may have any colour you like provided you pay the extra price to have it resprayed. I did for this one to attract attention as I have a long furrow to plough. My goal is to tour Natal, opening agencies."

"I hope the development of the roads will catch up with your objectives. They have a long way to go," Donald said. "I'm puzzled to see that the car was made in Canada. I thought Henry Ford was American?"

"Canada and South Africa share 'British Dominion' rates for anything traded in these and other such countries. An American Ford would have been far more expensive –

that's why a Ford factory was opened in Canada to exploit the opportunity.

"My friend Jean-Pierre phoned to tell me that you were coming in this morning and asked me to pay particular attention to your purchase. This I welcome as I welcome you. I understand you are going to live in wildest Zululand and that the Model T is the only car which can withstand its punishment?"

"In the long run, yes, but first of all I need to understand how it works and how it performs in the wilds of Durban, before I make up my mind. Have you a demonstration model I may use for a few days?"

"Of course! This red one is our demonstration model. All you need to do is fill up with petrol before you return it and to leave me with a deposit of ten percent of the price of the car to cover insurance. I won't cash the cheque unless you prang it. Okay?"

A composite photograph of three men with their right elbows in plaster hung on the wall behind Chapard's desk "That's a rather unusual picture you have there. How come?"

"They are three prominent members of the DFFC – the exclusive Durban Ford Fracture Club. I put it on the wall as a salutary warning to all Tin Lizzie drivers. If the levers that control the engine are not set the right way the engine can backfire when hand-cranked and break your arm. The best way to avoid that is to pay the extra price of getting an electric starter fitted. You don't have to worry about that now, as the demonstration model has been fitted with one."

"And where was that other photograph taken. Of your family?"

"Ah yes. It was taken in a small town, Milly-la-Forêt in

the Essone region in front of my father's workshop. That's where I come from. You can see the sign over the big door behind my mother and little sisters and small brother. My father was a forgeron (how you say in English?) like his father and his father before him.

He always smelt of peppermint. How I arrived here in the subtropics via Madagascar to follow my father's trade could make a story of adventure – but we will save that for another time."

"I think the English for forgeron is blacksmith," Donald said.

"Yes, yes. Blacksmith! It was my intention to follow in my father's footsteps in Natal, but I found that I could improve my income by selling and repairing bicycles and so, bit by bit, I became a mechanic as well. Now the demand for the motor car is forever increasing so I fell in to the idea to be the first to sell and repair motor cars. Now I train my two young assistants (one of them an Indian, very good at his work) to become mechanics in this new field so that we can assemble the cars I am beginning to import from Canada. Today, however, my two men are very sick with the flu. It is fortunate that I have already had the sickness and recovered.

"If you wish to drive the car today you must have a driver's licence which I am authorised to issue to you. Let us complete the form together. The cost is five shillings. I will send the duplicate into the municipal offices when it opens again."

After an extended lesson, during which Chapard demonstrated the use of the three peddles on the floor ("beware the middle pedal; it's the devil! It puts the car into reverse! It can be dangerous if you are travelling forward") and the setting of the levers near the steering wheel, Donald drove the motor out of the showroom, very gingerly indeed into the side lane, with a shrill whining of the engine and gears, with Chapard's last words, "Keep to the left on all roads!", ringing in his ears.

He avoided a steam-powered truck and the rickshaws, many of which still cluttered the street despite the pandemic and drove cautiously up West Street and Marriott Road, turning such heads as there were along the way, with the car's whining progress and the odd sight for Durbanites of a wine red Model T.

Bernard Cole, Donald's bank manager, was small, nervous and smoked endless cigarettes, so that his ragged grey moustache was stained in the centre with brown tobacco tar. He occupied a dark brown wood and glass-panelled office out of proportion to his physical stature, and sat on a chair that had to be padded with an extra cushion made by his wife so that he could reach the pens, ink wells and telephones on his large desk. The fan suspended from the ceiling wobbled in its flight and Donald always avoided standing beneath it lest it chose that moment to come adrift.

"Hello. How was your Zululand trip?"

"As far as the future farm is concerned all went well, but the impact of the Spanish flu was fairly horrific. By the way, I see you have abandoned the idea of wearing a flu mask."

"Well, I am alone most of the time. Yes, the same could be said of Durban. Half the staff is down with this awful disease and three of our best (other than you) are dead. Two were the best comptometer operators we had – you will remember Basil Spencer and John Frost? Ghastly business. They just collapsed at work within days of each other, then the teller Bailey fell ill on the tram going home and never came back to work. In these circumstances can you delay your departure? I really do need some strong hands at the helm to weather the storm. I remember your saying that you had the Spanish last year, which suggests that you are immune?"

"That is correct and yes, of course I will stay on for a bit," said Donald, thinking that this was equally convenient for him in the light of his having to attend the League of Nations lecture on the following Saturday. There was also the matter of entertaining Emily which preoccupied his thoughts.

"Excellent! Then let's set a date for some time after this plague has burnt itself out."

"Well, with reservations, as I must get to the farm pretty soon to prepare the ground for planting or face financial hardship – ten days at the outside. There's lots to be done. Have the funerals taken place of our three staff?"

"They are today at St Thomas' graveyard. Can you go in my place? The service will be a combined one at the gravesides and very short. There's no time for a memorial service. The bank will obviously pay for the taxi and any other expenses."

"As a matter of fact, you will have to go. I have supped full of horrors and I cannot take in any more. The war, then this."

Donald related his Spanish flu experiences in Zululand and the witnessing of the shark attack to explain his refusal.

"I'll mind the fort here and ward off all intruders. How on earth are clients coping if they are unable to draw cash?"

Looking resigned, Cole said: "Most will have shop accounts and our customers all have cheque books, as you know, and – if anyone phones – for those who do not have overdraft facilities or whose credit is up to the limit the bank will consider extending credit to a maximum of another twenty-five pounds for a calendar month. Those food shops that have managed to stay open have been informed of this extension. As for the rest of regular trading ... it's a mess and that's no doubt. Even the cheque exchanges with the other two banks have been interrupted; but we will muddle through.

"There is the usual gallery of doubtful accounts which have developed well before the flu outbreak which I must ask you to look at (the files are on my desk), but there is one account of which I am most concerned because of the amounts involved – Umbilo Iron & Steel Works. I'm particularly worried about the new extreme variables in production, sales and turnover of the plant which has recently taken on a new manager. The ratios are all wrong.

"There's an unacceptable risk that budgets will not be met and something rather peculiar is going on; so as you are currently assistant to the Accountant (who's off sick), I would appreciate your bending your mind first to that problem and letting me have your conclusions. We will need a cash-flow report and a revised credit risk assessment.

"To say that we are on a skeleton staff has a macabre ring to it nowadays, but that is the truth of the matter."

"I bumped into Logan of Logan's Import & Export," said Donald. "He seems rather keen to get his hands on as much as possible of the cotton exports. He also mentioned that you two had had a conversation about me and my future Zululand prospects."

"That's true – but only in passing. Nothing like putting in a good word, is there? Look, I must dash if I'm going to get to that funeral," he said, as he reached for his hat off the stand. "Dreading it."

Donald had barely sat at his desk when Cole's plump secretary, Miss MacVicar, brought him a telegram. "It's for you," she said. The other girls called her 'Fatknickers' behind her back. She had a particular liking for mauve and every dress she wore was a variation on the same theme: dark mauve, pale mauve or just plain mauve. The status acquired by being Cole's secretary she exploited to the full. She was one of those women who linked batches of information with "and er", thus buttonholing the listener with little hope of escape.

He was galvanised by the message and glanced at the office clock when he read:

"ARRIVING DURBAN 6PM TUESDAY PLEASE MEET HOTELS CLOSED DEPARTING UNIONCASTLE THURSDAY EMILY"

– thinking of the things he would have to do in the time left, over and above his banking duties, not least reviewing in some detail the monthly profit and loss accounts read against the annual statements over the last three years of Umbilo Iron & Steel, with his thoughts wandering to the prospect and excitement of Emily's arrival.

He wondered – if the occasion arose of course – how to explain his absence from The Barbican to Judy.

He disliked deception but realised that that was precisely where he was heading.

Emily's train arrived more than an hour and a half late. In the gloaming, it was a ghostly sight to glimpse the engine driver and the stoker wearing flu masks, as were some of the passengers.

He saw her golden hair when she waved out of the compartment window. "Hello. Can you help me with this case?" she said. "It's bloody heavy."

When he made to embrace her on the platform she said, "Not now. We are being watched by that awful Anna woman. Vague acquaintance of my mother's. Shake hands for now."

After the luggage had been assembled and she had waved goodbye to the other stragglers, Emily said: "I told her that I was expecting my mythical university girlfriend's brother to pick me up at the station. I'm relieved to see that you aren't wearing one of those face mask things. The train was very empty and stopped at every tuft of grass on the way down. Sorry it's so late. What's the plan? Found somewhere for me to stay?"

"Yes. The Barbican, where I live on the Berea, is full – and putting you up there in any case would be a bit indiscreet as some of the juniors from the bank also stay there and two of the girls are down with the flu. No need to set tongues wagging; but a good friend of mine (we go sailing together) has an office-cum-flat overlooking the Bay. It's an easy walk to the reference library and the tram terminus. He keeps it for visitors and also stores samples there in a separate office-room for his trading business with Madagascar. It has a bathroom and a stock of food. Does that suit you? But let me fetch that porter's trolley over there first – they're all off sick – or worse, so I'll be the stand-in."

315

Donald was thinking to himself how reserved he was sounding and was wondering what was going through Emily's mind. She was wearing a beige knee-length dress, loosely gathered on the hips, low-heeled school-girlish shoes, and her left wrist sported a hand-carved bangle.

Seeing Donald looking at it she said, "Masheila gave it to me as a parting gift... I hope you didn't think it was a bit of a cheek asking you to find a place for me, but I so wanted to see you again and talk. Zeno's death has made Sonya retreat into a shell and her parents are now very distant. Sometimes I think Sonya blames me entirely for how he lost his life. After all it was I who encouraged everyone into the water. Good God! A red Tin Lizzie! Is that yours?"

A sleepy seagull was on the railing and flew away when they arrived at the Cavendish Chambers suite, which incorporated its own private balcony, at the end of the third floor.

"I'd almost forgotten what it was like being in a port city again with ships and shops and things. Not like Cape Town. The ships are so far away there, but here we're right in the thick of things. What a wonderful view of the harbour, and I like the telescope in the window. I'd become so used to the farm during vacs and so wrapped up in this bloody epidemic (she liked using that word), Indian and native families dying and a farmer-neighbour's wife, Mrs. Hennessey, too. It makes me feel endlessly wretched – on top of what happened to Zeno." She shivered, and said, "I'm famished."

"I think it's time we explored the larder," said Donald. "We'll talk more about that just now. It's going to be tinned stuff, I am afraid – except for rice, porridge and sugar. No milk deliveries so we'll have to make do with Klim. I would have asked you out to dinner, but nothing is open except for the cafe-de-moveon at the station, and I thought we could do better than its fried eggs and bananas by rustling up something here. Besides there's some wine and it's been kept cold in the icebox. All we need now is a candle, matches, knives, forks, two glasses and a corkscrew. Let's scratch around in the cupboards."

He turned from poking about on the shelves to find her close behind him, leading to their first unguarded long kiss and embrace, broken in time by her saying quietly, "Later."

"I'm only good at 'bush-grub' learnt up in East Africa. How are your cooking skills?"

"Pretty basic. Ntombi and Joseph do all the cooking on the farm although I did a lot of watching them as a child, followed by boarding school where they fed us on lumpy porridge and smelly cabbage. I only learnt to toast school-muffins there in front of the common room fire. Varsity hasn't exactly furthered my culinary skills either. Frying eggs and bacon would reach the perimeter of my ability but I'll have a bash, if you help me. There are tins of Fray Bentos steak & kidney pies in the cupboard, along with tinned peas and baked beans. Oh, and rice in a jar, up there on that shelf. I tell you what, you set the table. We can drag it over to the window. The twinkling lights and a glass of wine will distract you from judging what you're eating. You can open the wine if you can rumble around for the corkscrew, and set the water to boil for the rice. Remember to salt the water."

Emily kicked off her shoes and turned to watch Donald lighting candles on the table. "When are you leaving for Zululand?"

"The bank has asked me to stick around for the next ten days to help it cope. Officially, it's closed, but a few of us (those that are left and not prostrated by the flu or worse, dead) are working behind closed doors. The manager had to attend a combined funeral of three of our men today. He wanted me to go as the bank's representative but I managed to get out of it. I've supped full enough of horrors for the time being."

"And your friend, Toby. Has he gone back to Tam yet?"

"Not sure; we haven't been in touch recently. I have been caught up with events."

"My parents heard about your efforts – both yours and Toby's – at Ntambanana and Empangeni. Went down rather well."

"Well, burying flu corpses in a remote part of the farm and coping with distressed families must have been equally traumatic, for you, your father and Noel – and your helpers."

"Yes, it was. We could only see by the car headlights and then the battery went phut. Luckily there was a half moon, but groping our way back to the house was not much fun. I fell into a donga after scratching myself against a wag-'n-bietjie [thorn bush]. Look, you can see the scratches all down my arm and leg," she said, lifting a side of her skirt.

"The Indians were horrified when we would not allow them to burn the corpses of their loved-ones. I bet they dug them up again and burnt them when Daddy and Noel were out of sight. Bloody awful smell. (There was that word again.)

"Fortunately there were no natives to bury as they would have been equally upset with us, but we heard that there have been more deaths from Spanish Flu among the natives at the nearest kraal.

"Locally, the Zulu custom is for the dead to be drawn through a hole made in the hut wall and not the door. The hole is then sealed up again so that the spirit can't find its way back inside; and the burial is done in the early morning when the wizards are not about to snatch the body for evil purposes. If they go through the whole rigmarole it will be cause for more contagion.

"The Indians had to be buried so quickly to reduce the risk of infection that even some of the families of the deceased couldn't be present.

"Daddy will have to apply all his diplomatic skills to ease feelings in the weeks to come, supplemented, perhaps, by giving an abundance of food to the poorest. Daddy talked about offering an ox for slaughter to the Zulus, bearing in mind that beasts are still dying like flies from nagana so precious beasts will be hard to come by.

"Zulus dislike the dark and I predict that there will be much rumouring about ghosts in the months to come."

Conversation during the meal, washed down by wine, centred on the shark attack and Zeno.

"His death was so final and yet Sonya keeps on believing that his spirit is still there in their house. She talks about pictures falling off the walls and the slippers he loved, still under his bed, moved overnight to new positions. I hope she isn't having some sort of breakdown."

"It comes with grief. It takes time to believe that someone you were so close to has been snuffed out in a moment."

Donald described the background leading to the séance held in the Cohen house. "It was creepy ... everyone clutching hands and wearing face masks. Very sad too."

Emily giggled at the absurdity, despite the sadness, and Donald warmed to it. Her mirth was genuine and her laughter musical. "You can always tell a girl by her laughter," his father once said. "Can't stand girls who giggle when there is nothing to laugh about. They make giggle-sounds to each other like some tribal thing that excludes men."

Their conversation turned to Donald's plans for the new farm. He told her about having to shoot a green mamba in the Empangeni signal box which made her laugh again when he described the signalman's agitation, but said that while he was used to bush-bashing, life on a new farm might get somewhat lonely.

When he asked about Emily's intentions after graduation, she stretched out her feet and touched his and said what Donald had hoped against hope she would say: "This flat is very pleasant but I don't want to stay here alone. It could be creepy as there isn't another soul for miles, as far as I can see. Can you stay? There are two beds and I don't snore."

"Yes, I can but I will just have to slip down to the car to pick up a spare shirt I managed to buy today from an Indian shop, which miraculously, was open – the only one. I have to be at the bank looking spic and span at 8.30 tomorrow."

"That's a relief. I had visions of your bowing me a goodnight and vamoosing to the Barbican. I see there are dressing gowns behind the bathroom door, so I'm going to have a bath and wash off the smell of the train while you're out."

"Bear in mind that after I leave for work in the morning you're likely to stumble over a few lawyers and their staff in the corridor, those who are not down with the flu, as most of the chambers in this building are legal practices. I don't know how many will be about though, in the circumstances."

When he returned she was still in the bath, judging by the swirling noises, so Donald washed up as best he could with a scrap of soap he found, and moved to the balcony to gaze out at the bay at night.

The port light of a police launch far across the bay moved steadily northwards to the main docks. Stevedoring was going on, with night-time loading at some vessels accompanied by distant shouts, thumps and the whine of cranes coming across the water.

Wrapped in a white dressing gown, she joined him on the balcony in bare feet, holding two glasses of wine. "This could be our Balcony Scene," said Emily.

"Well, I hope we're not star-cross'd," Donald replied, smiling

"We're unlikely to be thwarted by a malign star, but those who are star-cross'd wouldn't be the ones to foresee that, would they," she said. "Do you have any malign characters lurking in the undergrowth?"

He said nothing for a while but took a sip of wine. "Well?"

He was aching to tell her about the encounter with Creighton and its consequences but said: "None that spring to mind, but there can always be a snake in the signal box to set the best schemes agley."

"Hmmm. My younger brother Nigel might prove bothersome though, but not malign," she said. "You haven't met him yet, but he used to follow me around like a puppydog when he was younger and he is still very possessive about his big sister."

Donald smiled, thinking of von Weldenburg and du

Quesne and the malign forces at work from a defeated Germany.

They barely noticed that they were drawn to one of the beds.

"I'm glad we didn't turn on the lights," said Emily as Donald slipped off her gown in the near-dark and got out of his clothes. Her shoulders were beautiful, he thought.

Small beads of sweat formed where their bodies touched.

She said: "While I may have seemed fast when we first met, I am not the liberated 'Twenties' girl you might think me to be. You're the first. There are two girls at 'varsity in Cape Town who are notorious for rolling in the hay, but I'm not one of them."

"I didn't think you were."

"Living on a farm, one can hardly avoid being educated into the practicalities of conception, birth and death, so I have to ask – are you equipped to prevent my falling pregnant? Sorry it sounds so archaic, but I have no wish to do my Masters in a flurry of babies' nappies."

Donald started awake in the small hours to find a naked Emily curled up against him. The blanket had slipped off and her body was faintly luminous in the dark.

Their love-making had seemed other-worldly, with Emily experiencing his gentle hands encouraging a growing excitement. At one point she was astride him, leaning slightly forward and rubbing her lower body against his. Donald remembered her shouting: "Better than horse-riding!" – then crying out and bursting into tears, before their rolling over, so that Donald was above her again. She went to sleep while the warmth within her hips began to wane pleasantly.

"Are you awake?"

"Sort of."

"Will you marry me?"

"Just let me go to sleep again now. I'll think about it," upon which Donald drew her body close to his and pulled the sheet and blanket over them.

"How much lobola will you pay my father?" she asked sleepily.

"Ten Nguni cows."

"Only ten?"

"Isn't that the usual bride price?"

"Oh. So I am just the usual," she murmured, falling asleep again.

It was the iceman who woke them in the early morning, with the sound of the flap being opened and a new block of ice sliding into place.

Donald raised himself on a straightened arm and looked out at the bay.

From the top of the window frame a speck descended on a gossamer thread, halting before touching the window ledge then clambering up again and across to continue weaving its web. He remembered being tucked up in bed as a child and how his father told him about Robert the Bruce who, despite the fact that he was a Campbell and not a McGregor, sheltered in a cave and being moved by a small spider's determination to spin a web against all odds, inspired him to rouse his men to drive the English out of his beloved Scotland.

At the yacht club three Indian fishermen were letting their rowing boat down the slipway in the misty half-light, a clutch of fishing rods protruding from the prow and a bundle of netting and other tackle in the stern. The heavy winds of the past days had disappeared, and the water was as still as a millpond. He distinctly heard the plop of a large fish.

Two steam tugs, dwarfed by their charge, were manoeuvering a merchantman out into the channel, their power displayed by churning wakes and the ease with which they could move a large ship. A small brown launch was already moving into position so as to retrieve the pilot after the merchantman was safely over the bar and released in the marine roadstead.

"Were you serious about marriage – or just 'flip'?"

"I am entirely serious" Donald said.

"Look, you must know a lot of girls – and have known many in the biblical sense as well. I can tell. Why me?"

"Just because, from the very first time I saw you I knew that you were the one. You are intelligent, educated and very attractive indeed. Not only that, I like your family very much. Your father is a courageous gentleman (I heard about his bravery in rescuing people during the Umfolozi floods at great risk to himself) and your mother has the sense of humour which could launch ships. There's always a twinkle in her eye – that is, when I'm not watching the length of ash at the end of her cigarettes. Over and above that, you have a good knowledge of the Zulus and the Indians and understand the challenges that come from farming in Zululand. And it looks as if you would like children of your own, judging by the way you got on with Noel and Lucy's children at tennis."

"Don't know. Too quick. Have to think about it in Cape Town. We have one big flaw as a family. We're colonial snobs.

Look down our noses at the Boers. Just instinctively. Don't mean to, but we do. Socially, we don't mix with them (except a few). Don't speak 'Die Taal'. Past still with us. Big schism. Takes a long time to change. Same applies to our attitude and ability to communicate with Indians and Zulus. We try hard but they could be creatures from another planet. Difficult to read their minds. I often wonder where the hell it's going to land up. And I know practically nothing about you and your family and that massive scar along your chest I first saw at Richard's Bay, just before Zeno was attacked."

"The scar is from a Schutztruppe bullet that got away."

"And that scar on your leg, and your slight limp?"

"That was from a bullet provided by another Askari which I managed to stop, so it made more of a mess – but as for the rest, here goes."

He told her about the farm 'Ansiud Tog' in Scotland. "That's a strange name. What does it mean?" Emily asked. "It simply means 'Yonder Farm', in Scots Gaelic."

"Perhaps you should call your new Zululand farm 'Yonder Farm', or perhaps just plain 'Yonder' – it is, after all, very, very yonder."

"Is there a Zulu word for 'Yonder'?"

"Yes – Lapho."

"And farm?"

"Ipulazi"

"What about "Lapho Ipulazi?"

"Bit of a mouthful. Prefer Lapho by itself."

"I like 'Yonder' most of all. Shall we choose that?"

"We? Well, go on."

He said that his mother had died when he was eight years old and that his father had remarried, and described how they had moved to Kew near London, while retaining the farm; how he was sent to Dulwich College; of his being several years junior to Ernest Shackleton; how his uncle had done well in London banking circles leading to Donald being shoehorned into the Capital & Counties Bank at London's 39 Threadneedle Street; of a disastrous love affair with a girl at the bank and his resigning and joining the London branch of the Natal Bank whereupon an opportunity arose for him to transfer to its head office in Durban. It was in February 1914 when he sailed for Natal.

While the German Kaiser's idiotic toy-soldier antics were viewed with dismay at that time, there was no inkling that Ferdinand was going to be assassinated in July or that the Kaiser would declare war on Serbia. The British press was far more concerned with the possibility of Ulster counties joining Home Rule in Dublin, nine life-boat men drowning off the County Wexford coast, and a suffragette slashing a painting of Venus in the National Gallery with a meat cleaver. War with Germany was unthinkable. The British Fleet was visiting Kiel Bay at that time, after all, and Queen Victoria's eldest grandchild, the Kaiser, in the role of an honorary Admiral of the Royal Navy, had inspected a British dreadnought.

Nevertheless, after Duke Ferdinand's assassination in Bosnia, news of mounting unrest in Europe had reached Durban, he said, and news of the arrival in Dar-es-Salaam of a distinguished German soldier, Lieutenant-Colonel Paul Emil von Lettow-Vorbeck, charged to command the Schutztruppe in German East Africa, had not gone unnoticed in British colonial circles. To the astute, it suggested that Germany was 'making ready'. He was the man, after all, who had ruthlessly suppressed the Namaqwa and Herero uprising in German South West Africa in 1904 on the instructions of 'Kaiser Bill'; although he took no part in von Trotta's subsequent genocide of both tribes.

Although 'the lamps were going out all over Europe', there was little inclination among the East African whites – German or British – to become embroiled in what was seen as a remote European imbroglio, even after Britain declared war on Germany early in August.

Most of the Dark Continent's natives remained either blissfully unaware or completely unconcerned at this danger to whites which had started so far away.

The Great Powers had formerly accepted that distant and undeveloped African colonies and protectorates would play no important part in any future war, and were seen as mere temporary land-grabs to serve as negotiation-pawns in some inevitable future peace settlement.

"I don't need to tell you that during 1914 one very seldom heard Dutch, or its little sister Afrikaans being spoken in Durban and the bulk of the local white population was instinctively pro-Empire and pro-British. Most of the Boers had left this part of Natal long ago.

"I remember someone asking me for directions in what I later found out to be Dutch-Afrikaans. He could have been speaking Serbo-Croat. I had never heard it before, although I did try to answer him in the smattering of German I had learnt in Hamburg, leaving both of us baffled by incomprehension.

"So, despite the fact that the bulk of the population is not white, you already know that most political power and opinion in Natal was in the hands of the English-speaking minority, and still is – not forgetting the support of the Asiatics, who still looked to Britain for their safety – with very few speaking Dutch-Afrikaans. Of course, in places like Vryheid the picture was different, which is still strongly pro-German Afrikaans; but no one in Durban paid much attention to the opinions of those living in what was considered remote and unimportant parts up north.

"When war came to Africa and Britain turned on Germany in East Africa, we were all caught up in jingoistic fever, not least me; so that's how I joined the British South Africa Police and landed up in East Africa in 1915 fighting the Germans, alongside the Portuguese and Belgians.

"I encountered Afrikaner-Boers in the BSAP and developed a great deal of respect for their toughness. They were intrepid in the face of enemy fire from the German Askaris.

"By 1917 most of us left alive were riddled with malaria and dysentery, some suffering from serious war wounds and mental conditions as well, brought about by the horrors we had witnessed. The conflict in East Africa was winding down and I was 'honourably discharged' at the beginning of 1918 when I contracted Spanish Flu which really did lay me low, on top of everything else.

"The Natal Bank had held my position open for me and that's where I landed up again after a slow recovery. Soon after, I learnt that my father had died not long after my step-mother and that I had inherited quite a lot of money, although my sister actually inherited the more valuable part of his estate, the Scottish farm and a share in a lace factory; so I decided to use my part of the inheritance here in Natal, encouraged by the grant of land I received in Ntambanana."

He told her about his French sailing friend, about the sisters who lived at the Barbican, about his friendship with Prue at the children's library – but not about Creighton or the girls he had made love to.

"Look, it's almost time for you to leave for the bank and barely time to wolf down toast. I'll be going to the reference library after doing some shopping – in the hope that some shops are open – which includes finding a new swimming costume in which to look stunning on board ship. Do we meet at lunchtime?"

This was asked as their bodies stayed entwined. "Of course, I'll look for you in the reference library... curious how our words are so far detached from what our arms, bodies and hands are doing. However, never ask me if I've wound the clock in these moments. Did I tell you that you have the most beautiful nose?"

"No you didn't. Not recently, although you did last night. But did I tell you that I am hypnotised by the curly hair on your chest and the way you walk across the room – especially when you are stark naked?"

Across the bay came a burst of inanimate groaning. "My God, what's that?"

"It's Old Groaner, the dredger. They've been making the channels deeper and wider for years and destroying the feeding grounds of the junior fish population in the process. No one seems to care. But there's still a central sand bank or two which you can walk on at low tide; so some of the fish will survive."

Down at pavement level they heard a woman's loud and grindingly coarse voice approaching from far off, shouting "He's gone and taken all my fuckin' money!" the voice crying, louder and louder between wailings, over and over again, until it dwindled down the street.

"You see," said Emily, "You can't trust men... I think I had better warn you that I might become unduly possessive."

"No Free Love then?" he said.

"Absolutely not. I predict I will not tolerate your casting lecherous eyes on any other girl."

"That poor woman below should have entrusted our bank with her money."

"But she's a tart! Don't they keep their money under the mattress?"

"Oh? How do you know she's a tart?"

"Well, by the sound of her voice."

"Could she not just be a rather ordinary whaler's wife from across the bay? What I like about money is that it is amoral. Banks guard our metal, not our morals. If it guarded our morals we'd all be broke. May I suggest that by lunchtime I scrape up a few sandwiches from the bank canteen to eat at the end of the Mole? Then we can plan what to do next; but I'll have to get back to the bank by about 2 o' clock. Agreed?"

"Agreed."

Emily had no idea of what 'The Mole' was, but remained in a state of enchantment sufficiently to agree to anything Donald might propose.

"It was a miserable business" said Cole. "Up until today, my experience of funerals has been cloaked in undertakers' 'respectability'. Yesterday was a matter of a few hasty graveside prayers among distraught relatives, coffins being lowered into a common grave as part of a queue of them. I don't think I could go through that again. All those weeping families. And the town is running out of coffins. By the way, what have you unearthed about Umbilo Iron & Steel?"

"Unearthed? Enough for us to consider calling in their overdraft. Not to put too fine a point on it, I think there is some sort of fiddle going on. In spite of its being a sound business up until now, the new manager seems to be making a mess of things – unnecessary purchases and so on – or pocketing some of the proceeds."

"All right. Do what you have to do. Just let me know when you call them in. I would rather like to be out of the office as I know their parents very well."

"You could be at another funeral, sir."

"Yes, I could, perhaps a grandmother's. Is the business worth rescuing?"

"Yes, I believe so, taking into account the inevitable surge we can expect in housing and the possible demand for pressed steel ceilings. May I suggest that we call in the directors and frighten the hell out of them? We can "reluctantly" permit a limited time to get their house in order, with the threat of terminating their overdraft hanging over them, and see what remedies they apply. The business should be able to prosper in this post-war environment."

"Right. Go ahead. I will be sorry to lose you, Kirkwood."

"Thank you. You may well see me back at my old desk if my agricultural aspirations turn to dust." The meeting with Umbilo Iron & Steel was arranged for the following week.

To extract something to eat from the Greek woman, Mrs. Papiagianapoulus, who ran the bank's canteen, proved difficult. "You can have cold escalope: thasallIgot, with some bread slice from my 'usband's bakery. He close now. Why you here, not Zululand? Better go there; we all sick here," she said and sneezed close to the escalope she was wrapping for him in greaseproof paper.

He found Emily in the reference library buried in a book about lobola and Zulu cattle. He thought to himself, "My God, how lucky can a man be," when she caught sight of him and smiled. The library was almost deserted.

"We have escalope," he said.

"What's that?"

"I don't know, but it's all that the lady in the bank's canteen, Mrs. Papiagianapoulus, had left to give me, plus some of the bread made in her husband's bakery; now closed for the duration. All I know is that it's a thin slice of some sort of meat, and flat, and she's Greek. I saw her beating it with a mallet as if her life depended on it then frying it."

"What a name! Well, let's go and flatten it further on the Mole – whatever that is."

The tide was in when they strolled to the end of the Mole to sit on an old concrete bench, pitted by salty corrosion. The swell lapped the barnacled rocks and the bay was all about them. Every time the swell sank it left with a bubbling-glistening sound.

"I haven't felt so happy and content as this since I was a child," Emily said.

"Nor I," Donald replied. "Hang on tight to your escalope or a seagull might snatch it. You know... about that green mamba."

"Yes?"

"I didn't complete the story."

"Go on."

"Well, after the natives had run away from the dead snake I climbed down and had a good look at it and it struck me that I had destroyed a beautiful creature. Have you ever looked closely at a green mamba?"

"Can't say that I have. Ran away from one once. At least, assumed it was one. Didn't wait to check."

"I was told that without them we'd be up to our ears in rats and mice. It was just an accident, confusing the levers of the signal box with the branches outside and, on reflection, I was very sorry I had to kill it. Perhaps, looking at it, there was a moment of resonance between it and the reptilian knob in my own brain. From time to time, I feel that we whites are much like that snake, unable to integrate with unfamiliar surroundings and a permanent threat."

"I suppose every story has a moral to it – as long as you can find it."

"As I'm about to live among or at least live beside the Zulus it would be a great help to know about their cattle culture. And then of course there is that other possibility of offering your father cattle as lobola for you."

"About that. Too early. Think about it in Cape Town," she said, leaning against him and looking up into his eyes. It seemed like a silent 'yes'.

"Well," she said, abandoning her usual style of incomplete sentences as she warmed to the subject she loved, "you already know that lobola is a bride price, which hinges on the cost of raising the daughter and the loss of someone to help with planting and tending of the crops. But the payment of lobola in a cashless society is always only done with cattle, and stems, in part, from the steady collapse of Zulu subsistence farming due to being forced into reserves where land is less arable.

"By the Zulus being drawn into the perimeter of white man's cash culture, the Zulu chiefs were quick to exploit the ready convertibility of cattle into cash so as to buy white man things. And of course, cattle also remain a valuable source of food."

"Hang on," said Donald, "You're not going into any details about the customs of lobola; you're just running around with the cattle."

"Be patient, my child, I'll get back to lobola in a minute. Cattle are the key. Another point is that, in the good times, cattle begot even more cattle and chiefs have not been slow, in the past, to build up large herds as a means of amassing considerable convertible wealth. But nagana is now decimating herds."

"And lobola?"

"Well, believe it or not, there is a thing called 'The Natal Code of Native Law' designed, in the last century, to bring some order and understanding by our Natal government authorities of Zulu cultural codes so that bewildering native disputes can be resolved within that framework.

"The rule book sets ten head of cattle for a commoner, fifteen for an induna, twenty for an appointed chief and no limit for a hereditary chief.

"I can see where this discussion is leading – I will barely be able to afford to pay the bride-price, despite the fact that I am having great difficulty in resisting making passionate love to you at this moment."

"Not quite the thing to do at the end of any barnacled mole, do you think? And why on earth is it called a 'mole' anyway?"

"It might raise a few eyebrows, I agree. Mole is a French word meaning a large mass projecting into the water. Venice has a 'Molo' which means just about the same thing. I looked it up."

"Eyebrows and passion aside, it is possible that you might never have to pay a bride-price to my father anyway.

He would rate as a sort of white chief so he could demand twenty cattle or more if the situation ever arose. Shall I go on about lobola?"

"Yes please."

"The present condition is that the herds are dying from nagana and the whole system of bride-price has been thrown into disarray – leading to bride-suitors being forced into offering goats, blankets or ill-afforded cash as temporary substitutes – and this is where I come in. My study covers the impact of rinderpest, nagana and East Coast Fever on Zulu society and regional variations of lobola implementation at a time when the herds are withering away."

"And?"

"I don't know yet. While the senior Zulu hierarchy controls much of the grazing land in the reserves into which they have been shunted, their grip over the young men suitors returning with cash from the goldmines has been compromised. You see it is becoming increasingly more expensive and difficult to buy cattle"

"Ah."

"Indeed 'Ah'. And then there's Sisa. You will be protecting me from burglars again tonight, will you?"

"Thank you. I will be there. What is Sisa?"

"A Zulu custom of kinship which applies to those who have access to land but no cattle. An owner of a herd is able to graze his animals, while allowing the land occupant to employ the cattle for ploughing and for milk. The owner is entitled to any increase in the herd.

"The custom staves off hunger for the lowliest members of the clan, or has done so before the whole system was thrown into disarray by the current disease.

"These are threads of my study, but I confess that I must sound a bit muddled as to what conclusions might be reached and how I'm going to summarise everything. I have a long, long, long way to go and a lot of reading and note-taking to come. Makes me nervous. Could you give me a lift this afternoon to the Killie Campbell Library at Muckle Neuk? It's the name of the big house on the Berea which a friend of Daddy's, Marshall Campbell, built after he retired from sugarcane farming at Umhloti. He died in Durban at the beginning of the war. I met his daughter Killie at an old girls' reunion at St Anne's. Although she had left yonks before me, we got talking about Zulu customs and found common ground. She knows far more than I do. Killie inherited the house in Marriot Road and has filled a section with Zulu artifacts which she and her father had been assembling for many years, backed by a lot of manuscripts on the culture. Her brother has also been helping.

"They even ran Zulu tribal history competitions for some years. Literate Zulu entrants (surprisingly, more than would have been thought, taking into account current illiteracy levels) had to write down as much as they knew of their ancestors. The San (Bushman) are also represented and now she is building up her Indian-settler collection, encouraged by her father knowing Gandhi rather well. Her father encouraged all-inclusiveness of the Natal communities."

Donald noticed that Emily's utterances were no longer abrupt and realised that that characteristic had been due to shyness.

"I phoned the house this morning after you left for the bank and spoke to Killie and asked if I could pop in. Both

Killie and William, her brother, have had the Spanish and have recovered and I assured her that we were 'clear' too, so Killie said come along. I'd like to delve into their records."

"Of course, but I must let the bank know first."

When Donald arrived in the Tin Lizzie to collect her again at Muckle Neuk, he found Emily and the older Killie sitting on cane chairs beneath a spreading flamboyant tree on the top terrace, high above the city. Killie's grand white house in neo-Cape-Dutch style served as a backdrop. It boasted twin gables and an enormous verandah, supported by white Doric columns.

"Hello. What's the name of your car? We could hear you coming up the hill," said Killie.

"Well, it's a Model T but I've already decided to call her 'Kelpie', a cloven imp which haunts Scottish streams and lakes. This mechanical marvel is a real she-devil to get used to."

Killie said: "We were discussing Indian musical instruments when you arrived and I was wondering, where I could find an example of an old sitar used in Natal to add to our Indian section. Any ideas?"

"What a beautiful place! Sitar. That's a kind of stretched mandolin from India, isn't it? Try asking Ivan Cohen. A sitar-player must have to replace broken strings from time to time, so he is sure to know the sitar community."

"Good idea. And my father knew Gandhi, so his associates would be another avenue to explore. I was saying to Emily that father and I – and now my brother William – have focused much of our attention on assembling relics and records of early Durban and Natal's indigenous peoples but we really have neglected the Indian community to some extent, perhaps because we viewed them as temporary 'imports'. On reflection, that might seem a bit muddled as my grandparents arrived in Natal only ten years earlier than the first of the indentured Indians.

"Nowadays, of course, they're everywhere and it's beginning to be quite posh to have Indian servants. They'll be running everything sooner or later. Granddad and Granny were both Byrne Settlers, you know, from Glasgow, arriving in 1850, whereas the Indians started arriving in 1860."

(Byrne, the originator of the scheme, was a minor cattle dealer in Dublin when he decided to cash in on the wave of emigration from Britain to North America and the colonies. He never visited Natal and his idea that 20 acres could provide adequate subsistence was based on the Irish and English ideas of a sustainable farm.

The settlers had to be either farmers or skilled artisans such as blacksmiths, wheelwrights, wagon makers and the like. Most immigrants, Killie's grandparents included, realised pretty soon that twenty acres was impractically small and moved to the towns of Durban or Pietermaritzburg to seek employment; with the result that Byrne's scheme collapsed in September, 1850.

With his knowledge of railway construction he brought from Scotland, Killie's grandfather secured the contract to build Durban North Pier in the harbour and was enabled to buy land on the Umhloti River north of Durban from the profits, where he developed a sugarcane farm. It was on a wide bend of the river so he called the farm Muckle Neuk, the Scots for 'Great Bend'.

Within his short life – he died at the age of 44 – he had become a prominent sugarcane farmer and miller.)

"Tea?"

"Yes, thank you."

"Emily tells me that you're another kind of pioneer – going to farm among the Zulus. That's challenging. Would you like a brief 'Cook's Tour' of my collection while you're here? Emily said that you were eager to learn as much as possible and seemed to have some particular interest in lobola? Emily, you've seen all this before so I'll leave you to your researches while I whisk Donald away for a short while."

Just as soon as they were out of earshot Killie paused and said, "You do realise that my Emily is quite smitten, don't you? She's rather young to be swept off her feet by a battle-hardened man-of-the-world and I am concerned that Ntambanana is so remote, but I am sure you will look after her. But another consideration is that she is at the end game of her first degree and there is every promise that she could go on to an MA or even a doctorate now that the university is recognising that women exist. Would she be the most appropriate person to share a life of early hardship with you out in the bundu?"

Donald was taken aback by Killie's caution and remained silent as they started the inspection of the collection, mulling over her remarks as much as the turn of events with Captain Creighton, two days before. Then he said: "I could say that – frankly, what Emily feels or doesn't feel is none of your business. She's nearly twenty-one and can think very much for herself. However, I appreciate your concern and must say that I have already gone over these considerations by myself and with a close friend. That I love her is fairly obvious. News that she loves me makes my heart leap up. That Emily is appropriate for a harsh Zululand life, I can't say, except that my instincts will say 'yes', while taking into account that opportunities for her field of study will surround us. She does come from a Zululand settler family, after all, and her parents would not be averse to her being reasonably close and supporting her through the adversities of farming in such a challenging area.

"For my part, I'll give uncompromising support to furthering her studies. If she has to attend university in Cape Town from time to time – so be it, though heart-wrenchingly tough her absence would be."

"Well said, Macduff, and in that case, I'll give you my blessing – whatever the future holds, although I still think that the age gap between you could be too great. But come and see what my brother William has been collecting."

She led him to a large kitchen at the back of the house where every level space, including the broad kitchen table and areas of the wide creaking floorboards, was covered with Zulu clay pots, arrows, beadwork, big and little cowhide shields, grass baskets, sleeping mats, snuff holders of horn and much else besides. The collection included a section devoted to artefacts of the vanished Natal San people whose last redoubt had been the caves and overhangs in the Drakensberg Mountains.

"Most of the evidence of their existence in Natal is in the corner of this room and the astonishing paintings they left on the overhang rocks in such places as Drakensberg's Ndedema Gorge. In this collection are small flaked stones used to scrape and cut, fragments of potsherds, a tiny bow and poisoned arrows made from reeds. The few San that did survive have retreated to the Kalahari Desert.

"The objects made by the Zulus, the San and some

other tribes in this funny big kitchen are treasures, not only for their intrinsic beauty, but because they're being discarded in favour of the white man's paraffin tins and similar paraphernalia. Look on them carefully, Donald, for they're going the way of the windjammer and the cannonball. You'll never see the likes of them again.

"Many were created by craftsmen who had never encountered a white person, insulated by time and distance from any European influence. Of course, there are some later pieces too – look at this bead piece with patterns hinting at letters of the alphabet, for example.

"Seen enough for the moment? Then come and inspect what I have been collecting for years and years," whereupon she led Donald to a panelled library filled with rare books on local history, racks of press cuttings, sepia photographs of sailing ships in the harbour and streets thronged with ox wagons and mule carts, explorers' maps and folder upon folder of letters that stretched back to before Natal's earliest settler days. "And there's Emily!" she said, who they discovered seated at an old Cape-Dutch table and poring over a leather-bound volume of The Natal Code of Native Law. Behind her were glass-encased bookshelves from floor to ceiling and wall to wall, relieved only by a painting by Angas of 'A Zulu Kraal at Inanda' and a display of early coin tokens. Donald was startled to see that one coin was stamped 'Creighton & Company. 6d'.

"Hello again," said Killie. "I have been dragging Donald through William's collection in the old kitchen."

Turning to Donald she said, "You see, like our father, my brother and I have always been collector-mad. For my part I am most attracted to manuscripts and documents reflecting the earliest settler days of Natal and I have been gathering such evidence from the time we lived on the farm at Mount Edgecombe, years and years ago."

As they drove away Donald said, "Dinner for two?"

"Dinner for two it is," Emily said, "overlooking our bay, of course."

Their lovemaking that night was tenderer and less frantic, two companions journeying without maps to the secret grotto. Before that, their small supper lit only by candlelight followed the same course as before, but although there were no more peas there was ample wine.

Donald was immensely conscious that his Scottish upbringing inhibited expressing the depths of his feelings for her except at the height of passion and with copious glasses of wine. He was bewitched by her youth and beauty and was swept up in the desire to shelter her, but the words that came out were, "Was the fish all right?" though he managed to add, "I love the cool wriggly feel of your feet."

At supper, he had half risen to lean over and kiss her on the mouth when his left hand sank into the wooden window ledge in a small cloud of dust, making them both convulse with laughter.

"Bloody termites! The whole of Durban is undermined by them."

And it was almost true. white ants eat away at wood a few millimetres below the surface so that, usually, their presence is only detected when a wooden framework collapses.

"When I was six, I told Daddy that I could hear white ants eating away under my bedroom floor at night on the farm. I was so insistent that he crawled under the house and sure enough discovered several ant heaps. What a palaver! He had to knock off the top of the mounds then squirt poison down the holes. They eat books too.

"The tennis court you played on at the farm was surfaced with the ant heaps he discovered ... makes a marvellous level surface for spectacular slides."

Once again, they had eaten barefoot with their feet touching, except when Emily mentioned that she had found some excuse to visit the Children's Library across the entrance hall, her toes withdrew. She had asked Prue Jardine, whom she recognised from Donald's description, whether there were any books on the Zulus in the children's section, explaining that she was doing something on them as part of her degree; whereupon Prue first led her to Arthur Mee's Children's Newspaper which had started publication for the first time on 22nd March 1919, as she thought she had seen an article on 'Cetewayo' under the heading 'Peoples of the World'; but she was proven wrong.

Prue had said that she would scour something she called the DDC indexes, but this would take a little time and she suggested that Emily should return an hour or so later, whereupon Emily thanked her but said that she was on a very short stay in Durban, would be leaving the following day and would be preoccupied with other essential things to do.

"Now why did you do that?" asked Donald.

"She's attractive, Donald. I just wanted to see what the competition looked like – or one of them. Pity about the birthmark on her neck."

Donald laughed and said, "That's absurd! No, we're just casual acquaintances. She takes the same tram to town every now and then and has asked me to accompany her to a rather dreary-sounding League of Nations talk this coming Saturday."

"That means that she is interested in you."

"No. She has been charged by the libraries to go to the talk and feels awkward about going alone. The discussion is expected to turn to Esperanto and Braille towards the end of the afternoon, in which the library service is expected to take an interest. Don't misconstrue the motive. Spanish Flu has made the centre of town unnerving on a late Saturday afternoon for a girl all on her own...I'm not trying to change the subject, but thinking of Braille, I wondered what you thought of Hubie and Frieda von Weldenburg? Frieda mentioned that she was a Braille teacher back in Switzerland when we met them on your parent's farm."

"I think Frieda is genuine but she's got dangerous legs ... and she knows it. I don't like Hubie at all and it irritates me that Daddy has got friendly with them, although I expect he believes he must make selected foreign newcomers feel at home in his role as this year's chairman of the Empangeni Cane Growers Association. I think Hubie is a fake. I'm sure he's not Swiss. I'm sure he's German and there's something sinister about that. Bright, yes. Charming manners, but he's just too bloody German for me by far, and has that ghastly interest in eugenics where it positions the Zulus and Indians. Ugh!"

Donald said, "Toby and I saw him at the Masonic the night before we had to leave for Durban, talking to a group of Dutchmen over drinks and dinner. He almost ignored us completely, although after Zeno's funeral I had returned a lost book of his in German I happened to come across in the hotel. He was so pleased then that he invited both of us to stop over at his new farm for a few days, on our way through to Ntambanana. The difference in behaviour between the two occasions was marked and barely explainable. What do you think of that?"

"A disposition for treachery?"

"You may have a point. Nevertheless Toby and I have agreed to take him up on his offer, primarily to take a good look at Frieda's legs again but also to get a peek at his farming methods. The German-Swiss are efficient, so it won't do much harm to pick up a few tips"

"My father, Noel and Eric are far better placed to steer you in the right direction, but you must do as you please."

"What are my chances of marrying you?"

"I told you that that subject would have to wait until I'm back in Cape Town and prepping for the ultimate exams. I need to put a distance between us to think clearly. On no account hint anything to my father or mother. That would be my business, if the time ever came to tell them what we might be contemplating."

"I give you my word."

"But do write. I will too. Often. You can even phone if the callbox in Res works. For a long time the girls used to stick a pin in the wires which had the same effect as dropping a coin in the tickey box, but one day it just stopped working. I must remember to give you the number. The phone's in the hall of the Res; not very private but it's better than nothing. Expect me to sound rather formal."

They fell asleep entangled and Donald was woken by strands of Emily's hair tickling his mouth. The rising sun had crept through the fronds of a palm tree, and the early breeze was shifting patterns of faint bubbly light it cast on a wall as he watched her soft breathing.

The mynahs had started up.

Emily stirred and stretched her arms then turned

over and drifted off again. Donald slipped out of bed and reached for a dressing gown then pulled the bedclothes over her.

The harbour was awake and he glimpsed the mauve hull of the Edinburgh Castle at B Shed. Above its white superstructure, wisps of steam were curling from its funnels.

The phone ringing in Jean-Pierre's office woke Emily finally and Donald said, "I think you'd better answer it, rather than me. It's probably Jean-Pierre and you, after all, are the official guest here. Good morning, dearest one."

"Morning," said Emily dreamily then kissed and hugged him while the phone continued to jangle. Donald fetched the other dressing gown and Emily stumbled to the phone just as it stopped ringing. It started ringing again a few moments later and Donald heard Emily say, "Yes, it's me and thank you so much for allowing me to stay here. It really has been a God-send. Wonderful view. Fancy waking up to this every morning."

Then "Yes, he's here. He's just arrived to make arrangements to take me to the boat later. Here he is," she said, looking at Donald and rolling her eyes, as if to imply 'what a dark black lie!'

"Hello JP. I've bad news. A moment after arriving I leant on the edge of one of your window ledges and my hand just went straight through. I'm very sorry, but it had been riddled by white ants. I'll pay for the damage."

"Please forget it," came the voice on the phone. "The whole building is supported by white ants. When they eventually decide to leave, it'll fall down. It's the penalty for not treating the wood with creosote because of the smell."

White ants proliferate in Durban's warm and humid

climate, eating untreated wood and paper, burrowing, just below the surface, through picture-frames, skirting boards, furniture and books. Some people resort to planting furniture legs in water-filled old jam tins as effective but unsightly termite barriers.

"When am I going to meet your future wife?"

"Well, she isn't convinced about that yet but I'm busy persuading her."

"I had a call from Judy which boils down to her asking 'where the hell are you?' I get the impression that she is more than a little concerned. She wondered if the Spanish Flu had taken you. You just disappeared without explanation. Shall I call her back and say that you had to hurry to your aunt?"

"No. Invent no details. Durban is forever full of whispers. Just confirm that all is well and I will explain later."

"When may I recapture my apartment?"

"Emily must be out of here by two o' clock when we have to leave for the boat. Does that suit you?"

"That's OK, but I would rather like to meet this girl, mon ami."

"Well yes, although I would appreciate you're not turning on your Gallic charm, if you don't mind. Perhaps we could meet here at about one?" Donald said, looking at Emily with raised eyebrows and responding to Emily's nod of assent.

"That's good. I'll be there."

It was Emily who took the initiative to draw him down to the bed with nothing on but their dressing gowns which were soon thrown aside.

"I'm glad we can see each other in daylight," Emily said.

"I'm not wildly proud of my body and I can't really see why you find me attractive – or at least you say that you do. Do you really love me or do you just like making love to me?"

"I love making love to you but mostly, I love you, my darling Emily."

"Here. Press this nipple very, very gently between your thumb and forefinger, so – and do it slowly and again and again. It's the sensation of an infant at the breast. Very gently. I just want to sense that."

In her mind's eye and deep in her body she felt an infant suckling and it was good. She imagined a baby by the man making love to her.

They fell asleep and were woken by post being pushed through the letterbox with a clap as the flap fell back. Bundles of mail dropped to the floor.

It made Donald spring off the bed, half awake, dimly aware that he should be doing something somewhere else. When his surroundings dawned on him he hurried into the bathroom to shave and wash before snatching a banana and eating it while dressing.

He explained to a very sleepy Emily that he had to leave immediately as he was already late for the bank and old Cole was a stickler for punctuality even though the bank was officially closed.

Emily kissed him longingly and sleepily, and said, "I am going to the library later and will come back to pack at about half-past twelve."

Chapter Fourteen

When Cole saw Donald arrive he buttonholed him into his office and stubbed out a cigarette in the brass bowl his wife had given him. It had a curved base. Donald was mesmerised by the way the bowl continued to rock to and fro on his desk with a life of its own.

Cole said that the bank would be opening for business on the morrow but for four hours only. He told him that the District Officer for Health had confirmed that there was every sign that the epidemic in Natal was burning itself out, although the Western Cape and Cape Town in particular remained very hard hit indeed and resources were still being strained to the limit. There was no relief either in such places as Kimberley and Johannesburg.

Donald thought immediately of Emily and wondered if she and her parents had made the right decision to risk her returning to university a week ahead of the third quarter. He thought her anxiety about her final exams should not put her life at risk.

"Donald, are you listening? You seem to be a million miles away."

"Sorry. I was."

"Children of some bank employees have lost one or both of their parents to Spanish Flu as you know, so the directors

349

of this and the other banks have agreed to establish a Bank Employees' Orphan's Fund as quickly as possible. While this is being prepared, it was agreed to provide temporary assistance to those in most urgent need (within limits of course) the costs being debited to a not-for-profit company immediately it has been registered.

"As we are the leading bank, I want you to formulate procedures as swiftly as possible on Monday and to act as temporary administrator, reporting to a small committee made up of an appointee from each bank. I have the other banks' agreement on this.

"Now I know you have to take this afternoon off, but I'll have to lean on you heavily during the days ahead, right up to your last day with us."

Cole asked him to arrange advertisements in the Natal Mercury & Commercial Shipping Gazette and the Natal (Mercantile) Advertiser announcing that the bank would be open the following day. Being very short-staffed Donald decided to walk to both papers himself. Turning from Smith Street at the forever bar-and-tobacco-smelly Central Hotel into Mercury Lane he passed a pie shop, a bespoke tailor – both closed - and a vacant office window on which a faded sign read

M K Ga ndhi &
R K K ahn
ATTO RNIES

The words were broken by a vertical part of the window frame. In small letters below was the legend 'Registered Office: Natal Indian Congress (1894)'.

There was a faded CLOSED notice pasted on the door,

directing clients to an address in Grey Street. Donald had heard that, before Gandhi's return to India in 1914, the solicitor used to walk to his Mercury Lane chambers every weekday from his house in Beach Grove.

He remembered someone mentioning that Gandhi, as a young man, was small with sticky-out ears and a moustache, his hair carefully parted and slicked down.

Gandhi, Churchill and Botha had all been present near a hill called Spioenkop during a battle for it in the First Anglo-Boer War on the 23rd and 24th January 1900, and Donald wondered how history might have been changed if any of the three had been killed.

Gandhi served as a stretcher-bearer in the Indian Ambulance Corps during the battle; Churchill, a journalist, acted as a courier in the South African Light Horse, and General Louis Botha (future Prime Minister of the Transvaal) was General Buller's cunning opponent.

After handing in a short notice at the advertising counter of the Mercury Gazette he walked to the Natal Advertiser, in its modest premises on Field Street, and bought a copy of the Stop Press edition which arrived while he was there.

Under 'Domestic Notices', deaths attributed to Spanish Flu in Durban and surrounds were extensive and there was no sign that the pandemic in other provinces was losing its grip, underscored by three reports which caught his eye:

NINETEEN DIE AT MINE

Johannesburg. 17th July 1919
At 3am today an operator was stricken by the Driedagsiekte at East Rand Proprietary Mine and

collapsed across the winding house machinery while the cage was being brought up, causing the cage to crash into the headgear and kill nineteen miners.

Driedagsiekte or 'Three Day Disease' is the more virulent form of the Spanish Flu which first presented in 1918.

FLU STRIKES REMOTE FARMS

From our Orange Free State correspondent
Smithfield. 16th July 1919

The entire de Wet family on the remote farm 'Waterval' in the Smithfield district of the Orange Free State was found to have died from the Driedagsiekte when the District Surgeon visited the farm yesterday afternoon.

He was accompanied by South African Police Sgt. Herzog, who had responded to appeals by distant relatives to investigate.

They found the whole place "as quiet as the grave" except for some coloured children, the family dogs and cattle out on the veld.

Mr and Mrs. Waltemar de Wet had died in their living room while their two adult sons had collapsed on the kitchen floor.

Many of their Coloured farm workers had suffered the same fate although their young children were not affected and were found to be starving and disorientated.

A spokesman for the Orange Free State Agricultural Union, Mr. Piet Verhagen, said that such discoveries were not uncommon, brought about by the second and more virulent wave of Spanish Flu and the isolation of many such farms.

He said that urgent new steps were being taken to establish regular contact with such remote communities in order to render assistance where possible.

AFRICANS SHUN FLU VACCINE

From our East London correspondent Cathcart.
16th July 1919
white relief workers in rural areas here have reported that they had been preceded by a 'witchdoctor' who had spread the word that the Spanish Flu was a clever 'trick' by Europeans to poison off the natives.

Medicines and anti-flu vaccine being offered by the relief workers were being shunned and mortally sick patients were being kept out of sight.

MUNICIPALITY COLLECTS CORPSES

Cape Town. 17th July 1919
According to the health authorities, more than 400 people are dying daily from Spanish Flu and municipal carts are touring the streets to pick up many of those who have dropped dead beside the roads.

Current deaths are ten times the usual rate of attrition.

Families of the bereaved have had to transport their flu victims to mass graves in the main cemetery by car, taxi and pony cart, and in many cases, wheelbarrows.

An Anglican Minister has been placed on permanent standby there as well as the Mayor's chaplain to officiate at funerals when no minister is available.

Walking back to the bank while glancing intermittently at the articles he practically bumped into Toby. "Good Lord! I was thinking about you yesterday and scratching about for your address. I am so pleased to see you again," he exclaimed, shaking his hand vigorously.

"Well, we're at least both still alive. Ghastly business all this, eh?" Donald said, gesturing to the newspaper articles. "I was asked to stay on at the bank for about ten days because deaths and illness had left it so desperately short staffed. I'm glad we've met up again. What have you been up to?"

"Well, not much, except helping out where I could, yet becoming more and more concerned about the new farm and wanting to get back there. I landed up staying at the Durban Club (yes, they actually stayed open unofficially for members, one of the few) after I shipped out of my old digs. I was shanghaied by some naval types hanging about in the bar into participating in a shattering naval 'sport' commemorating the Relief of Ladysmith during the Anglo-Boer War. It was a boiled-down version played out in the club's back garden.

"It seems that the craziness started when guns from HMS Powerful were dismantled and hauled over obstacles to Ladysmith by the ship's Naval Brigade. I learnt that 'The Flying Angel' was the nickname of the last man of each gun crew – and one of them turned out to be me on this occasion. God knows why. We didn't even have a muster for two teams, so we had to race against ourselves and a time keeper. Club furniture (you know those large chairs and tables that can be dissembled) was substituted for the real thing. Bloody heavy all the same, climbing over all those obstacles.

"When we landed back in the bar and after a couple more whiskies I found myself volunteering to patrol the lower reaches of Durban's docks with the few naval men staying at the club, on the lookout for sailors struck down by the Flu. It was like the 'Pangeni business. I never want to smell the stink of carbolic acid or Lysol again. Dead bodies at the docks; not lots, but some. Most were natives; some dying, and a couple of blind drunks. We had to lug them onto a push-cart and wheel them to a makeshift hospital in the Wesleyan Church Hall – it was the Old Point Road Railway Station. Bleak and draughty. This went on for days.

"I'm still at the Club, so let's meet up in the library for a sundowner… more comfortable than the bar. The kitchen's closed till further notice except for a kehla who makes rudimentary sandwiches and tea. Tastes like swill. That's all I can offer you – and whisky of course. As the club's officially closed you'll have to knock long and loud and ask for me. The Indian fellow left in charge takes his time."

"Thank you, but only after I've seen Emily safely onto the boat this afternoon. You and I have shared much, with more to come, so I look forward to picking up the traces again and in happier circumstances."

"Ship not boat please! A ship can carry boats but a boat can't carry a ship; however submarines are always 'boats'. Emily Bell? Good heavens, how did that come about?"

"I'll tell you all about it when we meet up later."

Donald explained that her father chose to book her on the Edinburgh Castle as he feared that the train via Bloemfontein would be unsafe at the present.

"Well, well, well. I expect to hear every detail, you sly old dog. Dress code is still a bit starchy, flu or no flu. Come in through the town entrance in Durban Club Place."

Jean-Pierre was at Cavendish Chambers when Donald arrived. The door from the corridor was ajar and he saw them sitting at the table by the window waiting for him with an opened bottle of wine and three glasses. There was cheese and bread too.

"Bonjour, mon ami!" he said, rising and shaking Donald's hand, causing Donald to shake Emily's hand in turn absentmindedly, much to her puzzlement, until he kissed her gently. "I arrived moments ago so within such a short while that I have been completely unable to sweep Emily off her feet, but I am already jealous of your meeting such a delightful girl.

"I brought some wine from my parents' vineyard in Madagascar and we've just opened a bottle to allow it to breathe a little. They make vin rouge from the Varousset grape at their Ambalavao estate there, and now it's ready to try! Here are some Madagascan cheeses to go with it and bread made this morning by Aysha in our kitchen. She is a brilliant cook and she says hello, and when are you coming to taste her curry again.

"Emily was explaining to me where you met and how people were dying in Zululand from the flu. Ach! We are all lucky to have survived. Fortunately it's beginning to burn itself out here, so they say. Come. Let's drink to that – and the morrow. As my good friend Ivan Cohen might say: Locheim! To Life, Good Friends, Love and Health Everlasting. But especially to you Emily and to you Donald."

Another bottle was opened and time passed until Emily glanced at Donald's watch and exclaimed, "Oh my God, I'll miss the boat unless we move now," leading to Jean-Pierre helping them with Emily's luggage to bump down three flights of stairs because the lift had stopped working and into the Kelpie.

"Have you got your flu pass ready? They'll demand it at customs, otherwise you won't be allowed aboard. Got your ticket?"

Emily looked hurriedly into her bag while Donald fished about in his pockets for the flu-pass he was given in Empangeni.

"Yes? Then hurry, hurry and au revoir and bon voyage and goodbye!"

The cabin on the twin-funnelled 'Edinburgh Castle' stank of fresh white marine oil paint. The ship had served as an armed merchant cruiser and escorted Atlantic convoys. After the war it was refitted. An earlier post-war voyage from Southampton had seen General Jan Smuts as a passenger, returning from his service in the British War Cabinet. A large framed portrait of him was attached to the outside wall of the purser's foyer office and caught the eye of most passengers coming aboard.

Missions to Seamen women were selling paper streamers at the foot of the gangplanks. Some passengers got confused and attempted to present their boarding cards to them.

Emily was to share a cabin with a fluttery girl called Marjory Wilson who had a pouter pigeon chest and pronounced eyebrows, who Emily immediately identified as a friend for the voyage; Helen Wiles, an Anglican minister's wife on a visit to visit her sister in Broadstairs; and Mabel Hansel, a plump woman who possessed a confusion of little parcels tied up with pink ribbon and who was already complaining about the heat and the smell of paint.

Donald had rushed the Kelpie (as best a Model T can be rushed) along the Embankment and down Point Road, past the phone box where he had met Luna and talked to Emily on the telephone and past Pickering Street until, waived through by Customs at the entrance to the docks, the car wobbled and bumped over forking railway lines before reaching the back of B Shed.

Unable to find a porter, he had grabbed a trolley and trotted the luggage up a ramp to a long low bench in the shed behind which sat a health official, an embarkation officer and several customs officers. After slapping 'Cape Town' labels on them, one of the officers was content merely to swipe a yellow chalk across Emily's cases after glancing at her ticket and flu-card. Then they were free to trample up the gangway, Donald clutching her valise.

They left the other women to fuss about in the cabin and went up onto the upper deck, past milling stewards and key-rattling passengers searching for their cabin numbers to lean on the railings facing the bay. This helped them to avoid the groups of streamer-throwers establishing 'last touch' with those soon to be left behind, their white faces staring up at them from the dockside. It was shortly after the ship sounded its fog horn for the first time that a clipped British loudspeaker voice ordered visitors off the boat – with the threat that gangplanks would be removed within fifteen minutes precisely.

Looking out over the bay, Emily said: "Haunting harbour sounds. Forever Our Bay. Our Leitmotif. Never happier. Don't hang about. Just say goodbye now. Said everything. Write. Got something for you. Don't open. Later."

She had reverted into her shy mode of truncated sentences which first attracted Donald to her. It was her way of bottling up emotions.

"I am going to drive as far as I can and park the Kelpie on the North Pier. You might want to wave. You never did explain the significance of Sisa."

"Unimportant. Well no. Not really true, but we've been concentrating on non-verbal matters recently, if you recall. Remember to write. Often. I'll explain by letter. Sisa. Awful system. Keeps lots of natives indebted to money lenders."

"I have something for you too," said Donald, "but don't open it now, either. It's rather small. Something to wear, on any finger you choose. It's my mother's wedding ring."

"I'll call it my Kula Ring – but this is one I'll never ever be parted from."

"Kula?"

"Malinowski. Too complicated to explain now. Just my whimsy."

"It's wrapped in a scarf. I love you, Emily."

They kissed longingly, body to body; then he left her staring over the bay as the ship's horn made the whole ship vibrate again with a powerful Beethovian blast. Just before turning out of sight he looked back and she waved.

He stood on the quay feeling singularly empty and watched the ship being manoeuvered away from the dock by tugs. "There goes my life," he thought. He glanced at his watch and saw that it was just after four o'clock.

A middle-aged couple stood beside him with several of their young children. The wife's horizontally striped dress dipped at the back. The husband stood with his hat raised in his right hand. Neither said a word and the children became restless.

Sitting in the Kelpie back at B Shed he contemplated opening Emily's small parcel but decided to leave it for later, so drove as far as he could to the harbour entrance.

The ship rose and fell gently on the first swells from the Indian Ocean as she began to leave the safety of the bay. He got out of the car and stood watching her passage. She was flying the Red Duster at the stern and a smaller Union Castle Line flag on the fore-masthead, opposite the new South African flag. As the mauve hull slid by he saw Emily leaning on the main deck rail, high above, and waved.

She pointed at the fingers of her left hand. She had wrapped the red scarf about her neck and it trailed in the wind.

It took a long time for the ship to pull out to sea, turn slowly to starboard and disappear behind the Bluff, so he took shelter in the Kelpie, even though it gave little protection from the buffeting wind, and opened Emily's gift.

It was a fountain pen.

Chapter Fifteen

"What are we going to do about Sonya and the Broccardos?" Toby asked. They were settled in the deep leather armchairs of the Durban Club library. Escorted by a turbaned Indian who had come to the door after much knocking and ringing, Donald had been led past a domed ceiling to find Toby reading the paper with his feet on the lowest bookshelf, a whisky at his side.

Most of the books had been removed long ago from that shelf as members repeatedly used it as a footrest.

"They must feel immensely let down. I thought of just arriving when we got back but things could go the wrong way. I'm particularly keen on reestablishing friendly relations with Sonya."

"I suggest we take the scenic route. Like you, I've a very good reason for writing to the Bells and the Reeds, a sort of bread-and-butter letter, thanking them in writing, belatedly (giving the interruption of Spanish Flu as the reason) for all their kindness – and letting them know that Emily got onto the boat safely. That would be a good starting point for mentioning that we wish to pay our respects to the Broccardo family. We can be sure that Emily's mother, Edna, is in touch with the family and so we can ask her to pass on the message."

"Ah yes; a 'bread-and-butter' rather than a 'Collins'. Agreed. I'll leave it to you to write. I know you'll pass on my best wishes too. I say, have you seen all this stuff in the paper about what's going on in Europe? What a mess! And here we are in 1919 thinking the fighting was over. Look at this one: 'Armed Peasants Marching on Munich. A great force of armed peasantry is marching towards Munich to destroy the Spartacus Soviet Republic', and here's another one – 'A Soviet republic has been proclaimed at Augsburg' and 'Rumoured Military Revolt at Berlin. Noske (whoever he is) making many arrests'.

"Here's a lovely one reported in that London paper I left open to show you -'Bolshevism in Natal. A message from Pietermaritzburg, the capital of Natal, states that Bolshevist propaganda is active in Natal and that Maritzburg is flooded with leaflets headed 'Bolshevists Coming' and calling on the workers, both black and white, to get ready for a world-wide Labour Republic'. What do you think of that?"

"Well, I think the term 'Bolshevism' means 'The Majority' and I gather Lenin's intention is to entrench a dictatorship of the proletariat majority in Russia before starting a world revolution; however the Mensheviks (meaning 'The Minority') are hell-bent on creating a 'Communist International' first; so the reporter should have referred to the Mensheviks taking over Natal, rather; but I suppose Bolshevism is a good all-purpose catchall word for the whole shebang. Perhaps Lenin, Stalin and Trotsky might fall out. Dim hope, I suppose.

"To answer your question – I read somewhere that the Government is paying for the travel expenses (including a free passage to Europe) of a Russian called Lahitzsky, his wife and their pet monkey. Lahitzsky has been addressing meetings in Johannesburg, condemning the Allied interference in Russia. The meetings conclude with the singing of 'The Red Flag'. It seems that the Australians are deporting such people and their monkeys and I think we should be doing the same. We have enough troubles here as it is, without foreign meddling. Lahitzsky's call is rather like the pot calling the kettle black."

"Well, there's nothing we can do about it tonight so let's have another whisky – if we can wake up the elusive Mr. Singh. He's a good old bloke. Try pushing that bell over there. If there's no response I'll have to search for him in the kitchen. What's your Tin Lizzie like, by the way? I only ask because I'll have to buy some sort of transport pretty soon."

"Goes uphill best backwards. Noisy. Reliable – when it works. Better than the one in which we travelled back to Empangeni. Are you thinking of getting a Model T truck or car? I couldn't help thinking that, as our farms are side by side, it would be handy to know that the parts of our vehicles are mostly interchangeable if something breaks."

"It's a thought. At least it would be a start. Where did you get yours?"

"It's not mine. Yet. Look here, one of the things I have to do on Saturday is to settle up with Chapard, provided he yields to the idea of my buying his showroom model. He had it specially painted wine red and modified as a kind of shop window wheeze. I'll also have to arrange to truck it by rail to Empangeni. Would you like to try driving the Kelpie tomorrow before we head off to Chapard's? We could go and have a look at that collapsed Umgeni River Bridge everyone is talking about, then wind up at Chapard's at about eleven, if you decide favourably."

"Kelpie?"

"Long story. Nickname."
"All right. Thanks. Good idea."
"Done."
"Cheers. Down with the monkeys!"
"And up with the Kelpies!"
"Down the hatch!"

The bridge near the mouth of the Umgeni River had been destroyed towards the end of the war by a flood which swept away people, cattle and snakes. One spectator claimed that he had seen a bellowing baby hippo caught up in the torrent, being carried out to sea.

Chapter Sixteen

Donald had telephoned The Barbican ahead of his return and spoke apologetically to the landlady Mrs. MacDonald about his disappearance, explaining that he was obliged to help a close friend at a moment's notice who had arrived unexpectedly and had been taken ill. This 'Bunbury' was as close to the truth as he could venture.

"Well you did cause great inconvenience and concern, and you might have telephoned," said 'Mrs. Mac'. We are very short of kitchen staff who had cooked meals for you. Judy and Dorothy were most concerned and I suggest you owe them an apology when they arrive home. Are you planning any more disappearances?"

"Well, you know that I have bought a farm in Zululand and will be moving there permanently in about a fortnight."

"Then you must please settle up in advance today for the full month. I am tempted to charge you for the wasted meals too." Mrs. MacDonald was grey. Her dresses were grey, her hair was grey and so was her face. Her large breasts weighed her down and she walked with a stoop.

Donald did his best to look contrite and Mrs. MacDonald appeared grudgingly mollified.

The explanation had to be given again to Judy and Dorothy when they arrived back from their first shopping expedition since convalescing from the flu, and it didn't go down well.

"Why didn't you phone? We called all sorts of people to help us find you – even that froggie friend of yours you go sailing with. We thought you might have dropped dead from the Three-Day," Judy said, and then started sobbing.

The revolving pedestal in George Chapard's showroom now displayed a sparkling clean and elevated example of the Ford Model T engine instead of the Kelpie. Large handwritten signs extolled its features and ruggedness. When the discussion turned to reliability George pointed out that Henry Ford had been raised on a farm so he designed the Model T to cope with the worst farm roads.

"The car sits on a steel triangle so it can flex like an ox wagon!" Chapard said. "All you need to keep it going is these few tools which come with the car."

He had hesitated to sell his Model T demonstration car to Donald when they visited until he realised that another sale seemed to be in the offing; so after much cordiality and paperwork they left the showroom with the knowledge that their new purchases – the wine-red Kelpie and a black Model T pickup truck – would be railed to Empangeni and Donald would hold on to his car and deliver it to Chapard for railing, late on the Tuesday. Toby elected to practise driving his pickup truck around Durban for the same reason, after he was sold a driver's licence.

Chapard had again talked grandly of establishing Ford agencies throughout Natal and Zululand, but subject to the province building roads to replace the country's haphazard infrastructure. "Meanwhile," George said, "if you run short of petrol you can run your truck on paraffin. Even whisky will work, they say, in an emergency. Some friends of mine tested that theory after a party last week."

Chapter Seventeen

The Jardine's house was high in Nimmo Road, a solid double-storeyed colonial pile of verandahs, edged by white-painted wooden railings on the ground and first floors. At the right was a three storeyed confection of Coronation brick pierced by generous sash windows. Drainpipes from the roofs led to buried water tanks on both sides of the house. There were French windows at ground level. Donald recognised early on in his approach that the Kelpie would not be able to cope with the very steep driveway to the house, so turned it around and reversed it up to between tall coconut trees and parked it on the gravel beside the front steps.

A sign in a flowerbed read 'BEWARE OF COCONUTS'. In the distance, a garden 'boy' was watering the flowerbeds. Aged about fifty and barefooted, he wore a white linen kitchen suit of shorts and top trimmed in red. His earlobes were ornamented with white ceramic cylinders. As Donald reached the verandah the French windows swung open slowly and a man's voice shouted: "In this way!"

Jardine, the Harbour Master, stood inside the drawing room at a transplanted ship's wheel on a pedestal which he had engineered to open the windows with a simple set of levers concealed beneath the floorboards.

Behind lay the sitting room cluttered with framed sketches, models and paintings of sailing vessels among the wife's collection of floral drawings, a framed 'Sea Fever' poem by John Masefield illustrated by small etchings, shelves of enormous South Sea Island shells, a wall mounted barometer, a costly radio telegraphy receiver, a pile of old Straits Times newspapers and a tripod-mounted telescope. Well-used and comfortable sofas showed that this was where the family clustered.

"Hello," he said and gripped Donald's hand. Jardine had wide-set eyes, was tall, gravel-voiced and sported a naval beard. Donald took to him immediately. "So you're off to build a brave new world, eh? Prue tells me you met on the tram. Well, that's as good a place as any. I met my wife buying an ice-cream in Singapore… always hot and humid there. Worse than Durban in February."

"Hello, sir. We're only going to listen to a briefing about the League of Nations. Nothing more. I'm the informal bodyguard."

"Prue tells me you fought in East Africa."

"Yes. In the BSAP."

"I'm told conditions were ghastly. So many casualties and even more deaths from disease. Now it's the flu taking over from where the war left off."

"It's not quite as grisly. And at least the flu seems to be beating a retreat in Natal; although I've heard someone call it The Orphan Maker."

"And no League of Nations will be able to fix that."

"One wonders what the League is expected to fix anyway, with Germany 'excommunicated'. Not that I like the Germans and all they stand for, but without them represented in some guarded capacity in planning for the future, it's rather like building a two-legged table. I think the world expects the League to be some sort of Deus ex Machina that will appear and resolve everything."

Prue came into the room and smiled. She had done something to her hair again and it suited her. She said: "Hello D-Donald," and turning to her father said, "Daddy, we're going to be late. We must leave chop-chop."

"Ah. Yes. You look a bit flimsy in that rig, Missy Dodo. Not much on, but I suppose that's the fashion. You will come back for a sundowner, though, will you Donald? Tell me all about it. Meet the wife. Cordelia's out spending all the money we haven't got at Greenacres at the moment. As a major concession they're staying open this afternoon, even though it's Saturday, so that my wife can spend even more money. I have no doubt something will come out of nothing. All on tick."

"Thank you, I would like that. What a beautiful view you have of the city."

"Yes it is. Best when the Jacarandas and Flamboyants are out; but I don't get much time to enjoy it. Most times I'm down at the harbour. Today, however, is one of the days I am not on duty. Next week will be particularly busy as we're getting the first visit of the SS 'Omar'. Used to be the German 'Koningen Luise'. Just renamed and cleaned up a bit. Now it'll be packed with Aussie soldiers going home, so Durban'll be swarming again. Last time the Aussies were here they got up to all sorts of pranks. Swopped babies in prams. Spot of anxiety for the mothers who had parked them outside a shop."

"Good heavens!" he said to Prue. "You're not taking a novel with you, are you?"

"No. It's just a copy of 'The Thirty-Nine Steps' I

promised to lend Donald."

"Ah. Bit tatty, don't you think?"

"Well, it will just have to do. You know what libraries are like after a war."

"Sorry about Daddy," she said as soon as she got into the Kelpie.

"Why?"

"He likes to control everything."

"I think he's a lovely fellow. And isn't that what Harbour Masters are supposed to do, control everything?"

"It depends. He tends to steer the d-domestic h-helm as if it's part of the harbour."

As they rode down into town, Prue said, "Your mind seems full of thoughts outside my ken."

"Yes. They were far out to sea and the hinterland of Zululand. Pardon me; but I'm delighted to see you again."

"I've never been in a Tin Lizzie before."

"Neither had I until recently. It's a mischievous wee beastie. My introduction to them was on a very bumpy road from Ntambanana."

"I'll hand over the Buchan novel after the meeting. B-Better not leave it in the car. It would be just our luck for someone to nick it. I'll keep it in my handbag."

"How did you get involved in the cloak and dagger business?"

"More like smoke and mirrors. Not many daggers."

"Well?"

"Can't tell you much, except that we spent many years before and during the war in Singapore. That's where I grew up and went to school and college. We enjoy living in Durban as a sort of s-substitute and it's less hot. N-Not quite as humid either. With eyes half-closed it's easy to imagine that the local Indians are the Chinese and Indians of my childhood.

"D-Daddy was Assistant Harbour Master supervising huge changes to the wharfs and warehouses. I was sad to see the lines of oxcarts being replaced by the railway... those poor coolies losing what little livelihood they had. He was more than busy so Mummy pre-preoccupied herself in the usual Good Works things that colonial wives did. Not least were efforts to regulate the supply of opium and reduce d-deaths of the poorest through the smoking of used opium dregs. Even now, half of Singapore's income is derived from opium. Obviously, she made enemies especially with a Chinamen called Hang Bun Soon, but I was the one who got caught up in the middle – l-literally – of a mutiny of the 5th Light Infantry regiment which was entirely Mahomedan, stirred up by Turkey entering the war on the side of Germany. I'm told it was all because Churchill commandeered two Turkish battleships being built in Britain – and paid for by public subscription in Turkey. Germany's cunning plan was to give two of its own battleships to Turkey as a substitute. As a result I think the Sultan issued a fatwa against Allied troops which d-d-didn't help things either.

"I was walking home one d-day in 1915, during my first year at the Nan-Nanyang Institute just before the Chinese New Year, when a crowd of sepoys from Keppel Harbour went on a killing spree. It was horrible and I was transfixed when I saw them rushing down the road towards me with sickles and pangas. Couldn't move. At that moment an officer from HMS Cadmus spotted me and swept me off to safety in the nick of time.

"The town was eventually rescued by sailors and marines from HMS Cadmus in the harbour and French, Russian and Japanese naval crews which responded to an appeal for help. There's more to the story but that will do!"

Chapter Eighteen

Prue and Donald were asked to give their names and occupations to two women wearing flu-masks, sitting at a small table in the foyer of the Arthur Smith Hall beneath a Workers Educational Association sign. Donald wrote 'Planter' against his name and gave his address as 'Yonder', Ntambanana, Zululand'.

"Hello. I'm Angela Palmer," one of the women said, "and this is my colleague Ruth Sneddon. For my sins, you'll see me sitting on the stage in a few minutes time. Welcome, and thank you for coming along. You'll get flu masks from Mr. Filatov just inside the door."

Prue whispered: "She's a friend of George Ber-Bernard Shaw and Emmeline Pankhurst, but when Virginia Woolf met her she said that all Palmer spoke about was a lot of 'peace, peace, peace drivel'. They're members of the Fabian Society in England and espouse gradual change in the same d-direction as the b-bolshevists, but much, much more slowly. In fact, the Fabian Society's emblem is the tortoise.

"As a Fabian, Angela pursues the goal of obtaining equal rights for the n-n-natives l-like the local socialists but much more at a tortoise-pace; nevertheless her stance causes much unease here," Prue said.

They were handed a copy of the League's Covenant of

twenty-six Articles to which was clipped a leaflet headed 'Saluton!' which described the work of the International Esperanto Society and efforts to make it the official language of the League (the French were objecting).

The last piece of literature was a tract from the Franchise Department of the Women's Christian Temperance Union (WCTU) advocating the right of white women to vote. There was no mention of voting rights for native or Indian women.

The dark green curtains of the Arthur Smith Hall gave it a musty Victorian air. As they entered, a man wearing a flu-mask introduced himself to Donald as Ivan Filatov from the Durban Industrial Socialist League, and pressed a newsletter into their hands with two flu masks from a basket at his feet. When Donald glanced at the title, 'The Socialist Spark' and Filatov then recognised and greeted Prue warmly, he wondered what on earth he was getting into. He had spotted such phrases in bold parts of the text as "equal rights for all" and lower down, "the black people of South Africa are the true proletariat of the working class."

Filatov was an intense whiskered splutterer with an unnerving habit, while talking, of coming within close nose-distance of his listener, a position he would maintain even when the other retreated. His fondness for garlic-laced foods made these encounters even less pleasant. It might have been an organiser's wry sense of humour which put him in charge of the flu-masks.

"This second wave of flu is waning in Natal, we're told," Filatov said, "but we're still ordered to take precautions. This is the first public meeting allowed since the flu regulations were introduced."

"Filatov brings his three children into the library quite

often," Prue murmured, while taking their places. "Now I know where his loyalties lie. He had mentioned he was a printer at the Natal Advertiser and that his dream was to visit Russia. Yoof! That smell of garlic!"

On each seat was a leaflet about the Durban Braille Society, illustrated with a black-and-white engraving of Sargent's painting of nine wounded soldiers, their eyes bandaged, blinded from the effects of a gas attack.

Below the illustration was an invitation to readers to 'Dine in the Dark with us' giving a date and venue and the cost of the fundraiser for blinded ex-servicemen. It was signed by the Secretary, Danielle Joubert.

"Oh, I know Danielle. She's the local 'Dutchie', see – there she is. We could talk to her afterwards and mention that 'Swiss' w-woman in Zululand. Could be useful."

From the proscenium arch hung a large blue and white star-within-a-star encircled by the words LEAGUE OF NATIONS.

On the stage, among a flutter of international flags on small poles, some of which had fallen over, sat the Mayor, Councillor Buzzard, several Technical College dignitaries, Angela Palmer and – to Donald's surprise, General Jan Smuts.

Prue whispered that Angela Palmer was endeavoring to develop, with colleagues, a university college. The city fathers had been inclined rather to encourage 'practical skills more appropriate to the challenges of pioneering Natal' – such as sanitary engineering, telegraphy and business training. A compromise had been reached by establishing a Durban Technical College whose first principal was a Benjamin Narbeth.

The Mayor stood and thanked those present for

attending and outlined the purpose of the briefing; then said: "We are honoured by the presence of a man who has travelled many miles to be with us this afternoon. As his time is particularly limited, I am going to ask our distinguished guest to speak first and set the perspective about the League and its role in the years ahead.

"So permit me to introduce someone who needs no introduction – mountaineer, botanist, philosopher, soldier, lawyer, statesman and politician, who not only participated prominently in the Paris Peace Conference but played a leading role in developing the League of Nations Charter: our Prime Minister General Smuts."

Smuts stood up and after the applause died down launched immediately into a description of the League's purpose and his legal reasoning behind the particulars of its formulation. He still spoke autocratically, like a barrister, staring into the middle distance with his ice-blue eyes, his high-pitched Malmesbury 'brei' attenuated by years at Cambridge, his Inns of Court exposure and his service in the Imperial War Cabinet.

"A Dutchman in Englishman's clothing," murmured Donald.

Smuts believed strongly in uncompromising cooperation 'by our two Teutonic nations – the Boers and the English, 'to form a united front against the teeming millions of barbarians in our Dark Continent,' a concept at odds with his high regard for Walt Whitman, although in later political life he did moderate his views on absolute separation from 'the dark races' as being impractical.

Someone quipped at the time that perhaps Smuts had stumbled across a few barbarians who had mastered Ancient Greek.

After outlining the formation of the League and touching on the Articles, he said: "I have no intention of dragging you through the Articles. You all have a copy of them, complete with an analysis of their implications, to take home and read at your leisure. What I wish to concentrate on is the subject of reconciliation and limited reparations.

"I must warn you that what I have to say now might inevitably fly in the face of current thinking and I sympathise with these sentiments. I am mindful that many of us have suffered extreme tragedy, and it is to them that I direct my thoughts.

"We all have in mind the noble desires to make the last 'War To End Wars' a reality, but I must ask how can the inferiority complex which is obsessing and poisoning the very mind of Germany be removed?

"There is only one way and that is – and this will shock you – by restoring her complete equality of status with her fellows. Not immediately, there are formidable reparations to be met; but we must work towards that goal.

"While one sympathises with French fears, one cannot but feel for Germany in the prison of inferiority. In my opinion, Germany's Versailles status will, in due course, become an offence in the conscience of Europe and a danger to future peace, while we are being distracted by the turmoil of Bolshevism.

"Fair play, sportsmanship and every standard of private and public life calls for a frank re-examination of the current bonds which will bind the future League and exclude Germany as a pariah. I fear that exclusion might well lead to the League's downfall unless we take into account a more balanced approach.

"As a result of our current strictures, I predict that unless we take a more realistic view concerning reparations, a new tyranny might emerge from Germany in years to come, disguised in attractive patriotic colours, enticing youth to a second war more devastating than the war from which we have just managed to emerge."

There was no mention of the far more ferocious reparations Germany was demanding of Russia. Smuts pulled out and glanced at his pocket watch then said, "Councillor Buzzard and Honoured Guests, please excuse me. I must leave immediately if I have any hope of fulfilling my second duty of the afternoon."

And he was gone even while applause followed him.

There were several lesser speakers who added little to Smuts' analysis of the role of the League, save for a nervous and spluttering presentation by Ivan Filatov, who gave the views on the League by the International Socialist League and the Communist Party of South Africa. Filatov had emerged out of the curtains onto the stage shortly after Smuts had left, clutching a sheaf of papers.

Introduced by Angela Palmer, he extolled the provision of equal opportunity within the framework of the League and the uplifting of the native people – 'the true proletariat'.

Natives and Indians were not allowed to attend white public gatherings and a buzz of disapproving muttering arose as he went on speaking until an Afrikaner stood up and shouted "Sit down, you bloody kaffir-boetie!" to which Angela Palmer reacted immediately by standing and saying loudly, "Thank you, Mr. Filatov, for that report on your movement and the most provocative and challenging perceptions you outlined," thus bringing to an abrupt end Filatov's garlic-laced presentation.

Some members of the audience began to drift away while a Mavis Taylor was making the case for Esperanto to be adopted by the League as a universal second language. She had an aquiline nose, was tall, ungainly and had a lisp, and invited members of the audience to learn the language at classes being held in the Trades Hall in Gardiner Street every Tuesday and Thursday evening.

"Communicating in Esperanto with a lady who lisped could be an experience," thought Donald, "but there is already an international language – Latin. Why not adopt that? Too difficult, I suppose."

Prue had started to fidget and said, "I really would like to leave now and go home. I think we should just say hello to Danielle before we go and deliver that message about the Zululand Braille woman. OK?"

"Agreed."

They caught Danielle as she was drifting out of the hall. She proved to be down-to-earth and welcomed meeting up with Prue. Donald liked her immediately. Prue mentioned Donald's meeting with Frieda von Weldenburg and her desire to meet Durban counterparts. On Danielle expressing keen interest in developing contact and providing her address, Donald said he would pass on the message to Frieda, who he was likely to see in the near future.

"Well done, Donald. We'll make a spy of you yet," muttered Prue (she seemed to like muttered asides).

Danielle was a natural blonde of about thirty, with a soft sympathetic figure. She spoke English with a 'skittery' Dutch accent, her eyelids flickering as she spoke, as if she were blind (which she was not).

"I hope Mummy hasn't bought everything in Greenacres. Let's see if you like her. She sounds a bit 'snooty colonial' but it's just her manner. She knows no other. Her father spoke like her. He was the Dean of St Andrew's Cathedral in Singapore, so please be tolerant."

"Why should I not be?"

"Don't know. You seem a bit aloof sometimes yourself."

"Put it down to reticence after four years of war in East Africa and all that. The company of women remains exciting but confounding."

"Do I excite you?"

"Yes, in a confounding way."

Prue lapsed into silence as the Kelpie whined its way up Nimmo Road and then backed up the steep drive to park beneath the coconut palms.

"Watch out for falling coconuts," she said, as they climbed out of the car. "It's the season when they do."

"I hear that you two met on a tram. Hello and thank you for taking Dodo to what must've been a somewhat dreary Saturday afternoon."

"Dodo?"

"Nickname. Long story."

"On the contrary, Smuts was there and he came out with some startling observations about German appeasement."

Cordelia Jardine smoked, spoke as a Roedean girl would speak, was fashionably dressed for a late humid Saturday in Durban and clearly took no prisoners.

"Tea and cakes or shall we cut to the chase and order in sundowners? I, for one, am for the latter. And I am sure Prue is too? I don't have to ask what that bearded man standing over there would like."

"Thank you. After listening to my erstwhile General talking appeasement for the Germans after he had led us into a long war of death, disease and attrition against them, I really would appreciate a drink."

"Alex, would you give Jeeves a call? His real Hindu name is Jeevan but he quite fancies our calling him 'Jeeves' because he reads books by PG Wodehouse in his room at night. We sometimes hear him chuckling. Given half a chance he'd call this place Blandings."

Their conversation paused when Jeevan wheeled in a dumb waiter with drinks.

"Thank you Jeeves. Ah yes. Smuts. Clever man," said Jardine. "I think he's leading us in the right direction, despite his rather Dutch views about black barbarians and trying to keep the races apart. Look around…swarming with blacks and Indians, and half-castes too. Won't work ultimately. Hasn't worked in Singapore in the form of suppression through shambolic neglect by the administration. The Indians and Chinese are far too damn clever to stand it for much longer. Drugging the Chinese with opium won't work in the long run either."

He said this while pouring his wife a whisky and soda without asking her what she wanted. They were sitting in cane chairs on the tiled front verandah overlooking the garden and the sweep of the town far below. The sun was setting and Prue had gone in to fetch a shawl for her mother and herself.

Inexplicably, Donald experienced a sudden flashback of killing a man he had shot in the throat. His opponent had collapsed with a bubbling groan beside him while enemy fire sang overhead. Donald jerked for a moment and he hoped the Jardines hadn't noticed.

"Drink? For a moment you looked as if you had seen a ghost."

"Whisky, thank you."

"Good man. Anything in it?"

"As it is, thank you."

"Ah. A true Scot"

"Some Greenacres customers I met this afternoon – you remember Mabel, Alex – are all agog about a film called 'Quo Vadis' coming to the Electric Theatre in Gardiner Street; and I heard that they are making something about four horsemen with Rudolph Valentino in it," said Cordelia.

"Oh yes. That should keep Cohen's Tinklers busy."

Ivan Cohen had the monopoly for providing a roster of piano players to accompany the silent films. The contract included the provision and servicing of the pianos too.

"Will they have that actress in it who keeps on taking her clothes off? What's her name again?"

"Audrey Munson. No, probably not. You know how 'prissy' American filmmakers are."

Jardine said to Donald that the only films he had seen were 'The Tramp' and 'Gertie the Dinosaur'.

"You can tell my husband's a cultured man, can't you," she said sarcastically. Everyone in the shop looked so silly with those damned flu masks. I wasn't allowed in until I put one on."

"Didn't stop you from buying the shop, Delia."

"Darling, it's only a few essential items. We were out of everything, including soap and toothpaste." Turning to Prue who had returned with shawls, she said, "Your father spends so much time down at the harbour that he doesn't realise that his household has been starving." – an exaggeration that Jardine chose to ignore.

Cordelia Jardine had weathered well, despite the harshness of Singapore and Durban sunlight, but her eyes told a different story. They reflected a determination to crush prejudice and right wrongs.

"What do you think of the Indian situation, Donald?"

"Oh here we go," said Jardine.

"I wasn't aware that there was one."

"You won't be aware then of plans to establish a South African Indian Congress as a united front, a direct result of the disabilities and inconveniences which burden the Indians?"

"No, I can't say that I am."

"I'm told that the congress will be opened by the Cape's last Prime Minister before the formation of Union, John X. Merriman – and for good reason, because he fought to retain qualified franchise for all adults irrespective of colour; but here the Indians have no vote and a lot of grievances."

"What does the 'X' stand for?" asked Prue.

"Xavier. I think the earlier Xavier did missionary work in India."

Turning to Donald, she said, "You will be aware, however, that sections of the South Africa Act in 1910 left anti-Indian and other discriminatory legislation against natives intact after the formation of the Union of South Africa?

"And that in March 1913 marriages not celebrated according to Christian rites were ruled invalid in the Cape Supreme Court, and that this rendered all Muslim and Hindu marriages not valid in law? (Admittedly, this was reversed some years later, but reluctantly and only after vigorous lobbying.) And are you aware that in 1913 all

Asiatic people were classified as Undesirables?"

"No."

"Last one: our Durban municipality, fearing that we whites might be overrun by barbarians, requires natives to register, carry a pass card at all times and be accommodated in single-sex hostels and townships.

"In the light of all these regulations designed to suppress and deprive, essentially in the interests of bettering the fragile Natal economy controlled by whites and the need for indentured labour, do you condone the suppression of rights of Indians and natives in favour of sustained cotton and cane production in Natal? And do you condone the treatment of the natives as outcasts in their own country?"

"Another whisky, Donald?"

"Thank you, it might help. This has certainly turned out to be a challenging afternoon . . . My answer to you must be 'not particularly', but such complex wrongs (and the world is bulging with them) cannot be righted with the snap of the fingers and I believe that the approach of the Fabian Society (slow but steady change for the better until equality is achieved) is the best resolution," he said, glancing at Prue.

"However, I do agree that, in this process, we should accordingly be resisting and countering any drift towards ever more draconian measures, and voicing the need to dismantle them."

"You're a man after my own heart, Donald. When do you leave for Zululand?"

"When the bank lets me go – probably towards the middle of next week. In the meantime, I'm obliged to start the establishment of an orphans' fund for those left behind by this awful flu."

"You mean the white orphans left behind, don't you?"

"Not really. The banks employ some Indian and Zulu people and I am confident that their needs will be looked after. It is, after all, my responsibility to set up the fund, and reinforced by this conversation and the general fairness of the bank I will satisfy myself that arrangements are made to care for all on an equal footing – and to hell with local prejudices and the government."

"Well said."

"However, the status quo of contracted labour and the permanent occupation of Zululand by us whites present situations beyond any very modest influence I might have. I am moving to Zululand to grow cotton or, if that fails, sugarcane. That will be my preoccupation. I did not come here to challenge the status quo or disrupt, but I will do my best to develop fair conditions for workers on my farm and influence those of my neighbours. That, I believe, is Fabianism in practice for the time being.

"I'll be farming among native communities still smarting from extreme injustices – and in the case of the marginalised Boer-Afrikaners, with highly conservative attitudes towards the natives and Indians – and I have no intention of antagonising everyone. And now I must thank you and depart."

"Must you go? Well, it has been a pleasure to meet you and we wish you every success for the future. I hope this will be an au revoir, rather than a farewell," Jardine said. "Do keep in touch and let us know how you're getting on."

"I will with pleasure, through Prue, if I may? We have agreed to correspond and I hope to meet you both when I'm next in Durban."

"Take the brolly you'll find in the hall," said Jardine.

"Protection against falling coconuts. You can hand it back to Prue."

Prue said, "My mother believes she has found a reformist spirit in you, so don't labour under the illusion that you've heard the last of this conversation!"

After Donald had left, Jardine said: "Delia, was it really necessary to embarrass the poor fellow?"

"I think that man is a good catch and I hope Prue has set her sights on him."

"Can you really see Prue stumbling about in mud behind a Zululand plough?"

"Perhaps."

At the car and out of sight of the living room, Prue said, "I did w-warn you about the zeal of my mother; but I think you've won her over. I can see Daddy likes you too. Here's the book and thank you for a rather interesting Saturday afternoon. We will indeed stay in touch."

"I strongly doubt that I'll ever have anything to report, but I'll keep you posted on my dove and pigeon observations. If there's ever something to claim for, I'll let you know via Creighton's rigmarole. It all seems unnecessarily complicated, but I suppose they know what they're doing. If I mention a 'Laughing Dove' be aware that something particularly hot is afoot. I spotted that bird in the list that Creighton gave me. Something Latin to do with Senegal."

Prue turned and kissed him, her mouth soft and warm, saying, "Trams are romantic things aren't they," looking directly into his eyes. "Good night and write when you can to this address. P-pop into the library before you go.. We can go up and see the dodo skeleton."

Donald watched her walk up the steps to the house holding the opened 'coconut umbrella' which had seen better days. Two of the struts had not opened properly.

Hadedas, with their Jurassic cries, were straggling across the dusk sky in an untidy imitation of an impeccable wedge of wild geese flying in the same direction.

In the house, Jeeves was sounding the dinner gong.

Chapter Nineteen

He decided to leave the Kelpie at The Barbican on the Monday and take the tram into town with Judy and Dorothy. When it arrived Donald went upstairs, but the two still-miffed girls rode below.

He had spent a large part of his Sunday sitting under an umbrella at Mitchell Park tearoom. He had strolled past smelly cages of a bored lion, a leopard and other creatures before settling into reading part of 'The Thirty-Nine Steps.'' after dipping into a journal on cotton cultivation. He had offered an excursion in the car to the girls but they had coldly resisted the excitement of riding in a Tin Lizzie and said they were walking to church.

On reaching the terminus on Monday, Judy walked ahead of him to the bank and Donald realised that while this was a declaration of anger and scorn, it might allow him to shed one lingering, though mildly romantic, responsibility.

Entering the bank, he was swept up by preparations for the onslaught of customers, the meeting with the Umbilo directors on the Tuesday and the formation of the orphans' fund.

'Fatknickers' brought him a telegram marked 'Personal' which she handed to him with an expressionless face while he was eating a hurried sandwich at his desk. The telegram read MAILED LETTER EAST LONDON LOVE YOU MADLY EMILY.

Miss MacVicker also gave him a sheaf of names, addresses and letters from adults bereft by the Spanish Flu, the few names of representatives from the other banks and a contact list of civic and religious leaders saying, "Mr. Cole asked me to hand these to you as a starting point; and there's a lady at the front who has asked to see you."

"Thank you."

When he got to the front counter all he could see was a small boy, just able to peep over the counter. "Do you work here?" the boy asked.

"Yes. I do."

"What do you do?"

"I just shuffle papers."

"What's 'shuffle'?"

"I'll show you." Donald reached for some blank deposit slips on the counter and proceeded to muddle them into three piles.

"Is that all? I could do that."

"No. I add up numbers too."

"Show me."

"What numbers would you like me to add up?"

"Two and, and, Five and, and, Twelve!"

"Those are certainly very important numbers. Now let me see," he said, writing down the numerals very large on a deposit slip and showing him. Donald assumed a heavy frown and adopted a pause for serious thought, then exclaimed "Nineteen!"

He was so engrossed in this discussion that he did not notice that a woman had come to stand near the boy until Cole arrived too and said to her, "Good morning, Mrs.

Buzzard."

"Good morning." Turning to Donald, she said, "Didn't I see you last Saturday at the League of Nations presentation? You were sitting beside that girl from the children's library, I think?"

"Why yes. You're very observant to have spotted us behind our flu masks. Thank heavens we no longer have to wear them."

She was dressed in white cotton. Even her stockings and shoes were white. The only relief from all this paleness was a floral ribbon around the crown of her straw hat. She was portly, but not unduly so.

"Mrs. Buzzard, may I introduce you to Mr. Kirkwood? I heard that you were coming in today after hearing about the development of the Bankers Society for Dependents and Orphans in the wake of the Spanish Flu. Mr. Kirkwood has been charged with establishing the fund.

"As you will know, Mrs. Buzzard is our Mayoress," he said to Donald.

"Ah. You are just the man I've come to see," she said.

"Then I'll hand you over to him – perhaps you would care to talk in our consultation room. Kirkwood, would you show Mrs. Buzzard the way?"

Donald bristled at being addressed as if he were a schoolboy, but said nothing. "What are all those people doing?" the boy asked.

"Oh, they're just shuffling papers and doing sums. Those are their jobs. Would you like to draw? I'll bring you some paper and pencils."

"What can I draw?"

"Draw anything you like, or perhaps you could sketch those ladies over there doing sums?"

"Sketch?"

"It's another word for draw."

After the small boy was settled she drew Donald aside and sat, before saying, "His name's Tommy. He lost both his parents from the Flu as well as his only older sister. The husband was a teller at the Colonial Bank and his wife was my close cousin. She died at about the same time as the daughter and so we decided to take him under our wing. We've started the rigmarole of being appointed guardians, but he's having great difficulty in coming to terms with the deaths. He keeps on asking when he can go home and when he can see his parents again. I've just come in to offer any kind of support I can give for other bank families so afflicted. My husband, being the mayor, could probably help to pull strings together if so needed."

"Thank you. It was most kind of you to call. Of course, the flu has hit the native, Indian and Mauritian families particularly hard, and the bank will be even-handed in providing a lifeline, but I'm floundering on the details for the moment, as this is my first day of coordinating everything. Unfortunately, I'll be leaving the bank to take up farming at the end of this week, so I have to act quickly to get things going."

She left after an exchange of telephone numbers, and the small boy in tow without the drawings which he left on a desk. They were troubled drawings of rudimentary people amidst large areas of scribbled blackness.

From that time on, for the rest of his stay at the bank, he immersed himself in the alien territory of founding an orphan's fund, interrupted only by a frigid meeting with the directors of Umbilo Iron & Steel. They had disclosed their discovery that the new works manager had been conducting a business on the side, unbeknownst to them, of selling pressed steel ceiling components from company stock. Donald was caught up in a world of committees and appeals from relatives of affected families. The only interruption he allowed himself was a lunch among the columns, arches and palm trees of the Winter Garden at the Marine Hotel with Andrew Wylie, one of the bank's solicitors, and a Paul Cunningham, a young architect cousin of the solicitor.

Cunningham often emphasised a remark with an unsettling crackle of his knuckles. He had thin hairy hands with pronounced veins.

Wylie had taken over the responsibility, pro bono, of the drafting and registering of the not-for-profit company.

"Somehow, I don't see you as a permanent administrator of an organisation for orphans and bereft parents, Donald. You'll be well out of it by escaping to Zululand! I've no doubt it's going to plague the minds of generations of joint bank committees to come. Sooner or later there'll be disagreement about support of dependent natives, Mauritians and Indians – and sooner or later the society will decide to build an orphanage."

Cunningham chose that moment to crack his knuckles again.

"Then what? You can't have native and Indian children living with whites! So what will happen to the 'undesirables'? And even they will arrive at a confrontation between Hindu and Mohammedan factions."

The management of the Winter Garden prided itself in offering 'the most succulent mutton curry in Natal' which all three had ordered. It arrived at that moment, borne by a turbaned Indian and his maroon-jacketed assistant, who had to emerge from the kitchens with food trays by pushing aside overgrown and noisy palm fronds concealing the entrance.

Wylie said, "To avert a confrontation I suggest we write a provision into the founding document which protects the 'orphanage rights' of our unwashed brethren from the outset. Agreed?"

Donald nodded but was distracted by the sight of a young Indian girl in a green sari behind the far counter. "My God!" he thought, "he made them such a beautiful race."

"Gandhi would be proud of you, Donald, but I doubt that they will accept any idea of co-opting an Indian onto the white committee," Wylie continued.

"What? Oh yes," Donald said, recovering from his reverie.

"Indian orphanages do exist already so it wouldn't be necessary to create another one," Wylie said. "The firm has dealings with a certain Parsee Rustomjee who has turned out to be quite a philanthropist. Among other things he's created the Rustomjee Orphanage and supports another one near the Umgeni mosque, as well as an orphanage for Indians run by the Catholic Church. There's even a Methodist day school for Indian children he takes an interest in. Provided he doesn't try to take over the whole shebang, it might be an idea to invite him to attend meetings of your advisory panel, as an observer, with the Mayoress as Patron? The society could support Indian employee orphaned children in such places and monitor their progress?

"That leaves us with the natives and the Mauritians – and of course stranded single parents having to cope," said Donald.

"I'd be reluctant to plonk 'untold riches' of child support into a local chief's eager hands, lest he just goes out and buys more cattle.

"Perhaps it might be an idea to talk to a missionary society? The Norwegians do a good job of running an orphanage for African children and they make a practice of consulting the local chiefs when it comes to relevant decision-making. Agreed? As for the Mauritians, they're not good on community responsibility and in my opinion they should just continue to be lumped together with those receiving benefits in white orphanages. We'll just have to steamroll over objections when they will surely come."

Paul Cunningham said, "Strange how we call them 'Mauritians' here; all based, I suppose, on boatloads of indigenous Mauritians and Madagascans who arrived and interbred with some Natal whites just after the abolition of slavery. Capetonians call their variety 'Bruinmense' [Brown People] or 'Coloureds'. The Dutch are inclined to classify everything according to skin colour.

"Interesting that the Cape 'Brown People' came from a rather different stock – more Batavian and Angolan slave origin plus local Hottentots interbred with white settlers. I believe the 'Hots' expanded down from Bechuanaland over the centuries, skirting the Kalahari Desert, unlike our Nguni Zulus who came down from the Congo."

"So, Donald, your committee will have to be in close consultation with appropriate welfare professionals," Wylie said, "and it will need a strong person at the helm."

"What are you drawing?" Donald asked Cunningham, who was pencilling in a strange building design on the back of a menu card. He was considerably younger than the other two.

"I heard that Durban's City Fathers are planning to erect a cenotaph to honour the war dead and there'll be a design contest."

"They don't need a slab of bloody concrete to do that!" Donald said. "Useless waste of money, and it's happening everywhere. A pile of concrete, fallen soldiers in bronze at the foot and a meaningless piece of sculpture at the top with the words 'Lest We Forget' decked out with a list of 'The Fallen'... once a year there'll be a gathering – flags, a Last Post and some clergymen prating. Then everyone will repair for tea and sandwiches – and forget.

"It's a pity that the ghosts of our men struck down as cannon-fodder could not march, limp or crawl down Station Road and assemble at the front of the post office instead. That would cause a stir among the 'key men' and war profiteers. A better use of the money would be to start an organisation offering survivors, the forgotten ones, the comradeship experienced in war to help them and their families adjust and get on with their lives, instead of all this empty tomb shit. It's no time for symbols."

Cunningham said nothing, put down his pencil and cracked his knuckles again. He stared at the tablecloth.

"Look. I realise you were too young to serve, but those who have survived actual conflict find it, to a man, very difficult to rekindle the comradeship they experienced now they've left the service. They need somewhere to dispel their sense of isolation and frequent deprivation. Next time you see a veteran, possibly with a leg or arm missing, perhaps even begging, remember what I said."

Cunningham excused himself shortly after Donald's outburst and Wylie said, "Poor fellow. He really did put his foot in it, didn't he?"

"I suppose I was a bit hard on him. Bloody monuments!"

"Well there's a rumour that Earl Haig is coming out to Natal next year to kick-start an ex-serviceman's league to satisfy just that purpose – something called the Comrades of the Great War – so don't be too hard on the locals. They mean well."

As they left, the sari-girl smiled a disappointing smile; her gums and teeth were stained red with betel nut juice.

Donald arrived back to find that the bank's auditors had descended on them unannounced. This meant that after the bank was closed to the public for the day a complete audit was to be completed, and that no employee would be allowed to leave until all books, and the cash, were balanced down to the last penny. The auditors and employees left at 9 o' clock that night and only after one weeping secretary had been escorted to the entrance of the bank, never to darken its doors again. Donald thus reached the Barbican close to ten to find the kitchen door locked and Judy and Dorothy asleep, judging by no light under their door. He wondered how Judy had got there ahead of him.

Before going to sleep he opened Emily's letter written on the ship's stationery:

'Dearest,' he read. 'It's ten o' clock at night and I am writing this in the ship's library before turning in. It's the only place I could find offering peace and quiet. You have no idea how a cabin-full of women chatter. Before coming here I was up on deck and leaning on the rail when a sister ship of the line passed on its way to Durban all lit up like a Christmas tree. Our ship sounded its foghorn in greeting as did the

other and I was immediately carried back to those last moments standing on deck with you, hearing the ship and harbour sounds and suggesting that these were our leitmotif. Remember? Oh, of course you do.

There is not much I can tell you that you don't know already, but Durban and Jean-Pierre's flat seem oceans away and drifting further and further. I do miss you so. When I came down by train I had hoped in my heart that things would actually turn out the way they did, and now I find every waking moment is filled with thoughts of you.

I was disappointed to hear that they only fill the pool after leaving Cape Town for Southampton so that smashing costume I bought to dazzle the ship's officers with will just have to wait until I get back to varsity – mind you, it will be cold there, probably raining and it gets dark very early at this time of the year.

We only dock in East London for a few hours, but that girl with the dark eyebrows, Marjory, and I plan to explore, and the first thing I will be doing on shore is posting this letter. Neither of us has been there before and I believe it's quite a pretty place although the natives are very poor and live in two slums out of sight on either side of a river.

Good night, darling. Do write, stay away from that pretty librarian and give my love to the Kelpie. Emily. PS: I didn't realise that a ship creaked so much. I can hear it while lying in my bunk at night, especially in rough weather.

The mosquitoes left him alone that night, probably

because he had remembered to dope the water settled between the leaves of the bilbergias outside his window with paraffin, but his dreams were filled with machines of war. At one point he lay with Emily in a shell hole trying to unravel her green sari when she turned to him and smiled, her mouth bloodied, and said 'it's only betel nut'. At another, he was counting pigeons flying overhead which were being shot at by Creighton and Cole. He woke up sweating in the middle of the night when an Askari tried to kill him with his bare hands because had got the code all wrong.

At breakfast he managed to make a disgruntled peace with Judy and Dorothy, so he drove them to work in the Kelpie, the latter being dropped off in Florida Road. He parked right outside the bank. On the way into town, Judy had said, "Will you write to me?"

"Yes, I will, if you like," Donald had said, thinking that this could make a perfect red herring to cover his sudden fascination with Zululand birds and the letters of covert knowledge sent to Prue.

He said, "For a long time, I've been fascinated by Natal's birdlife and I think I'll take up its serious study while waiting for the crops to grow. So if my letters contain rather boring stuff about Zululand birds from time to time, you must forgive me."

"All right, I will, but have you ever thought that it might be a spot lonely? Sitting on your verandah watching birds through binoculars and sipping gin and tonic? All alone?"

"Yes, I suppose so. Bit remote." He found himself saying, "You and Dorothy might want to visit me for a holiday once I'm up and running. It would keep a window open to the Durban highlife for a lone settler among the Zulus. But I don't think I'll be looking for any girl to share it with me just yet. Too much hardship. Very little social exchange." ("That was sufficiently blunt," he thought.)

"Perhaps," said Judy. "Depends on the woman."

After clearing his desk, being his last day, he was about to make his round of farewells when Cole asked him to pop into his office for a final chat.

When he opened the door he found some of the staff waiting there, including Fatknickers, all decked out in mauve as usual. She was standing immediately below the wobbling electric ceiling fan to keep cool. On the manager's desk the copper ash tray was oscillating again after Cole had stubbed out yet another cigarette.

Cole said: "It's not exactly a gold watch but we would like you to accept this barometer as a gift from all of us, in friendship and to thank you for your loyal support in trying times. We wish you good rains, sunlit days and bountiful harvests on your new farm. Perhaps every time you tap the glass you might remember us. To remind you, you'll find a small engraved plate mentioning us on the front."

A startled Donald found himself giving a stammering reply of thanks.

"I've come to see your Dodo," said Donald to Prue on arriving at the Children's Library.

"I won't mis-misconstrue that!" said Prue smiling. "Before we go upstairs I have two books for you, so I'm glad you found the time to call in. They're both second-hand and I found them in the rare books section of Adams bookshop.

"The first one is for presenting to von Weldenburg on your visit. It's (I can't pronounce it properly) 'Herrschaft und Knechtschaft', a famous passage from Hegel's 'Phenomenology of Spirit'. As he is so caught up with eugenics he is likely to appreciate it. You don't have to bone up on Hegel if you don't want to – just say that the man in Adams suggested it when you mentioned the theme of eugenics. I'll see that the man in the shop will recall your visit if ever asked. I think Hegel was inspired to write it after hearing of the Haitian Revolution, in which the slaves took over and killed all the masters. Nothing to do with eugenics, far more philosophical than that, but it could spark a lively dinner conversation about Untermenschen and slavery. Here's the address of the Braille girl we met. Please copy it out again and give the copy to Mrs von Weldenburg and say that she is invited to make contact with Danielle. Throw away my handwritten original, please.

"Then this second one's for you."

It turned out to be a beautifully illustrated volume of 'Natal Birds' by Robert and John Woodward, published in 1899.

On the flyleaf she had written 'With love from Dodo'.

"I think I had better explain the reference. You're familiar by now with my s-slight stammer on some days. Well, the writer of 'Alice in Wonderland', Charles Dodgson (pseudonym, Lewis Carroll), also stammered. You're familiar with the book?"

"Yes. My father and mother (although she died when I was very young) used to take turns reading it to us every night when we were tucked up in bed."

"The joy for s-stammering writers is that the impediment is not reflected in their writing. Dodgson used to make a joke of stammering over the Do-Do in his surname and would introduce himself as 'Do-Do-

Dodgson' until he just became known as 'Dodo'. B-But that's not the finish."

"He characterised himself as the D-Dodo in 'Alice' when describing 'the caucus race', in which every creature took part including the Dodo."

"My mother nicknamed me 'Dodo' for the same silly s-stammer when I was a child and the n-name slips out from time to time. She also used to read me 'Alice in Wonderland' at bedtime. I'm still self-conscious of the s-stammer but nowadays I just accept it. It's making a s-statement about Me."

"It seemed apt to make an oblique f-flyleaf reference as we have one of the only two complete skeletons of the Do-Dodo bird in existence, right here, a floor above the library. It arrived this m-month from M-Mauritius. Shall we go upstairs and have a look?"

Which they did.

"It's a kind of memento mori for wildlife isn't it," Prue said, as they gazed at the Dodo's enormous eye-sockets and powerful beak. The yard-high skeleton stood on a plinth beside a taxidermist's feathered reconstruction of what it was thought to look like.

"Strange to think that its ancestors originated in the Cretaceous Period 145 million years ago, yet mankind managed to bump it off by 1680 simply because it couldn't fly. Will you go around shooting things in Zululand?"

"Only for the pot or defence, not for sport."

"We don't look after 'all things bright and beautiful', do we? There were elephants on the Berea sixty-five years ago. Now where are they? Gone with the Dodo," she said, turning to him.

"Upstairs in the museum, he took her in his arms

beside the Dodo and kissed her lovingly," she said, after he had done just that. Breaking away gently, Prue said: "That could read as the first lines of a cheap romantic novel in the grown-up section of the library. Mind you, Hilaire Belloc wrote a child's poem about the Dodo's bones and beak 'all in the Mu-se-um', so it'll be in my library as well. It's in his Bad Child's Book of Beasts. That was a goodbye-for-the-moment kiss. I must go back downstairs again. Take care of yourself and think of me occasionally (rather than 'just for the Service')" she said, and walked away quickly.

Bibliography

It may seem a bit odd to include a bibliography at the end of a work of fiction, but this book and the ones that follow draw on research done by others. The opinions and conclusions voiced are not necessarily those of the authors listed below and the Eric Schnurr of the novel is an entirely fictional character. The story continues in Book Two, titled *What Happened At Yonder*.

Arthur, Max. *Lost Voices of the Royal Navy*. London: Hodder and Stoughton:1997 (originally published as *The True Glory: The Royal Navy 1914-1939*, the first of two volumes).

Berning, Gillian; Engblom, Peter; Konigkramer, Arthur; Buthelezi, Princess Magogo Constance (aka Dinizulu). *Know The Past, Wear The Future*. Durban: The Local History Museum: 1989.

Bizley, William. *Unsung Heroes, the Trek Ox and the Opening of Natal*; Natalia. Volume 34, (December 2004): pp 50-61.

Curson Med.Vet., Dr H H. *Nagana in Zululand*; 308-320. Pretoria; Digitised version University of Pretoria Library Services.

Dmytryshin, Basil. *A History of Russia*. Englewood Cliffs: Prentice-Hall, Inc, 1977.

Minaar, Anthony deVilliers. *uShukela!* Pretoria: HSRC Publishers, 1992.

Pager, Harald. Ndedema. *A Documentation of the Rock Paintings of the Ndedema Gorge*. Graz: Akademische Druck, 1971.

Phillips, Howard. *Epidemics*. Athens: Ohio, 2012.

Schnurr, Mathew. *The Boom and Bust of Zululand Cotton 1910-1933*. Halifax: Journal of Southern African Studies. 37:01, 119-134: Dalhousie University: 2011.

Wilson, Monica & Thompson, Leonard. *The Oxford History of South Africa*. London: 1969. Wiseman, John. The SAS Survival Handbook. London: 1991.

Natal's Famous Curry

Variations of the curry mentioned several times in the novel evolved over the years from the Madras curry recipes brought to Natal by indentured Indians in the second half of the nineteenth century. Nowadays it is ubiquitous and enjoyed by most people living in present-day KwaZulu Natal.

This recipe is by kind permission of Kevin Joseph, Executive Chef of The Oyster Box Hotel & Spa in Umhlanga, Durban.

These curries are usually spicier and hotter than those originating from other parts of India and are coloured with chillies, tomatoes and cayenne pepper.

The masala curry powder blend used here includes cumin, coriander, fennel, turmeric, mild masala, aniseed, cinnamon, medium masala and cardamom, although the proportions remain Kevin Joseph's closely guarded secret.

Preparation and cooking time takes about one hour and this recipe serves four.

INGREDIENTS

1 kg leg or shoulder of lamb (or 1 kg chicken) cubed

7.5 ml oil

1 onion, diced

2 cloves

2 cinnamon sticks (each 10 cm long)

20 ml medium strength masala curry powder

1 teaspoon of salt

10 g crushed garlic and ginger

4 curry leaves

5 g whole fennel seeds

250 ml water (one cup)

2 large potatoes, peeled and cut in half

1 medium tomato, skinned and diced

Coriander (dhania) leaves for garnishing

METHOD

1: Wash cubed meat or chicken and drain the water

2: Heat the oil and add the diced onion, cloves and cinnamon sticks

3: Add the famous masala powder, mix, stir and add meat to the pot

4: Add salt, garlic, ginger, curry leaves and fennel seeds, combining all the ingredients together by stirring

5: Keep the mixture on a high heat for 5 minutes, then reduce heat to medium

6: As excess water and juices evaporate, add another cup of water, followed by the tomatoes and potatoes

7: When the vegetables and meat have cooked for about 30 minutes, simmer on a high heat for another 5 minutes

8: Garnish the meal with coriander and serve with rice, green salad and roti

Printed in Poland
by Amazon Fulfillment
Poland Sp. z o.o., Wrocław

51674098R00251